You have a way of writing that draws the reader into the life of the characters and makes them so real, I sometimes forget it's a book.

- Kathy McGrew, Alabama

You have a very sensitive heart...I guess that's what makes you such a great writer. You have that special gift to be able to "tune in" to other people's feelings. Maybe that's why I feel like I've known you forever.

- Brynda Bridges, Mississippi

OTHER BOOKS BY
JOHN SHIVERS

Hear My Cry

Broken Spirit

Paths of Judgment

A Novel

John Shivers

CRM BOOKS
Publishing Hope for Today's Society

For Information:
CRM BOOKS, P.O. Box 2124, Hendersonville, NC 28793

Visit our Web site at www.ciridmus.com

Printed in the United States of America

ISBN: (10 digit) 1-933341-29-7
        (13 digit) 978-1-933341-293

LCCN: 2008937033

To Tracy McCoy

The best friend Margaret Haywood
(and my readers) ever had!

Her insistence that I make time to write,
and the flexibility she allows me on
the best job in the world as editor of the
Georgia Mountain Laurel magazine,
enabled me to continue the saga of
Margaret's search for freedom.
It was a long time coming,
but it's with pleasure that
I dedicate this book to you, Tracy.

Author's Notes

In February 2005 my readers were first introduced to Margaret Haywood in the pages of **Hear My Cry**. Her story of an unlikely domestic violence victim, and the deep denial in which she found herself, was evidently more commonplace than even I had realized. I soon lost count of the number of contacts from readers asking "How did you know what happens in my house?"

I'm certain that in some cases these abuse victims confessed their true situations to me, a faceless, totally unknown stranger, before they confided in even their closest friend or family member.

It was a sobering and troubling experience.

Equally amazing was the reaction from male readers. While their comments were in the minority numerically, I was surprised at the depth of their emotions, of the anger they expressed. That another man, one of their own kind, could be so cruel, so vindictive, so dogmatic, was deeply troubling to them. They asked, "How could a man demean himself so greatly, when it's his job to protect his wife and family – his most cherished possessions?"

The answer: abusers are created; they are a carbon copy of what they lived as children. Which is why the only true solution to this epidemic that threatens to unravel the very fiber of the family unit is with the children. Domestic violence is child abuse even when the child isn't physically harmed. Simply being a captive audience is often as destructive as the physical abuse itself.

Many readers have written, some with overtones of anger in their messages, to ask: "What happens to Margaret? I **have** to know... is she OK?"

Paths of Judgment picks up the story begun in **Hear My Cry**. In its pages readers can reassure themselves that Margaret does survive. However, the judgmental mindfield she must navigate as she seeks release from her abuser puts her in equally as much peril as the abuse itself.

You, the reader, will have to decide how Margaret fares. I'm sure I'll hear from many of you, and I welcome those contacts as I craft **Lift Up Mine Eyes**, the final book in the *Create My Soul Anew* Trilogy.

Just as with **Hear My Cry**, I'm just the typist for this book as well. The story flowed from my fingertips – sometimes as many as 13,000 words in a day. And, as always, I'm indebted to many friends and family members who encourage what can, at times, be a solitary chore.

To my brother and sister-in-law, Mike and Janet Shivers: Thanks for understanding when I must pull away and write.

To our children, Sarah and Lindsay Lewis, and the two most wonderful grandchildren in the world... Grant and Lillie: thanks for your love.

To Dale and Lynn Lowman, our "adopted" family: thank you simply isn't adequate. I've named a character for

Lynn in payment for the loan of Dale when I have to make road trips. They understand I have no sense of direction.

Another character is named Ann McCallum. She and husband Walter, my wife's brother and sister-in-law, have made their guest bedroom and their home cooking available on too many occasions to count, as we've traveled to book signings in Mississippi. Ann has also been one of my best marketing agents as well.

To Elmer and Corene Ritch and Catherine Ritch Guess: your love, your prayers and support, as always, are priceless treasures.

Last, the best critic, my staunchest supporter, and the woman who has encouraged me to pursue a dream when many others would have said, "Enough, already!" – my wife of 38 years – Elizabeth. Thanks, darling. Here's another one for you!

John Shivers
June 2008

He keepeth the paths of judgment,
and preserveth the way of his saints.

--PROVERBS 2:8

Vol. II, *Create My Soul Anew* trilogy

Paths of

Judgment

CHAPTER ONE

"Oh, no! No! No...!" Margaret Haywood's anguished wail shattered the quiet of the mausoleum atmosphere that haunted the elegant home. What she'd just seen felt like a sucker punch straight to the gut as she staggered and almost fell. "Just look at this," she cried. "Look what he's done to my beautiful house. How... how... could he?" The attractive blond woman with a framework of metal around her left arm clinched and unclenched her one good fist in anger.

The once fashionable family room that had earned decorator praise lay in shambles. Little had escaped the destruction. Margaret grabbed for the nearby arm of her friend, P.C. Dunigan. Then she closed her eyes and allowed her weakened knees to buckle, as she lowered herself to the floor. One mutilated wall in the family room provided support for her back.

Oh, God, please, when I open my eyes, let me see that everything was just my imagination.

But it was not to be.

The fabric covered sage walls bore evidence of many vicious slashes, too many to count. The machete that likely inflicted the damage was anchored in the middle of the chimney breast. Its sinister blade pierced an original canvas by one of Margaret's favorite north Georgia artists.

"Hey, friend," she heard through the darkness that strangled her. "Are you still with me?

Margaret opened her eyes, only to be terrorized again by the wrecked remains of what had been one of her favorite rooms in the Haywood residence. Three antique wall sconces she and Don had found in a New Orleans salvage yard caught her eye. Their delicate wrought iron frames were bent into shapes as grotesque as Margaret imagined the mind of the vandal to be.

Don, how could you have done this? Why didn't I ever see this side of you before?

"Oh, P.C. I would never... never have believed that Don would go... this far." The breaths in her chest came with ragged cadence and she feared she might faint. Even though she closed her eyes again, as she fought to maintain consciousness, the image of the decorator showroom that had been her personal creation still haunted her. What had once been a thing of beauty now hung in shreds of its former glory.

Just like my marriage.

"Hang with me, Margaret. Just stay here until your head clears and you feel like getting up again."

"Why, P.C.? Why would he have done this?"

Her friend's voice penetrated the haze that captured Margaret's consciousness. "Are you certain it was Don?"

"Well, yes. I mean... who else would have...?"

"Vandals, maybe? Teenagers? You're close enough to Atlanta that you probably have some gang activity here. And your house has been unoccupied for quite some time."

"No," Margaret answered. "This was Don. His fingerprints are all over it."

She could sense P.C. settling beside her on the floor in the house on Red Bud Way. Her house. Or at least it had been. Once. *Everything's changed. Nothing will ever be the same again.*

"Help me get up, P.C. I've got to see what else he's done."

If someone had been looking in, Margaret thought later, they'd have vowed the two women were under the influence of some illegal substance. Between Margaret's still weakened state, and the awkward cage of steel rods that encased her left arm, it was a cumbersome waltz as P.C. did all she could to pull her friend from the floor and help her to stand.

"You're convinced Don's responsible?"

"He's the guilty party alright." Margaret let her eyes roam the room where they had shared so many happy moments. It grieved her to understand they would never know such joy again. "If you know what to look for, you can see the pattern." Her breath caught in her throat. "Don had no intention of allowing me to put this house in the Tour of Homes. He's not about to do anything that would help battered women. Now he's made certain that I can't."

He was determined to show me that this is HIS house.

As if to validate her theory, she caught sight of the room's oversized sofa, its gold chenille upholstery hanging in threads.

"You're going to need to let Alice and Annie know that you're one home short." P.C. was referring to Margaret's co-chair on the tour committee and Annie Campbell, the director of the Carter's Crossroads Shelter Against Domestic Violence.

"I will, I will... just as soon as I can accept it myself." Margaret leaned against the doorway. "Everything that's destroyed is something we disagreed over. Don thought it was too extravagant to cover these walls with fabric. He wanted to use carpet. Naturally."

"That could be a coincidence."

"You don't see any damage to the large screen TV do you? But the three wall sconces were favorites of mine. And the sofa. He thought it was too massive for the room."

"His chair... at least I assume that brown leather recliner is his chair... isn't damaged either."

"Now you're seeing it the way I do. Come on, let's check out the rest of the house."

A few minutes later it was a heart-sick Margaret who sat at the foot of the back staircase to take stock of the situation.

"The family room window treatments, the beautiful gold and wine striped fabric she'd fashioned herself had been ripped from their massive wooden rods and lay scattered about the room. But the damage hadn't stopped there.

"You see what I mean, don't you? About how selective Don was in choosing what to destroy and what to spare?"

P.C., who had been checking out the kitchen, stuck her head around the doorway. "And can I guess that this kitchen – or at least what's left of it – was your personal kingdom?"

I hadn't even thought about the kitchen. Oh, Don, you didn't?

The evidence spoke for itself. Outside of the bed in the guest bedroom, which they had discovered in pieces and the shattered remains of the fiberglass jetted tub in the master bathroom, only the kitchen had been hit harder.

"I would have thought Don was too conscious of the dollar to have inflicted this much damage." P.C.'s hand traced around a deep depression in the stainless steel door of the sub-zero re-frigerator. "What made this, for pete's sake? A sledge hammer?"

Margaret sheltered her caged and recovering arm as she moved from appliance to appliance. There wasn't one single piece in the kitchen that didn't show evidence of wrath.

"He can do whatever he wants. He explained it to me the night he wrecked the family dining room; it's his money. And it's in his name. Besides, it's all insured."

Even now, weeks later, I'm still unable to believe how ballistic he got that night. But I can't deny he's capable of violence, because I've got the souve-nir to prove it. She fingered what her father called the tomato cage that encased her arm. *I just wonder how many more of his surprises I can handle.*

"It's all about control, you know. Absolute control. I fi-nally found the courage to deny him that, and he's determined to make me regret it."

Damn you, Don!

There had been a time when she would have been too goody-goody to use any swear language. There was also a time when she had two good arms. *Yes, times have changed. I just can't let this change me for the worst.*

"He's sick," P.C. announced. "We've said that before but now I'm convinced of it. He's dangerous, too."

"You're telling me? This is the same guy you had to pull out of a ten-day contempt sentence in Tennessee because he wouldn't listen to his very capable attorney. Surely you haven't forgotten that?"

"Representing Don Haywood is an experience I'll tell my grandchildren about. But I'm talking about a different kind of dan-ger. He's out to get you."

"I'm walking proof of that."

"Come outside with me. Now. We've got to get out of this house."

Margaret took one last look at the beautiful kitchen where she'd prepared so many meals for her family and friends. *I always tried to be here when the kids got home from school. I can still hear them piling in the door now.*

"He can't hurt me again, P.C. What more can he do?"

"Plenty." She held out an arm to Margaret who took it to steady herself as she came down the steps. "For starters, this could all be a set-up. He could be planning to pin all this property destruction on you."

"Me? Why would I wreck my own house? I love this place. This was home."

"Exactly. But whose name's on it?"

The light bulb came on. *He wouldn't stoop that low.* But in her heart, she knew now that Don was capable of anything.

P.C. pulled a cell phone from her pocket and began to punch the keypad. "I'm calling to report this. That's what we should have done the minute we found the damage. For all we know, he's hiding out there watching us."

The lawyer busied herself relating the pertinent information to the local police. "They're on their way. I just hope Don hasn't beaten us to it. Guess we'll find out."

Margaret listened to her friend's end of the conversation with only half her attention. The rest of her was focused on the events of the past few weeks, in which their seemingly perfect lifestyle had been brought to its knees, thanks to family violence. She had seen her children crushed and intimidated. And fearful. The man she had lived with and loved had transformed into a monster she didn't even recognize herself. He'd shattered her arm in one of his tirades. But the arm would heal, eventually. She knew that the marriage they'd had was forever broken. She would never be the old Margaret again.

Maybe that's good?

In the distance she heard the first wails of a siren that grew progressively closer, until a blue and white police car came into sight and turned into the drive. It drew to a stop near where Margaret and P.C. stood.

Two officers got out. One took their stories while the other officer made a quick walk-through of the house.

"The place is in shambles," the second officer reported. "Somebody invested quite a bit of muscle in there."

The first officer continued his interrogation. P.C. had hit the high spots for him, when he turned to Margaret. "When's the last time you were in the house, Mrs. Haywood?"

Like I could ever forget. She named the date.

"With all due respect, that's been almost three weeks. You expect us to believe you haven't been home in all this time?"

She didn't recognize the officer. *Is it possible he's the one person in Carter's Crossroads who doesn't know what happened here?*

"I've been in the hospital until two days ago." She attempted to swing her bad arm to validate her alibi. "My friend brought me over to get my clothes and some other items I needed."

"Who had keys to your home, Mrs. Haywood?" It was the second officer speaking. He had just returned from a walk around the house. "There's no sign of forced entry. Whoever did this got in with a key."

Margaret looked at P.C. who had advised her before the police arrived not to openly accuse Don. "It'll go better if they come to that conclusion themselves."

She turned to answer the officer. "I did, obviously. My oldest son, he's in high school. And my husband, of course. Just the three of us, although there may be a key in the key box at my husband's business, Haywood Tufters. You'd have to ask him about that."

"Have you called Mr. Haywood?"

"My husband and I are estranged, Officer. I haven't seen him since the night he broke my arm." She stared at the officer defiantly. *Why is he making me feel like I'm guilty?* "Haven't talked with him since that night either. I've got a restraining order against him."

The two policemen exchanged uneasy glances.

"You're sure there's no one else who has a key?" The question was posed by the first officer, while the second man returned to the patrol car where Margaret realized he was talking on a cell phone.

"My dad's been here several times to get clothes for my children, but he was using my son's key. You're welcome to talk with him."

"His name would be?"

"Harold Maxwell." She gave him the address and her parents' phone number. "I don't know what else I can tell you."

The officer asked a few more questions regarding neighbors with possible grudges. Had there been any other unexplained incidents of vandalism recently? Did Mrs. Haywood know where Mr. Haywood was?

To the last question, Margaret replied, "No, officer. I don't." *What's more, I don't want to know. Right now I hope I never have to see him again.* But she knew the chances of that were remote.

The officers left promising to be in touch and P.C. locked the house and slid behind the wheel. "I don't mean to add to your worries right now, but if what we've seen here is any indication of how far he'll go, you're going to have to make some hard decisions." She negotiated the turn out of the drive.

Margaret looked back at her house, the warm, mellow brick and the massive white columns that soared to the second story roof. The nausea in her gut threatened to erupt, but she knew she couldn't let her emotions seize control. She couldn't decide if the urge to vomit was from grief, fear or anger. Whatever, she didn't have time to indulge herself.

P.C.'s right. Whether I'm ready or not, I've got to get a handle on some of this and make plans for the future. And I've got to start today.

That's when the tears, unbidden and unwanted, began to wet her cheeks.

"Go ahead and cry, honey. As much as you've had thrown at you lately, you're entitled to a few tears."

"But I... I... don't... cry."

"Then you'd better tell your tears, because it looks like they're taking care of serious business."

The two traveled in silence until Margaret got control of herself. "At least the kids didn't see me lose it. I've got to hold it together for them."

"And you will, Margaret. You will. But remember, you're only human. And you can only shoulder so much before it affects you."

"I'll make it. I'm a survivor."

"Well, even survivors can't go without some down time. I'm going to take you back to your parents. You look like you could use a nap."

"You're probably right." Margaret watched the familiar landmarks of her old neighborhood disappear in the distance and was so weary she found she couldn't even grieve for what had been. "It's been a full day and..." she looked at the dash clock, "it's not even mid-afternoon yet."

Is every day going to be as hectic as this? I thought therapy this morn-

ing was hard, but that was a piece of cake compared to what came next.

P.C. helped her into the house and left, saying she had several errands to run. Margaret was too tired to wonder what her friend might have to do in a town where she was a virtual stranger.

She was about to stretch out on her bed when she remembered that she had to break the news to her committee. She dialed the number of the shelter and was connected with Annie, the woman who had stood with her at the hospital as they prepared her for surgery the night of Don's assault.

"Margaret..." Annie's upbeat voice actually helped to prop her up, Margaret discovered. *But then Annie has that knack.* "It's so good to hear your voice. I'm sorry I've been neglecting you, but we've got more victims in the shelter right now than we've ever had."

Margaret knew that Annie was totally dedicated to the women and children that she and her staff served, and could only imagine how busy the little woman had been. It made it that much harder to have to share bad news. But she knew she had no choice.

"Hate to add to your load, Annie, but we've got a problem." She went on to relate the afternoon's discovery. "I'm just sick about it. Alice has worked so hard and all the publicity is already printed and out there." Alice Hanover was also an abuse victim. Her husband had tried to burn her out when Margaret first met her and donated the clothes that Alice wore to her mother's funeral.

Their friendship had blossomed and, when Margaret was asked to chair a new fundraising effort for the domestic violence shelter, she'd asked Alice to serve with her.

"I'm sick for you, too," Annie replied, "but I'm also not totally surprised."

"You aren't?"

"Remember Margaret, at the end of the day, despite his money and his reputation, Don Haywood is an abuser. And abusers will stop at nothing to keep their power intact."

"I know... I truly do. It's just hard to accept it. He's always supported every community service project I ever attempted."

"But you've never undertaken one that threatened him literally where he lived."

"But what about the tour?" *The tour I was supposed to be chairing before my husband broke my arm.* "It's bad enough that I dumped everything on Alice. Not that she hasn't done a marvelous job," she hastened to add.

She could hear Annie speaking to someone in the background. *Poor Annie. Her entire day is nothing but one interruption butting in on another interruption. I don't see how she has sense enough at night to find her car.*

"I'm sorry, Margaret. We just got another victim and this one has a four week-old little boy. Her husband threatened to kill the child because the wife didn't respond to his physical advances."

"Thank goodness she had the courage to get out."

"Too many don't and that's why we have so many funerals for small children." She paused. Finally the shelter director spoke again. "I'm worried about you, Margaret. I think it might be best if you withdrew from the tour. For this year, anyway."

"You mean because of the negative PR my battle with Don could have on ticket sales?"

"Lord, no. I'm just enough of an opportunist to run you on a float down the middle of Main Street as the poster child for battered women." She chuckled. "Well, maybe I wouldn't go that far. No, it's not because we're ashamed of you. I just fear what else Don may do to you in his efforts to regain control."

Margaret knew that Annie was sincere, but she also knew

that she couldn't cave in to Don's intimidation. "Thanks for your concern, Annie. I mean that sincerely. But unless you fear that my association with the tour would hurt ticket sales, I'm going to stay front and center."

"And I respect you for that," her friend assured her. "Just promise me you won't overdo. You're still a long way from recovered."

"That's why I'm about to settle down for a long afternoon's nap."

"Pleasant dreams, then. We'll talk more tomorrow. But remember, if you need me... I'm only a phone call away."

Margaret was stretched out on her bed, almost asleep, when her mother tapped on the door. "Sorry to wake you, hon. But Dr. Michaels, your pastor, is here. I thought you'd want to see him."

Did Dr. Michaels call to say he was coming by and I forgot?

"Tell him I'll be right there, Mom." She pulled herself up from the bed, ran a brush through her hair, and straightened her clothes. Afterward, she regretted having made even that much effort.

Margaret had already accepted that she was going to be the bad guy. For sure, Don had spent a couple of days in jail. Now it appeared that the community was more concerned with his embarrassment and loss of prestige. Never mind Margaret's badly broken arm and the shattered lives of three children who had witnessed his physical attack on their mother.

As it turned out, Dr. Michaels' visit was only the latest chapter in that saga, the latest indication that Don's winning public personality and deep pockets were going to buy him a free ticket out.

What she hadn't expected was her pastor's admonition

that she needed to step away from the tour of homes and everything that it stood for. "You have allowed that den of feminists to destroy your marriage, break up your home and deprive your children of their rightful father."

Our home is broken all right. In many different ways. But I didn't do it and neither did Annie Campbell and her so-called band of feminists. Margaret knew from experience that it was futile to dispute the pastor. Besides, she was too exhausted to fight anything.

The dapper-dressed minister again turned a blind eye and a deaf ear to her concerns. "I wish you could understand my feelings, Dr. Michaels," she said as he left. Her plea has been addressed to her visitor's rapidly disappearing backside. No answer was forthcoming. Not that she really expected one.

Margaret knew the position of the distinguished salt and pepper-haired gentleman in the expensive suit, and she fingered the chipped red paint on the outside of her parents' front door and watched as the pastor's Lincoln Town Car disappeared down the steep drive. *I don't need your visits if you're not going to show me some compassion for all that I've endured.*

Tempting as it had been, she hadn't shared with him the destruction she'd discovered earlier in the day. And she didn't tell him about the letter from the children's private school that was guaranteed to break her children's hearts and disrupt their lives even further.

He wouldn't believe me. He'd just call it more of my misguided ranting and probably accuse me of trying to further hurt Don.

But she had been tempted to bring the pastor up to speed.

In the end, instead, she thanked him for coming as politely as her clinched teeth allowed, and closed the door with her intact right arm, thankful once again it had been her left arm that Don shattered.

Just like he had shattered our marriage.

Still, the purpose of Dr. Michaels' visit was his insistence that restoration of the Christian marriage was still possible. If only she would "cooperate" as God expected her to do, because of the sacred vows she'd taken. She crawled back onto her bed, but re-claiming the sleep that had almost been hers was another matter. Instead she kept replaying her pastor's insistence that she was in the wrong to punish Don for his actions.

Is it Christian marriage when the husband can stand on his head-of-the-home status to physically cripple his mate? To do what Dr. Michaels wants would mean dropping the charges against Don and taking him back as if nothing ever happened. What's more, he had the nerve to insist that I ask public forgiveness for the pain I've caused Don. What about my pain, God? Doesn't anyone care about me? And what about my children? Don is still trying to hurt them.

Margaret was still battling with the minister's comments when her daughter, Sally, appeared in the doorway.

"Mommie. I need to talk to you."

"Sure, honey. Come on in. Want to climb up here on the bed with me?"

She sensed that her daughter's visit was more than simply wanting to share time with the mother who had been absent un-til just a few days before. "I'm glad I'm home again, Sally. I've missed you. All of you."

Seizing her mother's reassurances as her opportunity, the young girl asked, "Mommie, when can we go home again? You know, to our house, so that things can be like they used to be."

The words ripped through Margaret's already breaking heart and far over-shadowed her throbbing left arm.

"All my friends are talking about us, Mommie. You're out of the hospital now. Can't we go home?"

Oh, Sally, if only you were old enough to understand all the reasons why I can't even begin to answer your questions. But come to think of it, I'm a lot older than you, and there's so much I don't understand either. Or is it that I still don't want to accept it?

Tears began to spill down the cheeks of the chestnut haired little girl and her two pony-tails tied with colorful green ribbons jerked with emotion. She moved closer to Margaret on the bed and snuggled. "I don't like the way things have been, Mommie. I just want to go home. I'm tired of being Grammy's little girl."

Oh, Lord, how do I tell her there's no home to go to? Can she ever understand that even if we could go back to our house, things will never be the same? Don can never live with us again.

"We'll talk about all of this in a couple of days, sweetie. You and Brian and Jason and me. I know you're ready to get back to your own room, and I'm sorry your friends are making you uncomfortable." She stroked her daughter's head. "But I promise you, there will be some answers soon. Can you trust me to wait a few more days?"

"Won't Daddy be here too?"

"No, I'm sorry, he won't."

"But he's still our daddy. Isn't he?"

No... No... No! He's not! Margaret wanted so badly to scream. *But I don't dare. Don is still their other parent, whether I like it or not.*

"Of course he's still your daddy. And he always will be. But he can't be a part of this discussion."

The little girl in the faded jeans and Atlanta Falcons tee-shirt climbed down from the double bed. The set of her shoulders spoke more eloquently than any words ever could. Margaret read her body language and it screamed that the little girl still had unasked – and unanswered – questions.

"It's because he hit you and he's been in jail." Her daughter's pronouncement held no trace of doubt, and it cut further into Margaret's already fragile heart.

"That's part of it. But there's a lot more besides. Come Sunday evening, the four of us will sit down together and I promise I'll answer all your questions then."

"Grammy will want to be there, too. She says you're doing daddy wrong, that he's been too good to all of us to be embarrassed this way."

Oh, Mom. I wish you could understand the damage you're doing to these children.

"I'm going to ask Grammy and Grandee to go out for the evening so that we can have total privacy. OK?"

"I guess I'll just have to wait then. But you watch, somebody will ask me again tomorrow. I wish this was the weekend so I didn't have to go back to school until Monday." Margaret saw her daughter flash her an under-the-eyelash glance that plainly questioned whether the little girl had scored with her guilt trip.

Margaret didn't respond.

"Well, then, I'm gonna go watch TV."

That's another thing, Mama has let them watch TV non-stop. I don't know how I would have managed without my parents, but I've got to find another place to live. And the sooner the better."

Sally got to the bedroom door and hesitated. Margaret could see the invisible question mark on the back of her head. She also sensed her daughter's hesitation.

"What is it, sweetie? I can tell something's still bothering you."

Again, the child hesitated. Finally she faced her mother. "Please promise me, Mommie. Please promise that we won't ever have to go to the public housing project like Mrs. Hanover and her children. I just couldn't live there and besides, my friends at school would never understand."

Oh, God, I didn't need this right now. Not after what I discovered today.

"We'll talk about it Sunday night, remember?" *I can't promise that because public housing is exactly where we may all end up. If we're even that fortunate. But at least the ridicule of your friends won't really matter, because you won't be at Mt. Zion School either.*

Margaret could tell from the slump of her shoulders that her daughter was a very unhappy little girl, but she didn't know how to answer the child without lying.

Don... Don. Do you have any idea what your violence has cost us; what it has done to your children?

CHAPTER TWO

"You need a lawyer. A good one."

P.C. Dunigan lounged in the slipper chair next to Margaret's bed, her left leg tucked beneath her. At Ruby Maxwell's insistence their Tennessee lawyer friend had eaten with the family earlier and now she and Margaret were alone.

"Sure, I need an attorney. I just wish you could represent me."

"Well I can't, I'm not licensed in Georgia. So we need to find someone who can."

Margaret was rifling through a bundle of papers secured by a rubber band. She fingered an enveloped mid-way through the pack and pulled it free. "But, you can take a look at this. It came today."

P.C. accepted the letter, opened it and as she read, her eyes widened. "You have got to be kidding! He's refusing to pay the kids' school tuition?"

"That's about the size of things. I can understand him wanting to hurt me, but to do this to his children is a new low."

"What will you do?"

"I'm not sure, but I can tell you what I won't be doing. I won't be paying their tuition. I don't have the money."

What I'd like to do is strangle Don Haywood, Lord. Only that wouldn't solve anything. But I've got to do something.

P.C. handed back the letter and got up to pace the room. "You should be able to get a court order to force him to continue paying their expenses until everything is settled."

"But that will take an attorney and they cost money. And I would imagine the better the attorney, the higher the fee."

"You're half right. Only you don't have to pay. Your attorney can sock Don with your legal costs and you get the best of both situations."

"So where do we find this legal wizard? I can guarantee you there's not one attorney in Carter's Crossroads who'll go up against the great Mr. Haywood. He's underwritten too many favorite causes and greased too many skids."

P.C. slammed her fist onto the small tea table that sat next to her chair. The single-legged table shimmied, but didn't collapse. "We don't want anyone local. For something like this, you need a big gun from Atlanta."

"Atlanta?"

"A big dog from the big city is what we're going to get."

Margaret considered P.C.'s advice. *I know she's right, it's just that I never thought I'd find myself in this position. Lord, I don't even know how to begin.*

The two women talked further with P.C. leaving shortly

afterward, the promise that her one goal for the next day would be to find the right attorney.

"Get some rest, my friend. You've been through the mill today."

After getting dressed for bed, Margaret went to be certain her children had finished their homework and were in their pajamas.

"As soon as this show goes off, she told the trio, it's bedtime for all of you. Tomorrow's a school day."

"Aw, Mom."

"Jason, my man, you know the drill as well as I do. Just because we're at Grammy's doesn't change the rules. If we'd been at home, you wouldn't have gotten to watch TV at all."

"Yes," Jason answered, "but we're poor little children and Grammy says we need all the petting we can get.

Margaret chose to ignore her mother's second-hand opinions and after a few more half-hearted protests that Margaret felt were offered because it's what children did, they agreed to their mother's directive.

Back in her room, Margaret tried to follow her own orders, but her mind wouldn't cooperate. Instead, she replayed the events of the day, beginning with the discovery that the home of her dreams had been trashed. She questioned again if all of it could possibly have been her imagination. *Is all of this a bad nightmare?*

Sleep finally captured her, although it was far from restful and she greeted the new day with bleary eyes and something less than the energy she knew she'd need later, during therapy. *Who knows what else I'll be met with today.*

Before she got sidetracked, Margaret settled herself in the small bedside chair that had been her Grandmother's and opened her Bible to read for a few minutes. Since the accident, she'd found it almost impossible to overcome the many challenges that had confronted her without encouragement from the Scriptures.

I can't believe I went for years without this addition to my life. I need to hear God's voice before I get involved in my everyday activities.

After reading and a time of prayer, where she shared concerns and her joys with her Heavenly Father, Margaret fumbled her way into the bathroom and got ready for the day. Shortly after breakfast, P.C. arrived to take her to the hospital.

"I've got several phone calls to make while you're in therapy, but I'm planning to have an attorney for you by the time I see you in an hour."

∽

"Today you probably hate me, Mrs. Haywood, but when you have the use of your arm a few months from now, you'll thank me."

The words were offered by a bouncy, blond-headed young woman who wore her hair in pigtails. A blood-red and white striped lab coat over her regulation white pants gave the first appearance that she was an overstock from the candy factory.

"No... Candi... I could never... never... hate you... but I can... see... how it would be very easy... to do."

The last words were said with much strain and grunting, as Margaret attempted to lift the dumbbell to the height her therapist had indicated. "You really know how... to hurt... a girl... don't you?"

"I am pleased when my patients can reach the goals I believe are attainable. But I don't get any pleasure when they're hurting. My reward comes when I can see them recovered and using their injured limb."

""I can appreciate that you would look at it that way. God must do wonderful things through you."

Margaret saw a wave of dismay sweep across the therapist's face and she wasn't quite sure how to interpret it."

As Candi began to massage Margaret's hands to help bleed the pain out of her body, she asked, "So why don't you hate me? I can tell you with certainty that many of my other patients do, and often tell me so to my face."

She completed the massage and began to stretch Margaret's fingers, the final step in each session. "What's your secret lady? As badly as I've hurt you during some of our work-outs, you ought to hate my guts." She paused for a second, obviously thinking before she spoke. "That's how I'd feel if you caused me this much pain."

"It's no secret. I'll be glad to share it with you. Or with any of your patients for that matter."

Candi patted Margaret's shoulder. "Honey, I wish you would. When the going gets rough, as it often does, the patient's attitude can make a bad situation tolerable." She flexed Margaret's thumb. "Attitude really is half the battle, you know."

"Your hand massage is so relaxing. I'd love to have it on a regular basis even if I weren't in therapy." She smiled at the young lady whom she assumed was in her mid-20s. She was single, that much Margaret knew for certain from earlier conversations. "It's almost worth the torture just to get to the hand massage."

Margaret lay back on the table, still breathless from all the exertion. *Thank you, Lord, for holding my hand through another very painful treatment.* Then, without opening her eyes, she said, "It's prayer, a simple prayer that I say before we begin each session."

Candi, who had been gathering up her rubber balls and lotions turned with a start. Disbelief was clearly written across her naturally upturned nose. You're telling me that because you say a prayer what we do here doesn't hurt?"

Margaret turned in the direction of her therapist's voice and opened her eyes. Looking the other woman straight in the face, she said, "Oh, it hurts. Believe me, it's very painful." *I've got to get this out before I lose my nerve.* "You see, I don't ask God to take away the pain. Instead, I ask Him to be with me while I do my therapy and to help me stand the pain."

"And He does that?"

Margaret smiled, while inside she was bursting. "When I'm bending my elbow or squeezing that little red ball you think so much of, I can feel Him moving with my arm."

"You're serious?"

"Without God, I'd have given up a week ago, but He's promised me He'll be with me. With His help, I know I'm going to make it."

Candi stopped loading her equipment and turned to face her patient. "If you had hit me with this the first day or so, I'd have written you off as a semi-deranged crackpot or at least a couple of sandwiches shy of a picnic."

"And you don't think that now? You don't think I'm a little strange?"

"Oh, I'd like to. Believe me, I really would." Candi pulled a chair alongside where Margaret had risen to a sitting position. "You see, God talk usually turns me off." She played with the gold charm bracelet that dangled from her left arm."

"That's a beautiful bracelet. I had one years ago and the chain broke and I lost it."

"Thanks, it was a gift from a very special lady in my life. I guess she's part of the reason when anyone starts to talk about God like He lives in the house with them, I want to turn and run in the opposite direction as fast as I can."

Lord, please put the right words in my mouth so I can glorify You without coming off like a goody-two-shoes.

"So... there's the door. Take off. I promise I won't be offended."

Her new friend was struggling, but Margaret didn't feel led to say anything that would lessen her discomfort. Instead, she reached out her good right hand and took hold of the therapist's hand. And held it.

Finally, and with what appeared to be a great deal of effort, Margaret was rescued from counting squares of ceiling tile when Candi said, "I don't know why, but I can't run this time. I really can't. I don't even want to?"

As she twirled one of her ponytails, she added, "It's like my body refuses to move." She looked back at Margaret with an accusatory tone. "Say, what gives with you anyway? You sure don't strike me as a Bible thumper."

Margaret realized the other woman was blushing.

"I'm sorry," she offered. "I don't mean to insult you, or your religion either."

Lord, please put the words that Candi needs to hear in my mouth. Use me, Lord.

"You haven't insulted me. Or my religion. But why don't we get down to the nitty-gritty here and stop tiptoeing around the real issue?"

"I'd like that. I'm just confused and I'm not your average Christian either, although once I called myself one."

"So how am I not average? I'm not even sure I'd recognize an average Christian if I met one."

Candi struggled with her thoughts. "Other Christians I've dealt with were almost snooty acting, like they were better than me because they had religion and they assumed that I didn't."

She brought her hands up beside her face and a grimace of frustration marred her usually chipper expression. "They're judgmental and they always spout verses at me like they have a license or something because they know God." She blushed again. "But to me they look like first class phonies."

"And I'm not like that?"

"You sure aren't. You see, those other Christians would talk to me like I was a dog because I asked them to do something that hurt. But not you."

She wheeled on her heel and stuck out her right hand, her index finger only inches from Margaret's face. "Tell me the pain hasn't been excruciating. You know it has. But you've never once complained or refused to do what I asked. Why? That's what I want to know."

Margaret attempted to gather her wits yet again, a task made more difficult because she was tiring quickly. *Even with God taking the treatment with me, it's still exhausting. A nap would be so nice.*

"The only answer I can give you is the truth. I have to recover from this because I don't have any choice. And the only way I can reach that goal is to do everything that you ask of me, and more if possible."

Candi reached for Margaret's good right hand. "But you don't even whimper. How do you stand the pain?"

"I ask God to help me bear it and He's right there, hurting right along with me."

"You really believe that."

Margaret smiled. "Without Him, I could no nothing, just like the hymn says."

Candi looked away. "Then why wasn't He taking care of you when your husband beat you up?"

So that's where this is really going.

This time she was ready with an answer. "I can understand how you might see it like that. But you see, I believe He was there."

"You're not serious?"

"Look, my three children weren't harmed. There was only one blow which, admittedly, was a severe one. But Don stormed out. He didn't hang around to hit me again. I was able to summon help and get my children to a place of safety."

Margaret smiled at the young lady who truly had, whether she realized it or not, become a soul mate through the difficult times they had endured together. "So you see, I know God was right there with me."

Almost as if unwilling to concede her position, Candi countered. "But if He was there, why didn't He stop your husband from assaulting you?"

It was a question she had asked herself more than once during those first few days in the hospital. The answer had arrived from a most unsuspecting source. There had been a knock at the door late one afternoon, shortly after the physical pain medication had been decreased and she was in major discomfort. But the pain in her arm paled in comparison to the pain in her heart that she couldn't seem to resolve.

"You won't think less of me if I admit that I asked that same question in the beginning?"

"Evidently you got an answer."

"A minister acquaintance of mine, a lady as a matter of fact, from out of state, dropped by to see me on her way to a conference in Atlanta." Margaret could tell she had Candi's attention. She couldn't help smiling as she recalled that special afternoon when P.C.'s pastor had lifted her spirits in more ways than one.

"I don't understand."

"This minister is herself a former battered spouse. When I asked her why God allowed this to happen, she threw it back in my lap."

"I've always heard that victims provoke their attackers, but I don't agree."

"Neither do I," Margaret affirmed. "And neither does Pastor Janice. But that's not how she meant it."

The look on Candi's face clearly asked for more. It was, Margaret felt, a request that sprang from the very depths of the young therapist's confused soul. Exhaustion was close to claiming her, but she knew she couldn't stop. *Stay with me, Lord. Please. We're so close.*

"God had been dealing with me for quite some time about the state of my marriage and the need to confront a bad situation that was rapidly getting worse. If I had followed His guidance, this might never have happened." She paused to catch her breath and realized that the starch was draining quickly.

"You see, Candi, it's only been in the past few weeks that I've come to realize that God expects us to help Him to help us."

"But God is supposed to be all powerful." The statement was made with very little room for doubt, Margaret observed.

"And He is. God gave us brains and heart and hands and feet, to be used as His instruments. God expects me to know better than to walk willy-nilly into rush hour traffic on I-75 and depend on Him to miraculously keep all the cars from hitting me."

Candi was quiet for the longest time and the weary patient questioned whether she had gone too far.

"You're something else, Margaret Haywood."

"Is that good or bad?"

"I'd have to say it's good. Very good, in fact." The therapist gathered the last of her equipment and headed for the door. "Gotta go now. I'm late for my next session." Her striped lab coat was swirling about her legs as she reached the door, then turned and said. "You know, I've heard a good many sermons growing up. My mama believed you were in church every Sunday, unless you were dead. And then you were there for sure."

She flashed Margaret a toothy grin. "Most of 'em left me cold and empty. And questioning. But this the first time I've ever seen a sermon."

Then she was gone, but the echo of her words replayed themselves in Margaret's head as she finally surrendered to the sleep of exhaustion. She would recall later that it had been one of the most peaceful sleeps she had ever enjoyed.

It was also to be the last peace she knew for quite some time.

"Wake up, Margaret. I've got you a lawyer."

Exhausted from the therapy and from the emotional encounter with her therapist, Margaret had allowed herself to drift off into a twilight sleep where there was no pain and trouble was a seven-letter word that didn't fit into her vocabulary.

"A lawyer?" Her voice was slurred and thick sounding. *Why do I need a lawyer?*
"Let me nap just a little longer," she begged, anxious to recapture the euphoric slumber she'd been enjoying.

"Margaret. It's me, P.C. Wake up. We've got to see this attorney today if you expect Don to pay the kids' tuition. Otherwise, he's going to abuse you again."

He's going to abuse me again. Don's going to abuse me... abuse me...

abuse me.

She felt the damp cold of a rough cloth assaulting the warmth of her face and she jumped from shock. *Oh my gosh, Don. I've got to stop him.*

"P.C.! P.C.? You gotta help me, please. The sound of unleashed fear in her voice made her even more afraid and panicked. "Please!"

P.C. grabbed Margaret by the shoulders, being careful to avoid the injured arm. "That's what I'm trying to tell you. I've got you an attorney in Atlanta and we have an appointment for 3:30."

It was P.C. who was washing my face. "Can we make it? What time is it now?"

"We can and we will, but not before you finish your nap."

"Don't say that. I don't have time for sleeping. This man has got to stop Don and the sooner he knows, the sooner he can do something about it."

"I agree," P.C. said patiently. "But right now, I'm taking you back to your parents. You need a good nap so you'll be on top of your game when we see Jim Deaton."

That's his name? Jim Deaton?"

"He specializes in spousal abuse divorces. What's more, he comes highly recommended."

It didn't occur to Margaret at the time to ask who had given this attorney such a glowing reference. Instead, she said, "I really am tired... Guess I've sort of overdone it today. A nap would be nice."

"Then here's the game plan: You go home and sack out. Take a good long nap. I'll wake you in plenty of time to get you some lunch and we'll still make the appointment."

· "When I got married, Mr. Deaton, I assumed it would be for life."

"And you no longer believe that?" The question came from a young man whom Margaret guessed would be about 35, maybe 37. When he looked at her, as he was doing now, the cobalt of his eyes gave him a twinkle at the same time that she saw a look of ferocious determination. *This man doesn't pull any punches and I suspect he doesn't allow others to do so either. But he's so young. Don't I need someone older, more experienced?*

She faced the man who, while he played pick-up-sticks with the paper clips in the dispenser on his desk, still had not taken his eyes from her face. Those all business blue eyes.

"At the same time that I answer your question, Mr. Deaton, I have to tell you that this is the first time I've really admitted this to myself. Given the severity of the physical injuries my husband inflicted on me, never mind the emotional scars that my three children and I will carry with us always, I have to question why I would want to remain married to my abuser."

I've always been so proud to tell people that Don was my husband. There! I've said it.

"Then we'll proceed accordingly."

Margaret had immediately liked the sandy-haired gentleman with the Dennis the Menace haircut. He met them personally in his waiting room, which had University of Georgia Bulldog memorabilia of every description on the walls and table tops.

He didn't try to reason with me or get me to change my mind. I wonder why?

Instead of asking him, and satisfying her curiosity, Margaret said, "I really appreciate you seeing us on such short notice."

"Hey," he answered good-naturedly. "When you specialize in domestic violence work, you sometimes have to throw an appointment book out the window. After talking at length with Ms. Dunigan, I felt your case was one of those."

Margaret patted P.C.'s hand in appreciation, while the Tennessee attorney was strangely quiet, sitting composed and not at all intrusive in the chair next to Margaret.

"From what I understand, you need some representation now, not next week or next month, if your children are to continue in their present school with their tuition paid by their father. As well it should be."

He doesn't mince words.

"I really like what I'm hearing. But I don't imagine you work for free Mr. Deaton, and I have very little money of my own."

There was that laugh again and Margaret decided he sounded like some actor she'd seen on TV, but at the moment, she couldn't decide who.

"The name's Jim, that is, if I may call you Margaret. And no, I make it a practice never to work for free. The creditors hate it when you do that and can't make your Jag payment on time."

Margaret guessed he was cracking a joke, at least about the Jag. "I can call you Jim, I think, but I still can't pay you."

"I don't want your money, Margaret. You're going to need every penny you've squirreled away. But I do intend to get paid." He dumped the paper clips again and began a new game of pick-up. "You see, Don Haywood is going to pay my fee, and for him, it ain't gonna be cheap."

That's what P.C. said he could do, but I didn't really believe her.

"Then you'll take my case?"

"I thought you understood. I've already started the file." He held up a manila folder with "Haywood, Margaret" in large black block type on the tab. "You've got yourself an attorney."

"So where do we begin?

"I want all the details of what happened the night your husband arrived home on that evening when he later struck you and broke your arm."

For the next two hours, Margaret spoke almost non-stop. The attorney filled one legal pad with notes and began writing in a second one. Occasionally he would interrupt to ask a specific question, but for the most part, he simply let Margaret talk.

P.C., who had maintained her silence, finally interjected herself into the conversation as Margaret began to wind down. "So what about the tuition? It's due by the first of the month, almost $5,000.00. Margaret simply does not have those kinds of resources."

"Did you by chance bring the letter with you?"

Margaret handed over the offensive letter and the attorney quickly scanned it.

"I'll have a conversation with the school on Monday. This is Friday evening and I'm sure they're gone for the day. Meanwhile, let me make a copy so that you can keep the original."

When he left the room, Margaret turned to P.C. Speaking quickly, she said, "He's exactly what I need. But how, out of all the attorneys in Atlanta, did you find him? And so quickly, too."

P.C. grinned. "Promise this will go no farther?"

"Sure, but..."

"You'll understand. Joe Busbee put me onto him. It was the mention of Joe's name that got him to see us today."

"Did you call Joe or did Joe call you?"

There was that awkward grin again. "I called Joe. Seems he and Mr. Deaton, Jim, are close friends and Joe knew he was who you needed."

"Poor Joe."

"Poor Joe is right. You don't know the half of it. He's a real alright guy who is caught in the middle of a very awkward situation right now and wishes he could escape to an uncharted desert island somewhere in the South Pacific."

"I guess I didn't know how Joe felt about all of this. I didn't even consider asking him to represent me."

P.C. twisted in her chair. They could hear Jim Deaton's footsteps coming closer. "I'm glad you didn't. In the first place, his specialty is business. And in the second place, Don is bombarding the poor guy with demands that he represent him, and then ranting at him because he won't."

"Poor, poor, Joe."

"When this is all over, you need to let him know that you appreciate the position he's put himself into, refusing to help Don, his long-time client, and slipping information to me at the same time because he feels an obligation to you."

"I never dreamed it would all play out this way."

"Neither did Don. That's why he's so frantic."

Attorney Deaton returned and handed Margaret the original of her letter from Mount Zion School. After he has taken his seat, Jim Deaton pulled open a drawer in his desk and extracted a number of pamphlets. "Here's some reading matter for you about the practicalities of the divorce process." He grinned. "And they also prepare you for the peculiarities as well, because there are many."

"Thank you. I didn't realize there was a divorce manual. Something like *Divorce for Dummies* or something?"

He grinned again. "It's an unofficial manual at best, but it does help take some of the surprise out of the ordeal. Some of those brochures deal specifically with divorce where spousal abuse is the primary grounds. You'll want to pay particular attention to those."

Margaret realized that the amount of natural light filtering through the Plantation shutters was greatly reduced and guessed that it was well after Jim Deaton's normal business day. Still, there was one other item she had to ask about. Shoving aside what she assumed was embarrassment, she posed her question.

"Do you mind if I ask you something rather personal?"

"Don't guess we'll know 'til you try, so shoot."

"Why do you specialize in domestic violence divorces? If I'm hearing between the lines correctly, this is a topic that's especially important to you."

The grin returned, wide as ever, but this time it didn't extend to his piercing blue eyes.

Uh oh, I've hit a nerve. Why didn't I keep my mouth shut?

"It's really very simple," he answered, after taking what Margaret considered an extraordinary amount of time. *Was he trying to figure out how to say it politely, or have I made him angry and he needed time to cool off before he spoke?*

"I grew up in an abusive home where my father controlled every time any of us breathed. The few times I told anyone, they didn't believe me."

"Didn't believe you?"

"My father was a judge."

"A judge?" Margaret and P.C.'s response was in perfect stereo.

"And because of his prominence and the public image that he projected, he didn't fear getting caught."

"Is he still practicing?"

"No. He was disbarred several years ago."

"And your mother...?"

"Jim Deaton hesitated ever so slightly and his face assumed what Margaret could only describe as a mixture of deep love and abject misery. "My mother is dead."

"I'm so sorry. I really shouldn't have asked." She grabbed P.C.'s arm. *I need reinforcement.*

"He hit her in the side of her head with a two-by-four on the same day I graduated from high school."

Both ladies were silent, uncertain of what to say. P.C. was the first to find her voice. "But why, Jim? Why?"

"He had a very good reason, at least that's what he told the jury. She had dared to defy him and give me permission to go on my high school senior trip after he had forbade me to go."

"Oh, how awful." Beside her, Margaret could hear P.C. reacting as well.

"They convicted him of murder in the second degree. I think, in truth, the D.A. was too intimidated about having to prosecute 'Hangin' Joe Deaton' to push for murder one and the death penalty."

"Is he still in prison?" P.C. was the first to speak.

The young attorney swiped at his brow. "He served 11 years of a 15-year sentence and was paroled. The man lives as a bitter recluse in the same house where he killed my mother. And he blames her for his disbarment."

"You're kidding? He blames her because he killed her?"

"He would tell you right now, if you were to ask him, that she'd still be alive today if she had just recognized that he was the head of the house."

"He's sick!" Tears were streaming unbidden and unchecked down Margaret's cheeks.

"My father didn't intend to kill my mother. She waited on him hand and foot and he believed he was entitled him to that level of servitude. But that one time when his anger got away from him, he lost control. And my mother died."

"I'm so sorry."

"That, Margaret, is why I specialize in domestic violence cases. Partially to render a service that is desperately needed, and partially out of guilt."

"Guilt?"

He was a study in misery. "I couldn't do anything to help my mother, but there are other victims that I can help. You are one of those because you managed to survive."

"You don't mean...,?"

"Make no mistake, Margaret, Don had no intention of killing you that night. But had his anger been stronger, and had he persisted in beating you, you might be talking to my mother right now instead of me."

Dead? I never thought it through that far.

Like I said, Don wouldn't have meant to do more than scare you into submission, but if he went too far, you'd have been dead either way."

The fragrance of rich soup stock and cornbread baking assaulted the two ladies when they returned late from their mission into Atlanta. Peeping into the pot, Margaret was reminded that many of the family nights from her childhood revolved around Ruby Maxwell's homemade soup. Tonight it was vegetable beef. *But I can remember potato soup. And the big pots of chili that always made you go back for seconds.*

"You're just in time," her mother crowed. "The soup's been simmering all day, my cornbread is just about done. And for dessert we've got homemade apple pie."

"Umm, Mom... it does smell wonderful. I'm so tired, I was

going straight to bed, but bed will have to wait."

"Then sit and I'll serve it up in a jiffy. You, too, P.C., nobody leaves without eating."

"Gee, Mrs. Maxwell, I'd love to stay if you have enough."

"It's not a question of enough, but is it good enough. It ain't fancy, but if I do say so myself, it'll be good enough."

As the cook went to the doorway at the top of the stairs, P.C. took another look around the Maxwell kitchen. "You're mother is very transparent, did you know that?"

Almost asleep, with her head lying in her soup bowl, Margaret asked, "Transparent? How do you mean?"

"Just look at this kitchen. I've heard of people matching their possessions and this is one of those cases."

"I don't get it."

"Just look at her cookbooks. They're all dealing with downhome southern and country cooking. There's not a French one or a gourmet one in the bunch."

"That's because Mama's a meat and potatoes cook."

"My point exactly. She has the accessories that speak to who she is. I think it's wonderful."

The cook under discussion was, in the meantime, rapidly becoming provoked. "Harold Maxwell. You down there?"

"We're here, Ruby. What's got you so bothered?" The words wafted on a sea of audio from the basement, up the stairs, to where one little woman stood, vexed, with her hands on her hips.

"Come on up Harold. Margaret's just about asleep at the table and the soup's gonna get cold. Now bring those children and come on up."

"Be there in a minute..."

"Honestly, when he gets to playing with those three, I gain

another grandchild!"

But the four missing diners were soon in place, the blessing said, and bowlful after bowlful of delectable soup consumed, until at last, Margaret yelled surrender and retired to her bedroom where the she was asleep almost before her head hit the pillow. The soup provided fuel for weird, and at times, hilarious dreams.

At one point, when she wakened during the night, Margaret was able to recall snatches of the dream she'd been immersed in. *It's almost like I was able to pick back up from this morning.*

If Margaret had doubted the need to retain an attorney so quickly, those doubts were put to rest the next morning, even before the family finished with their traditional Saturday morning breakfast.

Her father had responded to the rather strident summons of the front door bell and returned to the kitchen accompanied by two men in suits. Margaret recognized one of them as an officer on the Carter's Crossroad's Police Force.

"Mrs. Haywood?"

I don't have a good feeling about this.

"Yes, I'm Margaret Haywood. Is there a problem?"

"Detective Collins, Mrs. Haywood. And this is Detective Anderson. We have a few questions we need to ask you."

What has Don done now?

"Certainly, won't you have a seat? Can we get you a cup of coffee?" She hoped her speech didn't betray how frantically her heart was pounding. *Where are the kids? I don't want them hearing whatever this might be.*

"We'd rather talk in private, Mrs. Haywood."

"Anything you have to say to me, Detective Anderson, you can say in front of my parents." She looked to her father, hoping she didn't appear as frantic as she felt. "Dad, where are the kids?"

"The boys left about 15 minutes ago with that group from your church to play football and Sally has gone with Mrs. Martin and Audra. She said you'd given her permission."

I don't remember giving her permission, but if she's with Mrs. Martin, I won't worry. Those girls have been best friends forever. I'm glad to see that all of this hasn't hurt that relationship.

If facial expressions and body language were any indication, Margaret judged, both of her visitors were extremely uncomfortable. "Really, Mrs. Martin, we must insist. We have to talk with you alone."

This IS serious. "Am I under arrest?"

"No ma'am, you're not under arrest, but we do need to ask you several questions and we would prefer to talk with you privately."

"I can assure you, my daughter has nothing to hide." The tone of his voice told Margaret that her father was highly upset. "And I'm not at all comfortable with the way this is sounding."

"Please, Dad. It's okay. Like you say, I've done nothing wrong and I have nothing to hide." She put out her good arm to Detective Collins, who helped her stand. "Right this way, gentlemen. We can talk in the living room. However, I only have a few minutes to give you, because I am due at therapy in less than an hour."

"We'll be as brief as possible."

She seated herself while offering each of the detectives a seat. Margaret was more than a little alarmed that they positioned themselves on either side. *Why do I feel surrounded?*

"Mrs. Haywood, how much do you hate your husband?"

"Hate my husband? I don't hate him at all. It's his actions that I have a problem with." *Where are they going with this?*

"Would you say you hate his actions enough that revenge would be an option?"

"I'm not certain I understand what you mean."

"You said yourself that you have to be at therapy in less than an hour, so let's not play games. You seem like a reasonably intelligent woman, and the question is simple enough."

What is it that I am supposed to have done?

"Someone has done a number on your husband and given the circumstances, you're the primary suspect."

"I'm afraid you're still talking in riddles. Just what is it that I'm supposed to have done to Don? It's been three weeks last night since I've even seen him."

"Someone has vandalized his home and inflicted tens of thousands of dollars in damage. I don't suppose you'd know anything about that."

P.C. was right, Lord. He's trying to make me the bad guy. She couldn't decide whether to be speechless or angry.

"That was **our** house, Detective Collins. And, no, I had nothing to do with that damage." She fought to catch her breath. *How dare Don do this to me.* "Why would I have done such a thing to the home I love? It doesn't make sense."

"On the contrary. It makes great sense," Detective Anderson replied. "As time worn as it is, there's nothing more volatile than a woman scorned. You wouldn't be the first wife to figure if she couldn't have it, she'd make sure the husband didn't have it either."

"That's absurd and I'm insulted that you would even suggest such a notion. You make me sound like a raving lunatic."

"Is it that far-fetched? The home is in your husband's name only. You could easily have found yourself on the outside looking in if you didn't reconcile with him."

So that's what this is about. I can see Don's hand. He's set this up to force me to take him back and he'll let the insurance company take the fall for the damages that "unknown vandals" did to the house.

"Whether I reconcile with my husband has nothing to do with this as far as I'm concerned." *Where is P.C. when I need her?* "Just when am I supposed to have done this dastardly deed? I was hospitalized up until about 24 hours before my friend and I discovered the damage. And my whereabouts between the time of my release and our call to 911 yesterday can be substantiated."

She attempted to wave her imprisoned arm to emphasize her point. "Besides, even if I had the time, I didn't have the strength or the balance required to wreak all the damage I saw yesterday."

"Oh, no one thinks that you personally wrecked the house." Detective Collins' grin was really more of a smirk, Margaret decided. "But you could easily have gotten someone else to do it for you."

"That's both ridiculous and an insult. I can assure you that my circle of friends doesn't run to hoodlums and vandals."

"No. How about Annie Campbell?"

"Annie Campbell? *This is becoming more bizarre by the moment.*

"You do know who she is?"

"Certainly I know who she is, Detective Anderson. "Annie is my friend and the director of the battered women's shelter here."

"And there's nothing she wouldn't do to help a "victim" as she calls them. We've had dealings with her before."

"You think Annie Campbell vandalized my house?" Margaret found it almost impossible not to laugh in the men's faces, as she visualized short and plump Annie swinging a machete. *If this weren't so serious, it would be hilarious.*

"From what your husband tells us, she's got a lot of low-life going through her shelter doors. She'd have the connections to get it done."

Margaret drew herself up with every ounce of righteous indignation she could muster. *It's one thing for Don to try to make me the bad guy, but to widen his vendetta to include Annie and the shelter is too much.*

"I've never heard anything so preposterous and I'm not going to dignify your accusation with a response. Surely you men have better things to do with your time than to run around spouting such ridiculous theories."

"Your husband doesn't think it's that far-fetched. In fact, he's been very cooperative in our investigation and is just sick that someone has violated his beautiful home in such a despicable way."

I'll just bet he's been cooperative. What did he do, bankroll some pet project for the police? Margaret immediately regretted her rush to judgment and was glad she hadn't voiced that opinion out loud. *But Don always has believed that Haywood money could buy anything needed or wanted in Carter's Crossroads. At the time, I thought he was just being civic-minded, but in reality, it was all about Don being in control.*

"If you've come to question me solely on the basis of my husband's sick accusations, you'd..."

"You'd better go back to square one and start again." P.C. Dunigan materialized from the back of the house. "You gentlemen have your nerve coming her to harass Mrs. Haywood who is trying to recover from injuries, severe injuries I might add, that were inflicted by her husband."

The two officers blushed, but Margaret couldn't be sure if it was they were ashamed or angry.

"From the sound of things, you've done about all you're

going to do here this morning, so why don't I show you both to the door?"

"And who might you be?" Detective Anderson's smirk had changed to a sneer.

"I'm Mrs. Haywood's friend and she wants you to leave. I'm just trying to help her."

"Hey, you're that lawyer woman with initials instead of a name. D.C. something. Ain't you?"

"It's P.C. and I'm still showing you to the door."

"Yeah, we heard all about you from Mr. Haywood, too. Only thing is, you can't practice law in Georgia, so you don't have no standing in this case."

"We might ought to look at her," Detective Collins answered his partner. "I'll bet she could have done it."

How far will Don's sickness go?

"You're welcome to investigate me fully. I have no more to hide than Mrs. Haywood. And as for my legal standing in the case, you don't have to be licensed to be a friend. And I'm offering her advice that I think she needs, strictly friend to friend, of course."

Margaret had finally found the voice that had left her when P.C. rode into the room on her mystical white charger. "Am I ever glad you got here. They think I'm behind all that damage at the house."

P.C. placed her hand on Margaret's now trembling shoulder. "Your dad called me. Said I ought to get over here. Looks like it's a good thing I did."

She confronted the two detectives. "Do you have a warrant? Is Mrs. Haywood under arrest?"

"No, she ain't under arrest. We're just following up on the leads her husband gave us."

"Well, I'd suggest that you carefully consider the source

of those leads, and if I were you, gentlemen, I'd widen my investigation." Then she smirked at them. "Not that I'm giving legal advice. It's just a tip between friends. We are all friends, aren't we?"

P.C.'s arrival had added starch to Margaret's backbone and she stood, unsteadily at first. "I've tried to be cooperative, but I think this entire conversation had gone very far into left field." She pulled herself up to her maximum height. "Now I'm going to ask you to leave and any further communication with me must be through my attorney. My *Georgia* attorney."

"Who's that?"

"He'll be in touch with you, Detective Collins. That's a promise."

"Can't you tell us who he is?"

Why? So you can run straight back to Don with the information?

"He'll be calling you shortly. Now if you don't mind, I think it's time you left." To emphasize her position, Margaret turned and headed for the kitchen. Over her shoulder she called to P.C., "Be sure to lock the deadbolt after Detective Collins and Detective Anderson leave."

Back in the kitchen, Margaret found her father standing, gripping the back of his chair so hard he was white-knuckled from the exertion. "Oh, Dad, thank you for calling P.C."

"Honey, I know it's not right to eavesdrop, but I knew those two were up to no good, so I stood around the corner and listened. I figured you needed her."

"Pretty low, isn't it?" P.C. asked as she plopped down in an empty chair at the round oak pedestal table where Margaret had eaten as a child. "They're gone, but this isn't over. You're going to have to be on your guard, because Don Haywood is one desperate man."

"I never thought he'd stoop so low, but it looks like he'll

do anything including implicating his wife in something that could leave her with a criminal record." Harold Maxwell reached for Margaret's hand and her heart began to melt from the expression of love and anger that she saw mirrored on his face.

"It'll be okay, Dad. We're going to make this work." *And we sure do have a lot to fix.*

CHAPTER THREE

Throughout the day, as Margaret endured yet another round of therapy at the local hospital and then huddled in a con-ference call with her attorney, she found herself revisiting the events of the past few weeks, talking them over with God in the conversational manner she had found so therapeutic for her soul.

Certainly I'm at fault here in several ways. I've never tried to dodge that. But Lord, nothing I've done has given Don the right to rip our entire family to shreds simply because he is a man. He may be a male, but real men don't deliberately cause pain.

Jim Deaton, when they reached him at his weekend home on Lake Oconee, quickly assured her that she had handled the matter exactly as he would have wanted. "Give me their names and a phone number and I'll make certain you aren't bothered any more unless I'm present."

After a few more shared comments about the vandalism at the house, the attorney said, "I'm filing a petition on Monday morning asking for an injunction to force Don to pay the kids' school expenses, and their health costs, too, until all of this is settled."

"When will that be?"

"Your divorce petition will be filed by the end of the week. My paralegal will begin drafting it on Monday, and as soon as it's complete, you'll get to see it before the finished document is printed."

"You're doing this in Atlanta?"

"No. In Carter's Crossroads."

"You mean all of this is going to be splashed out here for the entire community to know about. Why can't you do it in Atlanta?"

Margaret could hear the wheels in her attorney's head turning, but she didn't know how to read the silence that preceded his answer.

"We're doing it in Carter's Crossroads because such action has to take place in the county where the defendant resides."

"Why?"

"The law protects defendants from being named in frivolous lawsuits by requiring plaintiffs to bring suit in the county where the defendant lives."

"Why does Don need protecting? I'm the injured party here. That is, my children and I are."

"Don doesn't need protecting. Unfortunately for us, the law is written to protect defendants in general. Which, in this case, just happens to be Don. Didn't you read any of that information I gave you?"

Margaret had to admit she hadn't. "I just haven't had the

time. I was too tired last night and then the day started this morning with my two visitors."

The attorney advised her to read them thoroughly. "Whenever we get into court I want you there when I ask that Don be ordered to pay for his children's needs."

"You want me there with this hardware item on my arm, looking like I'm anorexic?"

"You bet I do."

Margaret spent the remainder of her day resting, reading the brochures she'd gotten at the attorney's on Friday, and educating herself on what was to come. P.C. was there for part of the afternoon, and by the time the evening meal was on the table, Margaret knew more than she had ever hoped to know about obtaining a divorce in a contested case.

"I thought it would just be a matter of Jim drawing up papers and presenting them to a judge for his signature. I didn't realize all of this would be happening as well."

P.C. explained, "In a situation where both you and Don agree that you don't want to be married any longer, especially when there are no children present and the property settlement is a simple one, that's just about how it goes down."

"Going down. That's what I feel like I'm doing."

"It's overwhelming, sure. But it's also reality. You want a divorce. Don doesn't. You believe you have justifiable grounds. Don doesn't agree. And there are three children whose rights and welfare must be considered."

"I know. I know. I read it all in the manual Jim gave me." She flashed her friend a searching look. "Level with me, P.C. Is there a chance the court won't give me a divorce? Could they tell me I have to stay married to Don?"

"They could...," She held up her hand to stop the rebuttal

she could see forming in Margaret's mouth. "But in your case, it is somewhere between highly unlikely and impossible that you won't get your divorce. What is up in the air here is how much responsibility Don will be made to shoulder for his children. As for you, will you walk away with nothing, since you never held gainful employment to contribute to the marital coffers, or will Don be forced to deed some of his wealth to you?"

"Whew!"

"That it is. And there's not a thing we can do about it. Besides, I heard your mom call 'soup's on.' Has she made another pot of that delicious soup since yesterday?"

Margaret giggled. "Probably not. 'Soup's on' is the standard call to chow around here, regardless of the entrée. Last night it just happened to really be soup."

The two women made their way back to the round table in the corner of the kitchen that Margaret had come to see as an anchor, since it reminded her of happier days in that house.

"Hey, Mom, Brian crowed as the three Haywoods bounded through the back door from outside. "Congratulate me! I scored three touchdowns this afternoon and we won the game."

"Hey, I'm impressed. So 'congratulations', son."

Jason giggled. "Ask him who he was playing against."

A light bulb came on. "So who were you playing against?"

Brian blushed and shot his little brother an "I'll get you later..." look. "It was just Butch Truman and his brothers."

"Isn't Butch younger than you?"

Brian's face changed color a couple of times. "Well, yeah. I guess so. What's that got to do with anything? I scored, and that's what counts."

Looks like it's time for the "It's not whether you win or lose but how you played the game" talk. But not tonight. Not now.

Margaret changed the subject instead and the good-natured talk around the table ranged from a dress that Sally just had to have to her father's announcement that he'd been asked to go back to work part-time for the accounting firm where he'd retired several years prior. Before Margaret could inquire further, Brian interrupted.

"Tomorrow's Sunday, Mom. Are we going to our church?"

Church! I haven't even thought that far ahead. She felt beads of sweat consume her as she thought about what it would be like to make an appearance in church with her arm in the awkward brace.

"They went to church with us last Sunday, but I know rather they'd rather go where they know folks their own age. But it's up to you," Harold Maxwell offered.

Everyone at the table was looking to her for an answer. She took a deep breath. "We're all going to our church tomorrow, provided P.C. can go with us."

"Well, sure, I'll go. Thanks for the invitation." She grinned. "Did you invite me because you really want me to go or because you needed a chauffeur?"

This time it was Margaret's turn to grin, although she fought the impulse before finally conceding defeat. "Both. Are you sure you don't mind?"

"Got to go to church somewhere. It might as well be with the Haywood Gang."

The alarm sounded before Margaret's exhausted body was ready and at first, she couldn't remember why the clock was disturbing her sleep. *The doctor said I needed as much rest as possible.*

Then she remembered. It was Sunday and she was about

to go back to her church where, for the first time in the more than 15 years, she worried if she'd feel welcome.

With some effort and momentary recall of the hard day she'd had on Saturday, she pulled her protesting body out of bed and shuffled off to the shower. With a garbage bag securely wrapped around her left arm to shield it from the water, she managed to bathe herself sufficiently. *Even taking a bath is a challenge when you're one-handed.*

When the family finally gathered in the breakfast room, Margaret could sense the tension in her brood. Brian, who had raised the subject of church the night before, seemed to be in a black mood and said little. Sally was complaining that her dress didn't fit right, that the color of her shoes clashed with her purse. She wondered aloud if she was getting a pimple.

But it was Jason who broke his mother's heart. The little boy who had been more like his old self for the past few days was suddenly looking at her with eyes filled with terror. *Is this how they really feel, or are they just mirroring my tension?*

Breakfast was soon finished and the five of them on their way. P.C. pulled in beneath the portico and discharged her passengers. "I'll go find a parking space and be right back."

The children, at Margaret's urging, went on to their Sunday school classes while she waited for P.C. *After all, she's never been here before.* Or was it because she was suddenly uncomfortable at the prospect of entering alone? The church, where she'd once felt as much as home as she did in their house on Red Bud Way, was frightening and intimidating.

If first impressions counted, Margaret was to reflect later, her entrance into the Sunday school classroom should have spoken legions. For one thing, those assembled looked at her as if she had three heads instead of a bum arm. But most troubling of all was the presence of Don Haywood, who sat in his customary seat at the front and who was in total command of the room.

"Well, well. Margaret. It's good to see you. You, too, P.C." He hadn't bothered to rise, but his voice boomed and Margaret felt herself becoming nauseous.

"Hey, folks, let me introduce you to my friend, P.C. Dunigan, the best little lawyer in Tennessee, even if she is a woman."

I'm not believing this.

"Good morning, Don. Everyone." P.C. acknowledged her introduction for only as long as it took to say Don's name. "I'm glad Margaret felt up to coming today. She's one of my best friends and I'm glad to be here visiting with her."

The two women took seats near the door in the back and when the class was over, Margaret couldn't even remember what the lesson had been about. On the other hand, Don's gall was unforgettable.

The class dismissed, but few in the group did anything more than mumble good-byes as they passed, as quickly as possible, their heads down and their eyes averted. *Every one of these people called themselves my friend, but they're avoiding me.* Margaret waited until the classroom was nearly empty before beginning the cumbersome task of rising and getting out.

However, if she thought she'd heard the last of her abuser, she was mistaken.

"It's so good to see you Margaret." Don's voice boomed, on purpose she suspected. He wanted others to hear. "I've missed you and I'm here for you if you need anything, Anything at all, just ask. Of course it goes without saying that whenever you're ready to put our family back together and come home, I'll be waiting for you."

Her face alternated between spasms of white-hot fury and blush red embarrassment as she and P.C. made their way into the sanctuary. Margaret didn't speak to her friend about what had just happened, for fear of totally losing control. Hysteria was surging just below the surface.

As Margaret fought to retain her composure, she was at the same time scanning the large worship area, looking for her children. What she saw was a smiling Don escorting the three younger Haywoods to a pew very near the front, where he slid in with them.

"He's using my children to make himself look good," she screeched under her breath to P.C. "What do I do?"

"Without coming off like a shrew, there's not much you can do."

The entire worship service was a nightmare and no more so than when Dr. Michaels, during the intercessory prayer, mentioned Don by name and then, as what appeared to be an afterthought, prayed for Margaret's healing "in every area of her life."

Mercifully, Margaret thought, the service finally ended, but not before she had to endure her husband's public plea to the children for reconciliation.

"Your mom is the one who's keeping you from living in our house. If she would just agree to come home, everything would be just like it used to be."

I'll just bet it would. Just like it used to be.

"I can hire someone to cook and clean until her arm is better," he added, apparently intent on sweetening the pot.

It was a somber crew that climbed into P.C.'s car for the ride back to the Maxwell home. They were almost there when Sally raised the question. "Are we still going to have our meeting tonight?"

Tonight? Is it tonight already? But this is Sunday and I did promise we would talk. Guess I better deliver.

"Yes... tonight... just the four of us. I'll order pizza so Grammy won't have to worry about cooking, and we'll talk about what we're going to do."

"Pizza sounds like a good idea, but I already know what I want to do. I want to go back home and Daddy says we can."

Oh, Sally, if only it were that simple.

"And make Brian stop making faces at me."

Margaret twisted to look into the back seat.

"Daddy says our rooms are all ready and waiting. Now Brian's sticking out his tongue."

"Son..."

"But Mom, Sally never knows when to keep her mouth shut."

"That's neither here nor there and we won't talk about it right now. Just don't make faces at your sister or stick out your tongue."

This just doesn't get any easier.

Margaret took a deep breath. "Things just aren't as simple as Daddy made them sound, but we'll talk about all of this tonight. Right now, I'm sure Grammy has a delicious lunch waiting and we don't want to spoil her good food."

Just as Margaret had predicted, her mother had baked chicken and dressing and more vegetables on the table than could be counted.

While the adults talked about a number of different matters, none of them related to the crux of the problem. Margaret noticed more than once how quiet her children had become. It grieved her that their loyalties were being pulled in differing directions. *Don, is there no end to how you will abuse your children?*

The table had been cleared, the homemade peach cobbler and ice cream was history, and the two were alone in the den when P.C. brought up the subject. "What are you up to this afternoon?"

"Looking for courage. I'll need to lay it all out on the line for my kids." Then she thought for a moment. "No, make that the courage I'll need to deal with the aftermath. Compared to that, telling them will be a piece of cake."

P.C.'s got something on her mind. Her body language says it all. "So what's bothering you? Go on. Spit it out."

"Knowing what all Don has done, makes me curious about what all we don't know. And I've got a sneaky hunch that he's been moving assets and erecting barriers to cut you off financially."

"Once upon a time, I would have rejected that idea. I'd have said you were wrong. But that was then and this is now."

As the afternoon sun swung lower in the sky and the hour of reckoning approached for Margaret, she and P.C. made a list of everything she could remember that Don had ever owned, ever invested in.

"As far as I know, while my name never appeared on any-thing, Don never made deals or excluded me from knowing what he was doing. *Except when he made the deal to sell Haywood Tufters and didn't tell me until it was almost over.*

"I'm going to get this to Jim in the morning and let him know our suspicions."

Margaret knew that her friend was about to leave and felt suddenly consumed by panic. "Do you have to go?"

"Yeah, unless you want me to stay and help you talk to the kids."

"I'd love that, more than you know. Except I promised Sally that it would be just the four of us. No Grammy and Grandee, and especially no Don." She patted P.C. on the shoulder. "Sorry, guess that excludes you, too."

From the lower level of her parents' split-level home, the two women could hear sounds of raised voices and disagreement.

"It doesn't take a rocket scientist to figure what they're arguing about."

P.C. was on her way to the door. "Careful, Margaret, don't let your maternal instincts cloud your judgment and cause you to do something you'll regret."

Margaret paced the short distance between the room's massive brick fireplace and the door to the rear foyer. "It's just not fair to have to burst their bubble."

"Maybe not, but it is reality. We don't have any guarantees in life that everything will always be smooth sailing."

"But my children...they've never had to face anything unpleasant."

Margaret realized that P.C. was staring at her. "What?"

"No offense, Margaret, but they'll be ill-prepared for life in the real world if they're never exposed to the rougher side of things."

"So you're saying?"

"Be honest. Above all, be honest. Let them know that for once they're going to have to accept situations they don't want and don't like. But reassure them that your love will always be there unconditionally."

"That's easier said than done."

"Better done now and dealt with, rather than creating false impressions and have to disappoint them later."

The pizza had been devoured, although Margaret had

found it difficult to enjoy. P.C. had left earlier, but not before extracting Margaret's promise to call after the family confab.

Harold and Ruby Maxwell had left shortly behind P.C., saying they would be out until at least 10 o'clock. Their departure was not without turmoil, however, when Margaret had had to listen once again to her mother's list of reasons why the marriage should be repaired.

Her number one reason was to spare Don the ridicule of having his dirty laundry aired in public. But what about me, Mom? What about my feelings? My embarrassment?

Margaret knew the community was already rife with gossip about them. *But I also know that not one of those details came from my mouth.*

Brian had disposed of the empty pizza cartons and the four of them were gathered in the den. As badly as Margaret dreaded what had to come, she knew that P.C. was right. *Honesty is the best policy.*

Sally, it appeared, already had her mind made up and she wasn't bashful about letting it be known. "I want to go back home and I want to go tomorrow. Daddy wants us and Grammy says we're hurting him if we don't do what he wants."

"Sally, you dope."

Margaret could read the anger in her eldest son's manner.

"Have you forgotten that Dad slapped you? He hit Mom so hard he broke her arm in seven places."

Sally went on the defensive. "No, I haven't forgotten and don't call me a dope." She stuck her tongue out at him. "Besides, Daddy said he's sorry."

"No more sticking out our tongues, okay?"

"But Mommie..."

"Sally. You heard me."

Even as she was speaking to Sally, Margaret had been keeping her eye on Jason. He hadn't spoken a word so far and actually
appeared to be in a world of his own. *This has actually been the hardest on him, I do believe.*

"Jason? You aren't saying anything."

Her youngest looked at the floor and scrubbed his shoe
against the nap in the carpet. Then, in a soft voice so low she had
to strain to hear, he answered. "I'm afraid to go back home."

"Well, I want to go back home to Daddy," Sally interrupted. "He says he's all over being mad."

*You're far too young to be a typical abuse victim, but you're sure
sounding like one. Annie Campbell says they call it the "Stockholm Syndrome"
where victims actually defend their abusers. I guess she learned it from me.*

"Like I believe that," Brian countered angrily. "Dad's made
that promise before and he's also broken that promise more than
once."

Margaret sensed that he was about to put her on the spot
and she didn't have time to dodge the blow.

"So what are we going to do, Mom?"

It's now or never. "I hear what all of you are saying and I know
already that none of you are going to be satisfied with my answer.
Please try to keep in mind that whether you agree or not, what I
am about to tell you is the truth." *And somehow, Lord, I've got to do this
without trashing their father, although my very human inclination is to do
just that.*

Over the next fifteen minutes Margaret addressed a trio
of faces that became increasingly troubled. She explained the severity of her injury and the struggle of the recovery period ahead.
Then she detailed the damage inflicted on their home and the suspicion that had been cast on her as the most likely culprit.

"That's crazy," Brian interrupted. "You were stuck in the

hospital. Besides, you love that house. You'd never destroy it."

"The police think I got someone to do it for me, since it was obviously done by someone who used a key to get in."

"I've got a key too, except Grandee has it. And Dad has a key, too."

"Yes, all three of you had easy access, too." *Thank you son for saying what I couldn't.*

"Can't we just buy new furniture" Sally's perspective was centered solely on her wishes. It was obvious she wasn't listening to anything being said.

"It's not that simple. We can't buy new furniture because we don't have the money. And while we're on the subject of money, unless I can find over $4,000.00 in the next few days, you're all going to have to withdraw from Mount Zion and enroll in public school."

"But Mom, I'm going to state in debate. If we change schools, that will ruin everything. It's not fair."

"I couldn't agree more, but the truth is, I don't have the money to pay your tuition."

"Dad will pay that."

Margaret fished in her pocket for the well-folded letter and held it aloft. "Not according to this letter."

"What do you mean, Mom?" Brian's eyes were sharp with suspicion and all of the color had drained from his face.

She read aloud from the letter, refusing to stop even when she heard the sharp intake of breath from her oldest son. *If I stop reading, I'll never get through this.*

"Dad wouldn't do that." Brian was insistent although Margaret noticed that his voice quavered. "He wants us to go to school at Mount Zion."

"I'm sorry, son. All I can do is go by the letter the school sent me. And I've heard nothing recently that tells me anything has changed."

"Daddy loves us," Sally insisted. "You just don't want us to go back home."

Jason said nothing, but his face showed more conflict than anything he might have said.

"If Dad isn't paying our tuition, does that mean he won't pay for me to go to debate competition, either?"

I wondered how long it would take for you to make that connection, son. "Your guess is as good as mine. I can't speak for your father."

"So who can you speak for?"

"Just myself, son. Just myself at this point." *And I hope for all of us.*

That question had been posed by a young man whose confidence had been severely shaken. He was wandering the room, picking up first one item and then another.

If only I could spare him this. "I've retained an attorney and will be filing for divorce in just a few days. My attorney is going into court tomorrow to ask the judge to order your father to pay your tuition and all your other bills until this whole matter is settled."

She took a deep breath. "As for where we'll live, I don't have that answer yet. But it won't be back at our old house, I'm afraid."

Margaret saw the horror in each of her children's eyes. It was an incident that she would revisit in the days to come.

"I may not be able to answer all your questions until after the divorce is final and we know how the court has ruled. After all, I'm going to have to get a job, you know."

"Mommie... we won't be living in the projects, will we? Please say we won't." Sally's voice had tears in it and the mother's heart broke because she couldn't offer that promise.

"For right now, we're fortunate that Grammy and Grandee have room for us here. But we do need to find our own place as soon as possible." She took a deep breath. "And that may have to be public housing, until we can do better."

"I can't live in that place. I'd be too ashamed," Sally wailed. The child struggled to her feet and left the room on a run. "I won't move to the projects," she screamed, "and you can't make me! I'll go and live with Daddy. He loves me and you don't."

Margaret wanted to go after her daughter, but between the cumbersomeness of arm brace and her fatigue factor, she couldn't easily get to her feet. In the meantime, Jason scooted across the floor and placed his head in her lap, making it impossible to rise.

"I just want to be with you, Mommie. Please let me stay with you. I don't care where we live."

Brian's face was red and Margaret could only imagine the emotions doing battle inside his too-old-to-be-a-teen, too-young-to-be-a-man body.

"Dad can't do this. I'm going to call him."

Margaret was unable to dissuade the boy and finally, despite her pleas, Brian left the den vowing to get a straight answer out of his father.

"Brian is mad," Jason offered, his head still in her lap. "Why can't he just be happy the way things are?"

"We're all upset, honey." She stroked his hair with the back of her hand. "We've got so many decisions facing us." With her finger, she lifted his chin. "But we will get through it."

Jason said nothing, but hugged her tighter. *I believe he's afraid to turn loose.*

"Tomorrow's a school day. Do you have all your homework finished?"

That's the first normal sounding thing I've said in longer than I can remember.

"It's all done, I guess. But I don't want to go back to school there... Can't I just go to the public school tomorrow?

"Why would you want to do that?"

"'Cause."

"Because isn't a reason."

"The little boy looked up at her. "Well it's the only reason I've got."

Further conversation between the two was curtailed when Brain sailed back into the room, his face lit with satisfaction.

"I knew there was a misunderstanding. Dad's planning to pay our tuition. He said he didn't know how the school got the idea he wasn't."

Margaret felt the rug being pulled from beneath her. *There was only one way they could have gotten that idea. From Don.* "Are you sure?"

"Dad just told me so. And guess what else? He's going to pay for our entire debate team to go to state, just like he always has."

"But Brian..." Margaret struggled to keep her equilibrium. "You heard what Headmaster Hunt said in his letter. How could there be any confusion?"

"Beats me." His face wore a wide grin. "I'm just glad we got it all straightened out. Dad said if we were all living together, it probably wouldn't have happened."

I'll just bet there wouldn't have been any misunderstanding. Don, have you no shame? You're hiding behind your own children to fight your battles. But she bit her tongue. "I'm happy for all of you, because I didn't want you to have to leave Mount Zion. But I didn't have the money to pay your tuition, either.

Brian headed out of the den, and over his shoulder Margaret heard him say, "Don't worry about that any more. Dad's going to take care of everything." As he descended the stairs, his words continued to float back up to her. "By the way, Mom, Dad said to have you call him. Said he had something he wanted to tell you."

I'll just bet he does! There are several things I'd like to tell him too, Lord. But I won't. That's why I've got an attorney.

She chose not to answer Brian and turned her attention instead to Jason who still cowered beside her. "It's going to be okay, son. I promise. Now why don't you go and get your pajamas on? It's soon going to be bedtime."

The boy pulled her head down to his and kissed her. "Night, Mommie. I love you."

Margaret watched as his tow-head dropped out of sight down the stairs. "But I still want to stay here," she heard him say.

Margaret hobbled to the top of the stairs. "Brian, will you please send Sally up here?"

It was several minutes before the little girl with the tear-stained face and pigtails askew topped the stairs. *From the sound of things, Brian had to force her to come talk to me. Lord, I don't want my children to fear me.* She didn't add that it was their father they should fear.

"You didn't want me, did you?"

"It's okay. Come here, baby."

Still, the child held back until finally, after additional coaxing, she came within arm's reach.

"I'm sorry you're so unhappy, but things are what they are. Brian has talked with your dad and he's going to pay your tuition." She fingered one of her daughter's pigtails. "You won't have to change schools."

"But Mommie," she wailed, "if we have to live in the

projects, I'll still have to change schools. My friends would make fun of me."

Why you little snob! "There's absolutely nothing disgraceful about living in the projects. Everyone can't live in a mansion."

"But we can. Daddy told me so. All we have to do is move home."

Margaret knew she was on overload with Don's manipulation of the children. She spoke carefully, choosing her words. "Listen to me once and for all, Sally. We are not going back to Red Bud Way, not unless the court gives me that house. Maybe not even then."

"I thought you loved me." Sally's scream was shrill and she stuck her fingers in her ears and danced hysterically. "But you don't love me. I hate you! I hate you!" The child broke and ran back downstairs. Margaret heard the slamming of a door and felt like she had been in the door when it shut."

Unable to deal with the grief, she hobbled down the hall to her bedroom. Then she remembered her promise to call P.C.

"I was getting worried."

"And well you should."

"Bad, huh?"

"You don't know the half of it. None of them are happy and good old Don made me look like a liar in front of my own children."

"How so?"

Margaret explained, to which P.C. replied. "Don's an abuser, Margaret. He does his dirty work by keeping you off balance. He needs a good case of court-mandated justice."

The court! Oh, my gosh. "But P.C., there's no need for Jim to go into court tomorrow. I've got to get word to him."

"You need to let him know what has happened tonight,

but I vote to allow him to go ahead with the petition."

"But Don told Brian he'd pay their tuition."

"Exactly. He told Brian. He didn't tell you and he didn't put anything in writing."

"So?"

"You've got no assurance that he'll keep the promise he made to Brian. But you do have it in writing from the school that he informed them he wouldn't pay."

"But that's not from Don."

"You don't think the school made it up, do you?"

"Good point. Okay, I'll call Jim first thing tomorrow, and if he wants to proceed, I won't object."

They talked for a few more minutes and, after she'd ended the call, Margaret reflected on the events of the day. *Don will stop at nothing to get his way. If I had good sense, I'd stay awake tonight and worry.*

Instead, she turned in her Bible, to the book of Proverbs, and read again the words of promise, *whoso harkeneth unto me shall dwell safely, and shall be quiet from fear of evil.*

I'm going to have to hold you to that promise, Lord. You're the only source of security I have against Don and his underhanded ways. Without You, I will fail.

CHAPTER FOUR

Breakfast the next morning was a mostly silent ordeal. Margaret attempted to make conversation with her children, but it was obvious, even to their grandfather, that the Haywood kids weren't in the mood for polite chit-chat. "What's the matter with them?" he asked, after they had left to meet the school van. "Didn't hardly say two words. Even little Jason didn't ask me what we were going to do after school."

"They're upset, and who can blame them," Margaret's mother interjected, cutting off Margaret's reply. Ruby Maxwell glowered at her daughter. "What you're doing to your children is criminal."

"What I'm doing is criminal? Just what have I done that's so bad?"

"You're trying to turn them against their daddy, after all

he's done. That beautiful house and plenty of money." The older woman busied herself at the stove. "There's lots of women out there, honey, that don't have it nearly as good. Think about what you're throwing away."

Margaret felt her anger rising and struggled to contain her emotions. *Hate the sin and love the sinner. Hate the sin and love the sinner.* She repeated the mantra silently, symbolically throwing her mother's favorite expression back at her.

She raised her injured arm. "If you knew everything, Mama, I'm sure you'd think differently. As for me, I don't think I had it all that great. Especially not the last time."

"Ruby, I thought we had agreed this was Margaret's decision to make. We didn't live with them and I, for one, don't like it a little bit that Don beat her and left her like this. And then him trying to charge her with all that damage at the house."

"Now Harold, I'd expect you to defend her. She's always been your little girl." Ruby Maxwell had moved to the sink and was swishing dirty dishes through the hot sudsy water with a vengeance that underscored her anger.

Margaret watched her mother's body language and pondered what to say, how to diffuse the situation. *Oh, Mama, if only you could fight as hard for me as you fight against me. If I didn't know you loved me, I might take it personally.*

The older women deposited the cleaned grits pot in the dish drainer with more force than was necessary, turned, and grabbed the tail of her apron as a towel to dry her hands, then faced her husband and daughter. "But you don't know the latest. She wants to move these children into public housing. Over there where she'd have who knows what kind of trash for neighbors. It's not safe and it's not necessary."

"What are you talking about, Ruby? That's pure nonsense."

Which of the kids complained to Grammy?

"You think it's nonsense? You just look right at your daughter and ask her why, if she's so concerned about their safety, does she want to take her children over to the projects instead of back to that beautiful home Don built for them."

Margaret felt the intensity of her father's sudden shift in attention.

"Ask her, Harold."

Margaret decided it was time to take the offensive. *Lord, control my mouth because if I say what I want to say, it will be the start of something ugly.* She beat her father to the punch.

"What Mama says is partially true, Dad. But only partially."

"Go on..."

"I don't know which one of the kids decided to recruit Mama to their side this morning..."

"It was Sally. That poor little thing came dragging in here this morning, couldn't hardly eat her breakfast, she was so upset. Kept tearing up until finally I got her to open up and tell me what's bothering her."

My poor, poor Sally. My little drama queen. I would have guessed as much.

"As I was saying, Sally was only partially right. I did tell them when we talked last night that it might necessary for us to go into public housing. But I didn't say it was definite and I haven't even inquired if there's a unit available.

"But why do you have to move anywhere? We're just rattling around in this big house and it's been great fun having you and the kids here."

Lord, help me not to hurt this gentle man that I love more than he will ever know.

Margaret hesitated, knowing that once the words were

spoken, she couldn't take them back. "It's just best for everyone, Dad, if we're in our own place." She rose from the chair and went to embrace him as best she could while balancing her bad arm. "Gosh knows I don't know what I would have done without you both, and this house to come to. Being back in my old room has been good therapy for me. But it's time to move on."

"But why public housing? If you have to go, can't you rent an apartment or a decent house somewhere? I agree with your mama. That's not the safest part of town."

Ruby Maxwell pulled out one of the breakfast room chairs and sat down. "It sure isn't safe. Why I'd have to sit up all night with a loaded gun across my lap if I had to spend even one night in that place."

Margaret caught the grin that threatened to erupt on her father's face as the two of them pictured "little" Ruby defending the home place. Her mother, who had never so much as held a gun, let alone used one.

"It's finances, Dad. Money, pure and simple."

"But you and Don are some of the wealthiest people in Carter's Crossroads."

Margaret picked up the yellow bisque saltshaker that had been on this same table when she was a child and rubbed it with her thumb to feel the grooves and indentions that reminded her of a less stressful time.

"Correction, Dad. Don is one of the wealthiest people in town. My name isn't on anything we own, and all I have that I can call mine is a few hundred dollars that I've managed to squirrel away."

The expression on her father's face spoke more loudly than words ever could. *I've shocked him.* Then she saw the red of anger begin to flood his normally placid features, as the look of surprise was replaced by one of fury.

"Do you mean to tell me that after your mother and I loaned you and Don the $20,000 you needed to start Haywood Tufters, none of the profits have your name on them?"

Oh, Dad, this was one thing I'd hoped you would never need to know.

"Don's position was that once we paid you back, with interest, just like a bank, it had no bearing on the future. So, no, nothing... the house or the cars, or even the bank accounts, have my name on them."

"But you've never wanted for anything, either," Ruby Maxwell reminded, unwilling to drop her campaign against the divorce.

"Well, Mama, I guess that depends on your definition of wanted, because there have been plenty of times that I've wanted Don to stop abusing me, to understand the toll his anger was taking on our children and on our marriage."

"Don't call it abuse, Margaret." Ruby Maxwell wrung her hands as she spoke. "You make it sound so dirty, like what happens in those families over in the projects. You and Don just had disagreements and sometime he went... well...went farther than he should have."

Margaret just looked at her mother, unable for the moment to speak. Then she said, "I called is abuse, Mama, because that's what it is."

She rose from her chair, noting that the rooster clock said it was time to call her attorney. "I'm sorry if you can't accept the truth, but the reality of the situation is that he beat me, repeatedly. He verbally belittled me and he used me. What's worse, he physically assaulted his own daughter and nothing you can say will make me believe that it's any more dangerous for my children in public housing that it was in our upscale home in the right part of town."

I'm sorry, Lord. I had to tell it like it was. Margaret bent to kiss her mother's head. "I love you, Mama, but you've got a blind spot when it comes to Don. And believe me, abuse happens in more homes than you could ever realize."

She was on the phone, about to dial Atlanta, when there was a slight knock at the door.

"Come in."

Harold Maxwell entered the room wearing a hat-in-hand look on his face. Then he realized she was about to use the phone. "I'll come back when you're finished."

"I'm just calling my attorney. Won't be but a minute. Sit down and wait."

Her father said nothing, but settled rather uneasily, she thought, on the small chair in the corner. *Dad never came into my room that much when I was growing up. I wonder what's up?*

In a manner of seconds she heard her attorney's voice and she relayed the message Don had sent through Brian the evening before.

"I'm not surprised," Jim Deaton replied. "It's not that he doesn't intend to pay as much as he intends to keep you off balance."

"I didn't think about it like that."

"We need to go ahead into court so that we have a judge's order requiring him to provide for all the children's needs. That way we can severely limit his arsenal of emotional weapons."

"That's basically what P.C. said, too. Only I understand it much better when you explain it that way."

"You also need to understand that every time we win one against him, he's going to become more desperate to find a way to retaliate. He's already proven how dangerous he is. Don't give him a chance to hurt you again."

"You really are concerned, aren't you?"

"Don is an abuser, Margaret. He's not going to change and abusers are at their most dangerous when they're backed into a corner and robbed of their ability to create havoc. You watch yourself. And the kids. He could be unstable enough to deliberately hurt his own children, because he knows how much it would wound you."

"So what do we do next?

"I'm going ahead and file this motion with the court to compel him to support his children during this interim period and I'll be back in touch as soon as we have a court date."

"Thanks, Jim. Don't know what I'd do without you."

"Just take care, Margaret. We'll talk soon."

Margaret ended the call and turned her attention to her father who still sat quietly in the corner. *He looks like he's sick.*

"Thanks for waiting, Dad. I needed to catch Mr. Deaton before he got busy."

The turmoil on her father's face was heart-wrenching and Margaret noticed that his lips were moving, but no words were emerging.

"Margaret... daughter... oh, Margaret... why didn't you let us know how bad things were? Maybe we could have helped and things would be different today." He got up and began to pace the room. "I can't believe we didn't suspect anything."

Margaret joined her father and placed her good right arm around his shoulder and drawing him to her, planted a light kiss on his cheek. *This precious leathery cheek that looks considerably older than it did just yesterday.*

"I love you, Dad, but I couldn't tell you because I wouldn't even admit it to myself. I used to think it was because I was ashamed, but the truth is, I was in denial big time. It was only in the last couple of weeks before he broke my arm that I came to grips with the demon that lived in our house."

Her father's shoulders seemed to visibly stoop the more she talked, and she hated what her personal problems were doing to this man, one of the more gentle souls she'd ever known.

"Now Don is refusing to pay for the children's school?"

Margaret laughed. "If you ask me, or Mount Zion, the answer is that he won't pay one dime toward their tuition. But he clearly told Brian on the phone last night that someone was confused. He even assured Brian that Haywood Tufters would be paying for the state debate meet again this year.

"So where's the real story?"

"My attorney says he's doing it to keep me emotionally off balance. He believes if we get a court order that forces him to pay all of their expenses, then we take away a large part of his power to harass me."

"I'm going to be in court with you."

"You don't have to, Dad. I love you, but I'm a big girl. Besides, my attorney and P.C. will both be there. I'll be okay."

Her father waved her words away almost as if he were shooing a pesky insect. "I said I'm going to be there. And I will."

"You won't be able to say anything."

"Don't want to say anything. Just want to look Don Haywood straight in the eye and make him look back at me. This is my daughter he's abusing and I want him to know I'm a better man than he is."

Dear Lord, I've never heard such fighting talk out of my daddy. Indeed, she had been almost 15 before she realized whenever she heard one parent say to the other, "I beg to differ with you," that they were having an argument.

"Okay, Dad. I look forward to having you go to court with me." She tucked her right hand through his left arm and pulled him to her. "Do you remember when I was a child and the dentist scared me so bad I went into hysterics any time I had to go?"

He grinned at her. "Do I remember? I still have muscle weakness in my other arm from the way you fought every time you had an appointment."

"But you never gave up on me. You took me and more importantly, you stayed with me. I couldn't have done it without you."

"And you're not going to do this without me, either."

"Thanks, Dad. I love you. And you know what? I think I'd almost rather go back to the dentist than have to face this. At least at the dentist I know what's coming. I've never even served on a jury; I don't have a clue what to expect in court."

"You'll make it, Margaret. But you won't have to do it alone because I'll be there with you."

"I'm counting on it." She glanced at the clock. "Oh, my gosh, I'm going to be late for therapy."

"Then let me get out of your way." He started for the door and just as he opened it to leave, Margaret heard him say, "Got to try and make Ruby see this like it really is. But she can be so hard-headed when she decides to differ with me."

Margaret laughed as she stepped into the shower. *Dear, sweet Dad. God truly blessed me but it's taken all of this for me to truly appreciate how fortunate I am.*

As she stepped into the shower she tried to emotionally brace herself for the endurance test that therapy had become.

Stay with me, God. I need you.

Therapy was as rough as always, but Margaret took comfort that just knowing made the task easier to bear. *Besides, what choice do I have? I may be about to be a single parent, but I've got to have both my hands.*

One bright note came near the end of the morning session when Dr. Carr, the surgeon who had operated on her badly broken arm, stopped by to visit with her. "Your charts are looking encouraging, Mrs. Haywood. I'm impressed with how much mobility you've already regained."

Margaret, who was in the middle of ten arm-lift repetitions, struggled to answer him. "Uh... uh... thanks for the... encouragement. It means a lot... right now."

"If you liked that, then you ought to love this," the physician said as he fiddled with the stethoscope that hung around his neck. "Based on your x-rays and the progress you're making, I think we may well be able to reduce some of that hardware you're carrying around when you see me next week."

Margaret was so startled she stopped mid-repetition. "You're not kidding, are you?"

The doctor chuckled. "Never been more serious in my life. Let's give it another week and I think we'll be safe to make life a little easier for you. In fact, you'll probably be able to begin to try driving again."

Margaret thanked the doctor and reclaimed the dumbbell, determined to finish her assigned ten. *Guess that's something else I'm going to have to face. My arm may be healed enough to drive, but I don't have a car, so it really doesn't matter.*

Margaret always turned her cell phone off when she reported for therapy and when she powered back up, the display showed four missed calls. One was from her father. *I don't think he's ever called my cell phone before. Is something wrong?*

The other two calls were from P.C. and the last showed that Jim Deaton had attempted to call her less than five minutes earlier. Despite her concern over her father's call, she immediately punched re-dial and was rewarded with the sound of ringing.

Her attorney reported that he was in Carter's Crossroads and that he had filed the complaint in the courthouse summoning Don Haywood to court. After a short conversation, Margaret agreed to let him take her to lunch, and gave him directions to the hospital.

"I'll be waiting under the main front portico."

She made her way outside, knowing it would take the lawyer at least ten minutes to cross town. Once seated where she could wait in comfort, she dialed her parents' number. Her mother answered.

"Mama, my cell phone showed that Daddy tried to call me. Is anything wrong?"

"Just a minute, let me get him for you."

As usual, Mama didn't answer my question.

"Hey, honey. How was therapy?"

How was therapy? Since when does Daddy call me on my cell phone to ask about my therapy session?

"Dad... Is something wrong?"

"No, nothing's wrong. Why would you think that?"

"Dad, why did you call me?"

"I was going to pick you up after your session. I've got a surprise for you."

Margaret could feel vibrations of satisfaction through the phone. "A surprise? Dad, what have you done? You knew P.C. was planning to get me."

"I called her and told her not to, that I'd be there instead."

I'll bet that's why she was calling.

"Dad, what did you do? What's this surprise you've got for me?"

Gosh, I hope he hasn't met Don in some dark alley somewhere. Then she almost snickered aloud, picturing her father, who winced when he swatted a fly, physically attacking his son-in-law.

"You'll see," he chortled. "I'll be there in a few minutes."

"Wait a minute, Dad. Jim Deaton is in town and he's on his way here now to take me to lunch. He filed papers at the court-house this morning."

"Oh."

Margaret could hear and even visualize her father's de-flated spirits. "Can you show me after lunch? Will that be too late? I really need to talk with Jim before he goes back to Atlanta."

"No... the secret's permanent, so it'll still be there this af-ternoon."

It's just that you've done something you're so proud of and it's al-most like punishment to be denied the chance brag about it right now.

She agreed to call her parents as soon as she and Jim were finished and her father promised to retrieve her and explain all about the surprise.

Try as she might, in the short time before Jim's black Mercedes pulled up next to where she was sitting, Margaret could not imagine what had made her father so proud, so animated.

They were en-route to the restaurant she had suggested when her cell phone rang. She had been telling Jim about her father's big secret. "I'll bet that's him asking if he can reveal all before you and I have lunch."

But it wasn't her father. Instead, when she punched the talk button, it was P.C.'s voice she heard.

Gosh, I forgot all about calling her back.

"P.C., I'm sorry. I got so I involved with my dad I forgot to call you." She laughed. "He's done something that's totally out of character for him, and he's so proud he's about to bust to show me what it is."

"That's why I was calling you. He didn't tell you what it is?"

"You mean you know and I don't?"

"Like you said, he was about to bust and I think he trusts me. So he spilled his gut and I figured I'd better get to you before he did."

"So what exactly has he done that's got him in such a state?"

Margaret listened, and as she did, her lower jaw dropped and then dropped some more. Finally, she said, "P.C. I'm going to have to call you back."

She ended the conversation and sat, looking at her attorney, who made no attempt to hide his curiosity.

"I don't know what he did, but it must be a doozey."

It was ever so long before Margaret could find the ability to speak. And when the words finally emerged from her lips, they were delivered in squeaky, high octaves.

"He bought me a house."

"A house. Did you know about this?"

Even as she said the words, Margaret's mind was forming words of protest. "How could he do that? More importantly, how did he do it? They aren't that flush with money."

"Maybe he has assets you don't know about."

"Trust me, Jim. There are no secret assets. I just hope he hasn't closed the deal, because this is too much."

They were almost to the restaurant when resolve seized her. "Jim, do you mind terribly if we don't go for lunch? I feel like I need to get to the bottom of all of this and I'd like to go right home."

"No sweat," the young attorney said. "You direct and I'll drive. Have you there in no time."

As she recalled those few minutes in the days to come, she felt so embarrassed that she'd basically commandeered her lawyer's car and his person, but at the time, all she could think about was canceling the sale. *Dad bought me a house?!*

They arrived at her parents shortly before Noon and Margaret was out of the car loping across the back drive to the house, before she remembered her manners. "Oh, Jim. What must you think of me? Would you like to come in?"

They were in the house when Margaret's mother looked around the corner from the kitchen, where she was preparing lunch. "I thought Harold said you were having lunch with that lawyer you got in Atlanta. Is something wrong?"

Margaret performed the necessary introductions and asked, "Where's Dad and what is this surprise he's so proud of?"

Ruby Maxwell crossed the kitchen and called down the basement stairs. "Harold... Harold! Come up here. Margaret's home."

In just seconds they could hear footsteps on the stairs.

"You haven't had time for lunch," her father said as he entered the room.

"Just call me the cat that curiosity killed, but I had to know what this big secret is." *I don't know whether to be excited or frightened.*

"It could have kept 'til after lunch," he said, but his body language proclaimed otherwise. "And who's this feller with you?"

Margaret introduced Jim Deaton to her father and explained that they had detoured on the way to lunch to see what all the excitement was about.

"Ruby, we got enough lunch for these two?"

Margaret's mother placed her hands on her hips. "Harold

Maxwell, when have you ever known me not to have enough for a couple of extra mouths? Of course we do, so you go on and show Margaret what we did, and I'll be dishing it up. "I hope you like plain country cooking, Mr. Lawyer, 'cause that's all you'll get in this house."

Jim Deaton grinned. "Haven't had any real country cooking since my mom died? So yes ma'am, I'm sure I'll enjoy it. I just hope we're not inconveniencing you."

"Ruby is happiest when she's feeding folks, so let's leave her to what she does best and we'll go out through the back yard."

"The surprise is in the back yard?" Margaret asked.

"Not exactly," her dad said, helping her down the patio steps. "It's actually on the other side of the back fence."

Margaret considered his words and found herself more confused than before. *If that's possible.*

Harold Maxwell led them across the yard, through the grape arbor and around the side of the fence, in the direction of the street on the other side of the block. Once they were on the public sidewalk, he turned and pointed to the small bungalow that Margaret remembered had always been behind their house.

"This is the Goswick house. Mr. Fred and Miss Esther Goswick live here, or at least they did," she explained to Jim. "Mr. Fred died a few years back and Miss Esther lives here alone now. They've been Mama and Daddy's backdoor neighbors since I was a child."

"Correction," Harold Maxwell said with obvious pride. "She **was** our backdoor neighbor. Only now she's going to an assisted living facility and this will soon be known as the Margaret Heywood house."

The magnitude of her father's words hit Margaret with the impact of a dump truck doing a body slam.

"It's going to be whose house? Please tell me you haven't bought this house!"

"Not yet, we haven't. But we have given Miss Esther a deposit and we'll close as soon as the lawyer can get the papers ready.

"Dad, how could you?"

"It all came together this morning after you left for the hospital. Your Mama was talking to Miss Esther's daughter, Myra, and she told Mama they had to sell before Miss Esther could go to the assisted living facility."

I know where this is going. God, I'm going to look like an ungrateful brat.

He continued, "Your Mama came and told me, we came back and talked to Myra, she made us a price and I wrote her a check. It was a done deal in less than 20 minutes."

If his chest expands any more it's going to burst. But it's going to burst anyway because I've got to get him out of this.

"Dad," she said and encircled his waist and pulled him toward her, "I know you meant well, and I really appreciate that you're trying to look after me, but I wish we could have talked this over before you obligated yourself."

Just the negative edge of her voice caused the old man's face to lose some of its glow. "You don't like the house? Ruby and I thought it would be perfect. We can put in a gate between the two back yards and none of us will even have to get out on the street to go back and forth."

"It's not that I don't like the house. But it just wouldn't work. Besides, you don't have that kind of money and I'm not going to let you tie up all your savings in a house for me and the kids. We'll be okay. Honest."

"Not if you have to go live in those nasty projects, you won't." The words came from Margaret's mother who had walked up behind, unnoticed. "You are not going to take my grandchildren to that side of town where they've got drugs and killings. And that's that. Now come eat before everything gets cold."

It was a subdued Margaret that maneuvered the path back to her parents' door. Her father wore a dejected look about his shoulders and he shared details about the house with Jim Deaton, almost as if he hoped that the attorney could change Margaret's mind.

"This is some of the best meatloaf I've had in sometime, Mrs. Maxwell." Jim Deaton had heaped his plate with the catsup and brown sugar-topped meat dish and surrounded it with fresh mashed potatoes, fried okra and Cole slaw.

"Here, have some of my Parker House rolls, Mr. Deaton. Everybody says they're to die for."

I'm glad Jim can enjoy Mama's cooking. I've got such a lump in my throat 'til I'm not even sure I can swallow my tea.

The four of them ate in total silence until, when Mrs. Maxwell was dishing up banana pudding, her husband brought up the subject that was on everyone's mind.

"So tell me, Margaret, did I do wrong buying Miss Esther's house? It seemed like a no-brainer."

Margaret sighed. *I'm going to be the bad guy regardless.*

"It wasn't so much wrong as it was premature, Dad. Why didn't you at least wait and talk it over with me before you wrote them a check?"

Her father rubbed his hand across his brow, the frustration he felt clearly evident. "Myra was going to list it with an agent this morning and I knew we could get it cheaper if I dealt directly with her."

Jim Deaton, who had been finishing his pudding, asked, "I'm just an outsider here, but you are going to have to have a place to live, Margaret. Perhaps you're not looking at this as logically as it really is."

How can I explain to Jim that in the three weeks my children have lived here, their grandparents have spoiled them past redemption. We don't need to live where all they have to do is cross through the fence to get more spoiling.

"I mean, you're not foolishly thinking you're going to be able to go back to your house when everything shakes out?" Jim asked.

Margaret thought again of her beautiful home and of the wanton destruction she had discovered and knew that what once was could never be again. "No, I'm totally grounded when I say that we will never live on Red Bud Way again. And for more than one reason."

There's too much hate there for me to ever be able to overcome it. As if I could afford to maintain such a huge house.

Her father was speaking again. "Look, Margaret. If you're truly against this, I'll cancel the deal and tell Myra she can keep the deposit. It was only $2,000.00. But I wish you'd think about this. You're probably going to have to go to work when the dust settles. It would be so much easier for us to help you with the children if you were just across the back yard."

I hate to admit it, but he's just given me the one reason that I can't dispute.

"I agree, totally, Dad. But what if I don't always want to live there? You'll have your nest egg tied up in that house and I'd feel guilty if I didn't live there more than a year or two."

"We talked about that," her mother volunteered. "This neighborhood is solid and we can easily get our money out of it when you don't need it any longer."

"Or we might turn it in to rental property. With us right

here where we can keep an eye on things, it could be a good investment," her father explained.

Margaret threw up her hands. *I might as well surrender, because I've got bigger fish to fry before all of this is a done deal.*

"So when do we get possession?"

"Thanksgiving is this Thursday and the lawyers will probably be closed from Wednesday on. I'd think we should close shortly after the first of December, although Myra plans to move Miss Esther to the assisted living facility on December 1."

"Either way, Margaret, you'll be in your new house for Christmas." The speaker was Jim, who went on to say, "I really think this may be the best course of action. From what I've learned about Don, I would think he'd be less inclined to bother you if he knows your folks are just a few feet away."

Christmas! Oh, gosh, I hadn't even thought about Christmas. This will be our first one as a splintered family. For that matter, we've got to get through Thanksgiving first.

"You don't really believe Don would do any of them further physical harm?" Mr. Maxwell asked the attorney. "Surely he wouldn't."

"With all due respect, Mr. Maxwell, I put nothing past Mr. Haywood. My mother is dead because she under-estimated what measures my father would take to enforce his belief that he had a God-given right to be in total control."

Margaret saw her father's face flinch and felt sorry that he was being exposed to so much that was foreign to him.

"I'm mighty sorry to hear that, young man. I'm sure it's something you don't easily forget."

"No sir, you don't forget it. And you aren't nearly as trusting of an abuser ever again. Trust me, Mr. Maxwell, Don Haywood is a classic textbook abuser."

"But he's so charming and intelligent," Ruby Maxwell protested. "He's not some lowlife trash. Don Haywood is one of the most popular people in this town. How could he be an abuser? I just don't understand."

Jim poured himself a second glass of iced tea before he answered. "Mighty good sweet tea, Mrs. Maxwell." He took another long swig. "You might be interested to know that my father was a superior court judge, but he still beat my mother in the head with a piece of lumber. He went to jail and my mother went to the cemetery."

He smiled the sad smile that Margaret understood so well. *There are times that being right just isn't worth the price.*

"Don Haywood has already proven he's capable of equally volatile behavior. And as for his popularity, I'd have to question whether the people in Carter's Crossroads respect him as much as they do his checkbook."

Knowing that her attorney needed to talk further with her, and then get back to Atlanta, Margaret decided to take the bull by the horns.

"Okay, Dad, I accept your temporary loan of a house, but just until I can get my sea legs under me and began to fend for myself and the kids."

Harold Maxwell flashed a big, contagious grin that Margaret both saw and felt. *Dad, I didn't want to hurt you. You did what you did because you love me and you thought it was in my best interest.*

"But there are two conditions. First, I don't want anything said to the kids until after the house is vacant and we can go in." She turned to look at her mother. "This includes you, Mama. I don't care what kind of sob story Sally gives you about being too ashamed to live in public housing, they are not to know about the Goswick house until I give the word."

If they don't know it, they can't talk it. Otherwise, I might as well call Don's cell phone right now and give him the latest news bulletin.

"What's the other condition?" her father asked.

Margaret waggled her finger in his face. "That you, the most wonderful father in the entire world, agree not to make any more major decisions for me without talking to me first." She smiled and showed her teeth in a grin that matched her father's.

"Agreed."

That night, after most of the house was dark and quiet, Margaret finally settled in her favorite chair with her Bible. It had been a full day, between the doctor's news, Dad's surprise and the conversation that followed with her attorney. Even now, as she fingered the pages of the worn leather Bible that had become so precious to her, she recalled Jim Deaton's words: "It's going to get tougher before it gets better."

Dear Lord, if anyone were to ask me, it's already been a pretty tough few weeks. I've lost my husband, my home and car and the financial security that I took for granted. My children have found themselves trapped in a breaking home where they've been asked to choose which parent will have their allegiance. Now Jim says the roughest part is still ahead, and I guess in some ways it is. All I can do, Father, is to put all of this in Your hands and trust that Your will for our lives will be done. I don't know what I'm going to do to earn a livelihood, where we'll live once we move from this house that Dad's bought, or even how I'm going to get transportation to get back and forth to whatever job I can find. Thank you, Lord, for my parents, for P.C. and Jim Deaton, for Alice Hanover and for my children, three of the biggest blessings any mother could have. Hold us all in the safety of Your hand and guide and direct us in the days ahead. Thank You for all the blessings that we have. In Jesus' name,

Amen.

As she finished her nightly talk with the God who had become so much a part of her daily life, she felt again the blessed sense of peace she got whenever she unloaded onto His shoulders all the burdens that were too heavy for her. *What a wonder it is that Your shoulders are never too weak or too tired to carry our loads.*

After reading for a few minutes in the Book of Psalms, where she found the most salve for her troubled soul, Margaret climbed into bed, being careful to tuck her injured wing where it wouldn't be hurt, put out the light and slept.

CHAPTER FIVE

Margaret awoke with a start. The light peeping through the shuttered windows hinted that it might be later than she thought. A quick glance at the bedside clock confirmed her worst fear.

7:30! How did I manage to oversleep? Got to get the kids off to school. Thank goodness this is their last day before Thanksgiving. At least the pressure will be off for a few days.

Grabbing her robe across the foot of the bed, Margaret stopped only long enough to examine the mutinous alarm clock before throwing the robe across her shoulders and heading for the kitchen.

Guess if I'd remember to hit the "ON" button before I went to sleep it would wake me!

She could hear her parents' voices as she neared the kitchen and she found them sitting at the old round table enjoying their second cup of coffee. "I'm so sorry I over-slept. I was so tired last night I forgot to hit the alarm button."

As Margaret offered her apology, Ruby Maxwell rose from her chair and crossed to the stove. "You obviously needed the rest. Don't worry, we got the kids off on time." The entire time she spoke, the older woman was spooning food onto a plate. "Here, eat this. You need nourishment, too."

"But I need to be the one getting the kids ready for school."

"And you will be. Soon," her dad interjected. "Right now, your main job is getting well and getting your strength back." His normally gentle face took on an unfamiliar hardness. "Besides, you've still got to face the worst before it gets better."

It hurt Margaret to see her parent so troubled, but she knew he spoke the truth. "I know, Dad. I know. I'm just sorry I'm having to drag you and Mama through it with me."

"Sometimes bad things happen to good people and you just have to get past it."

Truer words were never spoken!

Margaret enjoyed every bite of the scrambled eggs, bacon, grits and her mother's cat-head biscuits, while her parents compared their task lists for the day.

"Your dad and I are going grocery shopping this morning," her mother volunteered. "I've no desire to buy my Thanksgiving groceries on the day before, so we're going to get that behind us this morning. Is there anything you need from the store?"

She thought for a second before she answered. "Nothing from the store, but on your way can you drop me at the hospital for my therapy and save P.C. a trip?"

"Sure thing," her dad answered. "Get yourself ready while your mother and I double-check our list."

A quick detour through the shower - as quick as someone whose arm was encased in intricate steel rods could manage - and Margaret was dressed and ready to leave. She had called P.C. to tell her of the change in plans and her friend promised to be waiting when the morning's torture session was over.

"Have you invited P.C. to join us for dinner on Thursday?" Ruby Maxwell asked her daughter on the way into town. "We'll be eating around three."

With a sick feeling of guilt, Margaret admitted she hadn't. "I feel like a heel, but I didn't. To be honest with you, I can't even realize that day after tomorrow is Thanksgiving."

Neither of her parents answered at first, but Margaret saw the look that passed between them. "I'll ask her this morning, when she picks me up at the hospital. I promise." *How could I have been so deep in fog that I've forgotten that P.C. is away from home just to help me?*

The next sixty minutes felt more like sixty years as Margaret strained and groaned and performed as the therapist directed. *In all honesty, the pain doesn't seem as severe as it was when I started. Maybe I really am getting better.*

"Another great session, friend. You are really surprising all of us, you know."

Margaret, who had finally managed to stop breathing hard, smiled at the always cheerful Candi dressed that day in a paisley smock of autumn colors. "Do you know how much like Thanksgiving you look today? And I am thankful for you and all that you're doing for me."

Her therapist grinned and dropped her head. "I'm just the tour guide, you're doing all the work."

Margaret returned the girl's infectious grin. "I won't argue with you about the work part." Then a thought hit her. "So tell me, what are you doing for Thanksgiving? I assume you'll be off duty that day."

Candi's smile faded a little, Margaret thought. "Afraid not," she answered. "Hospitals don't shut down for the holidays, as much as we and our patients who can't be at home might wish otherwise. I'll see you Thursday morning as usual."

"I just assumed we'd skip Thursday and pick back up on Friday."

"Why? Is there a problem? You're not going out of town, are you?"

"Me? No. All my family is here. I just hate for you to have to work on a holiday for me."

Candi grinned again. "If it wasn't you, it would be some other patient. So I'll see you same time, same place, as they used to say. Besides, you aren't the only one I'll be working with that day."

Curiosity consumed her, and she had to ask. "So when will you celebrate the holiday? Isn't there a turkey somewhere with your name on it?"

"The hospital will make sure we get a Thanksgiving meal and besides, since both my parents are dead and my only sister is on the west coast, I don't do a lot of celebrating."

Mom says she always has enough for an extra mouth or two. She won't mind.

"What time do you get off on Thanksgiving?" she asked.

"Three o'clock. I'm working a short shift Thursday. Why?"

"Because you going to join my family for dinner. Mom isn't planning to eat until at least 3:00 o'clock, so that will work out perfectly."

"But I couldn't."

"And why not?"

"I just can't. It's too much of an imposition."

"It most certainly is not," Margaret argued. "You might as well accept, Candi. I don't give up easily, so why don't you make it easy on both...?"

"Are we through for another day?" a voice interrupted. It was P.C.

"We are," Margaret answered, struggling to rise from the low chair where she'd been sitting. "I was just insisting that Candi eat Thanksgiving dinner with us Thursday, and according to Mom, that same command performance is expected of you," she said to her friend.

"Sorry to disappoint you and your mom, but I've got to head back home this afternoon for a few days. I've got things in my office demanding my attention and I can't leave my own Mom alone on Thanksgiving."

P.C. spoke to Candi. "I envy you, friend. Margaret's mom is an awesome cook. If what I've had to eat there recently is any indication, you are going to chow down on some serious good eating Thursday."

"Oh, P.C. Can't you go get your mother and bring her back here so that both of you can eat with us?"

P.C. helped Margaret into her jacket and hat. "It's cold outside she advised. Feels almost like snow." The two ladies exited the physical therapy department after Margaret had extracted Candi's promise to be their Thanksgiving guest.

"No can do," P.C. finally answered Margaret's question. "Mom is really frail and she doesn't travel well. In fact, I'll probably take the both of us out to eat. I'd have to cook if we ate at home, and my dear mother is in poor enough health without having to endure my cooking besides."

"I take it you don't cook?"

"Don't. Can't. Won't. Just ask my ex-husband. It's a wonder our marriage lasted as long as it did."

The two ladies made their way to P.C.'s car, and as she drove to the Maxwell home on the other side of town, the attorney brought Margaret up to speed on all that she'd discovered. When she finished, Margaret felt both stunned and angry.

"You're telling me that if I put my ATM card in the machine right now, it's going to reject it?"

"That's about the size of things. And Don closed out the checking account and re-opened a new account. His signature is the only one on the new account."

"How could he do that?" Margaret wondered aloud.

"Ethically, the Don Haywood I know would have no problem. Legally, since the account was in his name alone, and you were just an authorized signer on the account, he didn't have to have your consent."

"How'd you find all of this?"

P.C. concentrated on navigating the final hairpin curve before reaching the Maxwell house. "Thanks to the power of attorney you gave me, the bank had to talk to me." She grinned. "You could tell it made them very uncomfortable, but they had no choice but to comply."

"In other words, I really am broke." Margaret used her good right hand to open the passenger side door. "I don't have any access to funds." The last was said more as a statement rather than a question.

"For the moment you have no use of Don's money, but that will change as soon as Jim gets you into court. I promise you, the judge will take a pretty dim view of such manipulation." She grinned again. "I called Jim as soon as I left the bank. He's already working on it and has a date before the judge for next Monday."

"I wish I felt as confident as you do. All the judges know Don. And how generous he can be with everyone but his estranged wife."

"Don't worry, hon. Jim can handle it. You've got to trust him."

Margaret let herself into the house, after bidding P.C. good-bye and cautioning her to drive carefully. "I'll be back next Tuesday," her friend had said in parting. "I've got some papers to file at the local courthouse when it opens Monday. Then my calendar is clear for a few days."

Margaret had a horrible thought. "You mean you won't be here to go to court with me on Monday?"

"...'fraid not, sweetie. Work calls. I've done all I can do from here. But your dad will be with you. And Jim will look out for you."

Margaret wasn't comforted as she watched from the breakfast room window as her friend's car headed toward Tennessee. *I feel so lost and alone. At least nothing should happen between now and court on Monday anyway.*

Her pity party was soon ended, as she heard her parent's car pull into the garage. She helped them unload by putting away all the groceries she could manage with one hand while they brought in more bags than Margaret could count. Soon Ruby Maxwell was putting the finishing touches on lunch and the three settled down to enjoy roast beef sandwiches and potato pancakes.

"P.C. won't be here for dinner on Thursday," she shared with her mother. "But I did invite Candi, my therapist. She gets off work at 3 o'clock and doesn't have any family locally."

"She'll be most welcome," Ruby Maxwell assured her daughter before Margaret could apologize. "Is P.C. going back to Tennessee?"

"She's already gone." Margaret looked at the chicken clock on the wall. "She's been gone almost an hour and a half. But she'll be back next Tuesday." Then she shared with her parents the financial news P.C. had uncovered and finished with an announcement for her father.

"We have a date with the judge next Monday morning, Dad." She took one last bite of her sandwich. "Mom, that roast was delicious." She wiped a blob of mayonnaise from the corner of her mouth. "Will Monday work for you, Dad?"

"I'll make it work," her father answered. "Just let me know what time."

Margaret couldn't decide why, but following lunch, she felt totally at loose ends. *Maybe it's Thanksgiving Day after tomorrow? It's certainly not going to be like any of our previous holidays. Perhaps it's just that everything is finally ganging up on me.*

In the end, she escaped to her bedroom, where her intent was to nap until the kids got home from school. She was about to stretch out across the bed when her eye spied her Bible on the bedside table. Instead, she picked up the precious book and settled in the little rocker.

I need You right now, Lord. Only I don't know why it feels so urgent.

Opening the Bible that had come to be her most constant companion of late, she read at random, first one verse and then another, wherever her eyes happen to light. And as she read, the feeling of gloom that had enveloped her continued to dog her emotions. But instead of becoming more troubled, she felt an all-consuming peace settling around her. *It almost feels like a suit of armor. The enemy is still there, but I'm shielded from the spears they may throw.*

"Margaret. Margaret! Can you wake up? Please, it's important."

That's Mom's voice. What does she mean can I wake up? I haven't been asleep. Margaret turned her head. *OUCH!* Her neck was stiff. *Maybe I have been asleep.*

"Wha... what... what is it, Mom? What's wrong?"

As she focused her eyes, Margaret discovered her mother's troubled face peering at her. "Honey, you were sleeping so soundly, I hated to disturb you. But the kids haven't come in from school."

Margaret tried to clear the sleep from her eyes and her brain. "What time is it?"

"Almost 4:30. They should have been here at least 45 minutes ago."

"And they didn't call?"

"Your dad and I have been here the entire afternoon and the phone hasn't rung once. Don't you think you'd better call the school?"

The news that her children were late arriving home had shaken the cobwebs from her brain and motivated her to action. Reaching for the bedside phone, Margaret dialed the number she had memorized so many years before, when she first began to volunteer at Mount Zion School.

"I just hope someone's still there," she worried as she listened to the phone ringing. Just as she was about to admit defeat, the breathless voice of a man answered "Mount Zion School. This is Headmaster Hunt."

Oh, thank goodness!

"This is Margaret Haywood. My children haven't come home." She launched into the conversation without any of the requisite etiquette that she normally observed. "Surely they aren't still at school this late."

"Oh, hello, Mrs. Maywood." The voice had an edge of ice to it.

"Mrs. Haywood?" When I was raising thousands of dollars for his

school, my name was "Margaret." So let me guess... what's changed?

"No, the children aren't here. Mr. Haywood picked them up a few minutes before dismissal. He sounded like he had a full holiday weekend planned."

Don has the children? How dare he!

"Mr. Hunt, Don had no right to get the children today. I certainly wasn't consulted. Why wasn't I notified?"

The line was dead on the other end and Margaret wondered if the headmaster had hung up. Finally, there was a response. "Mr. Haywood is the children's father. I know that you and he are going through a rough time right now, but Mount Zion School would prefer not to be caught in the middle."

Or deprived of the Haywood largesse, I would assume. Margaret was immediately sorry for her snap judgment. Regret, however, didn't mean she was off target and she suspected being right on.

"No one is trying to put the school in the middle," she defended herself. "I'm their mother and they don't arrive home and no one calls. I think I have a right to be concerned."

Again, there was a long silence and she knew the headmaster well enough to visualize him forming his words. "Let me ask you something? Is there any restraining order in place that would prevent Mr. Haywood from claiming his children today?"

"A restraining order?" she answered dumbly. "No. No, there isn't."

"Then perhaps this is something you should take up with Mr. Haywood."

You can just bet I'll take it up with Mr. Haywood.

"Thank you for calling, Mrs. Haywood," the educator volunteered, clearly ending the call. "Have a wonderful Thanksgiving and drop in to see us when you're recovered. We've missed seeing you."

I'll just bet I'm missed!

Margaret turned to her mother. "Don got them from school and he hasn't even had the decency to call me. How dare he!"

"What are you going to do?"

Margaret didn't answer. Instead she was punching in the numbers to Don's cell phone which began to ring almost immediately. It seemed an eternity, but in truth, she had to admit that Don answered on the third ring. *About normal for him.*

"Yes, Margaret. I've got the children. I got lonesome for them and met them as they were about to get on the bus. We're going to celebrate Thanksgiving as a family. Wouldn't you like to join us?"

"Don Haywood. Where do you come off kidnapping my children? And you needn't think you can blackmail me into taking you back."

"Now, Margaret. They're **our** children and I have just as much right to them as you do. As a matter of fact, you've rather hogged them for the past few weeks."

Margaret was doing a fast burn and it took everything she had to keep from assaulting him verbally. "You couldn't have called me to let me know what was happening so I wouldn't worry?"

There was the sound of a low chuckle on the other end. "I knew you'd figure it out when they didn't arrive."

How callous can he be?

"Don, I want those children brought home right now. Do you hear me? Right NOW or I'm calling the cops."

Margaret both heard and felt Don's sharp intake of breath. "'Those children' are at **their** home. In **their** house on Red Bud Way." He bore down on the word "their" each time. "As for calling the cops, you go for it, Margaret. I'm their legal father and they're at the address where they've lived for years. Tell me what the police are going to do." The last wasn't a question... it was a challenge.

They're going to do exactly nothing because I don't have a legal leg to stand on and even if I did, Don's money would still call the shots.

Margaret didn't know how to respond and yet, she felt like some kind of reply was necessary. "Are they OK?"

"They're fine because they're finally at home, where they all want to be."

Margaret could visualize Don stroking his ego as he spoke.

"And if their mother was as concerned about her children's welfare as she pretends to be, she'd be here with them, getting ready for a family Thanksgiving."

"Even if I wanted to, how could I host a holiday dinner in that wreck of a house? You've fixed it where no one could live there!"

"Not me. Margaret. Surely you don't think I'd destroy our beautiful home that I've worked so hard to provide while you sat on your butt and were Mrs. Haywood?"

Margaret could see where the conversation was going and had no desire to reach that point. *Physically, nor emotionally... I can't handle this right now.* She changed the subject. *I'm not going to give him the pleasure of provoking me any more than he already has.*

"So when will you be bringing them home?"

There was silence. Then, "I told you, Margaret, they **are** home. I'll drop them at school on Monday and they'll ride the bus back like usual."

"Monday! You mean I'm not going to be with my children over Thanksgiving? You can't keep them that long." Margaret felt the room begin to spin around her and she dropped onto the edge of the bed to steady herself. "Besides... besides, they don't have any clothes except what they're wearing."

She heard a chuckle on the other end. "Don't worry about the clothes. I'm taking the three of them shopping tonight for enough clothes to last through the weekend. They need some to keep here anyway."

Again, Lord, his money can always solve the problem.

"As for Thanksgiving," Don was saying, "I know the children would love to have you join us. I'm having the meal catered in, since you wouldn't be able to cook if you were here." He chuckled again. "After all, that's the kind and considerate husband I am."

Rage consumed her and Margaret couldn't hold her tongue. "The kind of husband you are considers no one but himself and doesn't hesitate to use his children as pawns!"

"That's your opinion," Don replied. "But in the eyes of the court, I've made it possible for my children to celebrate the holiday in the only home they've ever known. And the parent who will clearly be missing is their mother. Think about it, Margaret."

There was a click and the line went dead. Margaret, with tears running down her face, turned to look at her mother. In a manner totally uncharacteristic for Ruby Maxwell, she had stood by, silently.

"Oh, Mom," she blubbered. "Don's got the kids and he plans to keep them over Thanksgiving. I'm not going to get to spend the holiday with my children." She put her head down on her chest and sobbed.

Margaret felt her mother hugging her, and the attempt at comfort only caused her to cry harder. "I don't think anything has ever hurt me this badly."

The two women sat there for several minutes, until Harold Maxwell's voice was heard coming from the hallway. "Are you two ladies back this way?"

Before either woman could answer, the owner of the voice

entered the doorway and stopped short. "My gosh. What's wrong?"

Margaret was still crying too hard to answer and it was her mother who responded. "Don got the children from school this afternoon without saying anything to Margaret and he refuses to bring them back."

For the rest of the day, Margaret wandered the house in a daze, unable to concentrate on anything other than the absence of her children. She only picked at her food that evening, and then went to bed early.

Lord, I know I'm supposed to trust You in everything that happens, but I can't understand why Don can be rewarded and me punished so severely when I'm only trying to keep my children safe from his violence. Please forgive me for my lack of faith, but tonight I'm questioning everything. In Your son's name. Amen.

She was about to step into the shower when her cell phone rang. It was P.C. calling from Tennessee. Margaret had reached out to her the previous evening to tell her about Don's latest abusive tactic. While Margaret counted many in Carter's Crossroads as her friends, she had to admit, that as a whole, none of them had attempted to contact her during the entire ordeal. *My grandmother would have called them "fair-weather friends." I'm so lucky to have someone like P.C. in my corner.*

"What's on your schedule this fine morning?"

"Therapy, as usual, then I've got to meet with Alice to see exactly where we stand on the tour of homes." She surveyed herself in the mirror and couldn't miss the pale, thin face with lines around the once brilliant blue eyes that stared back. *Do I know this person?* "I'm not really in the mood for any of this, but I don't guess I have a choice."

"Then I better let you get on your way. Don't be so rough on yourself and call me when you have a few minutes to talk. Sounds like you might need a shoulder?" *It's nice to have someone you can be so comfortable around. God, thank you for P.C.*

When Margaret's father dropped her at the hospital's out-patient physical therapy entrance, she immediately spotted Candi, her therapist. She had, she realized, come to depend on the slight young woman with hair the color of corn silk who always wore it pulled back into two ponytails and tied with gingham ribbons. *Or am I just feeling extra needy today without my children?*

After hugs and greetings, the therapist asked, "How tight on time are you this morning?"

Margaret thought quickly. "Not terribly." *Especially the way I feel right now.* "I do have a meeting at 11:30, though... about 15 minutes from here."

"Can you give me a few minutes?" The infectious smile was gone from her usually cheerful face. "We've got a new patient in this morning who's going through a pretty rough time. Her therapist is about to pull her hair out, but I think I can help."

"By all means. I can spare the time."

Margaret made herself comfortable in the out-patient waiting area. Despite her fatigue from a night of little sleep and a breaking heart, she became engrossed in a magazine article about women who had established successful businesses in the face of great obstacles. Then before she realized it, Candi was standing in front of her.

"Thanks for waiting, Margaret."

The words penetrated Margaret's visit to another world and she realized it was time for her torture treatment.

"I'll leave you alone for your prayer, then we'll get started."

"How did it go with the other patient?"

"Overall, it went well. She'll have more days when the prospect of what we ask of her will be more than she thinks she can handle. But we'll walk her through it again when that time comes."

"It's a lady, then?"

"Actually, she's a young mother of four children, all under the age of nine."

"What happened to her?" The words leapt from Margaret's mouth before she could catch them. "I'm sorry, that's strictly none of my business." *And I thought I had problems.*

"It's okay. I can tell you this much. She was in an automobile accident and her husband was killed. They were hit head on."

"Oh, how terrible. She has to get well for those children."

"That's what we keep telling her, but she simply isn't strong enough emotionally to be able to accept all that has happened and what she faces now. But now we need to get on with you. I'll just step around the corner and you can call me when you finish praying."

How can I be so ungrateful, Lord? Margaret thought quickly. "Can you tell me this young woman's name? Just her first name?" She could see the conflict written on the therapist's face.

"I definitely can't give you her last name, but her first name is Christie. Why?"

Margaret reached for both of Candi's hands. "Stay with me, please, won't you?"

"But you're about to pray."

"So?"

"I need to give you some privacy."

"I'd like for you to stay. Please?"

"You're the patient."

Margaret clasped her friend's hands tightly. *Lord, I thank You for Candi with an "i" and the difference she makes in the lives of her patients, particularly this patient. Help her to see how much a part of Your plan she is in the lives of all her patients. Father, please bestow Your healing peace on Christie and give her the strength and the courage, yes, even the will, to recover. Let her know that You will be there with her when the pain gets too severe and the demands are more than she can humanly tolerate. And be with me, Lord, as I begin the next session in my own recovery, just as You have been there with me every day so far. Help me to always remember that by hurting today, there's a better chance I can recover tomorrow. Thank You, God, for loving me, even when I am most unlovable, and thank You for Your Son who died for me. In His holy name, I pray. Amen.*

The expression on Candi's face when Margaret opened her eyes was one she would never forget. Her therapist's trademark smile was there, but there were tears in her eyes and an expression of disbelief written across her smile.

"I don't think anyone has ever prayed for me before. For certain I don't think anyone has ever thanked God for me."

"I hope I didn't make you uncomfortable."

"I'm not uncomfortable, exactly... just, I don't know... awed, I guess."

"Well are you too awed to begin my session? Remember, I've got to be out of here by 11:15."

"Huh? Oh, right. Yep, let's get down to work, cause we've got a lot to accomplish today."

An hour later, when Margaret emerged from the therapy room feeling just a little lightheaded, she had to admit that it had been the roughest one yet. But she also chuckled when she heard Candi say softly to herself, "She really thanked God for me and the pain that I put her through."

"See you tomorrow," she reminded her friend as she was

leaving. "Mama's already cooking."

Her dad was waiting under the portico when she emerged. Margaret gave him directions to the public housing complex where Alice Hanover lived. It was exactly 11:30 when his truck pulled alongside the curb and the two got out.

Alice was waiting in the open doorway and welcomed both of them warmly. Margaret introduced her father, whom she could tell was very ill at ease. At the same time she noted that packing boxes were in evidence in the edge of the living room.

"Are you packing?

"Uh-huh. We'll be going to mother's house later today, just in time for Thanksgiving. I'll move the rest of my stuff this weekend."

"That's great! So you got the estate settled?"

Alice explained that her mother left no debts and that since she was the only heir, the judge had ruled that she could occupy her old home place while the last of the details were being resolved.

"Margaret paid my rent here, you know?" she told Harold Maxwell. "When I didn't have anywhere to go and no money to rent an apartment, she was my angel. I don't know what I would've done if it hadn't been for her."

Actually it was Don's money, and that's one time he didn't give generously!

"She's a pretty special person, that's for sure. At least her mama and I think so."

Margaret, who was by now feeling both uncomfortable and a little guilty as well, said, "Enough about me. We can examine my qualifications for sainthood later. Right now I want to talk about the tour of homes. We only have about two weeks to get our act together."

"Have a seat, both of you," Alice Hanover offered. "I just need to check on our lunch and we can get started."

As Alice headed to the kitchen, Mr. Maxwell rose from his seat. "I'm going to run a few errands. Be back in a couple of hours. Alice, it was sure nice to meet you," he said and doffed his imaginary hat. "Thanks for taking such good care of Margaret that awful night."

Alice stopped in her tracks. "Lunch will be ready in about thirty minutes. Can't you stay?"

"I really do have some errands that my wife asked me to deal with. I thought I could do it while you two talk. Besides, you didn't know I was coming so I don't want to put you out."

"It's okay, Alice. Dad isn't offended."

Alice put her hands on her hips.

Is she really provoked or is she putting on?

"I figured three for lunch. You can't drive, so obviously someone had to bring you. Besides, it's just a mixed vegetable casserole and salad. There's a lot of stretch there and I promise there's enough for all of us."

"You're sure?"

"Of course I'm sure. So sit down while I add cracker crumbs to the top of the casserole and we can talk about our tour. Oh, Margaret, just wait until you see what I've done. I think this is just going to be great."

What she's done? For a moment, Margaret couldn't decide if she needed to be worried or not. *What could she have done?*

Alice returned from the kitchen with a bulging tan folio notebook under her arm. Margaret noted on the bottom corner the words, "God is our refuge and strength." *I don't know where you got that, but truer words have never been spoken.*

When the contents of the folder had been spread out on

the table, Alice began to pick up papers one at the time, offering an explanation with each one. "I hope I didn't assume too much, Margaret. But I had already decided your house wouldn't be available, so I called the Hortons who built that big place over by The Pocket." She paused to catch her breath. "They were thrilled."

Margaret knew the house. More than once, when she'd taken that route to town through the nature preserve, she had admired the massive Craftsman style home built by one of the area bank presidents. *How intuitive of you to realize that my house was out. I haven't even told you about all the damage.*

"No... no. That's fine. My house wouldn't have been a possibility, so I'm glad you handled it."

Alice went on to explain about the advertising she had placed, the free promotion they were getting both in Carter's Crossroads and in the Atlanta area. Tickets were already selling well, she reported from Annie Campbell. And the program books would go to the printer on Monday after Thanksgiving.

"Alice, I never doubted your abilities, but I can't believe you've managed to arrange all of this." Margaret was stunned. "I mean, this goes beyond my wildest imagination."

Alice was positively glowing.

Mr. Maxwell had been mostly silent, but when he finally spoke, he said, "Sounds to me like you have natural organizational skills. There are folks who would pay big money for your expertise. Remember that after you get re-settled and are ready to build a new life for yourself."

Margaret saw her co-chair drop her eyes, shyly, hesitant to acknowledge her accomplishments. *Another abused spouse with poor self-esteem.*

"Dad's right, Alice. What you've done here, and in such a short amount of time, is nothing short of phenomenal. You need to pat yourself on the back."

Her face flushed, but Alice did look up, unable to contain her pride. "I couldn't have done it without you," she told Margaret. "You're the one that picked me. I never would have attempted something like this on my own."

"I don't know why not?"

"Because this is the first time since I married that I've ever had a chance to do anything without my husband's direction." She grinned at Margaret. "This lady here trapped me in a moving car and informed me that I would help her. What choice did I have?" She reached over and patted Margaret's hand. "Only after I got into it, I realized how much I was enjoying myself." She blushed again. "And I liked how it felt to be good at something."

"Good at something doesn't begin to describe what you've done on this," Margaret insisted. "I knew I could depend on you to pick up and run with it after I got hurt, but you have far exceeded my expectations."

"Here, here," Mr. Maxwell agreed.

"Then I guess I should tell you that there's more?" The hesitancy in her voice was obvious. "I hope you'll approve."

What else has she done? "I'm certain I will, Alice. So spill it because now you've really got my curiosity aroused."

Her friend hesitated. "What had you planned... to do... about refreshments? Can't have a holiday tour of homes without holiday goodies, now can we?"

Gosh, I hadn't planned. Me, who thinks a visit by the exterminator calls for a reception totally forgot about the food.

"I hadn't thought," she admitted. "I don't want the hostesses to have to worry about the food. I don't know how we'll...,"

Her dad interjected, "There must be volunteers who would be willing to bake some homemade treats."

"Good idea," Margaret admitted. "I'm sure we can find ten or twelve people who will help us out. Mama will."

"But that's not necessary," her friend said. "That's what I've been trying to tell you. We're going to have nice refreshments at each home and no one has to bake anything." Alice grinned big. "What's more, it's not going to cost us a dime."

"You're kidding, right? Come on, don't keep us in suspense."

Her grin was so wide she was almost unable to talk, but finally Alice said, "I've gotten restaurants and caterers in town to donate finger desserts and drinks at each house. They'll even send staff to serve and clean-up. And all we have to do is give them publicity in the tour program and in the newspapers and they're happy."

"Alice Hanover... **you** are a genius. And I do mean that."

"You must be some super saleslady," Mr. Maxwell seconded.

Alice blushed again.

I don't think I ever knew Alice was so insecure. But then I've really only known her for a few weeks.

Her right index finger unconsciously twirled a curl in her shoulder-length auburn hair as Alice explained. "I was in the bakery the other day buying some donuts and it occurred to me that we hadn't done anything about refreshments." She turned to Margaret. "I started to call you, but you had just started your therapy sessions and I didn't think you needed anything else to worry about."

"Bless you, Alice, you truly are a God-send. But you should have called. I feel guilty dumping so much in your lap. After all, you've had your problems, too."

I must have been crazy to promise Annie that I could pull off this tour. If it weren't for Alice, I'd have egg on my face big-time right now. Lord, You knew what You were doing when You sent Alice into my life.

Alice patted Margaret's hand again. "Please don't feel guilty. If you do, I will too. And I've had too much fun pulling all of this together."

"So how did you get all these refreshments donated? Inquiring minds want to know."

"Well, like I said. I was in the bakery when I realized we'd overlooked that aspect. So I just asked the owner if he would be willing to donate refreshments in exchange for publicity. And I explained how I was a battered woman who had been rescued, thanks to the shelter."

Alice admitted she was battered. Man, that took some kind of courage. I'm not sure I'm ready for that.

"At first he was kind of hesitant, but after I told him I was a victim, he said he'd help us. That's when I realized he couldn't be expected to supply all of the homes and that I would need others as well. So I made a list and started making personal calls."

Margaret thought that Alice looked proud of what she had accomplished and with good reason. "You are the greatest, Alice. It took a lot of nerve to go that far out on a limb. I'm surprised you didn't get doors slammed in your face."

"Oh, I did. Several places told me they didn't agree with how the shelter breaks up families and would I please leave."

Where have I heard those words before? "So what did you do?"

Alice brushed at a piece of lint on the navy blue sweat shirt she wore. "I left, of course. But not before I thanked them for listening to me and promising that I'd be back next year to ask them again."

"You didn't?"

"You would have done the same thing, Margaret. You don't

take 'no' for an answer. Anyway, I managed to get one refreshment sponsor for each home on the tour and that's covered."

"So what else do we lack?" Margaret was frantically searching her brain that still wasn't functioning as smoothly as she might have liked. "Anything else that needs to be handled should be done this week, because we're only three weeks away from opening."

Alice excused herself to put the finishing touches on lunch, but called out from the kitchen. "Aside from an interview with the Carter's Crossroad's *Tribune*, that will run the Wednesday before the tour, I can't think of a thing."

Margaret agreed and asked for details on when the interview would occur. Then Alice called them in to lunch. As they were heading to the kitchen where a card table had been crowded into a corner of the small room, Margaret's cell phone rang. She looked at the caller ID and excused herself to the living room.

When she returned, Margaret said, "Ordinarily I'd hold off on this until you and I were alone, Dad, but I know we're among friends here."

Margaret felt herself going fuzzy.

"I've got to get hold of Jim Deaton." Margaret grabbed a chair to steady herself. She looked straight at her father. "Don has taken a warrant against me for wrecking the house."

"He what!"

"They want me at the jail this afternoon or they'll send officers to arrest me."

Alice looked from one to the other. "What's this about the house? What did Margaret do?"

"Margaret didn't do anything," the accused protested. "Don Haywood trashed his own house and is trying to say I did it."

She left the room again and when she returned, her face told the story before her mouth ever spoke.

"Jim's not available."

"He's in court in south Georgia. His secretary is going to try to get word to him and call us back about what I should do."

Despite Alice's insistence that regardless of what had happened, Margaret needed to eat to keep up her strength, Margaret found it difficult to do more than toy with the food on her plate. *The casserole is delicious and any other time I'd be begging Alice for the recipe.*

They had barely finished eating when Margaret's phone rang again. This time it was Jim himself and they spoke for a few minutes before she handed the phone to her dad.

"Looks like he intends to go for blood," her attorney observed after he said hello. "I'm sorry I can't get there, but I'm right in the middle of a case, and even if I could get a continuance, it would take at least five hours driving time to get to you."

"So what do we do? I don't want Margaret to be arrested. Especially not for this, for something she didn't do."

"I've called Joe Busbee to see if he will at least meet you at police headquarters to surrender her and get her out on bond."

"But he's Don's attorney."

"Only for business, and from what I've been able to understand, he and Don have had a parting of the ways. This isn't Joe's specialty, but any attorney can walk you through the basics and buy some time for me to get up there."

"Mr. Deaton. I can't believe Don's done this to her."

"Call me Jim. We're going to be too involved in all of this for titles. I'm Jim and you're Harold. As for Don's ability to inflict hurt, I'd wager we've just begun to see the full force of his venom. Margaret hasn't rolled over and played dead and that's getting to him."

"To think I used to think he was the greatest person I'd ever known."

"Why wouldn't you, when you had no reason to think otherwise?"

Harold handed the phone back to Margaret who promised she would call her attorney as soon as she bonded out.

Alice came around the table and put her arms around Margaret's shoulders. "It's going to work out. And I'm here for you."

Margaret stared at the grime on the outside of the kitchen window and marveled at how her personal life was suddenly as dirt encrusted as the outside of the public housing project. *Lord, I don't know whether I want to cry or throw something. Or both. But I'm going to need You this afternoon more than I ever have. But then I guess You've heard those words before.*

Margaret's phone rang again. "It's Joe," she said, looking at the Caller ID. After the two had talked, she informed the others, "Joe Busbee is furious. He'll meet us at the police station at two o'clock."

Margaret and her dad thanked Alice for the lunch, confirmed the last few details for the tour of homes, even though it was difficult for Margaret to focus, and departed shortly after 1:30. "We should make it with about ten minutes to spare," Harold said as he pulled away from the curb. "It's gonna be OK. I've got my checkbook."

Margaret caught the stony expression on his face and suddenly felt so very safe. *Dad's not in the mood for any nonsense.* She couldn't answer. The lump in her throat was too large to allow her to speak, and she knew if the lump moved, she would give way to hysterics. *I can't believe this is happening. To me of all people.* Then she realized how snobbish and entitled that sounded. *I'm a victim of domestic abuse. There is nothing my abuser wouldn't do to discredit me and empower himself.*

She didn't like what was happening, but reconciled herself to the reality at hand. Don had sworn out a warrant against her for criminal property damage. She knew that she was innocent and she was pretty sure who the guilty party was. Proving it would be another matter. She said nothing, but stared out the window at the passing landscape without really seeing the children at play in the schoolyard.

If anyone had asked her later, she wouldn't remember the sight of the fall foliage that bloomed so colorfully in the town square, either. For certain she didn't see the faces of the people on the sidewalks that recognized her and commented to those around them.

"Here we are." Her dad's voice cut into her thoughts and brought her back to the reality of the police yard. "There's Joe. He's early."

"Poor Joe, I hate to put him in such an awkward position." Harold helped her out of the truck and shut the door as Joe bore down on them. "Don't worry about Joe. He can take care of himself."

Joe reached them and enveloped Margaret in a bear-hug she thought would never end. *Although I have to admit, it does feel good to be held like someone cares about you.*

"Margaret, are you alright? Are you going to be able to get through this?"

"What choice do I have?"

"I'm here Joe, and I'm not leaving until we can take this poor child home." Her father's face was flushed a dark red and Margaret could see the veins in his neck and head standing at attention.

"Careful, Dad, I don't need you having a stroke on me."

"It's a wonder I don't have a stroke. If I could get my hands on Don Haywood, I'd...,"

"You'd ignore him completely and keep your hands to your-self. Do you want Mama to have to come down here to bail out the both of us?"

"No! Your mother's got no business here."

"Then watch your temper if we see Don. I need you Dad, worst than I've ever needed you before."

He hugged her to him and ran his hand through her di-sheveled hair. "The very idea of having my daughter arrested."

"I know, Dad. I know. I feel the same way. But it's happen-ing and there's nothing we can do but follow procedure."

The three of them huddled for a few minutes while Joe explained what would happen to Margaret and how he would respond.

"We'll get to take you home tonight, but it's going to be unpleasant at best between now and then. You better buck up. Just remember, we're here for you."

"Will they put me in a cell?"

"I'm certainly going to ask that they not do that, but ulti-mately they'll do what they wish. As much as it pains me to say it, I'm sure Don has called in every marker out there to ensure your total humiliation."

Margaret looked at her three rescuers. *I've imagined many adventures in my life, but going to jail hasn't been one of them.* "Then let's get it over with."

As she lay in bed that night with salty tears rapidly soak-ing her pillow, Margaret had never felt so alone and humiliated. It had been almost nine o'clock when she and her dad finally got back to the house. It was long past the normal dinner hour, but Margaret was in no mood for the hot plate her mother had waiting for the both of them.

"Thanks, Dad," she said hugging the tall gray-headed man who suddenly seemed years older than he had just hours earlier. "I don't know how I would have handled things without you." She kissed him tenderly on the cheek. "And I don't mean your money, either."

"I know, daughter. I know." He returned the hug.

The entire time, her mother had been peppering them both with questions.

"In a minute, Ruby," Harold Maxwell said to his wife, although not unkindly, as he settled himself into his customary chair at the kitchen table. "Margaret's been through a lot. Your curiosity can wait."

Ruby sucked in her lower lip, but said nothing to her husband. Instead, she turned her attention to her daughter who, by her own admission, looked like somebody who had just finished rolling in the trash dumpster. "Here, honey. Sit down and eat these pinto beans and corn muffins. I kept 'em hot for you."

There was a part of Margaret that was hungry, but a bigger part of her was so bruised emotionally, until she wondered if food would ever be attractive to her again.
"Thanks, Mom, but no. Right now I couldn't swallow anything if I had to."

The older woman made clucking noises with her tongue and teeth, but in a move uncharacteristic for her, didn't badger her daughter. Instead, she said, "Well why don't you go on to your room and get a shower. I'll check on you in a little while and if you want something, I'll get it for you."

Margaret hugged her mother, wordlessly, and bade both

parents good night. She did go and stand in the shower, but despite the fact that she scrubbed with soap and body wash until the water ran cold, she still couldn't rid herself of the sensation of filth that seemed embedded in her pores. She was even less successful at washing away the memories of more than eight hours in jail.

Oh, Lord, she prayed as she toweled off, almost torturing her bare skin with the large bath towel, *how could Don have been so cruel? Now it's all very clear to me... all of this was one grand scheme... his picking up the children from school without my consent to keep them over a holiday... of having me charged with a crime I didn't commit... and then him hovering in the background, egging on those officers to treat me like dirt. But, Lord, did you see that one officer who didn't want to do what Don ordered, but was afraid to disobey orders? I'm not imagining things.*

Once she was dressed for bed and under the covers, the full impact of all that had transpired since lunch grabbed hold of her heart, and Margaret wept in a way she had never known before. Before she finally closed her eyes to sleep somewhere along toward morning, and after she'd declined Ruby's latest offer of food, Margaret came to a shocking realization.

I feel like I'm cried out, and I should be exhausted and depressed. But I'm not. Instead, I'm at peace and I'm more determined than ever that Don Haywood will not defeat me. She got more comfortable in bed, for the rest she understood was imminent, and played back in her mind, in fast motion, the afternoon she had endured only a few hours before.

It was nothing like I'd seen on TV. In fact, it was so unlike the TV cop shows she'd watched and accepted as factual, she was as shocked by reality as she was by the demeaning attitude and actions of her arresters. Everything began very low-key. Joe had walked with her to the booking room and announced to the staff assembled that Margaret Haywood was surrendering voluntarily in response to the warrant issued for her. *He told me this would make them go easier on me, but I don't think even he truly understood how vindictive or cruel Don can be.*

Margaret closed her eyes at the memory of the shame she felt when a female officer led her into a small anteroom and ordered her to completely disrobe. Outside, she could hear Joe and her dad arguing with the officer who had booked and fingerprinted her. And she heard the man's barking threat that he could have them arrested for interference.

Just as the officer began the most invasive part of her search, Margaret heard the voice belonging to the man she'd once admired and committed to. She wasn't sure if the walls were actually that thin, or if Don was speaking more loudly than usual.

Does he know I'm in here being degraded and he's purposely raising his voice?

"Well, well, well, Joe." Margaret heard her husband say. "If it isn't **my** attorney who has a beautiful home, thanks to the hefty legal fees I've paid him down through the years."

"Hello, Don." The tone of Joe's voice was hard. "Don't you have better things to do than make Margaret's life miserable?"

She heard Don laugh in the way he did whenever he found something particularly funny. "You'd think, wouldn't you?" There was that laugh again. "Only this time, I'm the one on the outside and she's the one on the inside. It's about time she got to experience what it feels like to be treated like the criminal she is."

"Criminal...!"

Margaret recoiled as the word ricochet off the outer walls. "Margaret's no criminal and you know it!"

Don ignored his father-in-law.

"Hope you got that house paid for, Joe." Don's voice turned

vicious, and Margaret could see his expression as clearly as if he were standing in front of her. "Because you'll never see another red cent of my money," he snarled, "and by the time I get through, you'll be lucky to get a judge to appoint you as a public defender."

Margaret could both feel and see the silence in the other room.

The female officer had finished her body search. "You can put your bra and panties back on, but not your outer clothes," she ordered. "You'll have to wear this back in the cell." She tossed a dark green jumpsuit that Margaret could already tell was several sizes too big.

She felt all the color drain from her face, realized she was cold and faint. "In the cell? But I'm going to be released on bond. Aren't I?"

The officer grinned at her, but Margaret saw no humor in the woman's body language or the tone of her voice. "Maybe you are. Maybe you aren't. That'll be up to the magistrate judge. Tell him your little rich girl sob story. Right now, my orders are to take you to a cell, and until somebody tells me differently, that's exactly what I'm going to do. You got a problem with that?"

"I surely do," Margaret sputtered. "I'm not guilty of anything that should have brought me here in the first place. This is cruel and inhumane."

"That's a nice speech, Mrs. Haywood. But don't worry. We've got our most luxurious cell waiting for you, something that a high society woman like yourself can appreciate.' Again she laughed, but there was no mirth.

Margaret, feeling very uncomfortable in just her underwear, slid into the prison garb, only to be swallowed by its hugeness. *Must be a size 36!* Because of her arm and its wire brace, she had to let the arm hang inside the jump suit, and buttoning it was an ordeal. Through it all, the officer stood by uncaring and not offering to assist her. *And I won't ask her, either.*

The officer placed a handcuff on her good arm, an experience that sent terror straight to her heart, but Margaret was determined not to let her fear show. *That's what this woman wants to see. Oh, God, please help me.*

As she was led from the little room, shuffling along in the too-large uniform, trying desperately not to trip over the pants legs that dragged the floor causing her to step on them, she could see through a window that all was not well on the outside either. Her heart broke as she saw her father, his head in his hands, looking totally distraught. *Poor Dad. He's too old to go through this.*

Joe was in a heated argument with Don who, at just the wrong moment, raised his head, and Margaret's eyes met his. The triumphant expression on her husband's face was one of "Gotcha!" and his smile was, Margaret believed, pure evil. Either that, or he was possessed. *Is there really a difference?*

Her "luxurious" cell turned out to be a narrow, eight foot by ten foot space, with double decked bunks and a combination lavatory and toilet unit.

Margaret couldn't forget the degrading, the long hours she spent with a filthy old woman who kept asking if she was Henry and wasn't this Sunday.

I've never needed you more, God, than I do right now. Hold me close and protect me.

Finally, when she had come to terms with the realization she might actually have to spend the night in jail, despite Joe's earlier assurances that it should be a quick, in and out procedure, another female officer appeared. Margaret was handcuffed and led through the jail, out across the dark parking lot, and into the annex of the Carter's Crossroads' Courthouse.

It was there that she was reunited with Joe and her father, although she wasn't permitted to touch them, or to do more than assure them that she was OK. *I hope they believe me, because I'm not sure I do.*

Joe was recognized as her attorney. After a quick reading of the charges against her the judge, a short, bald man who could have been a twin to Uncle Fester on the "Adams Family" TV show, set her bail at $100,000.00. He didn't ask her if she was innocent or guilty and, when Margaret began to protest, Joe quickly placed his hand on her arm and indicated that she shouldn't speak. *How am I going to get $100,000.00? And why should I have to? I didn't do this. It's all a set-up.*

The judge banged his gavel, and the officer who had escorted her in, came over and took her by the shoulder.

"But I've been granted bond. I'm going home."

Joe turned to her. "I'm sorry, Margaret. It's going to take us a few minutes to get bail posted. You'll have to go back to the jail until we get everything ironed out. But I promise you, you are going to sleep in your bed tonight."

The attorney looked so miserable Margaret would have hugged him, had it not been for her shackled wrist and a nudge in the back.

According to the clock, she'd only been back in the cell about thirty minutes, although each minute seemed like an hour, when the same officer returned with Margaret's street clothes.

"Here you go, Mrs. Haywood. Get these on and I'll escort you up front where your people are waiting."

Margaret forgot her modesty and ripped off the jumpsuit as fast as her bum arm would allow, not caring who was watching. In a matter of minutes, she was being hugged by her father who, for the first time in her memory, was red-eyed and crying.

Joe hugged her tightly and whispered, "You're going to get through this and Don Haywood is going to pay. You can count on that."

Right now, I'm afraid to count on much of anything. For starters, these people still have a learning curve ahead of them where Don is concerned. And he's long gone from the starting gate.

Joe, who could hardly contain his anger, said to no one in particular, "Let's get out of here. Mr. Maxwell, you take Margaret home, but if she begins to act unusual or to experience any physical symptoms, get her to the emergency room immediately. She may still go into shock once she realizes all that happened. Posttraumatic stress in the morning wouldn't be uncommon."

Mr. Maxwell led his daughter back out into the night darkness. He opened the passenger door of the old pick-up truck as a bone-weary Margaret, with his help, managed to crawl onto the seat.

Joe followed. "You've been through an ordeal, so chill out when you get home. I'm on the way to my house for a conference call with Jim and P.C. Talk to you tomorrow."

Neither Margaret nor her father said anything on the short drive home, but as he pulled into the drive way, the old gentleman broke the silence. "Margaret, I don't care how much it costs. If I have to sell this house, I'll do it gladly, but we're going to make Don Haywood rue the day he ever struck the first blow. If it takes everything we've got and will ever have to bring him down, I'm going to do it."

"Now Dad, this is my...,"

"Hush, Margaret. You don't need to get excited. Like Joe said, you've been through an ordeal. You just need to know that we three, and I know your lawyer will make it four, we're going to see that Don gets everything that's coming to him."

Margaret said nothing, but in the silence of her acceptance, she heard her father whisper, "Only what Don thinks is coming to him and what he's gonna get are going to be two totally different things."

Now sleep was claiming her and, for the first time since she'd left the jail, Margaret wasn't afraid to close her eyes and go to sleep. She probably would have post-traumatic stress when she awoke, just as Joe feared. Only what Joe didn't understand was that this stress would be inflicted on Don, not by him.

Like Dad said, Lord, what Don thinks is rightfully his and what he's going to get are two entirely different things. Thank you, God, for taking care of me today. I couldn't have made it without You, and now I need You more than ever. Don Haywood is an abuser, God, and when abusers get away with their actions, it empowers them to greater acts of violence. He won't accept my fighting back as anything but an attack on him.

Then she slept.

CHAPTER SIX

When she looked back on it later, Margaret would realize that she had few concrete memories of Thanksgiving. The children were gone, and although she did try several times to call them, the phone was never answered at the house on Red Bud Way. Brian's cell phone was evidently turned off, because all she ever got was his voice mail. And the children didn't call her.

Jim Deaton had phoned early the next morning. "Don pulled a fast one on us," he commented, "but that doesn't mean he has the upper hand. Keep your chin up, Margaret. It's going to get better."

Margaret wanted desperately to believe him, but she also knew how determined Don could be when he set out to reach a goal, whether it was establishing a business from scratch or putting his wife in what he considered her place.

On Thursday, when her mother put a Thanksgiving feast on the table, it was a somber group of four adults, including Candi, who gathered not in the formal dining room, but around the kitchen table, to pick at homemade sage dressing and pumpkin pie.

Margaret couldn't help but remember with every bite she took the many similar meals she had lovingly and proudly prepared in her own kitchen on holidays past. Try as she might to hold it back, a sob escaped her lips, and she had to leave the table before she completely ruined the day.

Dear Lord, she had prayed minutes later in the privacy of her room, *why do I feel so alone, so abandoned? I know that You are here and that all I have to do is ask. But today, I feel so totally adrift in every sense of the word. I need You, God. Without You I cannot even get through this weekend. I feel like I'm suspended in animation and I can't figure out how to get out of this. The kids are a part of the problem. I miss them so badly, and yet I'm worried about them as well. Are they OK? Is Don on one of his tirades? Why can't I reach them? Why don't they call me? Will I have to go back to jail? Lord, I don't see how people who live years behind bars manage to breathe if all jails are as bad as what I had to go through. Please Lord, I hurt so badly. Touch my heart and heal the hurt and show me how to get through this. I pray in Your Son's name, just as I pray as well for my own children. Amen.*

Margaret slept off and on the rest of the day, leaving her bedroom only to go back to the kitchen for a late night snack of leftovers.

On Friday, her father again drove her to therapy. Try as she might, she couldn't seem to muster the positive attitude she needed for the exercises, and the pain was unbearable. Even Candi noticed the difference and asked what was wrong.

Suddenly Margaret couldn't hold it in any longer, and she began to weep, as she recounted the story of the children being taken from school by Don without her knowledge. When she told of her arrest for destroying Don's house, Candi was crying with her. She confided her fears for how far Don might go.

"That man actually had you put in jail. Like a common criminal?"

"He did. And it was something I wouldn't wish on my worst enemy. I was even handcuffed on my good right arm. When I asked them why, the police woman said that anyone who would hack up a house the way I'd destroyed Don's house was a danger to everyone."

"That's ridiculous," Candi snorted. "In the first place, you're not that kind of person. And even if you were, trust me, you haven't recovered enough strength yet to inflict that kind of damage. Your left arm is useless and your right arm is all you've got. From what you describe, whoever did that job used both hands to swing the blade."

Encouraged somewhat that someone agreed with her, Margaret said, "You know that and I know that, but Don Haywood's money has bought enough in this town that if he says that's how it was, he's going to be believed. In this case I've already been judged and I'm sunk if I can't prove my innocence." *If I go to prison, Don will get the kids!* The thought made her go cold all over.

"So what are you going to do?"

"At this point, I feel so defeated I don't know which way to go. My attorney will be here Monday and I'm hoping he can figure out a strategy. I'm exhausted."

"Well you tell him if he needs me to testify about your physical strength and capabilities, I'll be glad to. And I'm sure your doctor would as well."

Margaret was astounded. "You would do that for me?"

"Well, sure. Hey, you're getting a bad rap here and I've come to know you well enough to know that."

Margaret began to tear up. "Oh, Candi, you don't know what it means to have someone say they believe me."

The therapist patted her good shoulder. "Listen, Margaret. I wasn't going to say anything, but I think I should."

What does she know that I don't know? Is it about the kids? They're not in this hospital somewhere are they?

"... it was all over the hospital when I got here this morning. I didn't want to believe it, but I also knew that he was pretty dangerous." She patted Margaret's arm. "No wonder you were so down yesterday."

"Thanks for understanding."

Candi patted her shoulder again. "That's OK. I said, I already knew about you being arrested before you got here this morning, but I wasn't going to say anything."

Margaret went sick to the pit of her stomach. *The Carter's Crossroads' grapevine is alive and well, I see.* "I'll have to leave town before this is all over. Don's going to see to that."

"If you want to go, and you've got something better to go to, you might want to consider it," Candi offered. "But I wouldn't let Mr. Haywood run me off."

"What choice do I have? Don practically owns this town and money talks. Why even this hospital has benefited more than once from his checkbook."

"You listen to me, Margaret. While it's true that your husband has been very generous with his wealth, there are some people around here who are getting a glimpse of the real man behind the money. Believe me, they aren't impressed."

"What are you saying?"

The therapist flashed Margaret a searching look. "Before

you assume that everyone sides with your husband, you need to know that you do have friends here. Friends who are willing and ready to go to bat for you. So don't sell yourself short and don't short-change Carter's Crossroads, either."

Margaret left the therapy session sore and hurting in heart, mind and body. *Dear Lord, I didn't pray before we started this morning and You showed me how much of the burden You're carrying. I won't make that mistake again. Please forgive me for doubting You. Amen.*

On Saturday, Margaret realized she had a dilemma. The next day was Sunday and normally she would have been in church. She didn't want to miss, but neither was she comfortable going back to her church. P.C. called in the middle of this revelation, and she shared her doubts with her friend.

"It's not just one thing," she explained, after asking P.C. where she had been and what she'd been up to.

"We'll talk about that in a few minutes. Right now, I want to hear why you're having doubts about church. You're one of the strongest Christians I know. I never thought I'd hear you talk about giving up on the church."

"Not the church," Margaret clarified, "it's **my** church I'm having doubts about."

"You've lost me."

"My biggest fear about tomorrow is going to my church, because I'm sure Don will have the children there to show off to the membership that he is the solid father, protecting his children against their jailbird mother."

"Jailbird mother. Isn't that a little dramatic?"

"Maybe, but it's already out in town that I spent several hours in jail. From what I learned in therapy yesterday, the police are talking it all over town. Underwritten totally by Don, no doubt. That way his skirts are clean."

"Well, you knew that was bound to happen. So why not show up at church to prove that you're the same person you've always been."

"Because I'm not the same person. And I'm just now coming to realize that."

"This I've got to hear."

"You shall, and you're the first person I've said this to, because it's only been in the last few minutes that I've truly come to understand myself." Her friend said nothing, and Margaret continued... "It's only been since all this mess with Don started that I came to realize how far from God I'd gotten. Oh, I went through the motions, was in the right place at the right time in church, and called myself a good Christian. I realize now that I was really a pious hypocrite putting on an act."

"Aren't you being a little hard on yourself?"

"Nope. In truth, I'm probably a little afraid to be as rough on me as I deserve, because I've been walking in front of God, telling Him where I should go, instead of letting Him carry and guide me.

"I'm not afraid to be in church with Don and the kids tomorrow. But if I go there, it'll be for the same reasons I used to go: to put on show, to demonstrate that I'm not the awful person Don has made me out to be. That whole church is a façade; it's more like a social club than a place to worship God. About the only time anyone truly gets fed there is when there's a church supper."

P.C. chuckled. "You really are on a trip, aren't you?"

"Don't laugh at me, P.C. I'm serious. For the first time since I started therapy, I didn't pray yesterday before we started, and the pain was excruciating. I truly felt like I was going through it alone. I need a church that is more serious about worshipping God and less concerned about cosmetic aspects of the sanctuary and

making sure that every member puts up the appropriate appearance."

There was a period of silence before P.C. asked, "You're
really serious?"

"I woke up this morning and realized that I need a real
church, not the reality TV show that our church has become. Only
thing is, I don't know where that place is."

"How about your parents' church?"

"I thought about that, but it just doesn't feel right, either.
And don't ask me why," she said defensively. "Because I don't
know. Wish you were going to be here for church tomorrow."

"That's one reason I called. The matter I had to deal with
on Monday settled and I can come back tonight if you need me."

"Oh, P.C., I've imposed too much already. Then before her
friend could answer, she blurted, "Do you think I'm wrong to feel
the way I do?"

"Truthfully?"

"Truthfully."

"First of all, only you can know whether a church is the
right one for you, because only your soul knows if it's getting fed.
But if you're asking me, as an outsider, for my impression of your
church, I'd have to agree with you. It would never feed me for long."

Margaret was very clear with her friend, "I've always believed that when you march in the parade under a certain banner,
onlookers have the right to assume that you promote the views
that banner represents. And I can no longer in good conscience
march under the banner of my present church. Even if Don weren't
an abuser, I'd still feel this way."

The two chatted for a few more minutes, then P.C. said,
"I'll be back in Carter's Crossroads by bedtime. Just remember,
God is anywhere we ask Him to be. It's just that some settings

make it easier to feel His presence."

Margaret spent the rest of the day in her room, reading her Bible, napping, and jotting down some matters she needed to deal with come Monday, as well as some items she needed to talk about with Jim Deaton. Then, at the urging of the little voice that lived behind her left ear, she pulled out the telephone book and turned in the yellow section to "churches."

Reading down the alphabetical listing, she paid no attention to denominational affiliation, but to the name of the church itself. With each name, she identified its location, visualized the church building itself in her mind, and then tried to think if she knew anyone who was a member there.

Lord, I'm not looking for a church with the prettiest building or necessarily one that is in the "right" part of town. And there's no member I'm looking to impress or avoid. I'm looking for the place where I can feel Your presence, worship You, and feel You feeding me spiritually and emotionally.

She'd reached the bottom of the list and, at a loss for what to do next, went back to the top and started reading again. This time, as she read each name, she tried to visualize something that she knew about the ministry it delivered to its members and to the community.

About two-thirds of the way down the list, as she read the name of one church she would never ordinarily consider, a tingle coursed through her entire body. "Lord, are You speaking to me?" She read down the list and again felt a sensation of pure enjoyment course throughout her body. "Interesting, Lord. You've got me curious."

P.C. called late in the evening to say she was back in her motel room. "I'll be there to get you for church, wherever you decide to go."

Margaret, when she awoke the next morning, could smell

breakfast and for the first time in days, she actually felt hungry. *Could I actually be excited about going to a different church?* Before heading out to the kitchen, however, she opened the phone directory to the church section and scanned the list again. When she reached the name that had produced so much emotion the day before, she purposely skipped that line, only to experience an intense sensation of grief. She finished the list, then went back to the name she had skipped, and was rewarded with a rapid heartbeat and the urge to shout "hallelujah!"

I'm going to do it, Lord. I don't really understand why You want me to do this, but I'm going to follow Your lead and trust You to do what's best for me.

She dialed P.C.'s number and after three rings heard, "Good morning!"

"I know where I want to go to church," she babbled to her friend. "Get here and I'll tell you all about it. You won't believe how good God is."

"Then why don't you come down the hall to breakfast and tell me all about it. I'm sitting staring at a stack of pancakes that's getting colder by the minute."

Margaret practically ran to the kitchen, not even waiting to get her shower. Once there, she shared with P.C. and her parents where she wanted to worship that Sunday, and how she had arrived at the decision.

"But Margaret," her mother protested. "You don't have to go there to church. You don't know anything about those people. I understand if you don't want to go to your church, but you can go with us. You'll be comfortable there."

Her dad said nothing, but she could tell by his expression that he shared at least some of his wife's worry.

"You don't understand, Mama. I've trusted God to show

me where He wants me to worship today, and there's not a doubt in my mind that this is where He's sending me. I don't understand it myself, but I've had to put myself in His safekeeping and I have to trust that He is going to take care of me."

P.C. spoke up. "This is none of my business, and I'm sure there's nothing wrong with your church, Mr. and Mrs. Maxwell, but I have to agree with Margaret. She has to follow the Spirit's leading on this."

Margaret saw her father struggle to speak, and her heart went out to him. He was looking so old, and she wanted so badly to spare him any more pain. But his words surprised her.

"Our daughter's right, Mama. She has to follow where she feels led. We raised her to trust in God for everything and maybe we've kind of forgotten that ourselves."

Margaret reached across the table and brushed his hand with hers. "Oh, Dad, how can I ever thank you for understanding what I don't completely understand myself?"

Her reward was a wide but somewhat sad smile from the man whose approval had once been so important to her. "I might not have felt this way a few days ago, but when I see what you've had to endure..." he caught his breath, "being locked in a cell and treated like an animal because Don Haywood's money talks louder than common decency...," he choked, again, "and still, you come out smiling. There's a greater power at work."

Later that same morning, P.C. nosed her car into a parking space in a gravel lot next to a small, but neat, white concrete block building. "If the cars are any indication, this little church is going to be full," Margaret observed.

She and P.C. had left the Maxwell home with the usual admonition from Ruby Maxwell: Sunday lunch would be ready and waiting when they returned.

Suddenly I've gotten cold feet, Lord. Are You sure this is what You want me to do?

Margaret didn't know if she expected a thunderous answer from above, but all she got was a warm fluttering of her heart. "It's almost 11:00 o'clock. We'd better get in there and find a seat."

The two women picked their way across the rough lot to the front door of the humble little church that was, Margaret realized, the brightest spot in an otherwise blighted neighborhood. Directly across the street was a boarded up factory, and scattered around the church were older homes in various stages of distress. Vacant lots here and there, like teeth missing from a mouth, bore mute testimony to where houses once had been.

Why, Lord? Why here? Are You saying I'm as far down as this neighborhood?

Once inside, Margaret and P.C. slid into the first place they saw large enough for two, with room for Margaret's awkward arm, about half way down the aisle. The pews were wooden, old, scarred and had no padding on the seats. As Margaret glanced around the room, her decorator eyes took in detail that might have escaped other, less observant people.

The pews didn't all match in style or wood. Someone had done a poor job of affixing contact color to the windows hoping to create the impression of stained glass. And the chamois colored paint has obviously been applied by volunteer labor, because the transition from the wall color to the frosty white trim color wasn't always as neat as it could have been.

Despite its cosmetic flaws, Margaret realized the atmosphere in the room more than compensated for the lack of polish to which she was accustomed. *In fact, as much as it amazes me to say this, I feel totally at home here, even though I don't know a soul.*

As she looked around the small sanctuary, she estimated a hundred people were gathered to worship. She was surprised to see almost as many dark skinned faces as there were lighter faces. Young people and frail senior citizens filled the pews, some dressed more stylishly than others. *Everyone appears neat and clean, but I'll bet I'm the only one in here wearing a designer label.* Suddenly she felt uncomfortably affluent and just a tad over-dressed, even though she had deliberately dressed down.

As she was trying to look without being obvious, Margaret felt a tap on her good shoulder. She half-turned, wondering in a split second of panic if Don could possibly be there, to discover the smiling face of Annie Campbell, her friend from the battered women's shelter.

"Annie?" she mouthed the words?

Her friend squeezed her shoulder and whispered, "After church. We'll talk after church." Their opportunity for further conversation was curtailed when the pastor, a young man whom Margaret realized she'd seen somewhere in town, stepped to the pulpit and began to welcome the congregation.

This is Annie's church?

About an hour later, when Margaret felt her heart would explode if she were fed any more of God's love and grace, the pastor pronounced the benediction. As he made his way to the back of the church, Margaret felt a stab of icy fear pierce her heart, as she realized that walking beside him, hand in hand, was the female police officer who had escorted her into court five nights earlier.

Why is she here? And why is she holding his hand? Are they married?

At that moment, as she searched frantically for another

way out of the church, any way in order to avoid speaking with that officer, she found herself caught up in Annie Campbell's loving embrace.

"Oh, Annie. It's...it's so good... to see you," she sputtered. "Why is that police woman standing beside the pastor?" she implored.

"That's Susan, Samuel's wife. She has to be at work on Sunday at one o'clock, so she comes in uniform." Annie hugged Margaret again. "So why are you here?" Hearing her words, she hastened to add, "Not that you're not welcome, naturally."

Margaret grasped her friend's hand and held on for what she felt like was dear life. "Oh, Annie, I've got so much I need to talk to you about." Then, remembering her manners, she introduced P.C. who had made her way over to join them. "Annie, I can't go out that door. I can't speak to the pastor."

"But why ever not? Don't worry about being a stranger, I'll be glad to introduce you."

"It's not that," Margaret whispered. "Don had me arrested last Tuesday afternoon and the pastor's wife was one of the officers I had to deal with. I'm too embarrassed to face her."

The chubby little shelter director put her hands on her hips. "He did WHAT?"

"It's a long story," Margaret said, "and I don't want to get into it here. But I can't go through that door. Is there another way out of here?"

"There is," Annie assured her. "Here, take hold of my arm and I'll lead you. You come, too, P.C."

Before Margaret could stop her, Annie guided the trio straight for the back door. The little woman had such a grip on her good hand Margaret was helpless to get away. Given that the pastor's face had lit up as he saw his visitors approaching, it was obvious to Margaret that she was a trapped animal."

The three reached the doorway and Margaret saw bright sunshine and longed to make a break for freedom, but Annie's grip dictated otherwise.

"Brother Samuel," Annie said, addressing the young pastor whom Margaret placed in his mid-thirties, "I'd like you to meet my very good friend, Margaret Haywood, and her friend, P.C. Dunigan."

The pastor extended his right hand, a wide smile dominated his face. "Mrs. Haywood, I'm so happy that you could visit with us this morning." He shifted slightly, looked past her to P.C., and said, "You, too, Ms. Dunigan. I'd like to have you both meet my wife, Susan, before she has to dash off to her job."

Margaret forced herself to look the young uniformed woman in the face, and when she did, she was astounded to see an entirely different persona than she had met at the jail." *It would be just too bizarre that this woman is a twin and both of them work for the police department, but she was the nicest one there.*

Before she could decide, the pastor's wife spoke. "I'm so glad to know that Mrs. Haywood has someone in her corner," she said to P.C.

The attorney responded politely and then the officer turned back to Margaret.

"Mrs. Haywood, I want to apologize for the other night."

"I beg your pardon. You want to apologize? I'm afraid I don't understand."

The young woman was smiling, but there was a very concerned look in her eyes. "Your husband is poisoning your name all over town. None of us wanted to mistreat you, the other night, but your Mr. Haywood made it very clear to the chief that he would not hesitate to go to the top if we – in his words – 'coddled you.'"

The pastor, a puzzled expression on his face, asked, "You two have met at the jail?"

Margaret found her voice. "Yes, I was arrested earlier this week and your wife was one of the officers assigned to guard me."

The shock of what she had said was evident on the young minister's face. "You, Mrs. Haywood? You were arrested? Whatever for? While I've never met you, I certainly know who you are. And who you are is a person who would never find herself under arrest."

Both his wife and Annie Campbell spoke at the same time. "It's her husband..." they began. Then the pastor's wife stopped talking, and Annie Campbell continued. "Brother Samuel, I'm as shocked as you are, because I can assure you that if Mrs. Haywood was arrested, it was a huge mistake. I know this woman."

I can't believe I didn't call Annie through all of this? How could I have been so... so...?"

P.C, who had been silent, began to speak. "She wasn't guilty, but she is a battered woman whose husband is her abuser." She ran her hand across the mass of wires that held Margaret's arm in place. "He did this to her, and now that she's refusing to roll over and play dead, he's trying to ruin her reputation."

"So far he's doing a pretty good job," the pastor's wife added. "Don Haywood has dropped so much money in this town, there's hardly an important person here he can't persuade or intimidate." She turned to her husband, gave him a peck on the cheek. "Got to go, hon. Don't want to be late." She waited to accept his return kiss, then turned back to Margaret. "Mrs. Haywood, you need to watch your back. Mr. Haywood was bragging the other night that he would either get you back, or you would lose the children."

Lose my children?

Seeing her look of confusion, the young officer continued, "By having you declared an unfit mother. Now that you've been arrested and charged with destruction of private property, he's got the ammunition he needs. Don't give him a chance to use it."

Margaret looked first at P.C., then at Annie. "Is she correct? Can he take my children before I've even been judged guilty?"

Both women nodded their heads, and Annie spoke first. "Depending on which judge hears the case, he might very well be able to get the children, at least temporarily, because he could make the case that you might injure them. A court is going to place minor children's welfare over your guilt or innocence."

Margaret looked to P.C., whose facial expression seconded Annie's opinion. "That's exactly what Joe and I think he's planning to do," she told Margaret. "That's the main reason that Jim Deaton will be here by 9:00 o'clock in the morning. We were going to let him break it to you, but perhaps it's best that it's already out."

Margaret felt herself reeling, and if both Annie and the pastor hadn't put their hands out to steady her, she would have fallen. *This is just too much. How could I have been so blind to the monster I gave everything I had? Has he always been this way and I was just too much in love to see it?*

The pastor, his wide, smiling face filled with concern, took her hand. "If you need me for anything... anything at all, I want you to promise you'll call me. I'll give you my business card that has my cell number on it. You can reach me anytime, day or night, on that number."

"But... but... I'm not even your church member and you never met me until just a few minutes ago. Why would you want to help me?"

I'll never forget the expression on his face.

"You're one of God's children and you're hurting. I'd still be willing to help you if you were guilty, but I know in my heart that you're not. If my wife and Miss Annie here vouch for you, it can't get any better than that."

Now I know why you sent me here to church, Lord. You truly do work in mysterious ways.

Margaret thanked him, took his card, and after insisting that Annie follow them back to the Maxwell home for lunch, Margaret and P.C. left the church. On the way there, Margaret called her mom to tell her to set another place, then all was quiet in the car. They were almost to their destination when P.C. said, in a very off-hand manner, "Don's as crooked as we all think he is, but he hasn't won yet. So don't you go throwing in the towel just yet."

"But P.C., how could Don stoop so low? He's using the children as bargaining tools. That's... that's... despicable." She pounded with her fist on the car's dash.

"Don't kill the messenger, Margaret, but that's what abusers do. They find their victim's vulnerable spot and they target it. In your case, it's your children. I've got an idea that Don has been this way all along. Because he became so successful in a commodity as financially volatile as carpet, in such a short few years, means he didn't do it without stepping on people and crushing some of them somewhere along the way."

Margaret started to protest when, a stab of memory she'd long forgotten pierced her consciousness. *When he bought out another plant years ago, I can remember the couple who started it literally weeping as they signed papers at closing. They wouldn't look at either one of us and I wondered at the time why they were selling if the business meant that much to them. Could Don have set them up, just like he's set me up? Only they weren't strong enough to fight back?* Suddenly she knew, not how he did it, but that indeed he had done it. Realization that the luxurious home she'd had and the carefree lifestyle she'd enjoyed had been financed by cheating other people suddenly made her sick to her stomach.

Well, Lord, I know now why You sent me there to worship today. And You did feed my starving soul, so now I'm going to have to look to You to protect my broken heart.

"We can't let him win on this, P.C. It's not just me, it's the kids as well who are going to be hurt. And he doesn't care if he has to sacrifice them, as long as he wins."

"Hopefully Jim will arrive tomorrow loaded with ideas. But we'll all give it everything we've got. I promise you that."

Annie followed them into the drive, and Margaret led her in to the house where she introduced the shelter director to her parents. Later around the table, after everyone had eaten and dessert had been served, Ruby Maxwell asked, "Now be honest with me, Miss Campbell, don't you think Margaret ought to forgive and forget and reunite her family? After all, she's never going to find anyone who will provide for her as handsomely as Don has. So what if he has occasional temper tantrums? He works hard and he's under a lot of stress."

Margaret saw Annie draw in her breath and look at her. She signaled with her eyes that it was OK to speak her mind.

"Mrs. Maxwell," Annie said, "I mean no disrespect to you, because I know you only want what's best for your daughter and her children."

Margaret watched her mother's expression harden.

"Quite frankly, I'd rather see Margaret homeless and on the street with nothing, than to see her risk her life to go back to that marriage and that home."

Ruby Maxwell's mouth opened and closed, but no sound

came out.

Annie Campbell continued. "Don Haywood fits the profile of a classic abuser, and abusers simply don't rehabilitate. They just become more intense and more empowered each time they're successful. In my opinion, Don is deadly. Margaret is fortunate he just shattered her arm. Next time, it might be her head."

"Miss Campbell," her father interrupted, "do you seriously believe that Don would kill my daughter?"

"I can't judge what's in his head, or his heart. Only God can do that. He might not intend to kill her, but I can tell you that he is capable of behavior that, should it go to the extreme, could prove deadly. And Margaret is the most likely victim."

After a long, almost excruciating silence, Ruby Maxwell had the final word. "Well I never," she said as she rose to begin clearing the table. "I just never."

CHAPTER SEVEN

Despite her nightly Bible reading and her prayer time on Sunday night, Margaret slept fitfully and was awake long before the alarm shattered the Monday morning stillness.

I hope Don is up and has the kids ready for school. If only I dared call over there, but I don't think I'd better. Don't want him to find some excuse to keep them out of school so they can't come back to me.

As soon as eight o'clock came, she dialed the school. "Pam, this is Margaret. I need to leave a message for Brian, please." She and the receptionist had worked together on so many volunteer projects down through the years, they were on a first name basis. She could sense discomfort on the other end of the phone, long before the woman she'd thought of as a friend said, "I'm sorry Mrs. Haywood, but Mr. Haywood has instructed that no one but him may have contact with the children while they're at school."

Mrs. Haywood? Mr. Haywood has instructed?

As if she felt the need to justify her message, the recep-tionist blurted, "After all, it is his money that pays their tuition."

So we're playing this game to the hilt, are we? Margaret wanted to lash out at Pam, but knew that her friend was in a compro-mised situation. "Don't give it a second thought," she told her, "I'll just be in contact with Mr. Haywood. You have a good day."

While trying to decide whether to throw the phone at the wall, it rang, and Margaret almost dropped it before she was able to punch the "talk" button.

"Margaret, it's Jim. Jim Deaton."

The sound of the attorney's voice was all it took to shatter Margaret's resolve that everything would work out in her favor. Through tears and a shaky voice, she said, "Oh, Jim. So much has happened in the last few days until I'm so confused and torn. I don't know which way to turn or what to do for the best. And now it looks like I may lose my children as well."

"Who told you that?" the attorney barked.

Margaret recounted the conversation at church and ended with the earlier conversation with the school. "I don't have any doubt that if I showed up at the school right now to see my chil-dren, I'd be asked to leave."

"Margaret, listen to me." The attorney's voice was low-key and soothing. "Don's not doing anything I didn't expect him to do. He just got on a faster timetable than I'd anticipated."

"But Jim, my children. My precious children! I may never see them again if he has his way. How can one man be so evil and get away with so much?" Margaret could feel panic overtaking her, but every time she allowed herself to think that Don might have her declared an unfit mother, she simply turned sick at her stomach.

"Listen to me Margaret. You cannot go off the deep end now. Don doesn't have the children yet, and if you do what I say and follow my advice, I feel very confident he won't get them."

"But Jim..."

"No buts, Margaret. Like it or not, this is the way it is. We're going to have to play the hand that's been dealt us, but we've still got a strong case. Now I need you to pull yourself together, get yourself together, and I'm going to pick you up in about 45 minutes."

"I've got therapy this morning at ten o'clock."

"P.C. told me. I'll drive you there and wait for you. We can talk on the way, and I want you ready for action as soon as you've finished. We've got a lot of ground to cover and a very short time to do it in."

Margaret didn't argue further, but promised to be ready. She showered, dressed and picked at her breakfast before Jim knocked on the back door. Harold Maxwell admitted the guest. As the two men were walking toward the breakfast area, she heard her father say, "I don't care what it costs, Jim. I want Don Haywood out of all our lives on a permanent basis."

The two men appeared in the doorway and Jim greeted Margaret. Then, returning to the conversation with Mr. Maxwell, he said, "Well don't put out a FOR SALE sign just yet. I still think that Don should be shown for what he truly is, and made to pay the bill for it as well."

Margaret could tell her father didn't know what to say. "You could really make that happen? I mean, bring him down and use his money to do it?"

"If we work this right, I think we stand a very good chance of doing just that. The only thing I have to warn you about is that Don is an abuser and abusers don't ever give up – especially when they're challenged."

"So you're saying that we should put nothing past him."

"That's exactly what I'm saying. He will take advantage of every opportunity."

Margaret told her parents good-bye. "Just look for me when you see me."

"Will the children be coming here after school?"

"The pessimist in me says they won't, Mama. I don't think Don had any intention of ever letting them come back when he got them from school last week. But if they should show up, call me on my cell phone."

It was another depressed morning in therapy, but Margaret did take time to pray, and was sincere when she asked God to intercede between her and the pain. The comfort level was much improved. *Thank you, God. Why do I doubt that I should turn everything over to You?*

When she rejoined Jim in the out-patient waiting area, P.C. and Joe were with him. "Is this a private conference, or can anyone join in?" she asked with an attempt at levity.

"Just waiting on you," P.C. said. "You're the guest of honor."

"Then why don't I feel honored?"

"Because you've been knocked down one too many times, and we're planning to combat that," Joe answered. "We've been out here planning strategy. We needed you to go forward, so let's adjourn to my office and we'll bring you up to speed and get this show on the road."

"Your office? But you're Don's attorney."

"Was his attorney," Joe replied. "He fired me and even if he hadn't, I would have refused to handle anything for him after I saw the frame-up he built against you."

"That's sweet of you, Joe, but I don't want to cause you any harm."

"You haven't and you won't. Trust me."

"Joe has been nice enough to make room in his office for Jim and for me," P.C. volunteered.

Shortly afterward, the four were sitting around the huge oval cherry table in Joe's conference room. Jim Deaton began to outline for her the case he planned to build against Don.

Do I dare hope he can pull this off?

"Joe and P.C. have given me a good insight into what makes Don Haywood tick, what fuels his madness. We're going to turn that madness around on him and, we believe before it's over, he'll lose control at the wrong time and in front of the wrong person."

"When he does," P.C. interrupted, "it will do him and his public image irreparable damage. Remember, Margaret, he totally lost it over nothing in Tennessee a few weeks ago. Our guess is that when he's away from home, where no one knows him, he lets his guard down, doesn't have to pretend to be the great benefactor, and that little slip cost him dearly in Gatlinburg."

"I agree, Margaret. I think we can cause him to show his true colors, which will force the court to think twice before even giving him unsupervised visitation, never mind full custody." Jim Deaton was emphasizing his points with his finger as he spoke.

"There is an unfit parent in this whole picture, but Margaret, it most certainly isn't you."

By the time the group adjourned for lunch, Margaret was so full of details of what would happen that afternoon, she could hardly find room for food. Or maybe it was that her stomach was too nervous to accept food.

They had a very thorough plan, she had to agree. But she also had to worry about how all they intended to do would affect her children. Don had already struck Sally once. Would he do it again, being further challenged drove him beyond the point of reason?

Jim had managed a chambers-only meeting with the judge and Margaret signed several documents before they departed Joe's office. As soon as they finished eating, the three attorneys went their separate ways. P.C. left going to the courthouse to file the petition for divorce, a petition asking the judge to deal with child support and temporary custody, and a request for a restraining order against Don, forbidding him to come within 100 feet of Margaret or the children. She was also asking to be awarded the Red Bud Way house until the divorce was final, so that she and the children might live there.

Joe's assignment was to swear out a warrant on Margaret's behalf, charging Don with child abuse for the incident where he slapped Sally so severely and destroyed much of the everyday dining room. Fortunately Margaret had sent two of the chairs out for repairs, and they were still at the shop, waiting to be picked up. Joe was going to get a statement from the woodworker, as well as statements from Margaret's doctor and Candi, the physical therapist. Annie Campbell had also offered to provide a statement, and Joe was trying to find the cab driver who had transported Margaret to the hospital.

Margaret and Jim drove straight to Mount Zion School, where they circled the parking lot twice looking for Don's gold SUV. When they didn't see it, they took up a position outside the school, within sight of the student exit door. It wasn't long before they saw Brian coming down the covered walk, swinging his book bag.

Margaret leapt from the lawyer's car as fast as her bad arm would allow, despite his admonitions not to show fear or haste.

As soon as she was on her feet, she called, "Brian. Brian! Over here, son."

The young man heard her and began looking to locate the source of the voice he recognized. When he looked in her direction, she began to wave her good arm, and moments later he saw her and came running.

"Oh, Brian, are you alright?" She had her arms around him before he could answer. "I was so worried about you."

"Worried about me? Why? You're the one who was sick."

"Because I tried all weekend to call you and no one answered at the house and you didn't answer your cell phone." Then the light bulb came on. "What do you mean I was the one who was sick?"

"You know. You had to go back to the hospital because you were so exhausted. That's what Dad told us when he got us from school last week."

Margaret knew she was treading on soft ground, but she knew she had no choice but to push on. She put her right hand on her son's left shoulder. "Brian, look at me and tell me the truth. This is very important."

"I always tell the truth, Mom." Then, when she gave him a "don't try that one on me, I'm your mother," he continued, "Well, most of the time anyway."

Margaret forged ahead. "Your dad told you I was in the hospital?"

"Yeah, last Tuesday afternoon when we got out for Thanksgiving. He was here to meet us, before we got on the bus. He said the doctor had put you in the hospital for complete rest, that you couldn't even have visitors or phone calls."

"And you believed him? Is that why you went with him?"

"He said you'd called him and asked him to get us for the

Thanksgiving holiday because we might be too much for Grandee and Grammy."

"You were in the hospital, weren't you, Mom?"

"No, Brian, I wasn't. But I can't explain now." She began to scan the crowd of younger students who were just then exiting the building in a massive stampede. "Right now, we've got to find Sally and Jason."

Son and mother continued to try to pick out the two younger children, but there were several minutes of strained silence before Brian yelled, "There they are, Mom. See 'em, right next to that first column on the right? Before she could stop him the boy had put his fingers to his mouth and gave forth with a shrill whistle. "Jason... Sally. Over here." He waved his hand to attract their attention. "Over here. Come over here," he yelled.

In a moment the two younger Haywoods came dashing across the asphalt, their bookbags bouncing on their backs. "Mommie, Sally squealed. You got out of the hospital."

So Brian was telling the truth.

Jason, ever the shy one, hung back before finally grabbing his mother around her waist and holding on. She could feel him shaking with terror and her heart went out to her youngest, at the same time she cursed Don for caring so little about his children.

"Please don't ever leave me again, Mommie," the little boy begged in a whisper so soft Margaret had to strain to hear him.

"Is this your car, Mommie? And who's this man?" Sally asked. "Did you come to pick us up so we can all go home to our house and be a real family again?"

"Margaret ignored most of her daughter's babbling inquisition, zeroing in on the last part of her question instead. "What do you mean 'so we can all go home to our house and be a real family again?'"

The little girl planted her hands on her hips and gave her famous exasperated frown. "You know, Mommie. Like Daddy told us. He said when you got out of the hospital after Thanksgiving, you'd be ready to come back to our house and we could all be like we used to be. A family."

As she looked from one child to the next, she saw that both boys were nodding their heads, apparently agreeing with their sister. *Don has stooped even lower than I thought him capable.*

Sally, sensing trouble, pleaded, "We are going to our house aren't we? Isn't that why you're here?"

Margaret looked at Jim and said to the children. "We're not going to our house immediately, there are several things we've got to see about first. Right now we're going back to Grandee's. Remember, we all still have clothes and other things there."

The children accepted that explanation and piled in the back seat of Jim Deaton's car. Margaret introduced Jim as a man she had hired to help her out while she only had one hand, and the children spent the fifteen minute ride talking about the catered meal they'd had at Thanksgiving, things that had happened at school that day, and their excitement at being back at home again.

Margaret didn't have the heart to tell them the truth, but she knew that time was rapidly approaching. She needed to talk with Jim before she said anything, and she had to know that Don had been served before they could do anything.

Sally, ever the family news broadcaster, suddenly erupted with a question that made Margaret's blood run cold. "Mommie... Mommie! Did you know somebody broke into our house and did all kinds of damage? They chopped up walls and furniture and tore up everything in the kitchen. Daddy says the police caught the person that did it."

"Yeah, Mom," Brian joined in. "And would you believe it

was a woman. Dad said she must have had quite a few screws loose, but he promised us that the police had her locked up, and that it was safe for us to come home for good."

Margaret was doing a slow burn and trying her best not to show it. Jim reached across the seat and touched her immobile left hand. "Don't lose it now," he seemed to be saying. And somehow, Margaret held her tongue. Instead, she asked sweetly, "So did Dad say who the woman was?"

"He said she was an old homeless woman who was probably mad at the whole world," Sally informed her, proud to be the bearer of the news. "And you should see the house, Mommie. Daddy had all the damage fixed so you can't even tell it, except the house doesn't look like it did before."

*That makes sense, when you know how Don's mind operates. He destroyed all the things that were special to me. It makes sense he would remodel it the way he wanted it because, after all, it is **his** house.*

When the car pulled to a stop at the Maxwell home, Margaret turned to face the children. "Kids, there is a chance we won't be going to our house tonight. There are some things your dad and I have to work out."

"But Mommie..." Sally's eyes were huge and already running over with tears. "Daddy promised we'd all be there tonight. He said after your stay in the hospital he knew you'd agree that's where we all should be. I want to go home to my room."

Margaret chose to ignore her daughter's protests, knowing from experience that to respond only gave the child more fuel. "Look, you three, I want you to go on in the house, and be sure to give Grammy and Grandee a hug, because they've really missed you."

Sally looked like she was about to mount the second round, and Margaret held up her hand to say STOP. "Go on to your rooms, get your homework done. No TV until all of you have finished. That way," she said, manufacturing what she hoped would pass for a sincere and excited smile. "That way, if we do get to go home tonight, you'll all be ready."

Amid the obligatory protests, the three Haywoods departed the car and headed toward the back door. She let them get almost there before she called, "Brian. Brian? Come back just a second, please."

"You two go on in," she heard him say. "I'll be there in a second. Mom wants something."

Margaret had gambled that he would do just that and, as he approached the car, she asked him to climb in the back seat. "I have to talk to you, but I didn't want the other two to hear this conversation."

When the boy had settled himself, Margaret began what was one of the most difficult conversations ever. *How do I ask this child to choose between his parents? Am I any better than Don, when it comes to using the children?*

She and Jim Deaton had talked about it earlier, and Jim believed it was crucial that Brian corroborate her accounts of Don's violent behavior.

"I'm about to do something I don't want to do," she informed her son. "But I don't have any choice." She could clearly see the confused expression on her son's face. "Brian, I need your help, and it isn't going to be pleasant. Believe me, I wouldn't ask if I had any other choice."

The boy sat, almost stone-faced, but said nothing.

In a faltering tone, Margaret continued. "Brian, this man is Jim Deaton. He's my attorney."

"Attorney? Why do you need an attorney?"

"Because I'm filing for a divorce from your dad."

The boy's face twisted into an expression of distaste that gripped her mother's heart in a similar way.

"But I'm asking the judge to allow us to go back to Red Bud Way to live, at least until everything is finalized. I'm doing everything I can, Brian, you have to believe me."

"But that means Dad won't be there. Right?"

"I'm afraid so, Brian. If he's there, I can't be there."

"But we can. Mom, we're tired of living here with Grammy and Grandee. We want to go home to our house, and Dad promised us this weekend that after you got out of the hospital, we could all be a family again. Like it used to be."

Margaret could sense that Brian was on the verge of losing his composure, yet without him, her case was one of "he says, she says". *Doesn't he understand how bad things were the way they used to be?*

Jim Deaton turned in the driver's seat to where he could look into Brian's face. "Your mom wasn't in the hospital. She was in jail."

"Jail?" Brian's voice was on the verge of cracking. "In jail? That's ridiculous. Why would she be in jail?"

"Because your father had her arrested for the destruction at your house. She spent more than eight hours in a cell before we could see a judge and get her out."

The boy's face blanched white and then glowed red with fury. "You're lying," he screamed. "Dad would never do anything like that. NEVER!"

Margaret's heart was torn between wanting to protect her son and the need to protect herself. "But he did, Brian. I'm the crazy homeless woman who supposedly did all the damage to the house." She lifted her broken arm as best she could. "Me, with one arm, I took a machete and hacked the house to pieces. At least that's what he convinced the police happened."

"I don't believe you."

"Brian, do you believe your father knocked your mother to the floor and shattered her arm?" Jim Deaton entered the conversation again.

"Huh? I mean, well, yeah. But Mom provoked him right after the whole deal on the plant fell apart. All he did was hit her. She's the one who lost her balance and hit the wall."

Margaret felt her face go red with anger, but she bit her tongue. *Don has no shame. He has thoroughly brainwashed his children to believe everything that has happened is my fault.*

"Brian, we need you to testify for your mother. You have to give her story about your father's abuse some substance."

Brian began making motions to exit the car, even as he screamed, "No! You can't make me. Everything is her fault. She's the reason we're stranded here instead of being able to live at home." In his haste to get the door open, he slammed the side of his head into the header with a thud that made Margaret ache for him.

"Dad promised us we'd all be a family again this week, and she's trying to wreck everything," he charged. By this point his face was an alarming shade of purple and the veins in his young neck were engorged and prominent. "I'm going to tell Sally and Jason what's going down, and then I'm calling Dad to come get us," he screamed. By this time he was half way across the driveway, when he turned to deliver one last volley. "We're out of here, and if you don't come home with us, as far as I'm concerned, you're no longer our mother. We don't have a mother!"

Margaret broke down in tears and sobbed uncontrollably. *If I'm not a mother, why is my heart breaking right now?*

Brian had just disappeared into the house when P.C.'s car

pulled into the drive. She approached the Mercedes with a smile of accomplishment on her face. When she discovered Margaret in tears, her expression changed, and by the time Jim had brought her up to speed, there was a glint of anger in her eyes.

"I'm going in the house to see if I can reason with him," she announced. "You folks stay here. Joe's due any minute."

"What else can I do, Jim?" She unconsciously fingered her injured limb. "Obviously my children are firmly indoctrinated into their father's line of bull. He really did a number on them over the holidays."

Jim patted her hand. "Don't worry, we can do this without Brian. It would have been easier with his cooperation, but we aren't beaten yet."

"Yes, but even if I win, what about my children? I've lost them emotionally. Do you think I can successfully run a single parent household when all of my credibility has been destroyed?" She gazed across at the house, to the basement windows where she assumed P.C. was with the kids. "Even if I win, I lose."

"We'll just have to take it one incident, one day at a time. It's too early to give up and bail." There was silence, as if neither could think of anything else to say. Then Jim remarked, "Here comes Joe. Let's see what he has to report."

The other attorney pulled to a stop, got out, and crossed over to the Mercedes, where he slid into the back seat recently vacated by Brian. He wore a triumphant look on his face.

"Hey, guys. I'm happy to report success. I got everything I went after." Then he realized that neither Margaret nor Jim were reacting to his announcement. Jim related the events of the past few minutes. "P.C.'s in there now, trying to talk to them."

"I'm going in, too," Joe announced. "Don has sold those kids a bill of goods. Somehow we've got to get them to listen to reason and see this for what it is."

Margaret was lost in thought, trying to imagine what it would be like to live without seeing her children, and having difficulty understanding why she would even want to still be alive. *My children are my whole life. Lord, I thought when You gave me the job of being a parent I had the most important assignment in the world. Now what do I do?*

Margaret didn't know how long they sat there. It was the sound of the door opening, and P.C. and Joe sliding into the back seat that brought her back from the fog-shrouded thoughts of despair. One look at their faces told the tale.

Jim was the first to speak. "No luck, huh?"

"Those kids are adamant that their father is no abuser and they claim they've never seen him do anything destructive," Joe was saying. "Unless it was provoked by you," P.C. finished for him.

Joe picked up the thread again. "Even your mom is siding with them, Margaret."

Margaret's lower jaw dropped. "Mom got in on this? Even after Don had me arrested, she's still singing his praises?"

"She is, but your dad isn't," P.C. clarified. "As a matter of fact, we left the two of them arguing because your dad said she had butted in where it was none of her business."

Oh, Don, if only you could understand just how far the ripple effect of your evil extends. Now my parents are fighting and they never have a cross word.

"Uh, oh," Jim remarked, "here comes Brian and from the expression on his face, I don't think he's here to tell us he's come around to our way of thinking."

The young man approached the passenger side of the car and Margaret hit the button to lower her window. "What is it

Brian?"

Her son's face was twisted in anger, and the words that spewed from his mouth hit the side of the car and its occupants with the force of machine gun fire. "We don't believe your lies, Mom! And we're going home to live with Dad. He's on his way to get us, and I told him everything you said."

Margaret gasped. "Brian, you didn't"

"Can't stand being caught up with, can you Mom?" The boy turned and strode back to the house, his back rigid and straight. Over his shoulder, the occupants in the car heard him say. "Dad said you were a crazy old homeless woman, and he was right!"

Margaret collapsed in the front seat in tears. *Oh, Lord, how could things have gone so horribly wrong? What's the use of fighting any longer? When Don gets here, my only hope to have my children in my life is to beg his forgiveness and go back home with him.*

Almost as if she were reading her friend's mind, P.C. reached across the seat back and touched Margaret on the shoulder. "If you're thinking about throwing in the towel, Margaret, forget it. This is exactly what Don is expecting to happen, and if you think life was rough before, you ain't seen nothing yet!"

I know she's right, but how can I stand by and allow my children to go back into that situation?

It was Jim's voice that cut through the tension in the car. "Whatever we do, we don't need to be sitting outside here in this car when Don drives up. Can we all go back into the house, Margaret?

Raising her one good hand in a half-way gesture of confusion, she said, "I don't know if I've still got a home here or not, now that Mom and Dad are on outs over this. But I agree that we don't need to be out here like sitting ducks, so let's give the house a try."

The four got out and crossed the pavement, went up the back steps and into the back foyer. Harold Maxwell was approaching from the breakfast room and stopped when he saw them. "I was just coming to get you." His face was hard and set in a way that Margaret had never seen before. "I understand Don's on his way over here to get the children. All I can say is, he's got his nerve."

"That he has, Dad. And he's had it for a long time. Trust me."

"I really don't want him on the place, but Ruby's gonna pitch a fit if I call the police, so I'll let him come. But if he starts anything, whether she likes it or not, I will have him arrested. This is my property and I say what goes and what doesn't." Then, as if he suddenly remembered his manners, he said, with a more kindly expression on his face, "You all come on in the den and make yourselves comfortable."

As they were settling in, the three young Haywoods trooped through the room, their possessions draped across them like they were pack animals. *They obviously intend to make only one trip.*

"We'll wait outside for Dad," Brian announced. "We don't feel exactly welcome in here." Sally said nothing, but did flash her mother a triumphant look as she passed her. It was Jason, however, who tugged hardest at Margaret's heart strings. The little boy was the picture of misery and fear and, when Margaret called his name and rose from her seat to go to him, Brian intervened. "Jason. She's not our mother any more. She's telling lies about Dad," he barked.

The child cowered in fear, caught between the two of them, but finally turned resolutely and fell in line with his brother and sister.

Margaret began to sob uncontrollably and through her tears, she could hear her dad taking Brian to task for how he was treating his mother.

"But she's lying," Brian persisted. "She claims Dad had her arrested for destroying the house, and we all know that's a lie. She's so desperate, she'll say anything." His words cut Margaret to the quick. "Dad says she's dangerous."

"You ungrateful child," Harold Maxwell bellowed in a manner Margaret knew was totally uncharacteristic of him. "She was in jail. I paid $10,000.00 to bail her out, and your dad was there the whole time, grinning and gloating that he had her right where he wanted her."

"You're lying, Grandee! You're no better than she is! Our dad would never do anything like that. It's just like he says, you're jealous of all the money he's made and Mom's too ungrateful to appreciate all he's given her."

Like a busted arm that will never be the same?

"Yeah," Sally asserted, "Dad's been real good to Mommie and I love him."

Then they all heard the sound of an approaching vehicle, and the children abandoned their combative stance and piled out the door. All except Jason who gave the appearance of a condemned man approaching the gallows.

Margaret's heart ached so hard for him, she had trouble breathing, but all the fight had left her. She was exhausted and spent, and at that point, felt there could be no salvation left for her.

Just then her mother came back in from outside, where she had followed the children. "I'll tell you," she offered, "it makes a heart feel good to see a father reunited with his children. That's how it ought to be."

"Now Ruby...!" Harold Maxwell began. "We're not gonna...,"

"You listen to me, Harold. Those children love their daddy and Margaret doesn't have any right to make them choose. That's my opinion and I'll say it as many times as I want to."

In the end, P.C. guided Margaret down to her room, where she helped her friend dress for bed and stayed until Margaret had slid beneath the covers and dropped off to sleep. When she got back to the den, Harold Maxwell delivered the message that Jim and Joe had gone back to Joe's house, and wanted her to join them. "P.C., you've been a good friend to Margaret," the old man said. "I'm just sick that all this has happened like it has. I guess we all underestimated how vindictive Don could be."

"That we did, Mr. Maxwell."

"But this one thing I know: my daughter isn't a liar. If she says Don is an abuser, then I believe her. And I intend to tell her so when she wakes up. But right now I'm terribly worried about those children. They don't have a clue how he's using them, and I'm afraid they're in danger."

"They are in grave danger. Joe and Jim and I will work tonight to try and find a solution. Tomorrow is another day. I just hope it won't be any more difficult than this day has been."

As she drove to Joe's house, P.C. thought about Annie Campbell and decided to give her a call. The only number she had was the shelter number itself, and Annie had left for the day. At first the violence counselor who answered the phone didn't want to give out any information, but when P.C. mentioned Margaret Haywood's name, the woman's demeanor changed immediately. "Give me your cell number and I'll have Annie call you in the next couple of minutes."

P.C. gladly provided the number, after which the phone

connection severed. It was hardly more than a minute later that her phone shrilled.

"What's happened, P.C.? I know you wouldn't have called unless there's a problem."

P.C. filled her in on all the details. There were a few moments of silence, before Annie asked, "Would I be too presumptuous to invite myself to join the three of you tonight? I'm not sure what I can contribute, but I am very concerned."

"I was hoping you'd agree to come," P.C. said. "I have a very bad feeling about this whole situation. I wouldn't be surprised if it blew up in all our faces."

Annie assured her she was on her way.

The two ladies arrived at Joe's house at the same time. Later in the evening, over take-out pizza, the four of them compared notes and planned strategy, while Margaret slept the sleep of the exhausted.

Joe explained that he'd been concerned to know if Don had been served with the papers. A call to the sheriff's office revealed reluctance on the part of the deputies, many of whom had received perks from Don, to serve him. Joe asked that nothing happen until the next day, and was assured that his request would be honored.

"That's the beauty of a small town, I guess," he informed the other three. "Everybody knows everybody, although in this case it's turning out to be a double-edged sword."

When the group finally broke up around eleven o'clock, they had agreed that Jim Deaton would file an emergency request with the court as soon as the clerk's office opened the next morning. They would demand that Don Haywood surrender the children to their mother until more permanent custody arrangements could be negotiated.

"I just don't want those children in the picture when those papers are served," Jim explained. "And I don't care if the sheriff himself has to serve him, we're going to charge him and his department with obstructing justice if they don't do their job. It needs to be done while the children are in school."

The others agreed. Everyone exchanged cell numbers with the promise to call if the need arose, or should new information materialize.

"I just wish I felt better about all this," Joe said as he bade goodnight to Annie and Jim. P.C. remained for a few minutes more, during which time Joe explained that she and he probably knew Don better than anyone besides Margaret.

"I know he's capable of totally losing control, and I'm deathly afraid of what might happen if he does."

The two shared a hug, a quick peck on the lips, and P.C. was gone.

Joe put out the lights and headed for his bedroom. Only he knew he would sleep little. The thought of those children alone in the house with Don made him go cold with fear. He was still awake, and cold, when the phone rang at two a.m.

He answered it with trembling hands.

CHAPTER EIGHT

The cell phone on the bedside table whistled its cheery tone, but Margaret, deep in exhausted sleep, didn't hear it. It rang a second time, until it went to voice mail. Margaret had no idea she was being summoned.

"Wake up, Margaret. Please wake up!" Harold Maxwell was shaking his daughter's right shoulder, pleading with her.

"Huh...? Wha... what is it? Dad? Is that you?" Margaret struggled to open her eyes, uncertain why her father would be in her bedroom in the middle of the night. "What's wrong?"

Harold hovered uncertainly over his daughter. "You've got to call Brian. On his cell phone. He's been trying to call you, but you were too asleep to hear your phone."

"Brian's trying to call me?" Margaret tried to process what she was hearing, but there were still too many cobwebs. "Why would he be calling me at this time of night?"

Harold Maxwell didn't share his fears. Instead, he replied, "He didn't say what was wrong. He called our number when he couldn't get you to answer and begged me to have you call him right away."

"Help me up, Dad. Something's wrong. There's no other explanation."

Once she was in a sitting position, she reached for her cell phone with trembling hands and punched redial so it would automatically return Brian's call. It was answered on the first ring.

"Oh, Mom. Oh, gosh," Brian said in a loud whisper, although panic was evident in his voice. "Mom, it's Jason. It's bad, Mom."

Suddenly Margaret was wide awake. "Jason?" *What's happened to my baby?* "What is it, Brian? What's wrong with Jason? Is he crying for me?"

"Oh, man, Mom... oh, Mom...," he babbled, "it's worse than that."

Margaret felt a coldness go through her and she wondered if she would ever feel warm again. "Brian, tell me what's wrong," she ordered. "Now!"

"You were right about Dad. And I was so wrong... and now Jason...,"

"Brian!" she screamed. "What happened to Jason? You have to tell me!"

"He's hurt bad, Mom. And it's my fault because I didn't believe you."

Margaret knew that her eldest was very close to losing it all, and she still didn't know what had happened to Jason. "Listen to me, Brian. It doesn't matter whose fault it is. Right now we have to get help for Jason. Now tell me what happened."

If I were a fiction writer, I couldn't have conceived this.

She finally managed to get Brian calm enough to learn that for whatever reason, the sheriff's deputy served Don with all the papers shortly after midnight. *With all that's gone on, I'd forgotten about those suits.* Brian related how Don had returned to the house, his rage building with every step. It seems that Jason, who had been awakened by the noise, came to see what was happening. "Mom... Dad was so angry, when Jason asked what was wrong, Dad grabbed him up and threw him against the wall in the den."

He threw my Jason against the wall!

"Brian, where is Jason now? Let me talk to him."

"That's what I'm trying to tell you, Mom. "He can't talk to you." His words were tumbling over themselves. "I can't get him to wake up. I'm in my room, with the door locked...," a deep sob escaped his lips. "Mom, I can't get him to wake up. Oh, please, Mom... don't let him be dead."

Dead!

The word marshaled all of Margaret's resolve. Later she would marvel that she had been able to function so efficiently.

"Where's your Dad?"

"I don't know, Mom. The house got real quiet after he threw Jason against the wall. I haven't heard his SUV leave, so I guess he's still here in the house."

"Listen, Brian... hang up and dial 911 and ask for an ambulance. Tell the dispatcher exactly what happened, and tell them you're locked in your bedroom. Don't open the door to anyone unless they identify themselves as EMTs or unless you hear my voice."

"But, Mom. Suppose Dad won't let them in?"

"That's why I'm calling the sheriff's office to send the deputy back. And Grandee and I are on our way."

Harold, having sensed a trip in the offing, returned from dressing just as Margaret hung up with the sheriff's dispatcher. She'd had to argue with the man, but he finally agreed to dispatch an officer when she threatened to sue. Margaret jerked on clothes over her pajamas and, in a matter of minutes, they were on their way. She called P.C. on the way, who in turn agreed to alert the others. Then she would head toward Red Bud Way herself, she promised.

The next few hours were frantic ones. She and her father arrived at the house which had an all-too-eerie appearance in the early morning darkness, right behind the ambulance. They found EMT's trying to gain entrance, but no one was answering their efforts. Margaret remembered her key, and produced it. *Thank goodness Don didn't change the locks.* She gave directions to Brian's bedroom, and cautioned the technicians that the man who had injured her child was probably somewhere in the house.

When the deputy arrived and Margaret filled him in, he entered first, leading the EMTs. The medics found Brian sitting in the middle of the floor cradling the all-too-still form of a small, blond-headed child in his arms and crying. The deputy located Don, in the master bedroom, sleeping the sleep of the innocent. *Sleeping as if nothing had happened.* The court papers he'd been served were ripped into bits and pieces and strewn like confetti around the room.

Sally, who had slept through all the confusion, awoke just as the paramedics were wheeling Jason down the stairs. At first she locked herself in her bedroom and refused Margaret's pleas that she open the door. Only after Brian ordered her to do as their mother asked, did the little girl come out.

Brian, in a manner that was totally different from that he had exhibited the previous afternoon, was all too eager to explain to the deputy sheriff how Jason's injuries had occurred.

Upon hearing his son's damaging assertions, Don Haywood attempted to attack him and would have been success-ful, had the deputy not pinned him to the floor and handcuffed him.

In the meantime, P.C. and Joe, along with Annie, had ar-rived about the same time, with the word that Jim Deaton was on his way from Atlanta.

Harold Maxwell took Brian and Sally back to his house, while Margaret rode in the ambulance with Jason to the emer-gency room. P.C., Joe and Annie followed closely behind.

Don Haywood left his home on Red Bud Way in the back seat of a sheriff's car, still in a frothing rage, his hands and feet shackled to keep him from inflicting injury to anyone else more than to himself.

Once they arrived at the hospital, Jason was taken from her and Margaret could only sit with her support group in the waiting area. Waiting... and waiting.

By the clock it was only about 40 minutes, but to the bat-tered mother now having to deal with the abuse of her youngest child, every minute seemed to be a year long. Finally the doctor – her doctor, she was relieved to see – approached her. The expres-sion of pain on his tired face told her more than his words ever could.

"Mrs. Haywood," he said as he took a seat beside her, "I'm not going to deceive you. Your son is in critical condition and we really need to transport him to Children's Hospital in Atlanta. They're so much better equipped to deal with his injuries than we are here."

Critical injuries. Oh, Lord, how could Don have done this?

"Just what is the extent of his injuries?" she asked. "Is he going to die? Please tell me the truth. I have to know."

"I'd say Jason has a better than fifty/fifty chance of surviving," he assured her. "It's what shape he'll be in afterward that I'm most concerned about."

"You mean... you're... talking about brain damage?"

"Jason has experienced some severe head trauma. He's bleeding inside his brain, which has placed him in a deep coma. He definitely has a concussion, a bad one. I'll have to be honest with you, the chances of him surviving without some brain damage are not good. But the sooner we get him to Atlanta, the better his chances. Do we have your consent?"

Margaret was in a daze and had she not been sitting, believed she would have fallen. "My consent? My consent. Of course, do it. Now. May I ride with him?"

"I'm afraid that won't be possible," the doctor said kindly, "we're going to be airlifting because time is crucial. There isn't room in the chopper for you as well."

"Don't worry, Margaret," Joe volunteered. "We'll leave in my car as soon as we see him loaded into the chopper. We won't be that far behind them."

"I'll go, too," P.C. volunteered."

Annie Campbell, who had been strangely quiet throughout the entire ordeal left the room without explanation, only to return a few minutes later with a slip of paper, which she handed to P.C. "This woman's a shelter director in the vicinity of Children's Hospital, and she'll be glad to help you any way you need."

Margaret raised her good arm to Annie, who returned it with a hug that Margaret found so comforting. "I'll be down later in the day," she promised Margaret, who protested that it wasn't necessary. "I'll be down and that's that," the little woman asserted. "And in the meantime, I'll be praying for all of you, but especially for Jason. You can depend on that."

Praying...

"Annie, would you call Brother Samuel, after it's a decent hour, and ask him to be praying as well?

"Why honey, you know I will. Is there anyone else you need me to call?"

"No, just Brother Samuel... no, wait... could you call my dad and let him know what's happening? I know he's worried sick."

Annie promised to make both calls, then stood with Margaret and the rest of the group, watching. The sheet-draped gurney seemed to swallow the little patient as it was wheeled toward the helipad. The techs stopped just long enough for Margaret to kiss her son's forehead and bush back a lock of his beautiful hair. The left side of his little head was already grotesque and brilliant purple.

They stood by the window watched him being loaded. "My car's in the parking lot," said Joe solemnly. "Let's go."

The car was strangely quiet all the way, and it wasn't until they were almost into Atlanta that Margaret remembered about Don. "I'm going to have to come back to town as soon as the courthouse opens to swear out a warrant for Don's arrest," she said, torn between which way she could best serve her injured child. "He's not going to get away with this."

"And he won't," Joe assured her. "Don Haywood is already in residence at the local jail. I checked before we left. Brian's story of what transpired was all the deputy needed to take him in on an assault charge. Come daylight, there will be other charges added, but that one alone will keep him there overnight."

Thank you, Lord, for giving Brian the maturity to call me and to deal with the crisis. Please, Lord, if is Your will, spare Jason's life. I don't care if he's brain-damaged. I just want my little boy to love a while longer.

By the time they reached the hospital, Jason had been received and was in ICU. A doctor was waiting for them to explain what was happening and how he saw the situation. "There's no doubt about it, Mrs. Haywood, your son sustained a massive head injury. The fact that he did not bleed externally isn't in his favor. Instead, all the bleeding occurred inside his brain, and his brain has swollen because of the trauma."

I've never been so scared in all my life. Despite her best intentions, Margaret found herself trembling so hard she could barely manage to sit in the chair. She bit her clinched fist to try and keep her composure.

"But will he live?" she begged the doctor. "Please tell me... I have to know."

"The next 72 hours will tell the tale," the doctor explained. "He's already in a coma, but we're going to put him in an even deeper sleep, for his benefit. And I'm about to go in and try to drain some of the blood from around his brain, in an effort to relieve some of the pressure."

Three days. 72 hours. I have to wait three days to know whether my son is going to live?

She forced herself to ask the next question. "Three days... after that, what happens?"

"Depending on the MRI results, we can hopefully begin to bring him out of the drug-induced coma after three days. Then, and it may take two or three more days, hopefully he'll begin to wake from the coma caused by the brain injury. We won't be able to assess his condition completely until he is awake and can talk to us." He patted her shoulder, "Your son is critically injured, Mrs. Haywood. The person that did this is nothing more than an animal, in my opinion."

"Can I see Jason? Please?"

"We're getting him ready for surgery, but I'll give you one minute with him, as soon as they're ready to roll him upstairs."

The doctor left, and Margaret looked at her two friends. "So it's come down to this." The other two said nothing. *But then what is there to say? We all knew this was going to come to no good, but everyone was too intimidated by Don's money to listen to us.*

After what seemed like an eternity, the double doors opened, and Jason's bed was piloted into the hallway. Margaret kissed her child again. "Fight, Jason. Fight as hard as you can son. We need you and I promise you, Daddy won't ever hurt you again."

All too soon the two nurses indicated he needed to get into surgery, and Margaret was left, standing in the corridor, watching her son being taken away from her. Then the doors at the end of the hall swung open and swallowed up her little boy.

Will I ever see him alive again?

Outside the first rays of sunlight were chasing away the darkness, only the darkness in her soul would not be so easily dispatched, Margaret discovered. Her entire mind was tormented with "why's" and "what ifs" and questioning how she could have kept this from happening. *God, I feel so guilty. I've failed my son... I failed to do everything I could to protect him. And now, if he lives, he may be brain-damaged. And it's all my fault.*

"Mrs. Haywood? What can I do to help you?"

The sound of an unfamiliar man's voice jerked her from her pity party. She looked up into the face of Brother Samuel. Standing right behind him were his wife, Susan and Annie Campbell.

"Brother Samuel!" *Do I even remember his last name?* "What are you doing here? I told Annie to wait until it was business hours to call you."

He chuckled. "You might have told her that, but Sister

Annie knows me better than that. We would have had words if she hadn't called me when she did."

"But I'm not even a member of your congregation." She stammered, "I... I didn't... didn't mean for you to drive all the way down here. I just wanted you to pray."

"And I have," he assured her. "And I will continue to lift Jason's name up. But right now, I'm concerned about you."

"I'm alright," she answered at last. "But you really shouldn't have come. I'm not one of your church members," she said again.

"Maybe not," the pastor agreed, "but you are one of God's children... a child who happens to be hurting very badly right now. I'm one of God's ministers; therefore I came."

Margaret reached her one arm to him, and they hugged in an awkward fashion. Then it really registered with her that the pastor's wife and Annie Campbell were standing nearby. She motioned them to her.

Annie spoke first. "What's Jason's status? What are we praying for?"

Margaret related the doctor's report and the possibility of complications. "If we can just pray for Jason to live," she asked. "I don't care if he is brain-damaged. I'll spend the rest of my life caring for him."

"Then let's all pray right now, shall we?" the pastor asked. There in the ICU waiting area, the five of them gathered around Margaret where she sat, joined hands and hearts, and prayed silently as the young pastor took their burdens straight to God.

Dear Lord, the giver of all that is good and pure, we ask Your blessings this morning on Jason Haywood. We admit that we don't always understand why bad things happen to innocent people, but we acknowledge that through it all, You are in charge, and we bow to Your greater plan. We do pray, selfishly, we admit, that You will restore Jason to us in perfect health.

But we pledge here and now to accept whatever happens, knowing that You know best and that everything happens according to Your timetable. We would ask Your continued presence in our lives during these next few days, that no matter the outcome, we may be strong and a witness for You to all we come in contact with. Bless Jason, Father. Bless us, keep watch over us, and hold us all in the palm of Your Almighty Hand, just as You would hold the lowly sparrow. We love You and Praise Your name as the one Who sent His Son to die for us that we all might have eternal life in You. It is in His Holy name we pray. Amen.

Margaret was unable to speak, she was so overcome with the sense of peace that had descended upon her as the pastor prayed. *I know that whatever happens, I can deal with it. Thank you, Lord.* She squeezed the minister's hand, then was struck with a very uncomfortable feeling. "Brother Samuel, I'm ashamed to admit I don't even know your last name."

The young man laughed and said, "It doesn't matter to me, but to relieve your anxiety, it's Bronson. Samuel Bronson."

During the next few minutes, Annie and Susan Bronson persuaded Margaret to walk with them to the cafeteria to get breakfast.

Despite her protests, she finally agreed, after P.C. reminded her that she had gone to bed the previous evening without supper, and that she had to keep up her strength because she was still recovering herself. "You go eat something. We'll stay right here. If the doctor calls or comes, one of us will get you ASAP."

After they left, the pastor, Joe and P.C. had a heart-to-heart conversation, sharing all the incidents that precipitated the violent outburst that had injured Jason.

"And you say Mr. Haywood was asleep in bed when the paramedics got there? He hadn't even had the conscience to check on his son after such a violent outburst?"

"The deputy said he was so asleep he actually had to awaken him," Joe replied. "But why did they choose to serve those papers at that hour, especially after they had promised me they would wait until the children were in school today?" He shook his head, sadly. "All of this could have been so easily avoided."

P.C. agreed, "But it wasn't avoided, and now we have to be sure Don Haywood can't buy or strong-arm his way out this time."

The pastor was still shaking his head over all that he had heard. "He has done a lot of good for the town, but I agree, he must answer for what he's done. And I'm talking about more than just this latest incident."

"Look," said P.C., "isn't that Jim Deaton's car pulling into the parking lot?" Joe looked and agreed, and offered to go meet the other attorney. He left, while P.C. and the pastor continued to talk. "Brother Samuel, I want to thank you so much for making the trip down here." She faltered. "Margaret...,"

"I wouldn't have it any other way," the minister said. Then he looked quizzically at the young attorney, "But I get the feeling there's something else you want to say. You're among friends."

P.C. hesitated, then plunged ahead. "Margaret came to your church Sunday morning because she had grown disenchanted with her own church. The church leadership was upholding Don in all their troubles and accusing Margaret of being the offending party."

"I'm not totally surprised."

"She decided last Saturday that she wanted to go to a different church." P.C. then went on to explain how Margaret had settled on the little shabby, concrete block white church in the poor part of town. "She truly felt like God was leading her there."

"I have no doubt that He was, which is all the more reason

why I should be here right now. Let's just say I felt equally led to drive to Atlanta in the middle of the night." He laughed, "The longer I serve God, the more I realize that I only mess up when I don't follow those nudges He gives me."

"I'd have to agree with you," P.C. said.

Joe and Jim returned as Margaret and her escorts arrived from breakfast. Jim went straight to his client. "I feel like I've failed you," he apologized. "I just didn't move fast enough."

"None of us saw this coming until yesterday afternoon, and by then too much was already set in concrete for us to change. What happened, happened. Now we have to deal with it."

Joe had briefed Jim on Jason's condition and prognosis. "I've already talked to officials in Carter's Crossroads, and I think a new day has dawned there as far as Haywood money is concerned," he told the group. "Don has hurt an innocent child now. And it's public knowledge. He won't be able to buy his way out this time, Margaret."

"You have prevailed, Margaret," P.C. argued, "although I know that's little consolation right now."

They were still discussing what might happen with Don, when the doctor approached. "Mrs. Haywood?"

Almost afraid to look up, she answered, "Yes?"

The doctor squatted down on the floor beside her chair. "I've got news, and I'm afraid not all of it's positive."

Margaret held her breath, unable even to manage a response.

"Jason came through the procedure with no problems. He's a strong little boy. We have relieved the pressure inside his head considerably, but he still has no reflexes below his waist."

"So he's paralyzed." It was uttered more as a statement than a question.

"Perhaps. Perhaps not. It could be that the swelling still present in the brain is pressing on the nerves to the lower part of the body, and once that is reduced, he'll be able to respond. But..." he looked her straight in the face, "there is also the chance that this is how he's going to be. As I said, the next three days will tell the difference."

Margaret thanked the doctor. "Can I see him?"

"He's still in recovery right now, but he should be brought back to the floor within the hour. "I'll leave an order for you to have five minutes with him as soon as they get him settled and stabilized. But..." he looked her in the face again, "don't expect any recognition. His coma is so deep he couldn't respond if he wanted to."

It was just a short time before the nurse summoned Margaret and said that one person could accompany her.

"Brother Samuel? Will you go with me?"

The pastor took her by the arm and they followed the nurse past room after room filled with children in beds.

"It's almost depressing, isn't it?" she asked him.

"But isn't it wonderful that sick children have such a wonderful hospital that caters exclusively to their needs?"

Margaret laughed, for which the nurse gave her a frown of rebuke. "The old glass half full or half empty, huh?"

"Sort of."

They finally reached the room where Jason lay so quiet and still. *I'll never complain again when he gets overly-enthusiastic.*

"I'll be back in five minutes," the nurse informed them. "No longer."

"Margaret walked to his bed and took hold of his hand. It was warm and comforting, and she took encouragement from that small indication. "Brother Samuel? Quick, before the nurse returns, take Jason's other hand and say a prayer. That's all I want, is for him in the depths of his coma to hear that prayer, and for him to feel us holding his hands. I truly believe it can make a difference."

The pastor did as she directed. *Lord, we come to You again, to thank You for bringing Jason through the surgery successfully. We believe, God, that You have the power to heal Jason completely, and we ask You now, as You have directed us in Matthew 21, verse 22, "whatsoever ye shall ask in prayer, believing, ye shall receive." We humbly beg your continued blessings on Jason's recovery and on his family members who must stand by, helplessly, at this critical time. Our prayer, Father, is for Jason to be restored to us in full health. At the same time, Your will, not ours be done. In the name of Jesus the Christ, Your Son, the child You watched suffer. Amen.*

Then before Margaret was ready, the nurse returned to escort them out. As she closed the door behind them in the waiting area, she pointed to a sign posted nearby. "Those are the scheduled visiting hours. If you want to see him again, you'll need to be here at those times."

Margaret thanked her and studied the sign. She was dismayed to see that basically, she would only get five minutes with him, four times every twenty-four hours. *I'll take what I can get, Lord, and be thankful for it.*

She gathered her friends around her and informed them. "I'm staying here, and I don't want to hear any arguments. As long as Jason's here, I'm going to be here. But the rest of you have jobs and other responsibilities. So I expect you to be leaving shortly to deal with those demands."

Susan Bronson raised an objection. "But Margaret... may I call you Margaret?" When she saw a nodding head in answer, she continued, "You can't stay here alone. You're still recovering yourself. You need someone with you?"

"I've got someone with me. God has given me a peace that

I cannot explain to you. I don't know if that means Jason's going to recover, or simply that God is holding me to help me deal with whatever the outcome is. But I'm not alone."

"I'm not counting God out," P.C. piped up, "but Susan is right. You're going to need help."

"And I need several someones back in Carter's Crossroads. I've got two other children who are going to be very upset. Brian is already blaming himself. He needs someone to be there for him, and Sally may be brash, but I know my daughter. She's hurting, too."

"If Joe would introduce me to Brian, I'd be glad to talk with him and try to reassure him," Brother Samuel volunteered. "I can help with Sally," Susan offered. "Where are they now?"

"My father took them back to his house about 3:00 o'clock this morning, and I'm sure he and Mama are worried sick as well."

"Leave Mr. and Mrs. Maxwell to me," Joe Busbee volunteered. "Between P.C. and myself, we'll try to help them."

"What about Don?" Margaret asked.

"What about him?" Jim questioned.

"What are you going to have to do to make sure he doesn't get out of jail?"

It was Susan Bronson who answered. "My name's not Jim, but I think he'll agree when I promise you, Don Haywood isn't going to see freedom for some time. The guys back at the station will see to that."

Jim picked up the conversation. "My understanding is that Don will be arraigned later today. I came by here first, to find out how things were, before heading to Carter's Crossroads. I'll be in court when his case is heard, and I'm going to request, on your behalf, that bail not be granted, and that he be held in the county jail until his case comes to trial."

"You leave all the legal stuff to us," Joe volunteered. "You just worry about yourself and Jason. The two of you are all that matter at this point."

Margaret assured him that she would, then looked past him to see Annie Campbell and a woman she didn't recognize coming towards the group.

Annie took advantage of the pause in conversation to say, "Margaret. Everyone. This is Rachel Morris, a formerly battered wife from here in Atlanta."

"I'm glad to meet you," Margaret said, with the others echoing her.

"I'm pleased to meet you, too, the newcomer said. I'm just sorry it has to be under these circumstances."

Why is she here?

Annie explained, "Rachel is here to stay with Margaret today. She'll be here until 5:00 this afternoon, when she'll be relieved by another woman, who will stay until 7:00 in the morning." She touched Margaret on her arm. "You will not be alone here at all. Someone from the local shelter group of volunteers will be with you, for whatever you need."

"Annie. But I can't accept this. These people don't even know me."

"Oh, but they do, Margaret. Maybe not by sight or by name, but by circumstance they know you intimately well."

I have so many debts to repay when this is all behind us. Whenever that is. Right now I can't see the light at the end of the tunnel. I just have to believe it's there.

The visitor seated herself on Margaret's good side. "I've been right where you are right now. Trust me, I know how you're hurting. That's why I'm here; to hurt with you, to hurt for you, and to make sure that you take care of yourself."

Oh, God. I'm going to cry. I've been so strong, but I don't think I can hold it in much longer. It's just so overwhelming. Margaret began to sob quietly, and at her new friend's urging, lay her head on Rachel's shoulder and continued to cry, uncaring that someone might hear her.

"Why don't you all go on back to town," she heard Annie urging the others. "I'll be right behind you. Margaret's in good hands and we all have things to do for her at home."

Brother Samuel leaned over her and whispered, "God be with you, Margaret. We're as close as the phone."

Margaret didn't look up, but whispered her thanks, and was aware that the group had begun to move towards the doorway. But she didn't feel abandoned or alone. *I just feel empty. Used up.*

After a few minutes, when her tears had subsided, Margaret raised her head and surveyed the wet shoulder of Rachel's blouse. "I'm so sorry I got you all wet. I don't know what came over me, but I'll be glad to buy you a new outfit."

Her answer came in the form of a hearty laugh, much more robust that she would have expected from someone as petite as this stranger, who seemed so comfortable. *What has happened to me? I never get so emotional with someone I don't even know!*

"Don't you worry about this blouse, it'll wash and be good as new. Something tells me you'll be good to go, too, after that cry. God is so good. He gives us a way to just release all the emotions that are locked up inside us."

Margaret was speechless. "I've never thought about it that way."

"But you do feel better, don't you?"

I have to admit I do. I still can't see the light at the end, but I don't feel so frantic to find it.

The two women spent the next hour getting acquainted

and, at Rachel's request, Margaret told her all about how Jason came to be injured. "It's my fault. Don should have been called on his actions long ago, but I chose to turn a blind eye."

"Well," said Rachel, "you're at least half right. You did turn a blind eye. We all did."

"We?"

"Honey, I'm not just a volunteer at the shelter here, I'm a former victim. Only I'm not as fortunate as you are. My little girl didn't have a chance to recover. She was dead the minute my ex-husband shot her."

"Your husband shot your daughter? How can you even stand to talk about it?"

"Listen, Margaret. I'm not here by accident. When Annie Campbell called my director to say she needed people to sit with you, I volunteered the minute I heard the story."

"But why? You didn't even know me?"

"But I knew how you were hurting. Who better than someone who has walked in your shoes and knows how helpless a mother feels when she can't keep her children safe? Thankfully, my little Emily – she was five – died instantly. She went right to the arms of Jesus. And by helping you, I honor her memory and keep her alive for me. Otherwise, I'd go crazy."

Before Margaret could reply, the nurse announced ICU visiting time, and Margaret asked Rachel to accompany her. Once in Jason's room, his mother couldn't tell any change for the better or worse, which somehow gave her hope.

"He's a beautiful little boy," Rachel said, taking one of his hands in hers. "So let's say a prayer with him right now. He needs to hear voices in prayer for him. The two women each took a hand, and Rachel prayed. *Oh dear Lord, You are perhaps the only Father who can understand the pain and helplessness a mother feels when her child is in-*

jured. We lift up Jason to you now, asking that You would ease his pain and in Your own good time, restore him fully to us. We would ask also that you clutch Margaret close to You, revive and restore her as well. Her faith is strong, Father. Give her the strength of body to match, so that she is equal to the days ahead, knowing always that You who knows best is in charge. We pray this in the name of Your Son Jesus. Amen.

Back in the waiting room, the two continued visiting and getting to know each other. Margaret confided that she didn't know what to expect once they were able to return to Carter's Crossroads.

Rachel's reply was one she would never forget. "That's not your decision to make, you know. God already has it mapped out. And when the time is right, He'll share it with you."

She's right, isn't she God? I'm supposed to wait on you? Then she remembered the lines from an old hymn, "Silently now, I wait for thee, Ready my God, thy will to see, Open mine eyes illumine me, Spirit divine."

I'm waiting, Lord. When You're ready, whatever Your plan is, I'm waiting.

CHAPTER NINE

There was no change in Jason at the next visiting time, nor the next. But the doctor had said there wouldn't be until they could wean him from the drug-induced coma. *At least he's still alive. Thank You, Lord.*

During the hours between visits, Margaret talked with Jim Deaton, who assured her that Don Haywood would remain jailed for some time. "At the risk of upsetting you," the attorney told her, "he doesn't stand a chance of making bail until we know whether Jason's going to pull through."

"What does that have to do with anything?" Margaret asked, her sleep-deprived brain unable to process all that she was hearing.

"Margaret, don't you understand? If Jason doesn't make it, Don will be guilty of murder."

Don... a murderer! Oh, Don, how have our lives taken such a drastic detour? We could have been so happy.

Between catnaps, she also talked with P.C., and with her father, who called about mid-morning. He was crying so hard that Margaret could barely understand him at times. That her father, who had always been so strong, was reduced to tears over the critical condition of his youngest grandchild, was equally upsetting for her.

"Look, Dad," she tried to reassure him, "Jason is holding his own right now. We just have to keep the faith that he's going to make it and be our old Jason."

"But... for... Don... to... have done that... to his own... son," he sobbed, "I just can't... can't accept it. He has to... has to pay... for this."

"And he will, Dad. He will." *I'm not sure how, but he will.*

Later in the day, Joe Busbee called. After checking on her welfare and Jason's unchanged condition, Margaret could sense a hesitation on his part. "Is there something else you aren't telling me, Joe?"

The lawyer chuckled, although there was no trace of humor in his tone. "Remind me never to play poker with you," he remarked. "We've got another problem you probably haven't thought about."

"And what would that be?" *How can there be any more problems than we already have?*

"It's Haywood Tufters. There's no one to run it or to handle the day-to-day details. More importantly, there's no one to sign payroll checks."

The plant! How could I have completely forgotten? I guess it's because that was Don's, never mine.

"What can I do, Joe? That's Don's baby and my name was

never on anything down there. Even if I could leave Jason, which I won't, I have no more authority than any of the workers on the floor."

"I'm not suggesting that you should leave Jason. But you're going to have to have an income when all this shakes out, and if workers walk out because they haven't been paid, Don's business and your source of income takes an immediate nose dive."

He's right. But I don't know what to do. Lord, guide me on this, please.

"So do you have any suggestions?"

Joe hesitated. "Someone is going to have to be authorized to manage the plant and, more importantly, sign checks. And there's not much time."

"Well, Joe, I hope you don't think Don would accept either you or me, so where does that leave us?"

"I've given that some thought and I've talked to Jim. He believes we can petition a judge, on your behalf, to appoint a conservator – a neutral party – to manage things in the short term."

"Will that work since my name isn't on anything?"

"That's why we have to do it on behalf of you and the children. Jim thinks if we show that failure to take action now will cost Don's children big time down the road, regardless of how all this shakes out, the judge will grant it."

"It's an idea."

"What have you got to lose?"

Suddenly all that money, and the source for it mean nothing to me. But I can't afford to bury my head and pretend the problem doesn't exist.

"OK, Joe. Tell Jim to go for it... And Joe, do we know yet who Don has retained as his attorney?"

"That's the interesting thing, Margaret. He's going to have an attorney appointed for him. None of the lawyers in Carter's Crossroads will voluntarily take the case."

Who would ever have thought it would come to this?

"That's interesting, and more than a little sad."

"Hey, I don't take any joy in how far my old friend has fallen," Joe said sadly, "but we both know he was on a self-made path to destruction."

"That he was, Joe. I just don't know why it took me so long to see it."

"Don't beat yourself up over it. Things were good. You had no reason to suspect anything was wrong."

Oh, I had plenty of reason. I just didn't want to see it.

"That's not exactly the way it was, Joe." Margaret confessed. "I first saw this side of him several years ago, but I chose to ignore it, because domestic violence didn't happen in homes like ours."

She waited for a response that didn't come. *I guess I've made him uncomfortable.* "Who knows how much grief we might all have been spared if I'd been honest with myself. Instead, I chose to turn my head because the money was great, and I couldn't bear the public stigma of abuse." She laughed. "Now... that's the least of my worries."

"What's done is done, Margaret. I don't think there are any of us who were close to Don who didn't see signs that we chose, for whatever reason, to ignore. Well, I'd better go and tell Jim to get on this other matter. Don has employees who're going to want to be paid."

"Bye, Joe... and thanks."

This whole situation just continues to become more and more confusing. I don't even know where to begin to unravel things. But right now my children are more important than anything.

As the day dragged on, Margaret found herself turning more and more to Rachel to help her find balance out of all the turmoil. One thing her new friend said caused her antenna to stand at attention.

She had been talking about Sally and Brian, about how Don had treated them, when Rachel remarked. "I really feel for them right now. Their dad's in jail, and I'm sure the whole town is talking about it. Their baby brother was seriously injured right in front of them, and now you're down here with Jason. They've got to be feeling pretty lost and scared right now."

Oh, Lord, how could I have been so selfish? I knew the others were with Dad, but I hadn't given the first thought to how uncomfortable they must be feeling.

Her face must have mirrored her true feelings, because Rachel patted her hand. "Don't worry, you've had other things on your mind."

"That's true, but I can't ignore the other two when I know they need me. Brian was feeling so guilty because he led his brother and sister back to their Dad. That's what he said to me on the phone, "If I hadn't.""

Without stopping to question whether she should, Margaret punched in the number of her parents' home and after two rings heard her mother's voice on the other end.

"Mom?"

"Margaret!" Ruby's voice was more shrill than usual. "Please don't be calling with bad news about our precious Jason." Then she launched into how upset she was and ended with a scolding for Margaret. "You know, if you hadn't publicly humiliated poor Don, this might never have happened."

Lord, I never knew my Mama could be so blind. Now I know where I got it.

She took a deep breath. "Look, Mama, you're entitled to think whatever you want to. This is something we're probably always going to disagree on. But I don't choose to accept the blame for Don's violent and abusive actions that put Jason in the hospital." She paused to catch her breath and collect her wits.

"Just look what you've..." Ruby charged, beginning her tirade again.

"Mama," Margaret interrupted. "That discussion is closed. Right now I'm concentrating on my children... all three of them. Now, did Brian and Sally go to school this morning?"

"They didn't want to, and I thought they ought to stay home. After all, think of how humiliating this is for them. But your daddy, I don't know what's gotten into him lately. He keeps disagreeing with me. He thought they ought to go."

"That's what I needed to know. By the way, where is Daddy?"

"He's downtown somewhere. He doesn't tell me much and I don't think I like him very much right now."

"I'll call you later, Mama. Bye."

Margaret pushed the clear button on her phone and sat, pondering everything, lost in her own thoughts.

"Problems back at home?" Rachel asked, her query breaking into Margaret's trance.

"Problems? No... well, yes, I guess." She turned so she could look at her new friend. "Mama just cannot accept that Don is an abuser, and she conveniently turns a blind eye to all he's done. Even now, with Jason seriously injured, she's trying to tell me if I hadn't "abused" Don, none of this would have happened."

Rachel traced the design on the cover of a magazine she held in her lap. Finally she asked, "Do you accept her argument that you're the cause of all this?"

"No," Margaret replied with a conviction that surprised even her. "I'm guilty of ignoring it for too long, but Don is an adult and should be held accountable for his actions. Nothing I did or didn't do justifies his violence and scheming."

Margaret checked her watch. "Ooh... I was going to try to reach Brian and Sally at school. It's almost time for them to go back to class after their mid-afternoon break. I'd better hurry."

The phone at Mount Zion School was answered again by Pamela who, when she heard Margaret's voice, suddenly lost her friendly demeanor. Margaret asked that Brian and Sally be brought to the phone, only to be met with resistance.

"I'm sorry, Mrs. Haywood, but it's so close to class time I'm afraid I can't do that. Children don't come to school to talk on the telephone."

Shut my mouth, Lord. Or at least rein in my tongue.

"Pamela, I'm not sure what your problem is, but I would suggest that you bring my children to the phone. There's at least ten minutes left in the break, which is plenty of time."

"Marg... er, Mrs. Haywood, as I told you yesterday, Mr. Haywood has instructed us that you aren't to have anything to do with your children. I'll have to hang up now."

Margaret fought with herself over how to handle the situation. Finally deciding to err on the side of a mother protecting her children, something she hadn't done very well recently, she exercised game plan two. "Pamela, perhaps you haven't heard that Mr. Haywood is now under arrest for violently abusing Jason last night. Now I would suggest you either get my children to the phone, whether it makes them late for class or not, or I'll have my attorney pay a visit to the school this afternoon."

Pamela was, she knew, a highly nervous individual who constantly rearranged the ink pens on her desk to be certain they were all in proper order. *I've never known if she alphabetizes them or what. There are times her attention to detail is commendable. This isn't one of those times.* Margaret could picture the receptionist's hands fluttering as she tried to decide how to deal with the situation that had fallen into her lap.

Finally a timid voice replied, "I've sent a message for them. Please hold, Mrs. Haywood." Then, as if absolving herself of all responsibility, added, "You know I don't make any decisions around here. I just do what I'm told."

Margaret heard the canned music that indicated she was on hold, and after what seemed an eternity, heard Brian's anxious voice.

"Mom? Is that you, Mom? How's Jason?"

"He's doing OK, Brian, all things considered. But right now, I want to know about you and Sally. Is she there with you?"

"She's coming, she'll be here in a minute. When they told me it was you, I ran as fast as I could."

Margaret didn't want to spook the boy, but she did need to know how he and his sister were faring. "Brian, are you both alright? I was worried about you."

"We're fine, Mom. At least I guess we are." He paused, then stuttered, "I... I don't think... think I can ever forget last night."

Margaret could hear the grief and guilt in his voice. "Brian, I want you to listen to me. I am so proud of you for taking care of Jason and calling me. We got him here in time, but if you hadn't assumed an adult's responsibility, the outcome might have been very different."

"But, Mom," Brian pleaded in a soft voice. "It's my fault. How can Jason ever forgive me? How can you? I could have gotten Jason killed." A half-sob escaped his lips.

"Listen, Brian. Get hold of yourself. I know you're standing in the front office, so don't put yourself in a compromising situation. Just listen, and hear me well. You are NOT responsible

for your father's violent actions. Do you hear me? NOT responsible. So stop giving yourself a guilt trip."

"But if I hadn't...," he interrupted.

"No but's and no if's, son. Bottom line, you're not responsible. We'll talk about this later, just you and me. I wish we could
right now, but I can't leave Jason and I'm not sure when I'll be
back home. So you're going to have to help Sally cope. Will you
do that?"

"You trust me with Sally?"

His question tore at the very center of her mother's heart.
"I trust you completely and always will. Now promise me you'll
stop torturing yourself."

"OK, Mom," he answered, hesitantly. "Do you want to talk
to Sally? She's right here."

Before she could even say "Yes," Sally's subdued voice came
over the phone. Hello, Mommie."

"Hey, sweetie. I'm sorry to interrupt you at school, but I
just needed to hear your voices, and I hope you needed to hear
mine."

"Mommie, is Jason going to die?"

There was that heart tug again. "No, sweetheart, I don't
think he is. The doctor says we won't know for sure for a couple
of more days, but I've been talking a lot to God these past few
hours, and I..." *I've got to choose my words carefully.* "I think Jason will
soon be back at home with us as good as new."

*I'm stretching things a little there, Lord. But this child doesn't need
to know about the chance of brain injury right now. We'll cross that bridge IF
we come to it.*

"I miss you, Mommie. When are you coming home?"

"Right now, Jason needs me. So I'm going to have to stay
here for a few more days. But Grammy and Grandee will take good

care of you, and I'll call you once or twice a day, but from now on I'll call you when you aren't in school. OK?"

"I don't want to stay with Grammy and Grandee. They keep fighting about Daddy and I don't like it."

I'm going to have to have a heart-to-heart with Mama. Today. "They're both very upset, darling. That's why they're acting that way. I'll have a talk with them. But in the meantime, you're going to need to stay there until I can come home."

"Mommie... when you come home... can we... do we... oh, never mind."

"What is it, Sally? You can ask me anything. If something's bothering you, I want to know it."

She could hear her daughter's jerky breathing then, without warning, Brian's voice came on. "Mom, Sally's OK. I sent her back to her room. What she was trying to ask you, well, even I'm having a problem with it."

"Then just ask it, son. That's what adults do, and as far as I'm concerned, you're one of the more mature adults we have right now. Nothing is going to make me angry."

She heard him take a deep breath, "We don't want to go back to live at Red Bud Way. Neither of us."

"Listen, Brian. I understand what you're saying. Right now I can't answer that question either way, but I do understand. And before we do anything, the four of us will talk it over first. Deal?"

"Deal," he said, obviously relieved. *It couldn't be easy for her child-man to reverse himself after so strongly declaring himself to the contrary less than 24 hours earlier.*

"And, Mom. Did you know Dad's in jail?"

"Yes, Joe and Jim gave me the details this morning."

"The talk is all over town."

It's Carter's Crossroads, isn't it? "Son, I don't doubt that for one minute. But just remember… neither you nor Sally have done anything wrong, and neither of you should be held accountable for your Dad's actions."

"OK, Mom. Love you. I've got to get to class."

"I love you, too. And I'm proud of you. Now get to class before you get a tardy."

At 7:00 that night, Rachel introduced her to another woman named Dorothy, who announced that she would be with Margaret that night, until someone relieved her at 7:00 the next morning.

Margaret stood to awkwardly hug Rachel who, by this time, felt like a long-time friend. "I don't know what I would have done without you, today," she told the shelter volunteer. *How would I have managed to get food, get in to see Jason and all the other little details that Rachel handled so easily? How would I have kept from going crazy?*

"You have been God's angel, you know," she said to Rachel as the two walked toward the outside exit. "I don't know how I can ever repay you."

Rachel led them over to a bench in the foyer. "Look, Margaret, you're in a very uncomfortable position right now. One child is injured, you're separated from the other two. Your abuser, a pillar of the community, is in jail for family violence. But things won't always be this way. Trust me. Been there, done that."

"Right now that's hard to see," Margaret admitted.

"It sure is, but I know from experience. And at some point after your own recovery is underway – and it's a lifetime project, by the way – you'll encounter another battered woman who needs what I've done for you today. When you help her, I'll be paid back."

"And I will," Margaret promised. "I certainly will."

"Of that I am sure," Rachel agreed. "Remember, in the shelter business, the emphasis is about pass it on rather than pay back.

The help goes a whole lot farther that way."

Oh, God, how blessed I am. Thank you, Lord for Rachel. Margaret hugged her again, too choked up to risk saying anything else.

Once she got back to the waiting room, with its walls of institutional green and yellow, and the stylish but somewhat uncomfortable furniture, she and Dorothy sat down to get acquainted. After a period of visiting, it was time to go in to see Jason, who once again lay like a tiny, silent angel swallowed up by the bed clothes. *If I didn't see his chest rising and falling ever so slightly, I'd have to touch him to be certain he wasn't dead.*

Jason. Dead. It was a concept she couldn't get her mind around. Jason was supposed to bury her.

Dorothy encouraged her to get some rest. "After all, you've been up almost 24 hours. You need some sleep."

Margaret surveyed the straight-back arm chairs in the room and declared, "I think I'd be more comfortable stretching out on the carpet than I would trying to sleep sitting up in one of these hard chairs."

Dorothy laughed. "Oh, my dear," she said with just a hint of southern magnolia in her voice, "hasn't anyone shown you the accommodations?"

"Accommodations?"

"Her new friend indicated a closed doorway on the other side of the room. Once inside, Margaret discovered small cubicles, each holding a very comfortable looking, inviting recliner. On a shelf nearby were pillows and blankets.

Everything looked so tempting to her exhausted body and mind. "But if I'm asleep in here, I'll miss going in to see Jason."

"Not to worry," Dorothy assured her. "This is all part of the hospital's grand scheme. Remember... this is a children's hospital. Parents are an integral part of everything." Now let me show you how this works. All we do is sign you in on this computer. Here, let me type for you, since you've only got one hand." She looked up and got her bearings. "Cubicle 14 is unoccupied, so we'll put your name beside it."

"That's all there is?"

"This screen shows up in ICU, and when visiting time comes, a nurse will determine where you're sleeping and come get you.'

"God is so good," Margaret volunteered, more anxious by the moment to sack out. "Suddenly my body is giving up, I fear."

"Then you lay down here... I'll get you a pillow and a blanket... and you just snooze away."

"But where will you be?"

"Don't you worry about me," I'll be just around the corner, where I can keep an eye on you and the ICU door."

Margaret sat in the recliner and let Dorothy lower the back. Once she was covered and comfortable, it was only seconds before she began to nod off. Just as she was almost past the point of no-return, she remembered. *I didn't bring a toothbrush or any toiletries, and I'm still wearing the clothes I yanked on when Brian called in the middle of the night. What must people think of me?*

CHAPTER TEN

"Wake up, Margaret. I know you're sleepy, but it's time to visit Jason."

"Jus' let m' sleep a few mo' minutes," Margaret mumbled. "Sooo tired."

"Margaret, it's Dorothy. You need to wake up, honey, if you want to see Jason."

"Jason?" In her stupor, Margaret felt panic strangle her. "Is Jason alright?" She struggled to sit up, but the left arm, like dead weight, hindered her. Then she felt two arms lifting her.

She was finally able to get her eyes open and focused. "What's wrong? What time is it?"

A nurse Margaret hadn't seen before provided the answers. "Nothing's wrong, Mrs. Haygood. But it's visiting time if you want to see Jason."

"We hated to wake you, but I didn't think you'd want to miss a chance to see him," Dorothy explained. "Although three a.m. does seem to be a strange time to be visiting the sick, doesn't it? She laughed.

The nurse accompanied them into Jason's cubicle, where the little boy lay as if he hadn't moved a whisker since her last visit. But still, Margaret could see the slight rise and fall of his chest, and she whispered another prayer of thanksgiving.

"I just wish I could know that he's going to wake up soon," Margaret said, and she sucked back a sob. *Jason is not going to hear me cry, Lord.*

The nurse, who was hovering at the doorway, caught Margaret by the arm as she and Dorothy turned to leave. "Don't say I said it, Mrs. Haywood, but your little boy is actually doing better. I think the doctor is going to be very pleased with his vitals when he comes around in about four hours."

Margaret hugged the nurse. "Thank you. Thank you so much. And no, I won't let on that you told me anything."

Dorothy convinced Margaret to try and sleep for the remainder of the night, and the still-groggy mother offered very little resistance. When she woke for the second time, it was to see sunlight flooding through the window in the corner. Almost as if she had been summoned, Dorothy appeared from out of nowhere to help her into a sitting position."

"Do you feel better after a good night's sleep? I checked on your several times and you seemed to be resting well."

"Yes, I do feel better. Now if I can just get someone from home to bring me some clean clothes and toiletries, I might feel like a human being again."

"It's as good as done," Dorothy assured her. "Rachel is right outside to relieve me, and she has everything you should need to clean up."

"She does? But who...? How...?"

Rachel appeared at the doorway, a tote bag in her hand, and a nice looking outfit of clothes hung over her arm. "Here you go, Miss Margaret. Why don't we see if we can't get you looking more presentable?"

"But these aren't my clothes?"

"They are now."

"I'm afraid I don't understand." Then a troubling thought struck her. "Rachel, you didn't buy all of this did you? I'll have to repay you."

Rachel set down her burden and hugged Margaret. "Hey, I hear Jason's still holding his own. That's real good news."

It feels so good to have someone to hold on to? Lord, what would I have done without these two women?

"Now let's get you ready for the day. I have an idea the doctor's going to want a conference, and you don't have much time."

Dorothy, who had left the room for a minute returned, with her sweater around her shoulders. "I'm going to say goodbye now, Margaret. I'll be gone by the time you get out of the shower."

"Oh, Dorothy... you've been so wonderful. I can't believe you stayed up all night for me. I feel so guilty."

"The two women hugged and Dorothy assured her, "I got some sleep. But I didn't need as much as you did." She stifled a yawn. "I will go now and catch an uninterrupted snooze." She waved goodbye. "I'll see you again tonight."

"Good-bye, my friend."

As Dorothy left, Rachel suggested, "Are you ready to get cleaned up?"

"Did Dorothy say something about a shower? Can I really

clean up?"

"Right through here," the older woman said, and pointed to a door at the back of the room. "You'll find all the comforts of home."

Oh, a shower is going to feel so good. Then a problem presented itself.

"My arm, Rachel. I can't take a shower with my arm."

Her concern was rewarded with a wide grin. "Yes, you can." Her friend reached into the tote bag and pulled out a black square of plastic. "Here's one giant trash bag. It should more than cover all that hardware."

"You're amazing, do you realize that?"

Rachel grinned. "Not really amazing. Just experienced. There's a difference."

Margaret was shown to a private shower and dressing area. Rachel accompanied her in and hung the clothing on a hook and set the toiletry tote on a waiting counter. "If you'll call me after you're dressed, I'll be glad to help you with your hair."

The hot stream coursing over her weary body was a rejuvenating waterfall that cleared her mind and gave her a new outlook for the day. *I didn't understand how badly I needed this.* She stood beneath the shower until she realized that Rachel was probably worried about her, so she turned off the hot water, reluctantly, and grabbed her towel.

Several minutes later, she had dried and dressed as best she could with just one good arm, and was calling out to Rachel. True to her word, with brush and blow dryer in hand, Rachel soon had her ready to meet the world.

They had no sooner entered the ICU waiting area when a willowy, young woman whom Margaret hadn't seen before came towards them. There was a smile on her face.

Lord, who is she? Dare I read anything into her facial expression? Or am I so desperate to know that Jason is going to make it that I'm seeing what I want to see?

"Good morning, Mrs. Haywood, I'm Dr. Lynn Lowman."

"I haven't seen you before. Is something wrong?"

"The young doctor laughed. "Not to worry. Actually everything is looking encouraging. Jason's past the most critical stage and he's been assigned to me. I wanted to visit with you for a few minutes, if I may."

"Then something is wrong." *After all, this is day two, and they had said three days.* She grabbed Rachel's hand for support. *I'm taking Your hand, too, Lord.*

The doctor indicated several vacant chairs nearby. "Let's sit, shall we. I know you have to be tired."

If the news is good, why doesn't she just tell me so?

After the three had seated themselves, the doctor cleared her throat, hesitated, then began to speak.

Do I want to hear this? Until they tell me it's bad, there's always the hope that he's going to recover.

The doctor was speaking, "...he's doing really well, considering all that he has been through."

I've GOT to stop going off on tangents when people are speaking. "I'm sorry, Doctor, but could you start over. I was trying to prepare myself for the news."

"Of course, Mrs. Haywood." The young doctor fiddled with the pen in her notebook. "You've been through so much, don't apologize." She emphasized her sincerity with another infectious smile. "Jason is doing really well, considering how critical he was when he got here." Then the smile showed a little less brightly. "However, he's not out of the woods. Not yet, at least."

"Is he going to live?" Margaret blurted out before she could stop herself.

"I don't think we have to worry about that any longer," the doctor answered. "His vital signs have shown small but a steady improvement since last night, so we're headed in the right direction. He's going to make it."

Thank You, Lord. Oh, Thank You, Lord!

"However," the physician continued, "we still don't know for certain what we're going to find when he comes out of the coma. We've already started backing up on the medication we've been giving him to induce our own coma, so by this time tomorrow, he should be totally weaned."

"Then will he wake up?"

"That's what we don't know." The doctor shook her head. "We can place patients in drug-induced comas, but we don't have any means to induce the body to wake from a natural coma."

Margaret phrased her question carefully, ever mindful that Rachel still had a firm grip on her right hand. "If he doesn't wake up once the drugs are removed, does that mean he won't ever wake up?" *I had prepared myself for life with a brain-damaged child, but not a comatose one.*

"Comas are wonderful things, Mrs. Haywood. They are the body's physical form of denial. The brain perceives that the body has been damaged and it places that body into a coma to allow it to heal. Only when the brain determines that enough healing has occurred will it sound a wake-up call?"

"So if he doesn't wake immediately once the drugs are gone, that doesn't automatically mean that he is brain damaged?"

"But it doesn't mean he isn't, either. Look Mrs. Haywood, personally and professionally, I believe that Jason is going to make a near full, if not a complete recovery. But I can't guarantee anything. I'm just a doctor and a very human one at that."

Margaret took her hand. "And a very compassionate one, too, I might add."

"With a little darling like Jason, it's impossible not to be compassionate."

It wasn't difficult for Don. I'm sorry, Lord. I guess I'm just a little angry. No... I'm extremely angry. I just have to remember that righteous indignation is OK, it's judging Don that I'm not supposed to do.

"So where do we go from here?" Margaret asked.

The doctor consulted the chart in her lap. "Here's what I am proposing, and if we do this, you may not get a middle-of-the-night visit with him."

"I don't understand."

"I want to do another MRI, but I want as many of the drugs out of his system as possible. My thought is that we'll do it in the middle of the night tonight, which would likely occur during the normal ICU visiting period. Can you live with that?"

"As long as I know what's happening, I'm fine. Please," she implored the doctor, "do what you think best."

"I think we'll have a much better handle on his overall condition after that scan. Then we can make some other decisions."

"Such as what?" *I thought we were stuck in limbo until he woke up.*

"If Jason doesn't wake in the morning when the induced coma is lifted, we will be at the mercy of his body as to when he wakes. If he wakes. It could happen later tomorrow. Next week. Next month. Sometime next year. He might never wake and, with proper care, live to a ripe old age."

Oh, this goes so much deeper than I'd ever imagined.

"Within two to three more days, were he to awaken fairly soon, he would be where he could be released to the care of your local hospital."

"You mean he couldn't go home? He'd have to go back to the hospital?"

"Jason is still a very fragile patient. Just because he's awake, assuming he does awaken, doesn't ensure that he'll be strong enough to go home immediately."

"I hadn't thought about that. I just assumed if he woke up, he'd be back to normal."

"Jason's little body has been through a great deal of trauma. An adult who sustained the injury he did would still be shaky on his pins. Your son is going to be very weak when he wakes. And the longer it takes for him to awaken, the longer his recovery is going to be from the effects of the coma itself."

Dare I ask this? Margaret took a deep breath. "Doctor, please level with me. What is your gut telling you on this? What do I need to prepare for? I've got two older children at home who need me, legal issues with an abusive husband, and more other worries than I could even begin to list."

"Mrs. Haywood, my heart goes out to you, but I'll also take off my hat to you. I don't see how you've stood up under all you've endured in the past few weeks." She pointed to Margaret's caged left arm. "I understand this is also credited to your husband's temper." She said it as a statement, not a question.

"You evidently know something about me, then."

"What your local hospital didn't provide us, the *Atlanta Daily Journal* did."

"I'm afraid I don't understand."

"Have you not seen a daily newspaper since you've been here?"

"Uh...no, I don't guess I have. Why?"

"I don't know how to break this to you, but your story has received a lot of space, especially in today's edition."

Oh, Lord. I never thought about the newspapers getting hold of this. I'm sure my children are totally humiliated. I've got to get to them.

Margaret looked at her friend. "Rachel, would you go find me a today's paper? I've got to see what they're saying." As the shelter volunteer got up to fulfill that request, Margaret continued. "Doctor, I'm going to have to go back home. As much as I hesitate to leave Jason for even one second, will he realize that I'm not here?"

"This is my personal belief, you understand, but I think that on some level, every time you're with him, he knows. Now that doesn't mean he can grasp that several hours have elapsed between each visit, or that he will miss you if you skip a visit. Does that help?"

"Yes, I think it does. Now, I have a big favor to ask. I'm about to call back home to ask someone to come get me, and I will be back here by no later than this time tomorrow morning. Can you arrange for me to see Jason for just a minute before I go, even if it isn't a scheduled visiting time?"

The doctor chuckled. "We may be only lowly human physicians with little control over life and death, but we can pull rank in ICU. Certainly, I'll leave word at the desk that you're to be slipped in without it being obvious."

Margaret grasped her hand again. "Thank you so much, Doctor. You have been so wonderful."

"Mrs. Haywood, you need to understand something. I grew up in an extremely abusive home. I was the only girl, so my dad spared me the actual abuse, but my three brothers got my share and then some. Instead, I had to watch and listen to what went on. Sometimes being a helpless bystander can be worse than actually receiving the abuse. You feel guilty. Relieved. Angry. And it can get so bad, you convince yourself that your father doesn't love you as much as he does your brothers. Otherwise, why doesn't he treat you all alike?"

"But you're so happy, so bubbly, if I may say so? I would never have guessed."

"How many people in Carter's Crossroads, until the last few days, would have guessed what went on at your house? I'm willing to bet you're normally pretty bubbly and happy yourself."

She's got me there, Lord. "Touché."

"But let me assure you," the doctor hastened to add, "that I am very happy. And if I'm bubbly, well, that's OK too. But I didn't get this way by myself."

"I don't understand."

"I had therapy, Mrs. Haywood. An extended amount of psychological therapy to get to where I am today. That's why I chose pediatrics, as emotionally-draining as it can be some days. I couldn't help my brothers or me, but perhaps I can help other hurting children. Knowing that I make a difference makes me happy. Even on the most bittersweet of days, such as when I have to look at a precious child like Jason, and I feel his pain, because I witnessed it firsthand."

"Oh, Doctor. God surely caused our paths to cross. I feel better about Jason's chances more now than ever. And that's not false hope, because when you can put your trust in God, there's nothing phony about it."

"God is so good," I'll agree with you. "But there's another reason I told you this story. Are you familiar with shaken baby syndrome or shaken brain syndrome?"

"It's where a baby is shaken so badly the brain is torn loose from its natural position and sometimes bruising and swelling occur."

"Well Jason is suffering from a marathon case of shaken

brain. It can sometimes take months for the brain to reassume its normal position. No two patients are alike. Until then, the victim can suffer personality changes, seizures, migraine headaches, and fatigue, not to mention short term memory loss. Foods that they once loved may not interest them any longer. Hobbies that once enthralled won't hold any appeal."

"So you're saying that I need to prepare for a different Jason to wake up from that coma?"

"You need to prepare for the POSSIBILITY. Only after he awakens will we be able to assess the full extent of his psychological injuries, or the prognosis for their permanence."

"I see." *I see that this gets a lot deeper the more I learn. Lord, You really gave me a mountain this time!*

The doctor continued, "That's why, shortly after he awakens, once we can do an initial evaluation, there is no doubt that we'll hook him up with a child psychologist that specializes in childhood abuse recovery." She patted Margaret's hand. "Believe me, Mrs. Haywood, that psychologist – and your full cooperation – will be critical to Jason's recovery. No one can predict how long the sessions will go on, or to what degree the Jason you knew will be the Jason you'll have."

Margaret almost choked on her words. *I asked for the truth, Lord. And I got it. Now it's up to You and me to bring Jason back.* "I'll do whatever needs to be done. Whatever! Jason is going to have a fair chance at normalcy if it takes every last dime I can scrape together." *And I will do whatever I have to, because I've known for months that he was afraid of his dad, and I stood by and did nothing about it.*

"Then Jason is one very lucky little boy." The doctor shook Margaret's hand and stood to leave. "I'll let you make your arrangements to get home. When you're ready to see Jason, just whisper to the nurse at the desk and she'll take care of everything."

"Thank you, Doctor," Margaret said once again, feeling that somehow the words were grossly inadequate.

"It's been my pleasure," the doctor replied as she walked away. "You have a safe trip home. I'll see you again in the morning, and I hope then I'll have more definite news for you."

Margaret grabbed for her cell phone and dialed P.C.'s number. When she answered, her friend volunteered that she was already en route to Atlanta, feeling that Margaret needed to be brought up to speed and would possibly need to come home. While she was talking, she saw Rachel walking toward her, a newspaper in hand.

"I'm not sure you want to read this," her friend said. "It gets pretty ugly."

"You're right," she said, taking the proffered newspaper. "I don't want to. But if my children haven't already, the parents of their friends have. I've got to go home and do damage control." She scanned across the bottom of the front page. "A friend is on her way now to get me," she said. "I'm going home at least for the day."

"I think you probably should," Rachel agreed, but Margaret only half heard her. Her mind was already glued on the newspaper, where she read, "**Town Philanthropist Assaults 6-Year-Old Son**."

CHAPTER ELEVEN

Margaret took time to visit Jason, to hold his hand, and to whisper in his ear. "Jason... Mama loves you very much and she's here for you when your body is ready to come back. You don't have to worry because you'll never be hurt this way again. I promise." Then she whispered a short prayer of thanksgiving, and reminded the nurse on her way out that she would be back by seven o'clock the next morning. "You can reach me on my cell phone if you need me."

The ride back to Carter's Crossroads was surreal at best, Margaret thought. As she and P.C. left the hospital an assault by brisk, cold gusts of December wind reminded her that an entirely different world existed outside the hospital walls. That life had been going on as normal, even as she had been praying for the life of her child to be saved, had totally escaped her.

"You know, I didn't even realize how insulated I had become from everything until that cold hit me. And if it didn't convince me, the headline in this morning's *ADJ* certainly did."

"I'm sorry you had to find out that way. It's been a zoo back home. I need to tell you, it's not just the newspaper; the story has been on all the Atlanta and Chattanooga television stations, and I heard just before I left that the "Today Show" will have a segment on it tomorrow morning."

"Don didn't have a clue how far this could go, did he?"

"You sound sympathetic." P.C. had finally escaped the morning northbound rush hour gridlock and was beginning to make time. "We should be there in the next thirty or forty minutes," she promised.

"Part of me feels sympathetic, but it's not for Don." *No, I have no sympathy for him.* "I cringe for all the innocent people – my three children at the top of the list – who are on public spectacle because of all this."

P.C. agreed. "Town has been lousy with reporters. TV vans parked everywhere. And you'll love this, the sheriff, Don's good ol' boy buddy, held a news conference yesterday. He said it didn't matter how much money Don had donated in Carter's Crossroads, he would still be held fully accountable for his actions."

Like there should have been a question!

"So how are Brian and Sally?" Margaret inquired, conveniently changing the subject. "Did they go to school today?"

They were fine when I talked with them last night. Samuel and Susan took the both of them to their house for supper and to do homework. We were all afraid the news media might discover where your folks lived and come there looking for them."

Oh, gosh. I hadn't even thought about Daddy and Mama. I can just see Daddy trying to fend off a hoard of reporters and saying gosh knows what to them. Ugh!

"I need to see the kids first." She dialed her parents' home and when her mother answered, she said, "Mama... I'm on my way back to town for the day, I'll be to the house later this afternoon, at least for a little while. Right now, though, I want to see Brian and Sally. Are they at school?"

"They went, but I know they're not happy. You see what all you've caused?"

"Mama, you and I are going to disagree about this. I don't care what you say to me, but you are to say nothing negative to either of the children. Is that understood?"

Margaret heard a sniff on the other end. "I can remember when you wouldn't dare talk to me that way. Giving me orders and all. After we took you and those children in because you were too proud to ask Don's forgiveness and go back home where you belonged."

"Thank you, Mama. I'm on my way to the school and I'll see you later." *There's no sense arguing with her; her mind's set and nothing is going to change it.*

"Your mama still thinks you did the wrong thing?"

"You picked up on that, huh?"

"Yeah, especially after she called me yesterday to ask how much it would take to get Don out of jail so he could go be with Jason. Said she knew for sure that Don didn't mean to hurt him."

"Don't tell me any more, P.C. At least not right now. I'd like to be sane and in control when I see the children."

As they sped through the business district toward Mount Zion School, Margaret saw the congregation of press camped out around the jail and courthouse. She wanted to ask what was new with Don, but mindful of her need to be calm for Brian and Sally, she decided what she didn't know – yet – wouldn't hurt her.

Once at the school, she braced for a confrontation that didn't occur. Instead, Headmaster Hunt greeted her personally, asked about Jason, all the while sending student aides to bring both children from their classes.

Sally arrived first. When she caught sight of her mother, the big brown eyes immediately puddled up with tears, and by the time she flung herself at her mother, the child was sobbing furiously. Brian appeared about that same time, and the three of them were shown into Elizabeth Francis' office, the same office where, only weeks before, Jason had spilled the secret that Don was an abuser.

Jason is paying the biggest price of all. And it's not over yet. But Margaret couldn't allow herself to dwell on the unknown future. *We'll meet it... whatever it is, whenever it is, and we'll deal with it.*

Margaret hugged her son, who embraced her much more strongly than he had in some time. *He's a man in a boy's body, and he's scared.* Then she set about quieting her daughter, who was famous for hysterics. Once she had the both of them seated on the little loveseat, she asked, "How are each of you? I want to know. So tell me the truth."

Sally, ever the drama queen, was first to respond. "Daddy's in jail and everybody says he's gonna get the death penalty." Her eyes watered up again. "What Daddy did was wrong, but I don't want him to die."

Margaret put her arm around the little girl and drew her to her. "Listen, Sally, I can promise you that Daddy's not going to get the death penalty. I talked to the doctor just before I left Atlanta. Jason isn't going to die." Then she fudged. "He'll be coming home to us soon, but we don't know just when. The doctor says it's going to take him a while to get well. But he isn't going to die." She emphasized that point again, hoping both children got the message.

With Sally momentarily pacified, she turned attention to Brian, whose drawn, hollow-eyed face bore mute testimony to how difficult things were for the young man.

"Talk to me, Brian. Tell me what you're thinking. Nothing's off limits."

The boy had risen from the loveseat and began to pace the floor in the small room. *I never realized how much like Don he walks!*

"How much longer is this going to go on, Mom? It's been crazy. People are looking at us and talking behind our backs. I feel like I've been walking down Main Street in my underwear."

Margaret's heart went out to him, but she wisely read his body language and didn't rise to comfort him. He wanted to walk, to talk and get the nightmare out of his system. Best allow him to do that.

"Jason is really going to be OK? I was sure when he was laying in my arms that he was dead and I didn't know what I was going to do."

The thought of how terrifying that must have been for him squeezed at Margaret's heart. *Yet he never laid him down, as if he knew something had to be done.*

"Jason is going to live; the doctor is very confident of that. But he's in a coma."

"A coma?" Sally interrupted. "But that's a punctuation mark."

"You mean a comma, dummy," Brian barked at his sister.

Margaret chose to ignore her son's rudeness, but did make a mental note to say something to him when all their nerves weren't stretched so tightly.

"That's right, honey, the words sound a lot alike. And you're right, a comma is a punctuation mark," she said, hugging

Sally closer to her. "Jason is in a coma, which is a kind of deep, deep sleep."

"So why doesn't he wake up?"

Such a simple question but what a complex answer. How do I explain this? "When a person is badly hurt, like Jason is, the body decides that the only way it can heal is to go to sleep. You know how when you're tired at night and you go to sleep, the next morning you feel so much better when you wake up?"

The little girl, her eyes big with uncertainty, nodded her head.

"Well, a coma is a sleep that lets the whole body repair itself. Jason will wake up when his body feels he's strong enough. We just don't know when that will be."

"What's going to happen to Dad?" Brian's manner was direct, but the break in his voice betrayed his conflicted emotions.

"We don't know, yet, son. And that's the truth. I'm hoping to get some answers later today."

"Will he have to go to prison?"

"I would say the chance is good that he will spend some time in prison. But that's up to the judge and the jury."

"Are you going to drop the charges against him if Jason gets better and comes home?"

Margaret reached and took his hand and stopped his pacing. "Brian," she said, "look at me, and hear me well. You, too, Sally, even though you may not understand everything that is happening."

Both children faced her, their faces a complex mix of dread and confusion.

"The attack on Jason was against the law. I'm not the one who had your dad arrested. The sheriff's deputies did that on their own, and when he goes to trial, we won't have any say-so about the charges or what kind of punishment he gets."

"Will we have to testify?" The question came from Brian.

"What's testify? Sally asked.

"It means get up in court and tell about things that happened with Dad that night."

"I was asleep," the little girl offered in a quaking voice. "I didn't see anything."

She's terrified. "Don't worry, sugar, I doubt they would want you to have to talk to the court. But you," she said, looking at Brian, "you may well have to testify. Do you think you can?"

Her eldest son stared at her so deeply Margaret felt like he could see her internal organs. Then, with great deliberation, he said, "I can do anything they need me to do, as long as I'm sure that Dad will go to jail where he can't hurt any of us ever again."

Dear, God, how bitter this boy sounds. Please speak to his heart and remove the venom without harming the backbone he's showing.

"I think it's a pretty good bet your Dad won't be where he can hurt us again for a long time."

The three Haywoods talked for a few more minutes, before Margaret shooed them back to their classes.

"Neither of you have done anything wrong nor have any reason to feel ashamed," she reassured both of them. "I'm sorry that your dad's prominence has landed this family in the news, but we can hold our heads up and go on about our regular activities, because we aren't responsible for his actions."

"But it's hard, Mommie," Sally wailed, well-restored to her dramatic best.

"Yes, it is," Margaret agreed, "but it's not impossible. The only thing I ask of both of you is that you don't talk to anyone from the newspaper or the TV. The less we can say, the better it will be now... and later."

The two children left going back to class with their mother's promise that she would see them at their grandparents that afternoon.

Back in the car with P.C., Margaret asked the single question that had been burning a hole in her sub-conscious. "OK, don't hold anything back. Tell me everything I need to know."

"I just talked to Joe and he and Jim are at the office," P.C. volunteered, "why don't we crash over there and that way we'll all get the same updated information." She didn't wait for Margaret's response, but cranked her car and headed across town.

Once inside, both the men hugged Margaret and asked about Jason. She gave them a synopsis of the boy's condition and the prognosis. "Now, you tell me what's going on and what all do I need to know besides what I read in the *ADJ* this morning?"

"Some more story, wasn't it? Joe asked. "You may not appreciate the significance of it all, but as painfully-revealing as that story was, it has changed many attitudes in this town. Don's fallen from his pedestal and fallen hard."

"Believe it or not, guys, I'm neither happy nor sad about that. Don is old enough to be held responsible for his actions, and that's all I want. In the meantime, I have one seriously injured child in an Atlanta hospital, and I have two more children here who are seeing their entire world being blown to hell and back. They are all I care about."

"You know, Margaret, I never before saw that rigid side of you," Joe commented. "Congratulations."

"I haven't had it very long. As ashamed as I am to admit it, I protected Don's reputation because of the money, until he began including my children in his swath of destruction. That's when I got wise. Unfortunately, it's almost too late."

"Don't punish yourself too harshly," Jim Deaton advised. "You're seeing from hindsight, and, you're human."

"So where do we stand? I'm only in town for the day, so we need to make time count."

Joe led first by explaining that Jim's petition to the court, accompanied by a "friend of the court" brief from him, had convinced the judge that someone besides Don had to have control over the bank accounts and Haywood Tufters.

"Who did he appoint?"

"Andy Davis at the bank, who's been Don's personal banker for a number of years, probably has as good a grasp on the business finances as anyone besides the accountant. He's the primary conservator, and he and the accountant will approve payments and co-sign the checks."

Don was foolish not to have a back-up plan in place, but then he thought he was invincible. "Does this mean forever? And where does this put me financially?"

"Not forever," Jim interjected. Just for sixty days, then the judge will revisit the situation. As for you, you're in an excellent position. While you will have to look to these two gentlemen for money, neither of them is going to give you any grief. Trust me."

"In fact," Joe said with encouragement, "there's no reason you and the children can't move back into Red Bud Way whenever you're ready. The judge cleared it."

Talk about a roller coaster. I go from everything I want to being penniless and back to deep pockets. Funny thing, the money doesn't seem as important as it was before. I'll be glad to be able to pay bills, but beyond that.

"Thanks, fellows. Thanks for recognizing that problem and dealing with it. Because it was the farthest thing from my mind."

"Well," P.C. offered, "you had other things on that mind."

"True, true. But I'd totally forgotten that the Don's carpet plant even existed. I stayed away from there, so I've never really felt like it was mine. I hate to think of all those loyal employees not getting a paycheck because of all this confusion."

"Worry, not," Joe assured her, "the accountant is calculating payroll and cutting checks today. They'll be handed out at lunch tomorrow, just like as always."

"So when are you moving back to the house?" Jim asked.

I never thought I would ever hear myself saying this... "We won't be living there again. At least, not anytime soon."

Three pairs of eyes looked at her with shock.

"You're not going back to that beautiful house?" Joe asked.

"Joe, I can't say what we may do down the road, but right now, both Brian and Sally have specifically refused to go back there. Seeing as how Jason's going to have to undergo psychological counseling as soon as he's well enough, I can't see taking him back to the scene of the crime." *If I'm honest, Jason has been unhappy in that house for a long time. I saw it, but I didn't want to believe it or take it seriously.*

For a long time no one said anything, until P.C. asked, "Then where will you go?"

"I never thought I would be homeless, but Don was right when he lied to the children and told them that an old homeless woman, who wasn't right in the head, destroyed that house."

"But you're not homeless," Joe protested. "You can afford to...,"

"There's a difference, Joe, between homeless and penniless. And I am homeless. Right now, neither my children nor I have any place, save for the kindness of others, to call our own, to lay down and sleep at night."

Jim volunteered, "You've got that house your dad bought."

"I'm not living there, either," she quickly informed the three attorneys. "The strings attached are more than I want to deal with. I am going to let Brian and Sally continue to stay with my parents, at least for a few more days, until we see how things are going with Jason." She lifted her good hand in a gesture of "Who knows!" "But I'm not worried. God has brought us this far and He's not going to drop us now."

Their conversation was interrupted by a phone call that Joe said he had to take. Jim and P.C. occupied the time talking with Margaret about Jason's prognosis and what might be needed for his care over the next few months.

"Sorry about that," Joe said as he hung up his phone. "I'd been chasing that guy for over a week."

"That's not a problem, Joe," Margaret answered. "You do have a law practice to run, especially since Don Haywood isn't sending you his business any longer."

Joe managed a sheepish grin. "Actually, Don did me a big favor when he cut me loose. I'd been sick of working for him for some time, but I didn't think I could afford to walk away from the money. He made the choice for me."

"As he did for me as well," she answered. "So somebody tell me about Don. What's happening and what's going to happen? I've got to prepare my children." *I've got to prepare myself as well.*

It was Jim who took the lead. He explained that Don had been arraigned and the judge refused to consider bail. You ought to have heard Don's outburst. I thought sure he'd be found in contempt, and it'll probably happen yet.

"No attorney in town would agree to take his case and the judge appointed a newcomer to the local bar to be his counsel. But he also informed Don that the taxpayers weren't going to get stuck with the tab for his defense." He offered a Jimmy Carter smile.

"There's something else you're not telling me," Margaret accused.

Jim grinned again, a very wicked leer. There was no doubt he was enjoying a private joke. "Don's attorney," he said, "is a young woman who's only been out of law school about two years. Don, I understand, is livid!"

Margaret couldn't help smiling. "You know, I hate to say what goes around comes around, but it does seem like poetic justice." *Or will it backfire on us?*

When she expressed concern that an intimidated, inexperienced lawyer might actually do them damage, Jim told her not to worry. "Don still hasn't accepted that he's lost almost all the clout he had, that his money isn't greasing the skids any longer. The more he protests and disrupts things, the blacker a picture he's painting of himself. He's going to complain himself into a much longer prison sentence."

"Then he will be going to prison?"

The three attorneys looked at each other anxiously. "Without sounding callous, Margaret, he deserves to do time, and I don't think there's much chance that he'll escape with less than a year or two," Joe offered. "Between the attack on you and now what he did to Jason, there's no way he can plead accidental. If he is stupid enough to try that defense, there are enough witnesses to shoot him down pretty quickly."

Is that all? Then what happens when he gets out?

"I don't wish Don ill, but I do want him to pay the price for his actions. Somehow I saw him serving about 10 years." *Am I really saying this?* "One or two years is just long enough for him to work up a good lather. What happens to us when he gets out? What's more, can I still get a divorce if he's in prison?"

P.C. piped up. "Unlike you two, I've really seen Don at his

very worst, and I have to share Margaret's concern. If he isn't locked up long enough for his anger to die a natural death, he'll come out with blood in his eye."

I'd assumed if Don went to prison, we'd all be safe. Now it looks like we have to live with the axe hanging over our heads indefinitely. Something about this isn't fair, Lord.

Jim scratched his head. "I'd be lying," he said to the room in general, "if I didn't admit that I've worried about the same thing. Abusers almost never respond to rehabilitation. The best cure, if you want to call it that, is to lock them up long enough that they finally have to come to grips with what they've done."

The three friends waited for a reaction. She looked to each of them, knowing that they were solidly in her corner, before she said, "Well, we'll just have to deal with that when it happens, won't we?"

Jim continued to fill her in on Don's hostile attitude that was losing him friends by the hour. "He'll be in jail until his case comes to court." And he talked about the media coverage.

"I just hope they leave me alone," Margaret said. "I've got nothing to say to any of them." Then she saw the expression on her attorney's face. "What? Why are you looking at me that way?"

"Because you don't see this from the most positive angle?"

Now he's totally lost me. "I beg your pardon? What are you talking about?"

Jim knelt in front of her. "Think, Margaret. Think."

She rewarded him with a totally blank look.

Seeing that he was going to have to spell it out, the attorney continued, "What more bully pulpit could you have for the cause of domestic violence? Do you have any idea how much your local shelter would pay, if they had the money, to be splashed across the state's newspapers and area TV stations?"

"Well... well, I never...,"

"You've got clout, Margaret. Everyone thinks domestic violence only happens in low-class homes. You're the poster child to refute that theory and the media will eat up every word you say. Plus, it gives you the chance to state the facts of this case the way you want them heard."

"Gosh, Jim, I have to admit I hadn't looked at it like that. I just wanted to protect my children from any further humiliation and the only way I could see to do that was to say "no comment.""

"You might want to take a second look at that line of thought."

Yes, I might. But not before I talk with Brian and Sally, and Annie Campbell and Brother Samuel.

The group dispersed a short time later, with both Joe and Jim agreeing to contact Margaret immediately if anything occurred they thought she should know. "You need to go by the bank before you go back to Atlanta and get some money for the hip and be sure they've reinstated your debit card and credit cards that Don canceled."

Margaret and P.C. went directly to the bank, where Margaret found herself warmly welcomed. In a matter of minutes, Andy Davis assured her that she and her children would have access to Don Haywood's income, including funds to pay any of Jason's medical bills not covered by the insurance policy Don maintained on the entire family.

As he escorted her to the door, the bank officer said, "Your credit cards and your debit card are valid and active, and here is my card. My cell number is on the back. If you can't reach me through the bank number, call my cell. It doesn't matter what time it is. This bank isn't going to be a partner to any abuse aimed at you."

Margaret thanked him and, when he asked if there was anything else he could do, she replied, "Pray that my son will awaken from his coma without brain damage. That's the only thing I need or want at this time."

Then P.C. drove her to her parents, where she planned to grab a bite to eat, take a nap, pack a bag for Atlanta, have a show-down with her mother, and hug her children and talk to them. *In that order, too!*

CHAPTER TWELVE

It was amazing what some of Mama's cooking and a chance to lay down in her own bed could accomplish, Margaret thought, as she stepped in the shower before pulling more clothes together. P.C. had promised to drive her back to the hospital.

Margaret was glad she'd revived herself, because she knew that what was about to come would drain her starch in quick fashion. *Might as well get on with it. I don't know when I've dreaded anything as much.*

Margaret made her way down the hall, where she found her parents sitting in the den watching the early edition of the state news. Just as she rounded the door, she heard her name being mentioned by one of the TV reporters. What followed was so ludicrous she had to sit down to keep from falling.

"Mrs. Haywood, we've learned, has abandoned her injured

young son, who is a patient at Atlanta's Children's Hospital, in order to rush back to the side of her jailed husband. Hospital administration would neither confirm nor deny the report." The reporter, a young man who looked like he should still be in high school, went on to say that additional reports would be forthcoming during their six o'clock news hour from Carter's Crossroads, where Mrs. Haywood was reported to be holed up.

"I've never been so insulted in my life," she sputtered. "How dare they!" *It gives you the chance to state the facts of this case the way you want them heard.*

Jim Deaton's words echoed in her head, even as she heard her mother say, "Do you see what your stubborn refusal to forgive and forget has cost your family and this town? Not to mention us."

Trying her best to contain her anger, Margaret asked, "How has it affected you?"

The minute she closed her mouth, Margaret regretted the question. "Your daddy was downtown today and somebody mentioned that you were his daughter. He almost didn't get home without being mobbed by the reporters, did you Harold?"

"Now, Ruby, I told you not to make a federal case. It wasn't a mob. There was just two of them, and by the time I got through telling them it wasn't any of their business, that was it."

"It could have been a lot worse, if more of those nosy reporters had been close by," Ruby huffed. "And all of it could have been avoided if Margaret hadn't let things get out of hand."

Lord, bridle my tongue, because I've got to deal with this now.

She sat forward in her chair, to where she was within inches of her parents' faces. "Daddy," she said, choosing to address him first, "I'm so sorry for all the discomfort and embarrassment this entire ordeal has caused for the both of you. Believe me, I'd rather it had been different."

"It hasn't been so bad for us, except having to sit by while you and the children were hurt and talked about," he replied. "As you know only too well, when your children hurt, and you can't fix it for them, it's bad."

"Humph... maybe it hasn't been bad for you, Harold, but I've had to sit in the beauty shop week after week listening to the talk about Margaret and Don, and I don't appreciate it."

"Ruby, you know as well as I do that you've listened to far more than your fair share of gossip about other people down at that beauty shop. You probably chimed in your two cents worth to boot. Now you see how it feels."

"Harold, whose side are you on?"

Harold Maxwell swiveled in his chair and looked straight at his wife. "I'm on the side of what's right. And what Don has done to his family is about as wrong as it gets."

"But look at all the good he's done," Ruby persisted. "He's bought so many things in this town that we wouldn't have had otherwise. And he gave Margaret and his children a beautiful home. Everyone has a bad day and gets angry occasionally." She looked first at her husband and then at Margaret, "Why I've even been known to have a bad day myself now and then."

If this weren't so serious, that last comment would be hilarious.

Margaret grabbed the opportunity. "Regardless of what either of you believe, you were not present in my house to know all that went on long before the night Don injured me."

Her mother looked as if she were about to speak, and Margaret rushed on. "Yes, Mama, everyone, even you, has bad days. But when you have those days, you don't beat Daddy 'til he's black and blue. You don't destroy furniture and boast that you paid for it and can do anything you want. And even on your worst day, I never knew you to hit me with the force that Don hit Sally. Why, her...,"

Harold Maxwell half rose out of his chair, his face purple. "Don hit Sally?" His voice quivered with rage. "He hit that precious child? His precious daughter?"

"As much as it hurts, Dad, the answer is yes. For the past three or four years, Don's attitude has slowly changed for the worst. He let all those things he bought for the community go to his head, and he became more verbally and physically abusive. It came to a head the night he knocked me to the floor."

"I don't see how you can talk about your own husband, the father of your children, with such coldness, Margaret. I didn't raise you that way. And for sure you've never heard me talk about Harold that way, though Lord knows he has his faults. But I don't bandy them about the town and embarrass all of us."

"Regardless of what faults he has, I don't ever remember as a child him slapping me so hard I hit the floor. I don't think he ever bodily threw you against a wall, which is how this happened." She indicated her arm. "And it's what happened to Jason, too. Only he was smaller and the blow did more damage."

"But Don has been such a good provider. Just look at the beautiful home he gave you," Ruby pleaded. "Doesn't all that count for something? Maybe if you had been a more understanding..."

"Mama," Margaret interrupted, "we can argue this for the next five years which, given your refusal to see that Don has any faults, isn't a far-fetched scenario. So let me make it very clear to you."

"I don't think I like your tone, young lady."

"I'm sorry, Mama. Hopefully one day you will understand and forgive me. Until then, I can live with what I am about to do."

She saw the older woman lose all the color in her face.

"What are you about to do?"

"Right now, I've got to give my attention to Jason." She had brought her parents up to date on his condition earlier in the afternoon, so she saw no need to repeat it. "Because of that, the best place for Brian and Sally is here with you. But Mama, you are further confusing and tormenting two very upset children with your constant singing of Don's praises. You've got to stop telling them how disloyal I am to him."

She caught her breath, and swung her gaze to her father. "Daddy, you're not guilty of this, but I do expect you to help police this situation. "If I hear one more word about how good Don has been and how I'm running him down, I will remove those two children from this house if I have to put them with strangers. Do I make myself clear?"

"Why, I never..." Ruby's mouth pursed as if she'd just eaten a sour apple.

"Ruby," Harold Maxwell thundered, "didn't you hear Margaret? I for one intend to see that those children stay here, and I don't doubt for a moment she'll do just what she says."

"But Harold, Don's been..."

"Ruby, Don's behaved in a very bad way. You weren't at the jail when he had Margaret arrested. You didn't see him swaggering around, reminding everyone how much he'd paid for this and that. And you didn't see the way he looked at Margaret when he... saw... her... in... handcuffs." His voice broke and he had to pull a handkerchief from his pocket and wipe his eyes.

"You didn't see it, Mama. Our daughter locked up like a common criminal. You know as well as I do she didn't demolish that precious house of his, but he set her up. And it hurt me so bad that I couldn't stand up to him."

He blew his nose. "We've always considered Don as the

son we never had, but I'm afraid our faith was misplaced. And you're doing our daughter and her children a disservice."

Mama sat, her face a study in stone. "Have both of you finished taking me apart?" Her voice was equally as hard as stone.

Neither Margaret nor her father replied.

"Very well, I know when I'm out-numbered. I'll keep my opinions to myself, but that doesn't mean that I like it or that I agree. But I'll keep my mouth shut. And when both of you are proven wrong, when Don is found not guilty and gets out of jail, I'll make sure he knows how much you two supported him."

You know, Mama. I don't doubt that for one second. How did I go all these years without seeing how stubborn you are?

Ruby had barely uttered her edict when the back door opened and the sounds of footsteps approached. When the two children saw their mother, both their faces lit up, and their somber moods immediately lightened. Margaret hugged them both and suggested that they go to the kitchen to find a snack.

Once she had them settled in the breakfast area with chocolate layer cake and milk, she said, "I'm going back to my bedroom to make some phone calls. When you finish, rinse your dishes and put them in the dishwasher."

"Can I have another piece of cake, Mom?"

"May I have another piece, Brian. Not can..."

"May I, then?" He grinned at her in the same way he had since he was a toddler, but that grin never failed to melt her heart.

"You may have another small piece. You don't need too much sugar and we sure don't want to spoil your supper."

"Thanks, Mom. You're the greatest." *How long has it been since I heard those words? The only thing better would be if Jason were right behind him, echoing his words.* Margaret choked back a sob. *Can't give way right now.*

"OK, I'm the greatest. Now when you finish your snack and have cleaned up your mess, come on back to my bedroom. I've got something to talk to you about."

A look of concern crossed both faces, but it was Brian who voiced the question. "It's not Jason is it? Is there something wrong?"

"No... no... no." She flashed the biggest smile she could manage at that moment. "There's no change with Jason, and nothing else is wrong. We just need to talk."

Once in her room, she dialed Annie Campbell and asked for feedback from the shelter director who also promised to be on-hand if Margaret decided to carry through. Her second call was to Brother Samuel. "Good afternoon," she said when he answered. "This is Margaret Haywood."

"Margaret. It's so good to hear your voice. We went by the school to get the children but they told us you were in town, so we knew you'd want them. I trust Jason is still holding his own?"

"Jason is fine, although I am about to call the hospital to check in. And I'll be going back to Atlanta late tonight." She told him about the scheduled MRI and the planned conference with the doctor the next morning and he promised to be much in prayer.

"And I wanted to thank you, too, for helping with Brian and Sally last night."

"It was our pleasure." Margaret got the idea from the tone of his voice that he was indeed sincere. "They're great kids. I can't wait to get to know Jason."

I just pray that the Jason you get to meet is the one I've always known. But I'm not complaining, God. I'll take him any way I can get him.

Margaret shared her dilemma with the pastor, and received his feedback, along with his promise to pray for that as well.

When she called the hospital, she was fortunate enough

to get the ICU nurse who had slipped her in that morning. "Jason is doing just fine," the nurse reported. "His vitals are climbing very slowly, but each hour he's a little more stable." The nurse laughed, "For such a slip of a little boy, he's got one of the strongest wills I've ever seen."

"Jason is very special," Margaret agreed and thanked the nurse for her care and concern. "I should be back at the hospital around midnight."

"I'll be off duty by then, but you know he's scheduled for a middle of the night MRI. You'll probably miss getting to see him until morning?"

"I'm aware," she said, "but I'll just feel better if I'm back at the hospital while the scan is being done."

"Very well," the nurse replied. "Have a safe trip back and I'll probably see you later tomorrow."

When the children came down the hall, they found their mother sitting in her little bedside chair, staring at the wall.

"Everything OK, Mom?"

"Everything's especially OK now that I've gotten to see you and Sally," she answered. "And I just talked to the hospital and Jason's a little stronger than he was when I left this morning."

Both children grinned. "That's great," Brian responded with what sounded like a great sense of relief.

This boy is still blaming himself. I've got to show him he's not at fault. Maybe my idea isn't so half-baked after all.

"So what did you want to talk to us about, Mommie?" Both kids settled on the floor by her chair, Sally with her head on Margaret's knee, since her caged left arm took up all of her lap.

"Kids, I'm about to ask you for permission to do something, and I'll explain why. But if the thought makes either of you uncomfortable, I won't go through with it."

"Boy, that's a switch, Mom. Usually we have to ask you for permission."

She couldn't help but grin at her oldest son. Occasionally flashes of the old Brian would break through, and from that she held out hope he soon could overcome all that was burdening him.

"Here's the deal. As you know, the newspapers and TV stations have been making a nuisance of themselves. What's worse, some of the information they're putting out is as false as it can be. Soooo...," She took a deep breath. "I'm considering holding a press conference."

"But Mommie, you told us not to talk to them," Sally protested.

"You're right, I did. But that was before I discovered just how ridiculous it has gotten."

"How will you do it, Mom?"

"That's what I want to talk to you about. This afternoon Joe and Jim Deaton and P.C. encouraged me, because I could make some remarks about domestic violence and the needs of shelters. We understand that the "Today Show" will have a segment on our situation tomorrow."

"Would we be on TV, Mommie?"

"You could be, if you wanted to, Sally. But ONLY if you want to."

Brian's head picked up. "You'd actually let us be there? Cool."

"Here's what I'm thinking, and I've already talked with Miss Annie Campbell and with Brother Samuel Bronson, the man who took you to his house for supper last night. They both agree that it could be a good thing."

"Brother Samuel is a neat guy, Mom. How'd you meet him?"

"I went to his church last Sunday?"

"But we don't go to his church," Brian argued.

"Still, that's how I met him. So why do you think he's so neat?" she changed the subject slightly.

"He knows all about all the Civil War battles that were fought in Georgia. You ought to see some of the collections he has."

Well, Brother Samuel, looks like you made a good impression on the eldest Haywood child."

"Not to be outdone, Sally piped in, "Mommie, his wife, Miss Susan is nice too. Did you know she's a policeman?"

"Yes, I met her and she is nice. She and Brother Samuel came to the hospital yesterday morning and stayed a long time." *Which is more than I can say for our own pastor Dr. Michaels, or anyone else from the church staff. Not even so much as a phone call. Wonder how many visits he's made to the jail? You know, Margaret, bitterness doesn't become you.*

"So let's talk about the news conference. Here's my idea. I want to get everybody's attention away from our town. I think I should have a press conference at the hospital in Atlanta tomorrow, shortly after lunch. That way everybody will leave and come there. Maybe some of them won't come back to Carter's Crossroads."

"What will you say?" Brian asked?

"That's where you and Sally come in. If I'm going to do this, I want to talk about domestic violence and how it can happen in all homes – even homes like ours. But to do that, I'm going to have to share some things that went on in our home which might embarrass you. How do you feel about that?"

Sally's lower lip was already quivering. "I don't know, Mommie. It's been just horrible at school. Everybody's talking about us."

"Yes, darling, I'm sure they are. And they're talking in the beauty shop, the bank and post office and at the supermarket. It's something we're going to have to live with, at least for a little while."

"Look, Sally," Brian said gently, pulling his sister onto his lap. "We need to trust Mom to do what she thinks is best. I'm ready to stop pretending it all didn't happen and to tell the truth. What do you say?"

"Can we still be there, Mommie?"

"Do you want to be sitting there beside me? I don't want either of you to say anything to any of the reporters, but it would make what I have to say stronger if you are there."

"Then we'll be there, Mom. Won't we, Sally?"

The little girl didn't answer, but instead leaned across and hugged Margaret's knee.

"Very well, then. You two better get on with your home-work. P.C. is driving me back to Atlanta later tonight, so I can be there when Jason has his MRI scan in the middle of the night. Once I talk to the doctor and have a report, we'll begin notifying the news media."

"Do you want us to go to school tomorrow?"

"Hmmm, Brian, I hadn't thought about that. Whether you go to school or not, I've got to find some way to get you to At-lanta." *Brother Samuel? Annie Campbell?* "Tell you what, get on your homework and let me work on this. I'll give you an answer before I leave."

When the kids had gone, Margaret grabbed a legal pad to make some notes on what she wanted to say when she spoke to the press. After a while, she dialed Annie Campbell to ask her advice. In the course of the conversation, she discovered that both Annie and Brother Samuel were planning to drive to Atlanta to be with her. "Can you pick Brian and Sally up from school and get them back home?"

Having secured her friend's assurance they would transport the children, Margaret went back to packing and, as ideas and inspiration came, continued to jot ideas on her legal pad, which she was careful to stash in her tote. *Don't want to forget that.*

Supper that night was one of Ruby Maxwell's usually good meals, and it started out on a positive note. It wasn't until after Sally volunteered that she and Brian were going to Atlanta the next day, to sit by Mom at her press conference, that things began to go down hill. That's when Ruby, forgetting her earlier promise, began to berate her daughter.

"You have really gone too far this time, Margaret. The very idea of putting these children on display while you officially air all your dirty laundry to the whole world makes me sick to my stomach." She banged a skillet on the stove as if to emphasize the depth of her feelings.

"Mama, why can't you trust me to do what I think best? You heard some of the garbage being broadcast this afternoon. I mean...," she pleaded and paused for breath. "Have you ever heard anything so ridiculous as me leaving my injured child alone to rush back to be at the side of my husband who put him in the hospital in the first place?"

"Yes, it's ridiculous, and it doesn't deserve a response. You mark my words, you're only going to make things worse if you go through with this. The less said, the better," I say. "But then no one ever thinks I have an important opinion," she huffed.

"Ruby,"

Harold Maxwell's voice was low but, Margaret thought, almost deadly. *I've never heard Daddy ever use that tone before.*

"Ruby, I thought we settled all of this earlier today." Only it wasn't phrased as a question.

"Well... well, that was before... before Margaret dropped this latest hair-brained idea. I just won't stand for it."

"You'll not only stand for it," Harold informed her, "but you'll stand with her as well."

"Whatever do you mean?"

"Better call the gossip parlor first thing in the morning and get your hair curled, because you and I are going to Atlanta to sit with her and these children. And you can tell them that while you're in the chair. It'll make their day."

"You can go if you want to, old man! I'm not about to disgrace myself."

"Listen to me, Ruby. And hear me well. You and I are going to stand with our daughter and grandchildren tomorrow, as a unified family. I've never given you one single order in all the forty-one years we've been married, but this time I am."

There was total silence at the table, and Margaret held her breath. *Mama has always been a little stubborn, but he always humored her and kidded her along. This is serious. And it's all my fault. Well, mine and Don's.*

Finally, after what seemed an eternity, Ruby sat down at the table and looked at her husband. "What time do we leave? I'll have to get my hair done and buy a new dress. I'm not about to go on TV in anything the whole town has already seen."

If Ruby noticed the collective sigh that passed across the table, Margaret thought, she gave no indication.

As she told P.C. later in the evening, it was one of those watershed moments she would never forget. But hurt feelings seemed soothed somewhat, and since she hadn't yet told the children they would be riding down with Annie and Brother Samuel, she informed them that their transportation problem had been resolved.

"I can probably arrange to get you in to see Jason," she told her parents, hoping the prospect would lessen the bad taste in her mother's mouth. "I believe he can hear us, whether he's awake or not, so I always talk to him and say a prayer with him every time I visit. He'll be thrilled to hear your voices."

"I wasn't sure," she related to P.C., "but I'm almost certain I saw tears in Dad's eyes when I talked about Jason."

"You probably did. He loves all his grandchildren and this has to be hurting him. Only he's from that era when men don't show their true emotions, so he's grieving in silence."

"Hadn't thought about it, but you're probably right." Then, she reached for her cell phone and called Annie Campbell. Once she had explained the situation, Annie was fine to let the children ride down with their grandparents. "But Brother Samuel and I will still be there, just as we promised."

The rest of the ride was given over to plans for the news conference, as Margaret shared with P.C. the prepared script she had written in bits and pieces. "I'll polish it up and pull it together more between now and tomorrow afternoon," she promised.

P.C. made several suggestions, several of which they debated. Then they began to make a list of all the media P.C. would need to contact once Margaret knew the press conference was a go.

Before she realized it, the two of them were walking into the hospital, headed for the ICU waiting area. "If we hurry," Margaret urged her, "we may get there in time for late visiting. They'll let two go in at a time. That way, you can see him and give me your assessment."

Margaret was right. They arrived in the waiting room just as the nurse opened the double doors to the ICU hallway. "Good evening, Mrs. Haywood," she said in a cheery voice. "We weren't expecting you back this early, but Jason's waiting for you. He's gaining strength every hour. That boy's something, he is."

As she stood by her son's bed," she couldn't help but recall the nurse's words. *That's boy's something. Oh, Jason. I hope I do you proud tomorrow. Because when you get well, I want you to know how hard we all fought for you. I'm just sorry you had to get hurt before we understood how special you are.*

"He looks so peaceful," P.C. volunteered on their way out. "Jason isn't hurting, Margaret. He's getting better."

The sleeping lounge with the comfy recliners was almost empty that night, and Margaret was able to get P.C. to take one in the adjoining cubicle, so that they both might get some rest.

When she was almost asleep, she heard P.C. say, "Sleep well, Margaret. By this time tomorrow night, your face and your name are going to be household words all over this country."

Oh, Lord. What have I committed to? Or should I be committed?

CHAPTER THIRTEEN

Margaret was awake even before the doctor came in search of her. However, her first glimpse of the physician's face didn't tell her whether she could rejoice or worry. *It's like she's got a poker face. What does that mean?*

Margaret tried to get up, but without help, it was an awkward exercise. The doctor extended an arm, and together they quickly brought the recliner to an upright position. Margaret couldn't stand the suspense. "Tell me Doctor. What did the scan show? Even if it's bad, I want to know. I have to know what we're dealing with."

The doctor flipped open the chart she carried and scanned the results for what seemed to Margaret like minutes. *In reality, it was probably only about 15 seconds. Who knew seconds could last so long?*

"Let me say first," she began, "I'm encouraged. We're not

out of the woods yet, but I'm amazed at the progress he's made in such a short time."

"Which means what, specifically?"

"He is now totally off the sedation and has been since late last night. In another hour and a half that will be twelve hours. Which is enough time for the induced coma to leave him. What he's doing now, he's doing on his own."

"What kind of remaining damage showed up in the MRI?"

She consulted her notes again. "He is no longer bleeding in that area of his brain where the impact was hardest, although he still has a concussion. If he should awaken in the next few days, he will probably be bothered by blurred vision, headaches and some degree of confusion."

"Will the confusion be permanent?"

"If it's the result of the concussion, he'll slowly work his way out of that. If it's due to brain damage, it's too soon to tell."

Margaret started to speak, but the doctor held up one finger. Margaret hushed.

"Jason has feeling in all his limbs. We can prick him on his feet and legs, and on his arms, and there's involuntary muscle reaction. If he had any kind of paralysis or motor skills problem, he wouldn't react this way."

"So he's not brain damaged?" *Oh, please tell me he isn't!*

"I can't promise that. He could have full motor skills, but be handicapped in other ways. Speech skills, for example. He may have full use of his muscles, but not remember how to walk. Only time will tell. But I can tell you that I am greatly encouraged by what I see."

"I pray you're right, Doctor."

"That's my prayer as well." "But whatever comes, you need to know your Jason is a fighter. He doesn't give up."

Poor Jason. We all failed you so.

Margaret shared with Dr. Lowman her plans for the afternoon news conference and asked if she could possibly be present to answer limited questions.

The answer she received was nothing like she expected. "Have you cleared this with the hospital administration?"

"Well... no. I didn't realize I'd need to." She tried not to look as dumb as she felt. "I've never done anything like this before."

"I don't have a problem being with you," the doctor continued, "but generally the hospital likes to steer clear of any controversy. I'd advise you to check with them before you do anything further."

Gosh, I hadn't even thought about that aspect.

"I'll do that," Margaret promised. "Whom should I speak with?"

"Go to the administrator. Her name is Ann McCallum and she should be in her office within the next thirty minutes."

"If she gives her approval, can you be available at two o'clock?"

"Sure." She flashed a wide grin. "Unless an emergency should arise."

Just as the doctor was leaving, P.C. staggered around the corner from her cubicle, still rubbing sleep from her eyes. "Whaz...whaz goin' on? Howz Jason?" She yawned wide and mumbled, "I slep' too hard."

"Well wake up hard, too. We've got a lot to do and our first act is to go beg permission from the administrator to have my press conference."

"What? You didn't do that yesterday?"

"No," Margaret said, as she grabbed her toiletry articles.

"Didn't know I had to." She looked accusingly at her friend, who was still trying to get awake. "Why didn't you tell me?"

"I assumed you knew you'd have to have permission to do something like that. This is private property, you know."

"Well, I didn't."

"Then let's get ourselves looking presentable and get on up there," P.C. suggested. "We don't have a lot of time. Say, you never did tell me about Jason."

"He's doing better and the MRI showed significant improvement," Margaret answered as she closed the door on her shower area. "Now we just have to wait for him to wake up."

Without even stopping for breakfast, Margaret and P.C., showered and dressed, presented themselves in the hospital's executive suite, where Margaret had to beg to speak with the administrator. "But I have to have just five minutes of her time," she explained to the secretary. "I didn't realize I had to have permission to hold a press conference here, and I've already asked people to be here."

"I'm sorry, Mrs. Haywood. I sympathize with you, but Ms. McCallum has a very tight schedule this morning." The woman ran her fingers across the black keyboard on her desk and peered intently at the computer screen. "If you could possibly wait to see her at three-thirty this afternoon, she has a few minutes available then."

"But I already have the press conference set for two o'clock. Even if I delayed it until four o'clock, there wouldn't be time to get everyone here if I can't speak with her until after three o'clock."

The secretary fingered the heavy gold chain that hung around her neck. "I sympathize with you, I really do. But Ms. McCallum will be in a work session with the board chair all morning, and I really couldn't interrupt her."

"Could you possibly pass her a note?" P.C. interrupted.

Margaret could see conflict written all over the secretary's face. *I don't mean to put her in a compromising situation, but I'm in sort of the same boat.* "If you could just hand her a note, I'd be so very grateful." Then inspiration hit. "Surely they'll take a break at some point during the morning, and she'll check in with you. You could hand her the note then."

"That's a great idea," P.C. crowed. "That way you wouldn't be interrupting her."

"I guess... I guess I could do that. They will no doubt take at least one break and I'm sure Ms. McCallum will ask for her messages."

I've almost got her on my side. "If you can do that, I won't ask anything else. It's just that so many negative and totally incorrect news items are being presented as truth. I just want an opportunity to set the record straight."

"Then write your note and I'll place it here on her stack. If she comes out, I'll make certain she gets it." The secretary looked hard at both ladies, "But I can't promise that she'll come out, and I certainly won't presume to speak for her in this matter."

P.C. was of the opinion that they should be certain the administrator had all the information she needed to make a decision. In a matter of minutes they had found the story from the previous day's *ADJ* and attached to it a tersely worded note asking for permission.

They were on their way to the dining room for breakfast, when Margaret stopped suddenly in her tracks. "I didn't give her any way to contact me. I've got to go back."

P.C. agreed, and went on to order their food, while Margaret beat a hasty backtrack to the executive suite. When she explained the problem, the note was handed back to her. She added her cell phone number and, on impulse, a last line that read, "Battered women everywhere will appreciate your understanding."

"I don't know if I hurt myself or not," she told P.C. as the two sipped juice and ate sausage biscuits. "But I just felt led to write that."

Breakfast finished, they adjourned to the ICU waiting area in anticipation of the ten o'clock visitation. Margaret passed the time making additional notes on her speech, and worrying because P.C. couldn't be making media contacts. P.C., meanwhile, was busy on her cell phone, although Margaret was too distracted to wonder what kept her friend so occupied.

"Look at him, P.C.," she said, when they were finally admitted to Jason's cubicle. "You wouldn't know anything's wrong with him, if he didn't have that bandage on his head."

"No, he looks just like Jason with a crazy hat," she agreed.

Margaret bent low, near his ear, and spoke in a very low but upbeat voice. "Good morning, Jason. You look like you had a good night's sleep last night. You just sleep on as long as you want to, but when you're ready to wake up, Mommie will be here with you." She hesitated. *Can he really hear me?* "And Jason, you don't have to be afraid of daddy. He won't ever hurt you any more."

"That's a tall promise to keep," P.C. said after they were back in the waiting area. "But I think you were right to tell him that. We don't know that there isn't a psychological reason behind the coma."

It was almost eleven-thirty when Margaret's cell phone rang. The number that showed up was unfamiliar and Margaret hesitated before she answered. *Suppose this is some reporter who's gotten hold of my number? That's all I need.* Afraid to miss an important call, she answered cautiously.

"This is Ann McCallum," said a woman's voice. "Is this

Mrs. Haywood?"

"Yes, Ms. McCallum, this is Margaret Haywood." *At least she called me back.*

"I've read your note and enough of the newspaper article to understand what is happening here. I sympathize with your situation, but I hope you understand that we are a privately owned hospital. We have to minimize potential liability issues."

She's going to say "no." What is Plan B? Especially on such short notice. God, is this Your way of telling me You don't want me to do this?

"I understand," she choked out the words. "Thank you for taking time to call me personally."

"Mrs. Haywood, I'm not entirely unfeeling in this matter. It's just that we cannot risk disruption of this hospital's main job, which is making sick children well. I'm certain that what would occur should the press descend on us en masse."

"You do have a very valid point," Margaret admitted. *I can't believe I didn't consider that. Look how much confusion they've caused in Carter's Crossroads.*

"So could you possibly be in my office in the next five minutes? I'd like to have you meet my board chair and see if there's some way we can achieve a win-win situation."

"You mean there's still a possibility?" she gasped. "Yes, we... I can be there in less than five minutes. Oh, thank you, Ms. McCallum."

Without even taking time to explain to P.C. what was happening, she grabbed her friend's arm, "We've got to hurry. Ms. McCallum wants me in her office."

Margaret had imagined the administrator would be an older woman, perhaps in her mid-fifties or early sixties. *Probably has her mousy brown hair pulled back into a bun, wears a conservative suit and glasses. I can just see her looking over her glasses at me.*

However, her mental image of the woman who held the fate of Margaret's news conference wasn't anything like she had pictured. When the door opened and the administrator stepped out to greet Margaret, she was a petite blond, wearing a stylish dress by, she was almost certain, one of Margaret's favorite designers. She appeared to be no older than forty at most, and if she needed vision correction, it was achieved by contact lens. *Was I ever off the mark?*

Margaret hoped the chagrin she felt didn't reflect on her face. "Ms. McCallum," she said, "I can't thank you enough for seeing me. This is my friend, P.C. Dunigan, an attorney from Tennessee who's been giving me moral support."

P.C. and the administrator exchanged pleasantries and Margaret said, "I shouldn't be long, P.C." Then, to Ms. McCallum she explained, "P.C. will be the contact with the press if we can make this work."

"Oh, well in that case, she probably ought to join us."

Ms. McCallum explained that she and her board chair, a white-haired man who, Margaret estimated was in his early sixties, had to leave shortly for a luncheon with private donors, so the four of them were quickly seated around the conference table at one end of the large, spacious office. *If I didn't know better, I'd never guess I was in a hospital. This looks like the president's office of some major corporation.*

Ms. McCallum got right to the point. "As much as we understand your position and want to help, we simply cannot allow a contingent of reporters and camera crews inside the hospital. We don't have the security staff to ensure a quiet and orderly event. Under no circumstances can we allow anything that might be detrimental to our patients' welfare." But she smiled as she spoke the last sentence.

"I really do understand, and I am so sorry that I didn't think this completely through before I started making plans."

"However, Mr. Goldman here has an idea that I think has merit. We hope you will as well." She stood and indicated that Margaret and P.C. should follow her to the wall of windows at the opposite end of the room. "See the beautiful park on the far side of the front parking lot?" she asked and pointed to the right. We think that would be a perfect location. The day is sunny, and the weather is cooperative. If you held it there, reporters wouldn't have to enter the hospital. That's a city park, and as such, park police, assisted by our security force, can maintain order."

"Just a logistics question," P.C. asked. "Who do we have to ask to get permission and how long will that take?" She consulted her watch. "We've got less than three hours to pull all this together."

"As a matter of fact, I placed a call to the commissioner before I called you, and the park is yours if you want it. You just need to call him back and tell him your decision." She handed Margaret a note with a name and number scrawled on it.

Margaret didn't even stop to debate the issue. "We'll take it," she said, "but we'll delay the press conference 'til three o'clock." She looked at P.C. "You get started on those phone calls, I've got to finish writing my statement and make a couple of calls, starting with the parks' commissioner."

"I'm so glad we could negotiate this to everyone's satisfaction," Ms. McCallum said.

"So am I," Margaret replied. "I can never thank you enough." She turned to the gentleman and extended her hand. "Mr. Goldman, it was a pleasure to meet you as well. Please believe me when I say, my son is getting top-notch care here, and I'm not saying that because you two saw fit to help me out of a tight spot."

The board chair, who had walked with them to the door, replied, "We're very proud of Children's Hospital and the ministry of healing that we practice here. I'm so sorry that you're here under these circumstances, but we're glad that you're pleased with his care. You may know that we're all pulling for his complete recovery."

"As they were leaving, the board chair added, "Mrs. Haywood, if I might suggest something?"

"Yes, sir. Anything."

"When you talk with the parks' commissioner, you might want to invite him to attend your press conference."

"You mean so he can keep a personal eye on the situation?"

"Not quite." Mr. Goldman's mouth had a sad smile on it. "Mr. Chisolm's only daughter was killed by her husband three years ago. Domestic violence. I'm afraid the poor man has yet to stop blaming himself. He knew there were problems, but he was afraid to interfere. Said he didn't want to be a meddling in-law."

You never know when, or where, you'll run into abuse victims. "Yes, sir. I'll certainly invite him."

Ms. McCallum stopped by her secretary's desk to tell her where she would be for lunch. "Mrs. Haywood is going to need a couple of tables and some chairs and a public address system. Would you please call Mr. Robinson in maintenance and ask him to coordinate with her in getting everything she needs and setting it up for her?"

Well, duh. I didn't even think about that little need either. To think I used to put together large parties without even having to work at it. I guess this is slightly different.

Her first call was to the parks' commissioner, who not only gave his blessing to the press conference but, when Margaret extended the invitation, accepted in a quiet, sad voice. Then she called Annie and her parents and told them about the hour delay.

In the meantime, she could hear P.C. on her cell phone, making one call after another, while she went over all her notes one last time and organized the prepared statement she would read. *I never have any problem with public speaking, but I've never spoken on anything like this, anything so personal. Better that I read it and don't miss anything or worse yet, state something incorrectly.*

Then, almost before she was ready, P.C. was urging her to put her statement aside and change clothes and get ready. "It's two-fifteen," she said, as if to impress upon Margaret how close it was to time.

By the time they got to the park, people from home were beginning to arrive. She had stationed a hospital security guard at the entrance to direct everyone to the conference site, where maintenance staff had erected tables and chairs and a P.A. system *Why they even put white clothes on the tables. It looks very professional. And they situated the tables so that when I'm talking, the hospital will be in the background. Thank you, Lord.*

The first ones she saw were her parents and Brian and Sally. *Mama looks mad, Daddy looks uneasy, Brian seems to be holding together pretty well, but I'm almost afraid if I even say hello to Sally, she's going to burst into tears.*

Nevertheless, she hugged both of her children tightly and whispered to them, "It's going to be OK. I promise." Then she greeted her parents, making sure to comment on Mama's new emerald green dress. "How pretty that dress looks with your hair, Mama."

"Well, it wasn't what I wanted, but when you don't have any advance notice, you do with what you can. And Roxie was so busy at the salon this morning, she had to squeeze me in." She patted her hair. "I doubt I got my money's worth."

First she doesn't want me to do this, then she grouses about her hair and dress. Mama, you're awfully hard to love sometimes. Margaret was rescued from having to respond to her mother's complaints by the arrival of Annie Campbell, Brother Samuel and his wife, Susan, and Joe Busbee.

"Joe, I didn't expect you to take time away to drive down for this. You've lost too much work already."

"Wouldn't have missed it, Margaret."

Wouldn't have missed it, or wouldn't have missed P.C.? She noted that the two had gravitated toward each other immediately, a practice that had become more common of late, she decided.

Then Jim Deaton and Dr. Lowman walked up together, followed closely by Ann McCallum and Mr. Goldman. A tall, lanky African-American gentleman was with them who was, Margaret was soon to learn, Mr. Archibald Chislom.

Almost before she and the children were seated, along with Jim Deaton on one side and Dr. Lowman on the other, it was as if the floodgates opened and the press descended upon them in a thundering herd.

Having only seen such events on the nightly Atlanta TV news, Margaret was astounded at how quickly so many people set up cameras and recording equipment without getting in each others' way. *They've obviously done this before.*

Margaret suddenly wondered how she was supposed to begin. And when? A note quickly passed by her attorney relieved her immensely. "Let me lead off, then do as I do," it read.

While she waited for everyone to get ready and for the crowd to settle down, she looked over her shoulder. How good it looked to see her parents, P.C. and Joe, Annie and Brother Samuel standing behind her. *I don't want to feel like I'm in this all alone.*

"Good afternoon, everyone. Thank you for coming today."

Jim Deaton's confident voice pierced the many conversations going on in the group, and everyone immediately ceased talking and
turned their attention to the front. Margaret noted that camera
operators were adjusting their equipment, and she felt as if she
were staring into the face of a fly with a thousand eyes. Under-
neath the cover of the tablecloth, she found a hand for each child
and squeezed it, hoping to give them more confidence than she
felt herself. *I wonder how we'll look on TV. More importantly, will I come
across as sincere or like a fishwife?*

Jim Deaton continued to speak. "I am Jim Deaton, an attorney representing Margaret Haywood and her children, Brian,
Sally and Jason. Those of you here certainly know why Mrs.
Haywood's name has been in the news so frequently in the last
few days. For anyone who might not know, Mrs. Haywood is a
battered woman. An abused wife. The injury to her left arm, from
which she is currently recovering, was suffered at the hands of
her abuser, her husband, Don Haywood who is, as we speak, confined to the Carter's Crossroads' jail, without benefit of bond. In
the early hours of last Monday morning, Mr. Haywood, who was
angry because his wife had filed for divorce citing domestic abuse
as the grounds, took his wrath out on the youngest member of his
family, his son Jason. The boy is now in ICU at Children's Hospital here behind us, in a coma.

"Mrs. Haywood is here today because she's read your articles and listened to your broadcasts. In all of those, she has seen
herself, her family, and the circumstances of this case presented
in a manner that has been fraught with misconceptions and erro-
neous information. She wishes to set the record straight. Ladies
and Gentlemen, I give you Mrs. Margaret Haywood." With that,
he stood and gestured in her direction.

Mellow my heart and my tongue, Lord. Let me say what I need to say, but please keep me from making a fool of myself.

Then, with the early December mid-afternoon sun shining down on them, and with not even a breeze stirring to muffle her comments, Margaret began to speak. She thanked the press for giving her an opportunity to clarify the story, introduced her children, and the other guests gathered around her.

"I'm going to read a prepared statement," she explained. "Dr. Lynn Lowman will then give you an update on Jason's condition, and we'll try to answer any question my attorney thinks are appropriate.

She started with the incident where Jason was thrown against the wall by his father, told about the evening when Don threw her to the floor with such destructive force, and how he had abused Sally. She touched on his arrest in Tennessee for the restaurant altercation, and she recounted how he had held her prisoner in exchange for money and a comfortable lifestyle.

"If I'm honest," she concluded, "there were aspects of his behavior that were excessively controlling from the first week we were married, but when you're young and head over heels in love, you tend to ignore the two thousand pound elephant in the corner of the room. As you get older and celebrate a number of anniversaries, you find one excuse after another to overlook and even forgive abusive tendencies. After all," she explained, "you have so much time invested in the relationship, you justify away the danger."

She looked at the crowd, specifically right into the eyes of the many cameras, as she said, "I can't tell you exactly when the abuse – physical, emotional and financial – began to increase in frequency and severity. But I can tell you that they did. Now my youngest son faces an uncertain future as we wait for him to awaken."

Margaret could feel her children's arms around her waist, and she was comforted. *Thank you, Lord, for three wonderful children. I pray You will restore our family unit by giving Jason back to us whole and excited to live.*

"Before I turn this over to Dr. Lowman, I'd like to say two things. First, I could not have handled all that I've been dealt over the past few weeks without God, through whom all things are possible, and the support of both friends and strangers at the Battered Women's Haven in Carter's Crossroads and shelters here in Atlanta. What they have meant to me is more than I can explain.

"Which brings me to my second point. The only way I can ever repay their kindness is to refuse to cower in the corner, afraid to do what is right, even though my husband – in this case, my abuser – may get angry. One of the main reasons we have so much domestic violence – in upscale homes like mine and in families of every socio-economic level – is because abusers are not stopped in their tracks. Every time they get away with something that is so morally wrong, it actually empowers them. At one time I loved my husband. I still love the man I married, but I detest his actions which are evil, cruel and just plain wrong. This is why I will spend whatever it takes to ensure that none of my children follow in their father's ill-chosen footsteps."

Margaret paused to collect her wits and sip from the water glass that had been so graciously provided for each of them. "I wish my husband no harm, certainly no injuries such as he as perpetuated on Jason or myself. But I do wish him justice for his crimes, with the hope that the opportunity of incarceration will bring about in him a healing in attitude and spirit."

Then she introduced the doctor, who shared the nature of Jason's injury and the odds for a full recovery. She outlined how Jason might be impacted for life by the actions of his father, and explained how close to death Jason had come in the first few hours following the assault. "If his older brother hadn't gotten him and called for help, by the time the sun came up, Jason Haywood would either have been dead, or, in my opinion, his brain would have been so traumatized he would definitely have been left a vegetable."

Neither Brian nor Sally had heard the true extent of their brother's injuries, Margaret realized. *How I wish I could look into their heads and know what they're really thinking right now.*

Following the doctor's remarks, Jim Deaton called for questions. TV people were looking at their watches, calculating how much time they had to get the story and still get it up on the six o'clock news.

"Look," she said, "I won't answer any individual questions afterward, so if you have questions, better ask them now."

"Mrs. Haywood... Mrs. Haywood... Over here, Mrs. Haywood." Suddenly the crowd went wild with shouts and all manner of questions flung at random.

"Do you still plan to proceed with the divorce?

"Yes."

"Will you institutionalize Jason if he doesn't make a reasonable recovery?

"Absolutely not. Jason's father is a wealthy man with good insurance. I will use those assets in any way needed to care for Jason as long as the need exists. For the rest of his life, if necessary."

"Mrs. Haywood, will you remain in Carter's Crossroads?

"My parents are there, as are many friends. My children haven't known any other home. However, had you asked me three months ago if I'd be sitting here under these circumstances, I'd have answered "no." So I think it's premature to even speculate on what might happen down the road."

"Will you take your maiden name back?"

Margaret tried to see who had asked the question. Unsuccessful, she replied, "I don't really think that's either here nor there."

"Will you testify against your husband? What about your children?"

"If the District Attorney needs any or all of us to testify, we will certainly discuss that with him at the appropriate time. Certainly we'll cooperate any way we can."

"Where is your loyalty to your husband? Isn't it true he's provided a lavish living for you and your kids? In light of all that, will you ask the judge to go easy on him?"

Margaret glanced at Jim Deaton, trying to determine who had posed such a loaded question. His expression admitted he was as puzzled as she was.

"I will neither encourage the judge to "go easy" on him, as you put it, nor will I expect or insist on a sentence that is more harsh than would normally be meted out. The manner in which Mr. Haywood has provided for us has no bearing, in my opinion, on how he should be treated by the courts."

Jim flashed her a big smile, which she interpreted as "done good."

"Mrs. Haywood? Aren't you and your family big church folks? What does your church say about you airing your dirty linen in front of the whole community? Whose side are they on?"

"My family and I are Christians. And we have been very active in our church. However, while we may be Christians, that doesn't mean we're perfect. We're all sinners saved by God's grace. My husband's particular sin in this case, I'm sure, has grieved God's heart as it has mine. But I believe that God still loves him and will be dealing with his heart over the months to come. As for our church, you would have to ask them about their opinion."

"Have you spoken with your pastor since your husband was arrested?

"No."

"You mean he hasn't been to the hospital to see your son? Or to see about you?"

Lord, do I tell the truth? Or do I alibi for the church the way I did for Don all this time?

"It's been a hectic few days and I know the church staff is pulled in many directions."

"So no one has come or called?

Margaret took a deep breath. "No."

The same voice, who seemed to have seized control asked, "Has anyone from the church been to see your husband?"

"I do not know." *I think this thing has gone far enough.* "Thank you for coming today," she said to the group. "I'm going now because it's approaching visiting time in ICU and I'm anxious to see my son. I would ask that each of you say a prayer for Jason tonight."

She indicated to those seated with her that it was time to adjourn. As she and the children rose to walk away, the support group around her closed ranks, making her feel protected.

'For He shall give His angels charge over thee, to keep thee in all thy ways.' Oh, Lord, I don't think I've ever felt that scripture from Psalms 91:11 so deeply as I do right this moment. Thank you, God, for all these people, Your angels, who have stood with me.

Back in the hospital, Margaret saw security turning away die-hard reporters attempting to follow her for more questions and she was immediately glad that Ann McCallum's judgment had been right on target.

Dr. Lowman suggested that if Margaret were to go in with each child at a time, both Sally and Brian could visit their brother without stretching the two person visiting rule. Afterward, if Mr. and Mrs. Maxwell wanted to go in, they might have a minute with him as well.

Margaret and Brian went first, and it squeezed her heart to watch the color drain from her eldest son's face when he saw his little brother. She took his hand. "It's OK, Brian. He's sleeping very peacefully and they tell me he's feeling little if any discomfort. If you hadn't gotten him away from your dad and called me, we wouldn't have him with us."

"But, Mom. If I..."

"Stop. If chickens had teeth, they could eat steak. We'll have no "if 's" here. Our time is short. Bend down close to his ear and tell him how anxious you are for him to get well and come home. And tell him that your dad won't ever hurt him again."

Brian did as she instructed, and seemed, she believed, to feel better for having done so.

"Sally was next, and as Margaret had expected, she was already sniffling before they ever got to Jason's bed. Margaret didn't scold her, but she did encourage her to dry her tears and tell Jason what was happening at school. "Tell him you can't wait for him to come home."

When under fire, Margaret decided, Sally could perform, and she did at that moment. When they were back in the waiting area, she indicated to her parents that they should go back. "Please," she implored both of them, "be sure to speak into his ear and tell him that you love him and want him to get well and come home."

"Are you serious?" Ruby asked. "He's in a coma."

"Mama, the doctor believes he can hear what we're saying

to him. It won't hurt anything."

"Don't worry, daughter. We'll do whatever you want us to do," Harold Maxwell said. "Come on, Ruby. Let's go be grandparents."

Before she knew it, the window had closed and everyone was in the waiting area, ready to leave for home. Margaret hugged her children and parents. "Thank you," she told Ruby. "Whether you agree with me or not, thank you for being here today."

They left, followed shortly by Annie and Brother Samuel and his wife and Joe. Jim remained behind for a few minutes to talk strategy. Seeing P.C.'s crestfallen face when Joe walked away, Margaret was seized with inspiration.

"P.C. you don't need to stay the night. I'm only here because I want to see Jason every chance I get. Why don't you go on home tonight and I'll talk to you in the morning. I may need you to come back after me around lunch tomorrow so I can deal with several things at home."

P.C.'s face lit up. "Are you sure? I don't mind staying."

"I know you don't, but there's no need. I'm fine. Go on, before the rush hour traffic gets any worse."

"OK," her friend said, already half way up the hall, "but you call me in the morning and I'll come back whenever you say."

After P.C. left, she looked at Jim. "Is it my imagination, or have P.C. and Joe taken a 'liken' to each other?"

Jim laughed. "It's not your imagination. I just can't figure out who's more smitten."

Margaret smiled. *How nice that something positive and happy can come out of all this nightmare.*

When Jim was gone, Margaret found herself totally alone for the first time since the wee hours of Monday morning. She thought about the local newscasts and checked the waiting room

TV that was on the PBS channel. "Does anyone mind if I change to the news?" When there was no response, she took silence as a yes and turned to Atlanta's major news broadcast.

It just was six o'clock, and the anchors were teasing the news content to come. She didn't have to wait long to hear the male anchor say "This afternoon the wife of a north Georgia textile manufacturer told the media about the abuse that her husband inflicted on her and their son, abuse that has left the son in a coma fighting for his life. We'll have the complete story later in this hour."

A little more dramatic than the real story, but as long as they don't edit out too much of what I said, this ought to set the record straight.

She occupied herself catching up on all else that was happening in the world, and then a shot of her and the children flashed across the screen. An unseen announcer advised that the story would be presented immediately after the upcoming commercial break.

The advertisements seemed to run on and on until the camera zeroed in on the male anchor again. "Don Haywood of Carter's Crossroads is one of that town's most prominent citizens. Haywood, who made his money in the carpet business he started from scratch about twenty years ago, has been very generous to his town. However, even his generosity has proven no match for the legal troubles he faces following his violent assaults on his wife and youngest son. Tonight Haywood is an inmate in the Carter's Crossroads' Jail, while his six year-old son lies in Children's Hospital here in Atlanta in a coma. Doctors have been unable to predict when, or if, he will awaken. This afternoon Mrs. Haywood recounted what had gone wrong in the marriage that all of Carter's Crossroads considered an ideal union."

Then she saw herself and heard her own voice. Within

two minutes, the clip ended. *They edited out most of what I had to say, but the basic story was there. I'm satisfied.*

The anchor's face was back on the screen, and he concluded the segment by promising the station would continue to monitor the situation, as well as Jason's medical status.

She couldn't get interested in the remainder of the newscast and decided instead to go on to the cafeteria and get something to eat. As she slowly cleaned her plate, while mentally comparing the food she was eating to her mother's cooking, she thought about other families she had met during the short time Jason had been in the hospital.

One couple had been living in the waiting area for over three weeks, while their young daughter hovered between life and death as a bacterial infection ravaged her body. They would sleep there at night, in the big room with the recliners, then the husband would clean up, dress and go to work. He'd come by at lunch and then back to the hospital for another night once he got off work. They had another child at home whom they had not seen even once in all that time.

Lord, there but for Your grace go I. Or am I going to be just like them, living from day to day inside these disinfected walls, with no hope of when I can get out?

After finishing most of the piece of red velvet cake she'd chosen for dessert – which turned out to be too dry to really enjoy – she strolled back down to the ICU wing, prepared to spend what promised to be a long night. Alone. *This is the first time I've ever been this alone. Is this what it's always going to be like?*

On her way through the maze of halls, she met several members of other families, all imprisoned there under the same warden – the love and concern for their child that wouldn't allow them to walk away to their normal lives. As she approached the elevator lobby, she noticed a couple who had been walking the opposite direction stop, look her way, and then turn to approach her.

"Excuse me," the woman said hesitantly. "But aren't you Mrs. Haywood we saw on the news tonight?"

Wondering if she was about to be chastised for ruining her husband's life, she replied that she was.

"You have no idea how your story touched us." She reached out for Margaret's arm. "I was abused by my first husband for almost five years. I was afraid to fight him, or to report him, because he threatened to kill me. But when he assaulted my daughter, I had to get medical help for her and then the whole sordid story came out."

"I can understand what you're saying," Margaret replied, not really certain of where the woman was going with her story, or what she wanted.

"Unfortunately, my daughter will suffer for the rest of her life as a result of the damage he did. She's ten now, and we have to come into the hospital about twice a year for treatments." She stuck her right fist in her mouth, as if trying to staunch a case of hysterics. "My ex-served two years and now he's out, but my daughter will suffer for the rest of her life. I'm married to a wonderful man now..." she patted the man beside her... and he loves Carolyn as much as I do. He never begrudges the money we have to spend or the times when we call Children's Hospital home."

Margaret was touched. "You sound very fortunate. I'm so happy for you."

"Well, you be happy for yourself, you hear? I promise you there's a good man out there somewhere for you... and your children. Just be watching and God will show him to you."

"Why... why thank you," Margaret stammered. "Thank you

for stopping to talk, and I hope you'll soon get to go back home."

"We're praying for your son," the woman said, as they parted ways.

"Thank you," Margaret managed to answer. "I'll be sure to include Carolyn in my prayers."

There's another man out there for me? I hadn't even thought that far ahead. I guess I've been married to Don for so long, I can't envision anything except him or being single. I wouldn't know how to even begin to date again.

Margaret curled up with a good book she had brought with her, and when the nurse announced visiting privileges, she hurried to get to Jason's room. Just as she was about to enter the door, another nurse stopped her.

"Is something wrong? Jason's not worse?"

"No, no," the nurse said quickly, "but I did want to catch you before you went in. Dr. Lowman wants you to do something for us."

"Sure. OK. What?"

"Please walk in very quietly, go to the side of the bed, but don't greet Jason or ask him how he is. Instead, put your mouth to his ear and say 'Jason... move your hand.' We want to see if he will respond to your voice and your command."

With her heart in her throat, racing at breakneck pace, she did as she was instructed. To her amazement, she saw his right hand twitch ever so slightly. *Or did I? Lord, did he really move his hand, or do I want it to happen so badly I imagined it?*

She turned to the nurse for validation and was overjoyed to see a big smile stretched across the woman's face. "He did move his hand, didn't he?"

"It was very little, but his hand did move." The nurse pulled a notepad from her pocket and wrote. "Again. His foot."

Margaret braced herself and again spoke into her son's ear.

"Jason. Move your foot." This time both sets of eyes were glued on the two small feet. And a few seconds after Margaret made the request, they were rewarded by seeing the toes on one foot twitch.

Margaret grabbed the nurse and pulled her into the hallway. "What does this mean? Why did Dr. Lowman want me to do this?"

The nurse whispered quietly, "I'm not supposed to give medical opinions, but the doctor thought he would respond to your voice more quickly than he would any of ours. The fact that he obeyed you means he's not paralyzed in his extremities, he can hear what you're saying, and his brain is capable of hearing commands and complying."

"So he's not brain damaged?"

"It's too soon to rule on that. We won't know anything for certain until he wakes up, but this is definitely an optimistic sign. I can't wait to call the doctor. She wanted to know tonight."

Margaret thought quickly. "Does this mean he's closer to waking up?"

"That would be a logical conclusion. If he can hear and comply, he's not in as deep a sleep as he was."

Margaret visited with him again for a couple of minutes, talking to him the entire time. Just before leaving, she offered a prayer in which she thanked God for Jason's ability to hear and respond. Then she found herself back in the waiting area, unable to contain her excitement.

When she finally put down her phone an hour later, after making calls to everyone she could think of, Margaret felt as if she had been hit by a Mac truck. Taking her book and her Bible, she found a comfortable recliner and began preparations to bed down for the night.

Dear Lord, You continue to amaze us with how good You are. Thank

You for the way You have looked out for Jason, and for the many blessings we've received through him. Please continue to hold him close, and stay close to Brian and Sally, and to me. We need You now more than ever. In Your son's name. Amen.

As she settled herself for the night, her exhausted body that craved rest fought with her mind and her heart that couldn't wait until the next visiting time. But in the end, the body won, and she felt herself falling asleep.

Tomorrow is going to be a new day for us. Jason's going to wake up. I just feel it. And everything will be wonderful.

CHAPTER FOURTEEN

From somewhere far away, Margaret could hear a telephone ringing. She tried to block it out so she could go back to sleep. Then, as suddenly as it began ringing, it stopped. Satisfied that someone had answered it, she began to drift back into sleep, only to be roughly jerked awake a second time as the phone began to ring again.

"Somebody get that phone, please!" she called out. But no one complied. And then the ringing stopped again.

More awake now than she had been, Margaret suddenly realized that she had never seen a telephone in the sleeping area. When the phone began to ring a third time, she realized that it was her own cell phone, stashed in her purse that had awakened her. She reached for her purse, but the ringing stopped once again before she could get her hands on the phone.

What's happened at home? Is something wrong with the kids? Or Mama and Daddy? Daddy's old and this has been hard on him. Margaret could imagine all manner of problems.

Her hands were trembling, making it more difficult to grab the little flip phone and check the Caller ID. For sure she didn't think it was a wrong number. Before she could get the phone open, it began to shrill again, and she wrestled for the "Talk" button. Her eyes were still too filled with sleep to focus on the screen.

"Hello? Who is this?" she demanded.

"Margaret? Thank God I got you."

It's Jim. "What time is it, Jim? Something's wrong."

"Where are you right now, Margaret? Please tell me you're in the hospital somewhere."

"I'm in the sleeping lounge outside Intensive Care? Why? Is something wrong with one of the kids?"

"Don's escaped. There's a massive manhunt underway."

"Escaped? How? Jim, this sounds like a bad Grade B movie script."

She could hear him breathing heavily on the other end. "Sorry, Margaret," he said at last, "this is no bad movie script and it's no joke. Don bribed a deputy to open the cell door and he's out and gone."

Margaret was still in a stupor, partly from being awakened out of a sound sleep, as well as from the news she'd just received. "Gone. Where is gone?"

"That's just it, nobody knows."

The image that materialized in her mind's eye suddenly jerked her wide awake. "Jim! The children. My parents. Could he have gone there?"

"Those bases are covered. Search parties have been to Haywood Tufters and to the house on Red Bud Way. No sign of him. The sheriff has posted guards around your parents' home, but they didn't wake your folks, hating to alarm them unnecessarily."

I hope Don wouldn't be stupid enough to go there. There's no telling what Dad would do.

"I think it's best just to let them sleep, as long as you're sure the house is protected. But he can't have just walked away."

"That's the other worry we have." Jim paused, breathed hard again, then, "Do you know where his SUV is?"

Margaret thought back and a concrete image appeared in her mind. "It was in the yard last Monday morning when we got to the house. It was still there when the deputy hauled Don off to jail."

"It's gone. No trace of it. The Sheriff has broadcast a bulletin, but so far there have been no sightings."

Margaret felt a chill go over her body as she realized that she had developed a false sense of security as long as Don was locked up.

"We... that is the sheriff and I... we're afraid he's on his way to Children's Hospital."

On his way to Children's Hospital! "Why would he be coming here?"

"That's why we're so concerned. Don saw one of the news broadcasts tonight about your press conference and went absolutely berserk. The deputies finally had to restrain him in cuffs and leg irons."

Why am I not surprised?

"So you think he saw the broadcast and made up his mind to come after me?"

Don wouldn't hesitate to stalk me and kill me.

"It all makes sense. So you and P.C. must take precautions. Tell her to...,"

"P.C. isn't here," Margaret interrupted. "Remember, she went back this afternoon?"

"Ooh... that's right. I had forgotten." There was silence and Margaret, numb from the news she'd just received, couldn't manage to breach the gap. "OK," he said, "here's the plan. I'm on my way, but it will take me about forty-five minutes to get there."

"I'm safe. I'm far enough inside the hospital he'd have to hunt me."

"With all due respect, there's one lesson I've learned from all this: Don't underestimate Don Haywood's wrath or his abilities. It's almost two o'clock, a perfect time for him to enter the hospital unchallenged."

Curiosity was getting the best of her. "Jim, exactly how did he get out of the jail?"

The next sound she heard was a low chuckle, totally lacking in mirth. "The way Don buys his way in or out of everything. He bribed an assistant jailer who was having money problems."

"With what? Don't tell me they were letting him keep money in his cell?" *But then, this is Don we're talking about. He's always been able to get special favors no one else could get.*

"Nope, he didn't have any money on him, but he wrote the deputy an IOU and assured him that he would get his money. The deputy unlocked the cuffs and leg irons and conveniently left the cell door unlocked." Margaret heard a deep sigh. "You can guess the rest."

She could, and the cold chill enveloped her again.

"Listen, Margaret, here's what you do."

Following his directions, she found the ICU nurse on the desk and asked to be directed to a security officer. It was only a matter of minutes until Officer Bohannon, as he introduced him-self, came to her in the ICU waiting area. Margaret explained the situation and asked that he call the sheriff in Carter's Crossroads, who would fill him in on the details.

The officer agreed, and as he was about to leave, asked if she had a recent photo of Don. About to say she didn't, Margaret dug in her purse until she found the picture.

"I don't know what he'll be wearing," she explained to the guard. "He would have had on a jail uniform when he got out, but since they think he went home to get his vehicle, he could easily have changed into his own clothes. The one thing he won't have is a wallet or any identification, because it's locked up at the jail."

"Mrs. Haywood, I saw you on TV tonight, and I'm mighty impressed with the courage you showed out there. Don't you worry. You stay right here and you ought to be plenty safe. The only way into this hospital at this time of night is through the ER entrance. I'll take this photo with me, show it to my guards, and post two men at the ER. Then I'll call your sheriff."

By now Margaret was wide awake. And worried. Don had proven before that he was not a man to be crossed. That he would stop at nothing didn't surprise her. *He would kill me if he had the chance.*

It wasn't but a few minutes until her phone rang again. This time she recognized P.C.'s number. "Margaret. Have you heard?"

"That Don's out of jail and possibly on his way here? Yeah, I heard."

"He's on his way there?" *How do you know that? All we heard was he'd escaped.*

"Yeah, well, it goes deeper than that." Margaret filled her friend in on why they suspected he might be coming to Children's Hospital. Several times Margaret heard sharp intakes of breath from her friend.

"We'll be right there, Margaret. You sit tight. Frightening as it is, this sounds exactly like something Don Haywood would pull."

"We? Who is we?"

"Joe and I. We're on our way in just a few minutes."

"Nope, you stay right where you are. The security staff is on top of things here. Besides, the only way into this hospital is through the ER. They've got armed guards posted there, and they have a picture of Don I had in my purse."

"But I'd feel better if we came down there. You don't want to be alone."

"And I don't want my friends to be dead, either. The last thing we need is for the two of you to arrive at the ER while Don's there. The way he feels, he'd believe he had nothing to lose if he shot first."

Margaret finally convinced P.C. that they should not risk showing up at the hospital, and they ended the conversation. Try as she might, Margaret couldn't seem to find interest in her book, in TV, or even in going back to sleep. Instead, she pulled her Bible from the side pocket of her tote and settled in one of the straight chairs. She could see outside through the huge plate glass windows that overlooked the ER wing at the opposite end of the hospital campus.

Maybe it's because I'm closer to you, Lord, but I do feel safer here on the second floor. Lord, I don't like anything that Don is doing, but he is one of Your children. If he is on his way here, intent on harming me or anyone, I'd ask that You speak to his heart in a special way. It's obvious that human intervention isn't going to speak loudly enough to convince him to change his ways and abandon his destructive plans. You, Lord, are the only hope. I want him stopped, but I don't want him harmed. Be with me, Lord, with my parents and my children, and with Don wherever he is. If his heart is so hardened that he refuses to listen to Your guidance, protect all of us here, Lord, in accordance with Your will. I pray this, Father, in the name of Your Son who died for all our sins. Amen.

She sat for a few minutes after she ended her prayer remembering the good times they had enjoyed as a couple and as parents with children. *I wish I knew when Don started going wrong. You'd think I could remember, but I can't. Now he's headed here, and there can't be any reason except he has to extract revenge. I just feel it in my gut.*

Margaret felt totally at peace, despite the confrontation she believed was imminent and would probably turn violent, possibly deadly. *He's been missing long enough he should be here just about any time now, unless they've apprehended him. Surely someone would have notified us if he had been caught.* She found her cell phone and dialed Annie Campbell's cell number, knowing that she would wake the shelter director. She also knew that Annie wouldn't care.

It was a sleepy voice that answered on the third ring, but when she heard Margaret's voice, Annie was immediately awake. "What's wrong," she demanded. "Is Jason worse?"

"Not Jason," Margaret replied. "Have you heard that Don escaped from jail just before midnight?"

"Escaped? How did they let him get away?"

Margaret could tell she'd caught her friend off-guard. "The way Don usually achieves anything. He bribed a deputy, with an IOU, no less."

Annie was quiet for a long time. "That would be hilarious if it weren't so pathetic. Do they know where he is?"

"Sheriff Tuggle thinks he may be coming here. He evidently managed to get to the house and get his SUV, because it's missing." Margaret emitted a groan of fatigue and disgust. "It seems he saw my news conference last evening and was so livid they had to restrain him."

Annie agreed. "I think the sheriff is probably on the right track. But I'm not worried about Don. I want to know what's being done to protect you."

Margaret explained the hospital's game plan for dealing with her husband if he did appear. "I'm not too worried about myself. I'm far enough back in the hospital that he'd have trouble finding me anyway. With security on high alert, I don't think he'd ever get this far."

"Nevertheless, you need to take every precaution. Don Haywood won't let a few locked doors get in his way."

"You're telling me. I've just been praying for the safety of all those innocent people between the ER and here. They sure don't deserve to suffer because of Don's abusive mantra."

The two talked for a few more minutes. Margaret extracted a promise that her friend would call the local shelter and put them on high alert, "Just in case," she said. Annie agreed that she would and then volunteered that she would be on her knees praying, just as soon as she called Brother Samuel and put him on notice.

It felt so good to have someone to talk to at a time like this. I'm fortunate to have Annie as my friend. For that matter, Lord, I'd say I'm amply blessed with friends.

Too anxious to sit still, Margaret walked to the window wall again and stood watching the hospital grounds shrouded in blackness from the darkest part of the night when, out of the corner of her eye, she glimpsed movement across the parking lot. But when she took a second look, nothing was there.

I've got a good case of the jitters. This thing is bothering me more than I thought. Now I'm seeing Don crouching behind every tree. But she vowed to keep on scanning the landscape, and if she saw anything she couldn't identify, she would err on the side of caution and alert Security. *Thank goodness these windows are mirrored on the outside. I wouldn't want Don to see me standing here. But this sure is a good place to keep watch. Now I know why they have blockhouses in prisons.*

She was concentrating so intently on the outside she didn't hear the call for ICU visiting. It wasn't until after a compassionate nurse realized she'd missed the call and personally came to fetch her, that she abandoned her post.

"How's Jason?" she asked his nurse as she made her way into his little room. "Has there been any change? Good or bad?"

The young nurse, who didn't look old enough to have the title R.N. after her name, flashed a large grin. "I'm going to wait and let you tell me."

Margaret's heart did a flip and she stopped stock-still in the corridor. "Is he awake?"

"Not awake, but more responsive. We're anxious to see what sort of reaction you get."

She couldn't get to her son's room fast enough, and when she did, the first thing she saw was general body movement. *All the times before, Lord, he's been laying perfectly still. Now he's moving and turning a little. Oh. Thank you, Lord.*

Margaret couldn't get to the bed fast enough, but she forced herself to move slowly so as not to spook the boy if he was more alert than any of them thought. She reached for his right hand and began to gently massage it. Without her even having to say anything, the boy responded by gently squeezing her hand."

Oh, Lord. He squeezed my hand! It was very slight, but he did squeeze my hand.

"Has he done that before," she asked the nurse who was standing nearby.

"We think he did it about 30 minutes ago when we were talking to him, but you didn't even have talk to him."

Margaret was beside herself with excitement. She leaned over the boy and gave him a gentle kiss on his forehead. "It's Mommie, Jason. I love you."

The child rewarded her by moving both hands just enough that she and the nurse could confirm it happened. Margaret pulled up a chair and settled by the bed. Taking his hand in hers, she began to talk about everything in general. Grammy and Grandee and how glad they had been to see him the previous day. All the news Sally and Brian had brought home from school. She shared with the child about an especially cute puppy she'd seen earlier in the week and asked him how he'd like to have a cocker spaniel puppy when he got home.

Every time he heard his mother's voice, she took note, Jason made some kind of body movement.

"He's definitely responding to you and especially to the sound of your voice," the nurse agreed. "I think our little fellow here is on the mend."

Determined to take advantage of every second she had, Margaret continued to talk about everything she could think of. Christmas. Would they have a live tree or an artificial evergreen? Did he have his Christmas list ready to go see Santa? She wondered aloud what he might like to find under the tree on Christmas morning, and suggested that they might try to take a short trip between Christmas and New Year's.

With everything she said, the boy responded. Margaret searched his face with the determination of a detective looking for clues and, along toward the end, she thought she detected slight eyelid movement.

"Did you see his eyelids move?" she asked the nurse. "I'm certain he did."

"No," the nurse replied. "I wasn't watching his face. But it would make..."

Whatever observation she was about to make was cut short as the hospital PA system announced "Code Red." "Code Red."

Margaret saw color drain slightly from the nurse's face and the petite little brunette excused herself and fairly raced out of the room.

Someone must be dying. No... wait a minute... I think that's a 'Code Blue'. Caught up as she was in Jason's responses, and hoping against hope that she could see him open his eyes, Margaret began to talk to her son again. Only this time she was much more specific.

"Jason. It's Mommie. I know you can hear me, because you've been squeezing my hand and moving your hands and feet." *Lord, I know he can hear me. I just know it.* "Jason," she urged. "You can wake up any time you're ready. I know you want to. There's no need to be afraid. You can open your eyes because you're safe and no one is going to hurt you."

Margaret was so caught up in her encouragement to the small child, she failed to notice that his nurse had returned, accompanied by the ICU Charge Nurse.

"Mrs. Haywood?"

Margaret turned at the sound of the unfamiliar voice to find both nurses standing at the foot of Jason's bed. Thinking she had done something wrong, she said, "I'm sorry. I didn't mean to put pressure on him. It's just..." She hesitated when she saw the look on their faces, then continued in a rush, "It's just that I believe he's ready to wake up. He just needs to know he's not in danger."

Jason's nurse smiled at her, although Margaret thought it was a forced expression. "It's not that, Mrs. Haywood," the superior nurse said, "but we do need to see you in the hall for just a moment."

What have I done? Margaret didn't argue. Instead, she patted her son's hand and said, "Mommie will be right back, Jason." *And I am coming back, if only to say goodbye.*

She followed the nurses into the hallway and watched while the younger one closed the cubicle door.

Unable to contain herself, and a little annoyed that she was losing precious visiting time, Margaret asked, "Please tell me what I did wrong. I want another minute with him before I have to leave." As if to emphasize her resolve, she glanced at the clock at the end of the corridor.

4:09. I've got maybe two minutes.

It was the older nurse who spoke. "You haven't done anything wrong, Mrs. Haywood. It's just that we've been alerted by Security that your husband is in the building. He managed to get by the guards in ER, but not before he shot a bystander.

Oh, Lord. No! No! No! Margaret mentally pounded the wall beside her. *Lord, what am I going to do?*

"As he escaped the ER, he screamed that he was coming to ICU. Now the guards have lost him between here and there, and the entire hospital is on lock-down."

It makes sense, Lord. I just didn't think about it. On TV I said that Jason was in ICU. Me going on TV incited his anger. I gave him everything he needed except a map of the hospital. And now an innocent by-stander has been injured – or did they say the person was dead? Either way, it's because of me. I should have kept my mouth shut.

"Mrs. Haywood?" the Charge Nurse asked. "Are you alright? Would you like to sit down?"

Feeling numb throughout her entire body, Margaret slumped against the wall, desperate for anything that would hold her up.

"Why don't we go back into Jason's room?" his nurse suggested. "Security has ordered us to keep you in here, behind the locked double doors, so let's go talk to that brave little boy some more." Without waiting for an answer, the nurse took Margaret by the elbow and gently guided her back to the chair where she had been earlier.

Margaret sat, but she didn't move or speak. *Lord, I just feel so helpless. How has it all gotten to this point? Will it all end before someone is killed?*

The nurse bent to Margaret's ear and whispered. "Jason can pick up on your tension. Talk to him, but try to be calm. It'll help you both."

As she tried to block the terror she felt, and her concern for the poor person whom Don had shot, Margaret reached deep within herself to find the courage to go on. Then, before she felt she was truly ready, her mouth opened. She talked to her son about his favorite foods and how she would cook them for him as soon as he could eat. When that line of talk wore out, she brought up Christmas again and told him stories from her childhood. Where would he like to go if they took a short vacation after Christmas – just the four of them – Brian, Sally, Mommie and him? And between topics, she encouraged him to open his eyes, although it took everything she had to assure him it was safe to awaken from the protective coma.

Lord, I don't want to lie to this child. He isn't safe if Don's loose in this hospital. Neither am I? The last thing I want is for him to open his eyes and see is his mother being murdered.

Margaret stuffed her fist in her mouth to head off a sob she felt rising from within. *If Don has a gun, this is his worst act of violence so far? How much worse can it get?* For all Margaret knew, it had already gotten to that point. Whoever it was he shot could be dead. She didn't know. *If he's shot someone, he won't hesitate to do it again.*

The entire time she had been talking to Jason, she had been watching the clock on opposite wall, only too aware that the minutes were crawling slowly by. *I'm running out of things to say, Lord. Give me some words.*

Conscious that she might lose it and begin to scream hysterically, Margaret forced herself to concentrate only on her son's face – forget the clock – and she began to remind him of good times from his short childhood. She talked of friends he had at school and at church, and of how anxious they were for him to get well and come home.

When she didn't think she could continue the monologue another minute, the Charge Nurse opened the door. She didn't say anything, but indicated that Margaret should join her in the hall once again.

"I'll be back in just a second, Jason," she promised the boy, and kissed him on the forehead.

The uniformed Director of Security was standing in the hallway.

Something's happened.

"Mrs. Haywood," he began.

"Please, Mr. Woodson," she pleaded, reading his name from his badge, "Something's happened or you wouldn't be here. Don't try to spare me."

"Very well," he agreed, shifting the hat he held from one hand to the other. "We have your husband cornered on the second floor, not far from here. I'm afraid he is refusing to give up, and we have a team of S.W.A.T. officers en route. In fact," he added, consulting his watch, "they should be pulling up at any moment."

"Will they kill my husband?"

The man cleared his throat. "Their goal, Mrs. Haywood, is to remove your husband from this hospital property, so that he is no longer a threat of any kind. They will use every means to take him alive but, ultimately, how they proceed will depend entirely on how he cooperates."

Then he's a dead man, because he's so drunk with rage and power, he's not about to surrender. I know Don Haywood too well.

The thought of Don being shot by the armed commando team was more than she could bear, and she again sought the wall for strength. Seeing that she was wavering, the guard offered her his arm and she accepted it.

"Mr. Woodson," she asked after she had regained her balance, "did he shoot someone earlier? That's what I heard."

"Well, yes ma'am, I'm afraid he did. There was a gentleman who entered the ER immediately after he did and for some reason, that provoked your husband. As soon as he caught sight of the man, Mr. Haywood turned and fired without saying a word."

Something was beginning to penetrate Margaret's consciousness and as she added two and two, she felt herself go sick to the pit of her stomach. *No... NO! It couldn't be. That would be too much of a coincidence,* She was about to upchuck, too fearful to even voice the question.

"The man who was shot? Please, you have to tell me his name!"

A spasm of regret passed across the man's face. "I'm sorry, Mrs. Haywood, but HIPAA privacy regulations don't permit me to divulge another patient's identity to you."

"But you have to, Mr. Woodson. You see, my attorney was on his way to join me here. He was the one who called to alert me that my husband had escaped."

"I'm sorry, Mrs. Haywood, I simply cannot...,"

"His name is Jim Deaton," she screamed. "Please tell me the man he shot wasn't named Jim Deaton!"

Hearing her anguished voice, nurses responded from different directions, but the Charge Nurse was the first to reach her side. "Mrs. Haywood, I know you're upset, but I cannot allow you to disturb other patients on this floor."

At that point, Margaret didn't care who was upset, because the expression on Mr. Woodson's face was all the confirmation she needed. Jim was the victim.

It all fits. He saw Jim on the TV broadcast last night, so when Jim walked up at the wrong time, Don knew exactly who he was and took care of him right there. Only why did he have a gun, if he didn't come here intending to kill me? She hugged the wall again. *If he'd had his way, I'd be dead right now and my children would be orphans.*

The thought of what her husband's sinister intent had been frightened her and, at the same time, gave her a backbone she never knew she possessed. "Mr. Woodson, I respect the restriction you must function under, but your face also told me everything I needed to know... except....," She paused and took a deep breath, uncertain if she really wanted the answer. "Is Mr. Deaton dead or alive?"

"I can tell you this much," the guard offered cautiously, "because it will be on the early morning newscasts in just a few minutes anyway. "The victim, **whose name has not been released, pending notification of next of kin,** is in surgery at this hour at a nearby hospital. He sustained two gunshot wounds to the lower abdomen and is in critical condition. Doctors have not issued a prognosis at this time."

Two gunshot wounds. Critical condition. Margaret didn't care that her information came in the form of a news memo. As grateful as she was that Jim had survived the shooting, there was still no assurance that his wounds wouldn't ultimately prove fatal.

"What will happen to my husband?"

The security chief hesitated.

"What will happen to my husband, Mr. Woodson? I have to know."

"As I told you earlier, the S.W.A.T. team's goal is to take him alive. Provided they are successful, he will be placed under arrest and taken to the county jail. He'll be held there under assault with a deadly weapon charge and attempted murder. Those charges could be upgraded to murder should Mr. Deat...should the man he shot not survive."

"So once he's in police custody, I can breathe easy. He won't be a threat to either me or my children?"

"Mrs. Haywood, from what little I know, your husband is apt to be locked up for a long time. No ma'am, you're in no danger for several years, once he's...,"

The walkie-talkie strapped to his belt belched a coded call, and the security chief turned in mid-sentence. "You'll have to excuse me," he called over his shoulder. "I'm needed."

With that, the uniformed man left the ICU unit at a rapid walk, leaving everyone aware that something was happening. Only no one knew any details.

Margaret, assisted by the Charge Nurse, returned to Jason's room, when she was too spent to try and keep up the façade of conversation any longer. Instead, she sat by his bed, holding his small hand in hers, squeezing and stroking, but saying nothing. Periodically, she would feel the tiniest response from him, and the hope it provided made those dark moments bearable.

Lord, I'm so weary. You already know the needs I'm too exhausted to voice. Hold me, Father. Keep me. And protect Don if it is Your will.

She wasn't sure how long she sat there before the Charge

Nurse came to the door and motioned her back into the hallway. She was surprised to note as she rose wearily from the chair that sunlight was peeping through the blinds. *It's later than I thought.*

Once in the hall, she found herself face to face with not only Mr. Woodson, but Ann McCallum as well. *Well of course they would call the hospital administrator in a situation like this.*

"Mrs. Haywood," the administrator offered her hand. "I'm so sorry you've had to endure this ordeal."

"Thank you, Ms. McCallum." She didn't beat around the bush. "I assume you have news, or neither of you would be here right now. Whatever it is, I can take it. The not knowing is worse than anything you might tell me."

It was the security chief who answered. "Your husband has been apprehended," ma'am. It was a struggle, but the team was able to take him without firing a shot."

"Then he's alive?"

"Alive. Rabid with anger, spewing venom, and on his way to the big county lock-up downtown."

Margaret put out her hand and touched each of them. "Thank you so much for all you've done, but most of all for understanding. All I can do is apologize."

"None of this is your fault, Mrs. Haywood. So don't you even think about taking the blame for your husband's action," Ms. McCallum dictated. "He's big enough to answer for his own shortcomings."

"And that answer is going to be a doozey," the chief opined. "It'll take a notebook to hold all the charges they'll lay against him before it's over.

I hurt for you, Don. But it's not like people didn't try to steer you in a different direction.

"Well, those charges are his problem," she said to the two

of them. "I have children to worry about... children who may at this moment be hearing on the early morning news that their father has been arrested. I'd better go and call them right now."

"I couldn't agree more," Ms. McCallum said. "I'll let you get to that unpleasant task, but if you need me or my office for anything, my door is always open to you."

Margaret expressed her thanks, and was about to go to the lobby so that she could call out of earshot of Jason, when they all heard what sounded like a new-born puppy. "Mom... Mom...mie? Where... am... I?"

Jason!

Margaret turned in mid-step and raced back into her son's room, where she found the weak little fellow blinking his eyes, looking around as if he didn't know where he was. Or why. Close on her heels were Mr. Woodson and Ms. McCallum, along with Jason's nurse and the Charge Nurse."

"Oh, Jason," Margaret squealed, as she bent to kiss him and stroke his hair.

"Mom-mie?"

"Yes, darling, it's Mommie. I'm right here."

"Mrs. Haywood," the nurse interrupted, "I hate to spoil this moment, but we need to check his vitals right now."

"Of course." She bent back down to her son. "You're in a hospital, Jason. But you're OK. These nurses have been taking very good care of you and they need to check you right now. Don't worry. I'll be right back. I promise."

I hate to leave him right at this moment, but I've got to call the folks before Brian and Sally learn this news in the worst sort of way.

"Don't... leave... me?"

His weakened voice tore at Margaret's heart, but she knew she had to care for all her children.

"I'm just going out in the hall while this pretty nurse takes your temperature and checks you out. I'll be back in just a moment."

The administrator leaned around Margaret and said, "Jason. My name's 'Miss Ann.' Will you be my friend and let me stay with you for just a minute or two, while your Mommie takes care of a little errand?"

Jason looked at her through eyes Margaret saw were weak and sunk back into his little face. "I... guess...," he said at last.

Ms. McCallum moved over and took his limp right hand and flashed Margaret a look that clearly said, "Go. I'll be here and he'll be OK 'til you return."

She and the security chief left the little cubicle and Margaret apologized over her shoulder for running off and leaving him as she dashed down the hall. Once in the waiting room, she dug her cell phone from her slacks pocket and dialed her parents' number. Her dad answered on the fourth ring.

"Dad!"

"Margaret. Is something wrong? Nothing's happened to Jason?"

"It's not Jason, Dad. Do you have the TV on this morning?"

"No. Should we?"

"NO!"

"Margaret?"

"I'm sorry, Dad. Listen, but don't let on to anyone else, not even Mama, that something has happened. I'll fill you in." She related how Don had escaped the night before, how her parents' house had been under guard all night, and the conclusion of the story, including how Don had been arrested for, among other things, shooting Jim Deaton."

"What next?" was her father's only comment.

"But Dad, I've got some good news, too." She couldn't wait and the words tumbled over each other as she told him that Jason had just awakened a few minutes earlier.

"That is good news. I wish the other situation had turned out differently."

"I do, too, Dad."

"So what about Brian and Sally? How do you want to handle this? Do you want me to tell them?"

Margaret, who had pondered that very question as she was dialing the phone, was suddenly struck with inspiration. "Dad. Don't say one word to them about Don. And don't send them to school today, either."

"Don't send them to school?"

"If they haven't heard the news now, they will before they even get on campus. Nope," she said, making a snap judgment, "I want them brought here. They can see Jason and then I'll tell them myself."

"It's probably best that way," he agreed. "Want me to put them on the phone?" Without waiting for her answer, Margaret heard him calling, "Kids... each one of you get on a phone. Your Mom's calling and she's got some good news."

In a matter of seconds she heard two clicks and the sounds of two children. "Mom? Mommie?"

"Hey, kids," she said. "Guess what? Jason is awake? He woke up a few minutes ago. So how would you like to skip school today and come to Atlanta to visit him? I think it would make him feel better."

"You mean you want us to miss school?" Sally queried.

"This is a special occasion and that's exactly what I mean. Dad, are you still on the line?"

"I am."

"Can you and Mama drive them down? I figure Jason would like to see you both as well."

"You know we can. We'll be there in about an hour and a half."

"OK. See you when you get here. And Dad, drive safe. Don't you be listening to the radio and forget where you're going."

"Don't worry," he assured her. "My radio's not playing. I think a fuse is blown. I'll have to take it by the shop after we get back.

Good. Dad understood my code.

"See you when you get here."

Margaret hung up and raced back to Jason's room. *I'm not going to get but one chance to make us a family again, and this time it's definitely going to be a family without Don. He has taken that option away from us.*

When she re-entered the little room, Jason's eyes shown more brightly when he glimpsed his mother. Margaret thanked Ms. McCallum and sat down beside her son's bed."

As the administrator was leaving, she said, "By the way, the gentleman who was injured during the night is out of surgery and is going to be fine, after a few weeks of recovery." She smiled at Margaret. "Mr. Woodson told me you were concerned."

Thank you, Lord. Jim didn't deserve that, but because he was aligned with me, he automatically became Don's enemy.

A weak voice from the bed interrupted her thanksgiving, but without hesitation she turned her attention to the small boy who needed her most right then.

"Why am I here, Mommie?"

"Do you remember getting hurt?"

"No. I don't think I do. What happened?"

Thank goodness he doesn't recall Don's violence. At least not yet. But he is going to need professional help to deal with all this. I'll not have this child ruined for life because of Don's need to be in control.

Margaret was relieved to hear Jason sounding stronger already. "Tell you what," she suggested, "let's get you well and then we'll talk about it. Right now, you just need to concentrate on getting better."

"I will, Mommie. I just want to get well and go home."

Don't we all, son, don't we all?

CHAPTER FIFTEEN

When Dr. Lowman came around a few minutes later, her face was beaming. "I hear we've got a patient who's awake and talking."

"Not just awake and talking, but making sense, if you understand what I mean?"

I don't want Jason to find out that he might have brain damage.

"Well introduce me to this young man. I'm anxious to meet him."

Margaret moved aside to let the doctor step up beside the bed. She could tell by Jason's face that he didn't recognize the doctor. "This is Dr. Lowman, Jason. She's been taking very good care of you since you got hurt."

During the few minutes prior to the doctor's appearance, Margaret had noticed Jason feeling around and finally fingering the bandage that wound around his head. She could tell by his expression he didn't know what to make of it all, but decided to wait and let him ask. *I'll answer everything as honestly as I can, but only as he wants to know.*

"I'm very pleased to meet you, Jason. So how are you feeling this morning?"

Jason looked at her, his eyes wide, and asked, "Why do I have this wrapped around my head?"

The doctor grinned. "What's the matter? Don't you like the cap we made you?"

"I don't know," he answered shyly. "I don't know what it looks like."

"Well we can solve that problem." Her eyes searched the room until they stopped at a wardrobe door next to the sink in the corner. "Mrs. Haywood. Please look in that closet and see if there isn't a hand mirror on the shelf."

Margaret found the requested item and handed it across to the doctor, who held it in front of Jason. "Well, what'd you think?"

"My head feels kind of sore," the boy said. "Is it hurt? Is that why I've got a cap on?"

"That's exactly why," the doctor explained. "But you won't have to wear it but a few more days if you don't like it."

Jason reached for the mirror and admired himself from different angles. "I guess it's OK. I've never had a cap like this before. Have I, Mommie?"

"No... no, you haven't had one like that." *And you won't ever have one again if I have anything to say about it.*

"Tell you what, Jason," the doctor suggested. "I'd like to play a couple of different games with you. Do you mind?"

"I like games, but I don't know if I feel like sitting up." For the first time, he appeared to notice the IV line in his left wrist. "What's this for?"

"We've been putting medicine into your body through that tube to help your head get better. And you don't have to sit up to play this game. It's the perfect game for laying down."

"OK. I think... I think I'd like to play."

"Good. Have you ever played Simon Says?"

"Sure. Is that what we're going to play?"

"It's kind of like Simon Says." She explained she would stand so that Jason couldn't see what her hands were doing. "Sometimes I'm going to touch your feet and legs and sometimes I won't. Whenever I ask 'Now?' I want you to tell me if I really touched you or not."

For the next several minutes, the doctor performed her examination, periodically asking "now?" and being rewarded with answers of "yes" or "no" from the boy in the bed.

If the doctor's expression is any gauge, he's answering correctly.

When she finished, she said to the patient, "You did very well with that game. I couldn't fool you." Then she put her hands to her mouth in an expression of surprise, "I'll bet you can see with your feet and legs. That's why I couldn't trick you!"

Jason giggled.

Oh, Lord, that's music to my ears.

"That's silly," he said, "eyes are in your head, not in your feet and legs."

"Well then maybe I'd better look at those eyes in your head. Maybe you have very special eyes that let you see right through me."

Jason giggled again, but when she produced a penlight from her pocket, he obligingly let her peer intently into each eye, as he followed her requests to "look toward Mommie... look over my shoulder... look at your toes."

"Yessir, Mr. Jason. I'd say those are very special eyes in-deed. Do you know why?"

Jason started to shake his head from side to side, but quickly stopped as he cried "ouch" and his hand went to his head.

"Did that hurt?" the doctor asked.

"Uh-huh...," A guilty look crossed his face. "I mean, yes, ma'am."

"Not to worry," the doctor promised as she brushed the hair off his forehead, "your head is going to be sore for a few more days, so go easy on the head movements. OK?"

"OK," he said with a grin.

"Now, Jason, I have a very important question for you." The doctor looked like she was keeping a deep dark secret that she really wanted to share. "Are you by any chance hungry? Would you like something to eat?"

Margaret was astounded at the look that crossed his face. *It's almost like he just discovered food.*

"Yes ma'am, I am hungry. In fact," he said as he rubbed his stomach, "I'm starving."

She winked at him. "I just thought you might be." She con-sulted her watch. "If they don't have a breakfast tray up here in the next five minutes, I'll go downstairs and cook something for you myself."

"What's for breakfast, Mommie?"

"I don't have a clue, Jason. I'm not cooking this morning."

"Oh... that's right. We're spending the night at our house with Dad. He'll be cooking breakfast."

Margaret and the doctor exchanged glances, but neither said anything.

"You know what, Mommie? You cook better than Dad. He

burns everything."

Ordinarily I'd find that humorous. But not now."

"That's right. We spent the weekend with Dad while you were in the hospital." He was quiet for a few minutes and Margaret held her breath. "Mommie?"

"Yes, son?" Margaret dreaded to hear the next question.

"Where are Brian and Sally? Did they get hurt? Are they in the hospital, too?"

How do I answer him? And how much do I tell him."

"No," she said finally. "You're the only one who got hurt, but Brian and Sally, and Grammy and Grandee, too, will be here in just a little while to see you."

The door opened and a nurse walked in with a covered tray. "Here's your breakfast, Jason. Made especially for you."

The arrival of food cut short a discussion of what had transpired that fateful night, and of who was where, much to Margaret's relief. "Here you go, son. Let's see what you've got."

She lifted the lid as Jason exclaimed "Wow."

"Wow is right. Look at all this."

The two of them looked on a platter piled with silver dollar pancakes, bacon, eggs, grits and a cup of fresh fruit.

"That looks good enough to eat," she told her son.

"It sure does. I just don't know where to start first."

Anywhere you want, son. Anywhere you want.

"Why not let me pour some of this good syrup over your pancakes? You can start with them and take bits of egg and bacon as you want them. And, look," she said as she ripped the cover from a small beverage container, "chocolate milk. Your favorite."

Let's raise you up in the bed," the doctor said, and she began to hit buttons until Jason was in a sitting position. "Does your head hurt if you sit up?"

"It's a little sore, but it doesn't hurt." He looked at the two of them, as if he feared he had given the wrong answer. "But it's OK."

"Sure it's OK," the doctor agreed. "But we'll probably need to lay you back down a little after you finish eating. Deal?"

"Deal" he mumbled between a bite of pancake he had already speared.

"I was going to ask if you wanted me to feed you," his mother said. "But I guess there's no need."

There was no answer from the bed, save for the sound of a little boy making progress through a plate of pancakes and trimmings.

"Jason?" Dr. Lowman asked, "Do you mind if your Mommie steps out in the hall with me. Just for a minute. Then she'll be right back."

The boy never looked up, but kept on eating. "OK."

Margaret, unable to stop the tears that had sprung to her eyes unbidden, followed the doctor into the hallway.

"How can I ever thank you?" she blubbered to the young doctor. "He's awake and seems so normal."

The doctor smiled. "You did as much as I did. You never gave up hope, you never gave up talking to him. I'm convinced that you talked his body out of going deeper into the coma. And he is in remarkably good condition, considering."

"You sound worried. Is there something you aren't telling me? Did you discover something during the exam?"

The doctor held her up her hand, palm up, stop sign fashion. "Jason really is in good shape. However, he's obviously having some memory problems, although it was obvious in there that he is slowly remembering tidbits."

"Is that bad?"

"Over all, it's good. It's very good. The question becomes this: will the attack be something that comes back to him at some point down the road, or is the trauma of it so great that his mind has effectively blocked him from remembering it?"

"Which is worse?"

"Neither and both." The doctor led Margaret to a vacant bench nearby. "Sit, and let's talk a few minutes."

The doctor explained that some form of amnesia was very common following head injuries. She believed most of Jason's memory loss would be temporary. Her concern was that either the memory of how his father abused him might surface at the most inopportune time. "Specifically a time when you wouldn't be with him."

"And what if he never remembers it?"

"Repression of that memory will always handicap him, and because it's in his subconscious, he'll never understand why."

Margaret could envision both scenarios. In the first, he'd be at school and something would trigger that recall and he would be terrified. What's worse, his classmates, probably not even his teacher, would understand what was happening. As far as the second possibility, she knew adults who had never been successful. *Could some of them be handicapped by things that happened in their childhood and not know what it is or how to fix it?* The very thought of Jason in that situation made her insides ache.

"I fully intend to get psychological counseling for him, as soon as you give the word. I just don't quite know how to go about it."

"I'm glad you're still in agreement. We'll want to move on that pretty quickly." The doctor looked at Margaret with troubled eyes. "But if I may say so, Mrs. Haywood, I would suggest that all three of your children, not to mention yourself, could benefit from

some sessions with a counselor. After all, each of you either suffered abuse at the hands of your husband, or you witnessed it happening. Sometimes it's more painful to be the bystander than it is
to be the victim."

*I'm not against all of us going into counseling. I just hadn't thought
about it for anyone but Jason.*

"But, we can cross that bridge tomorrow. Today, we need
to celebrate the big bridge Jason crossed this morning. We're going to keep him here in ICU until shortly after lunch, then, if he's
still responding the way he is now, we'll move him to a room on
the floor."

"Oh, that sounds so wonderful!"

"But let's talk about a few things. Did I understand you to
say that his siblings and his grandparents will be here later this
morning?"

*I'm so overjoyed about Jason's improvement, I'd almost forgotten
about that. I've still got to tell Brian and Sally about their dad.*

She explained. "I wanted the other children to hear about
the situation with their dad during the night from me, not from
the news media or their friends at school. So I asked my parents
to drive them down this morning. Should I not have done that?"

"No... no, that's not a problem. In fact, it will probably cheer
Jason considerably to see them. But there are a few ground rules
which everyone needs to abide, and they're all for Jason's benefit."

"Go on."

"First, no one is to ask him about how he got hurt or try to
probe his mind for memories. If he asks, that's one thing. But no
questioning, no matter how gently it's done. While I agree that
you must tell the other children what happened here last night,
and I commend you for recognizing that, Jason cannot know anything about it. At this time," she concluded with emphasis on the

last three words.

"All things in good time."

"Exactly. Now get back in there and be with your son. He is precious and we've all fallen in love with him. Only now we get to meet him all over again as a real person."

She had barely gotten back into Jason's room, when her cell phone rang. It was P.C. Margaret glanced at her son, still eating heartily, and said, "This is P.C. I'm going up to the lobby where the signal's stronger."

"Uh huh," was the only answer she received.

Taking that to mean approval, she left the room and answered the phone as soon as she got around the corner.

"Margaret! Why didn't you call me? I can't believe that even Don was crazy enough to try and hold a hospital hostage. And now he's locked up in Atlanta."

"Good news first," she crowed in response. "Jason's awake. And talking and making sense. And, P.C., he's eating like there is no tomorrow."

"I'll bet his stomach feels like there was no yesterday," she chuckled. "Now back to Don. Why didn't you call me?"

Why didn't I call her? Last night is all a big, faint blur. I couldn't swear to anything that happened.

"To be honest, P.C., it came up so suddenly until I was involved before I knew what was happening." She related how she had gone back to visit Jason and then became a prisoner in the ICU because Don was loose in the hospital. "I just didn't think. I guess I was numb and in some ways, I still am. Just like when they told me about Jim...!"

Does she know about Jim? I've got to find out more on his condition. But how, I don't even know which hospital he's in?

"We would have come right on...,"

"I know you would," Margaret interrupted. "P.C. Do you and Joe know about Jim?"

"Jim? Jim Deaton? If we know anything Joe hasn't mentioned it. Why?"

"Don shot him."

"Don did WHAT?"

"Jim was coming here to stay with me, and they both happened up at the ER at the same time. Don saw him first and shot him twice in the stomach."

"Oh no! Did he... is he?"

"He didn't die. Unless he's died in the last hour or so. But I don't even know which hospital or anything about how he is doing."

"Atlanta news indicated he'd shot someone, but they weren't releasing the name until next of kin were notified."

"It was Jim," Margaret offered sadly. "And as for next of kin, the only family he's ever mentioned to us is his father."

"Who could care less," P.C. agreed. "Well, anyway, Joe and I are leaving here in a few minutes to drive down. Do you want us to pick up the kids? Do you need anything from your parents?"

The kids!

"P.C., I've got to run. I almost forgot. I didn't want the kids to hear the news about Don from TV, so I asked Mama and Daddy to bring them down. I'll bet they're out in the waiting room right now, wondering where I am."

"See you in a little while."

Margaret was already dashing for the door before she heard P.C.'s last words. Sure enough, as she rounded the corner, there the four of them sat. Waiting, and looking worried.

When Harold Maxwell saw her, he came running on his long, old legs, to hug her. "You scared me, when we couldn't find you."

"Sorry, Dad. I was back in Jason's room and, to be honest with you, I had so many interruptions between there and here, I totally forgot you were coming."

"Just as long as you're OK. That's all that matters.

"I'm very much OK, Dad. And I'm going to get better."

Her children had surrounded them, waiting their turn for a hug. Only Mama, Margaret noted, didn't bother to get up. *Poor Mama. She simply cannot accept that the man she "adopted" for a son would be capable of all he's done. I would hope she'd have the same stubborn attitude about my actions, but either way, this latest news is going to hit her hard.*

"Can we see Jason?" Sally clamored. "I wanna see Jason."

"I know you do, sweetie. And as soon as I can talk to the nurse, we'll get you back there to see him. But first, I'd like to walk for a few minutes. I'm tired of sitting."

She led the four of them down the hallway leading away from ICU, although Harold Maxwell had to insist that Ruby walk with them. She finally came, but not very willingly, Margaret noted.

She didn't really know where she was going, but when she spotted a directional sign pointing the way to the hospital's interfaith chapel, she knew that was where they should talk.

"Why are we going in there?" Brian asked when they rounded the last corner and Margaret indicated the chapel entrance. He looked suspiciously at her. "You're not going to tell us bad news about Jason, are you Mom?"

Might have known I couldn't fool him long. Guess I'll have to come clean.

The rest of her family stood in a group, saying nothing, but looking at her, clearly waiting for her answer to Brian's question.

"You're partially right, Brian. There is something we need to talk about, and I wanted some place quiet and away from the crowd." *Plus I need all the help I can get, Lord.* "But it's not about Jason, at least nothing bad. He's doing wonderfully, and you all will get to visit him shortly. There are a couple of suggestions the doctor has made to keep from overwhelming him, and we'll talk about those, too.

The family continued to stand in the hall way and she had to encourage them to follow her into the chapel where they were finally all seated around each other.

If I tell them about Don first, they'll never hear the instructions about Jason. So I'll begin with the doctor's instructions.

Margaret gave them an account of how and when Jason awoke, how he seemed to be feeling and reacting.

"Well if the child can eat like you say he did his breakfast, he's on the mend," Ruby Maxwell volunteered.

"Thank God," Margaret's father whispered.

"I do thank God," she answered, "and yes, for the most part he is on the mend. However, there are some things you need to know before you talk with him." She continued to explain about Jason's amnesia and the doctor's wishes that he not be bombarded with questions. "It's better that he remembers things on his own, as his brain recovers."

Brian started to say something, but Margaret held up her hand. "I do plan to be totally truthful with Jason. As he remembers and asks questions, we will answer honestly. But we're not going to force him to remember or confront those memories until he is ready."

"OK," Mommie. "We won't ask any questions." Sally had finally joined the conversation.

Why is Sally so reticent this morning? Usually she's like a verbal bull in a china shop.

"There's one other thing you need to know about Jason." She looked at her entire family. "As soon as the doctor says he's ready, I'm going to be taking him to see a psychological counselor to help him cope with all that's happened."

"You think that's the right thing to do, Margaret?" Ruby Maxwell's mouth was curled in an expression of distaste even as she spoke the words.

"I most certainly do think it's the best thing to do. In fact," she said, looking her mother squarely in the face, "I'm going to be going myself as well." Then she deliberately looked at her other two children. "And I hope Brian and Sally will agree to go as well, so we can all help Jason recover by seeing that his entire family is behind him." *And after I drop this next bombshell, I hope you'll all see the need.*

"Well no one in our family has ever had to get psychiatric help," her mother muttered. "God was good enough for any problems we had."

"God is good enough, Mama. And He's providing us this opportunity out of His goodness." *I'm not going to fight with you today.*

Harold Maxwell, evidently reading his daughter's thoughts, said, "Ruby, if this is what Margaret thinks they need, then I'm standing behind her. This isn't our place to say."

"Might've known you'd be on her side. Lately you don't care what I think."

Ignore it, Dad. Ignore that cutting tone of voice. She just wants you to mix it up with her.

Margaret grabbed the floor again, knowing that she was fighting a battle of wits with her mother. "But before we go see Jason, there's one other piece of news I need to tell you about."

She took a deep breath... *Help me, Lord...* looked at each child directly, and said, "I have to share something with you about your dad, and I'm afraid it's not good news."

She was watching for their reactions and saw the color drain out of Brian's face, while Sally expression was one of dread and curiosity.

"Is... is Dad OK?"

Honesty is the ONLY policy. "There's no easy way to tell you. I'm going to ask you not to interrupt me. But I promise I'll answer any questions you have once I'm through."

"So spill it, Mom. Let's get it over with." She could see the lines of suspicion on her eldest son's face.

Margaret began by telling then that their dad had managed to escape from the hometown jail the night before. She recounted the events that had unfolded at the hospital during the pre-dawn hours, including how he had shot Jim Deaton and details on how the S.W.A.T. had finally taken him prisoner."

Both children had expressions of shocked disbelief on their faces.

"Right now your dad is in the local county jail here in Atlanta, and while he'll still have to answer charges at home, right now he's Atlanta's prisoner."

"The man was pushed to it. Seeing his wife on television airing their dirty laundry and making him look like an animal." Ruby Maxwell wasn't holding back on how she felt.

"Mama!" Harold Maxwell's voice had a hard edge to it. "This is none of your business. Mine, neither. So we're going to keep our opinions to ourselves. All of them. Do I make myself clear?"

"But, Harold, you know...,"

"Not one word, Mama. Not one single word. We're going

to be here for Margaret and these three precious children, but we're not going to say one single, solitary word. Period."

Her mother didn't respond except to pooch out her lower lip, Margaret noted.

"I don't know what comes next for your dad, but I do know what comes next for us. For starters, we're going to...,"

"How is Mr. Deaton?" Brian interrupted. "Is he going to live?"

Margaret smiled. Her son's unspoken question was "Will Dad get the death penalty?"

"Jim... Mr. Deaton is recovering from surgery. You dad shot him twice in the stomach. From what I understand he'll make a full recovery but it may take a few weeks."

"I'm so glad," Brian whispered more to himself than anyone.

"As I was saying, we're all going to have to pull together. We've got to make sure that Jason gets well, and the best way we can do that is if the four of us..." she looked at her parents..."really the six of us, pull together and make a new life for ourselves."

"You mean, without Dad?" Sally asked. Her voice trembled as she spoke.

"I'm afraid so, sweetie. Look, you two, I'm not going to sugarcoat this, because we're all going to have to deal with this back in Carter's Crossroads. Between his attack on me, the way he abused Jason, and now this assault on Jim Deaton, there is no way in this world your dad can escape serving some prison time."

"Daddy in prison?" Sally gasped. "But he didn't mean to hurt anyone. He told me so."

"Sometimes when we make poor decisions, those decisions come back home to us in the form of consequences. That's where your dad is right now. And he will have to pay a price for those decisions and the actions he took." She gazed at each of them with what she hoped was a genuinely loving expression. "I wish I could tell you otherwise, but I can't. All of this is out of our hands now. And he's the one who is responsible."

No one spoke for a few minutes, then Brian asked, "Mom? If we're honest, we all know that for a long time Dad has been getting more and more violent. But why? Was it something we did?"

Oh, son... how wonderful it is to hear you acknowledge the truth. I know that had to hurt.

"I don't have all the answers, but I do think I can fill in a few of the blanks."

Sally hadn't picked up Brian's line of conversation, but she and Brian were both looking at their mother with expressions of pleading and curiosity.

"Your dad is an abuser. Now that I can look back, I see small signs of his controlling behavior even before we married. But I was too much in love with him at the time to see any faults, most certainly none as major as what we're talking about here."

"You mean Dad didn't really love you?"

"No... he loved me. But for some reason, his self-esteem was so low, he had to be in control so he could feel good about himself."

"But everyone in town loves Dad. He enjoyed meeting people and doing things for them." Brian was clearly confused.

Margaret hesitated then, knowing what she had to do, she plunged ahead. "That's exactly what I'm talking about. Your dad had to have money. People with money can call the shots. He was so generous because that way people would tell him how great he was, and he could deny to himself, at least for a little while, that he was a nobody."

"But he wasn't a nobody," Sally protested. "He was our daddy."

"That's not what Mom means, exactly," Brian explained to his little sister.

Lord, I'm amazed at how tender he was with her just now.

"When Mom says he was a nobody, she means *he* thought he was a nobody. So if he was generous and made everybody tell him how great he was, at least for a little while, he didn't feel like a nobody."

"This sounds cruel, Sally, but what your dad was really doing with his money was buying friends. And those kinds of friends aren't genuine. But they were the..."

"Mom?" Brian interrupted, "why did Dad think so little of himself? He was a really fun guy when he wasn't angry."

Thank God, Brian, that you can see there was a good side to him. I'm glad you'll have those memories.

"You're right, son. When things were good with your dad, we all had fun. But you'll have to agree, won't you, that when things were bad, we all suffered?"

Brian nodded his head in agreement. "But things just got worse. Even though we tried harder not to upset him, it was almost like he wanted to get mad." The young man shook his head in confusion.

Margaret knew she had to give him some relief for the torment he was feeling, and the only way to do that was with straight answers. "Listen, kids. I'm not trying to trash your dad. You love him, and you should never stop loving him. But I'm going to try and answer your questions as honestly as I can."

"But Margaret, you shouldn't...," Ruby Maxwell began.

Harold Maxwell put his hand on his wife's arm. "I thought we weren't going to interfere. Besides, I'm interested to hear what she has to say. I have to admit," he rubbed his chin, "I've asked myself the same questions since all this started." He looked around at the group and cracked a sheepish grin. "So far I haven't come up with any answers.

Ruby huffed, but said nothing.

Her face is saying everything her mouth isn't. How much more do you have to hear, Mama? I'm not asking you to stop caring for Don, but no one is as innocent as you make him out to be.

"Here's how I see it," she began. "First, abusers resort to violence because they must be in control, or in their minds, they're nothing. A nobody. Violence scares those around them, so they move out of the way and let the abuser do his thing."

"So then the abuser ought to be satisfied," Brian volunteered.

"You'd think so, wouldn't you?" Margaret agreed. "Only it doesn't work that way. In the first place, the feeling of being in control soon evaporates and the abuser is more frantic than ever to get it back. Also, and this is an important part of the picture, according to Annie Campbell, "every time the abuser succeeds in intimidating someone – usually his spouse or girlfriend..."

"Or his children," Brian volunteered.

"Or his children," Margaret agreed, "the abuser needs that next shot of control even worse than he did before. And, every time an abuser is successful, it empowers him to be more abusive the next time. Do you understand?"

Brian nodded his head, his expression indicative of a light bulb slowly coming on. Sally, on the other hand was still clearly confused.

"Sally, what don't you understand?"

"But... Mommie... Mommie, Daddy always said he was sorry after he got mad. If he wanted to get mad, why did he say he was sorry?"

"I can answer that," Brian answered. "He apologized be-cause he was afraid if he didn't, we would leave and he wouldn't have anyone to control.'

"That's right, Brian. As twisted as it sounds, that's exactly what it was."

"What I don't understand is why Dad was this way in the first place."

"We may never know all the facts, unless he decides to share them. At this stage in his life, I don't know if he would... or even if he could. But I have some ideas." She looked at her chil-dren optimistically. "You know, hindsight is so much better than foresight."

"Huh?" Sally asked, her entire face one giant question mark.

"She means you can look back and see things now that you couldn't see or understand then," Brian volunteered. "You got it now?"

"I... I think so."

"So what's your theory, Mom?"

Margaret explained how all during the time they were dating, their dad hadn't wanted to have anything to do with his parents. "Didn't you kids ever wonder why you only had Grandee and Grammy? Why you didn't have two sets of grandparents like most kids?"

Margaret had to laugh to herself at the amazed look that crossed her son's face.

"Gosh, Mom, you're right. I mean, you know, these two," he jerked his cocked thumb toward Harold and Ruby, "these two were always there for us. I don't guess I ever felt anything funny because we didn't have any other grandparents." Then the light bulb look crossed his face. "Do we have other grandparents?"

"Let me tell you a little story," Margaret said. "It won't explain everything, but I hope it will provide some of the answers.

"You know," Harold Maxwell volunteered, "I always did think it was strange that Don's parents just showed up for your wedding and then left and we never saw them again." He looked at his wife. "You remember, Mama...we tried a couple of times to invite them over, but they never came."

"That's right," Ruby agreed. "So we finally gave up."

"I tried one time to talk to Don about it. You know...early on. That's the only time I ever saw the man angry, but he was spitting bullets when he told me he'd rather not talk about it. So I never pressed it." He looked at his daughter quizzically. "You have anything to add?"

"Yes, I think I do. It's like this." Margaret recalled that during their dating, Don never once took her home to meet his family. "At the time, they lived in a little place called Valley City, a little town up in the northeast corner of the state. About a two hour drive. One of the worst fights we ever had before we got married was when I demanded to meet his family. I mean he'd already given me an engagement ring and I didn't have a clue what his parents looked like, if he had any brothers or sisters or any-thing."

"What happened, Mom?" Brian's face was a study in curi-osity.

"We drove up there for the day, with your dad in a foul mood the entire way. When we got there, it was obvious that he hadn't let them know we were coming. What's more, it was also clear they didn't know anything about me, not even that we were engaged."

"Were they ugly to you, daughter?" Harold Maxwell asked.

"Not so much ugly, Dad, as frigid. It was almost like they

didn't even have a son and we were two strangers who not only had dropped in unannounced, but who were infringing on their privacy."

"They don't sound very much like grandparents," Brian observed. "At least not like Grammy and Grandee here."

"Trust me, Brian, they didn't act much like any in-laws I would have chosen, and I wrestled the entire time we were there about whether I wanted to be a part of their family."

"You did?" Sally questioned. "But if you hadn't married Daddy, you wouldn't have been our Mommie. And I wanted you for my Mommie." The little girl reached her hand over and patted Margaret's hand as she spoke.

"And I wanted you for my little girl, too," she reassured the child. "Nevertheless, the entire time we were there, I had serious doubts. Your Grandmother Haywood made no effort to feed us anything, even though lunch time came and went. She didn't even offer us a glass of water or offer to show me where the bathroom was."

"What was Don doing all this time?" her father asked.

Margaret glanced above them at the modern art sculpture that hung from the ceiling in the little chapel. "I don't understand all that happened that day any more than I understand whatever that is hanging from the ceiling..." she pointed to the odd-shaped cylinder, "but for sure I couldn't wait to get out of there."

"You stayed longer than I would have," her mother said. "I don't stay where I'm not wanted."

"All in all, we were there about four hours. Must have gotten there about eleven o'clock that morning, and it was a little after two-thirty when we left. I was totally bewildered and your dad had steam coming off his head. Both of us were about to starve."

I'm not painting this as bad as it really was, but the kids wouldn't believe it if I did.

"We got in the car and I started to ask multiple questions. Your dad held up his hand and said, 'All I ask is that you give me a chance to find us some food, and then I'll do my best to explain.'"

"And did he?" Brian asked.

"About twenty minutes down the road, he found a nice-looking restaurant and we went in and got a table. After we'd given our order, he said, 'I didn't want you to ever have to endure that, but you insisted. So I'm going to give you a condensed explanation and then I don't want to talk about my family or why they're the way they are ever again.'"

She paused and still remembered as if it had been just the day before. "The server brought our lunch, but I couldn't tell you now what we ate or if it was good. What I heard made my blood run cold and destroyed any yearning for food. I ate only because my stomach was complaining."

"So what was the story?" Brian was impatient and Margaret understood why he might be. Having not been there, he couldn't begin to appreciate how heavy the tension was at that little café table that afternoon so long ago.

"Basically," Margaret continued, "your grandfather had never wanted children, never wanted the responsibility or the financial burden. But your dad came along anyway. He never forgave your grandmother and never missed an opportunity to remind your dad that he was an intruder."

"What's an intruder, Mommie?" Sally asked.

"Someone who's not wanted," Brian supplied. "Go ahead, Mom."

"Your dad never got spending money. His mother was forced to buy his clothes at yard sales and thrift shops. If your dad reached for a second helping at the dinner table, he was reminded that he should save that so he'd have something to eat the next day."

"That is so cruel," Harold remarked.

"Oh, according to Don, it got worse. He father refused to pay for school supplies, special projects. And on many occasions, according to your dad, he would be beaten so severely he literally couldn't sit down."

"Why?" Sally whispered.

"He said it usually happened when a utility bill would come in higher than your grandfather thought it should be. Or there was an unexpected car repair. He would take his anger out on your dad physically, but emotionally, too. The whole time he was hitting him with whatever the old man could lay his hands on, he was screaming that if it weren't for Don, the utility bill would be lower or there would be extra money for the car repair bill."

"Were they that poor, Margaret?" her dad asked. "They didn't look it the one time we saw them."

"They weren't poor at all. In fact, they had a beautiful home, very tastefully decorated. And the two cars in the driveway were some of the most expensive you could buy. Mr. Haywood was self-employed, but I don't guess I ever knew what his work was. If I did, I've forgotten."

"Then why did he act that way?" Brian asked. "I mean, if they weren't poor?"

"For whatever reason, your grandfather was a bitter man, determined to make your dad pay for that bitterness. It seems that once when your dad had an accident in the house that did minor damage, his dad hit the roof. He informed Don that he would pay to have it fixed. Only your dad had no source of income and his father knew that. His solution was that each night at mealtime, when your dad had filled his plate, his father would reach for it, before he had ever taken a bite. Your dad said he'd hold the plate up and make your grandmother tell him how much the food was worth. Then he'd cut that figure in half and tell your dad he could go to bed hungry and the value of his food would be applied to his debt. He would sit there and calmly eat the food on your father's plate before touching what was on his own plate. Just a different version of sending a child to bed without his supper. I'm sure your dad never told me the whole story.

The only other time I ever saw them was at our wedding. Remember, Dad. They refused to march in the processional as they should have, but slipped in behind everyone else and sat on the back pew."

"I knew then they weren't our kind of people," Ruby affirmed.

"As soon as the minister pronounced us married, they got up and left before your dad and I even had time to walk back up the aisle. And they didn't come to the reception."

"You never saw them again? Really? That sounds weird," Brian said.

"Haven't seen them ever again, to this day."

"Did you ever ask Daddy about his parents?" Sally asked.

"The few times I did, he'd remind me of the conversation in the restaurant that afternoon. He had no intention of talking further about them. When you were born," she jerked her thumb in Brian's direction, I mailed them a birth announcement. After all," she justified, "your dad was an only child. You would have been their first grandchild."

"What did they say?"

"The announcement was returned by the post office

marked 'Moved Left No Forwarding Address. When I showed it to your dad, he said he already knew. Said they'd moved about a year before, which would have been near the end of the first year of our marriage."

"So did you send it to the new address?"

"Your dad said he didn't know where they were and that was the way he wanted it. I don't honestly know if he knew where they lived, but if he did, he didn't choose to tell me. I don't even know if either of them are still living."

"That's deep, Mom," Brian offered.

"You're right, son. I always held out hope that if Mr. Haywood died first, your grandmother might reach out for your dad, and her grandchildren. If they've ever been in contact, your dad didn't tell me."

"But, Mommie," Sally interrupted. "If Daddy was treated so bad by his daddy, why was he so mean to us? Why did he hurt you and me, and why did he throw Jason against the wall? I don't understand."

"It does look like that someone who was abused wouldn't make sure they didn't do that when they got grown. Annie Campbell says she's certain your dad promised himself over and over that when he grew up, when he got out of there, he would never treat his family the way his dad treated him."

"So why didn't he?" Sally asked again.

"Because children pattern themselves after what they see and do while they're growing up. In spite of their best intentions, unless there is some kind of intervention, the abused child will usually be an adult abuser when they're grown."

"Mommie?" Sally pulled on her sleeve. "What's intervention? Does it hurt?"

Margaret pulled the little girl over to her. *For one so young, you're having to deal with so much adult information right now.* "Intervention is where a professional person, like the psychological counselor Jason and I are going to see, works with you to get all those bad memories out of your head so you can be a better grown-up. And, no, it doesn't hurt. Understand?"

The little girl nodded her head, but Margaret didn't know what that meant exactly.

"And that's why you want Sally and me to go too, Mom? Because you think we might grow up to be abusers?"

I've got to handle this very carefully. "I just want all my children to be the best they can be, and that can't happen if they're carrying around lots of bad memories and anger from childhood. The counseling won't hurt you and it could help you."

"I see..." was all Brian said.

"Don had it pretty hard, that's clear to see," Harold Maxwell offered. "Still and all, it doesn't excuse him from all he's done to hurt the people I love most."

"No, Dad, it doesn't excuse him. But it's not for us to judge him. He's going to be judged plenty in the very near future. I don't welcome it for him and I sure don't welcome it for us."

"What do you mean, Mom?"

"Think about it, Brian. Think of how much notoriety we got as a family after he abused Jason. Now that he's shot a man in an Atlanta hospital and then taken armed refuge in that same hospital before law enforcement could capture him, we will all be on the news big time."

Other individuals were coming to the chapel doorway, and seeing the Haywood group already there, were leaving without entering. *There are others in this hospital with more pressing needs than mine, Lord. I need to get out of here and let them have access to Your love and grace.*

"Do you all realize we've been in here almost an hour? Others need this space, and I know Jason is chomping at the bit to know where I am," Margaret explained to her family.

It was a silent, mostly somber group that departed the chapel. *Lord, I didn't mean to rain on everyone's parade, but these were things that had to be discussed.* "We'll talk about this further later today," she promised the kids. "Let me go see how your brother is."

Jason was ready to get out of bed and play. His nurse had her hands full trying to contain his enthusiasm. She looked at Margaret with a "what'd you do?" expression and said, "Someone needs to ask Dr. Lowman if this child is truly sick. You sure couldn't prove it by me."

"Hey, Mommie," the little boy screamed when he saw his mother in the doorway. "Where have you been?"

"Hey yourself, sweetie," she said. "You're not giving this nice nurse a hard time are you?"

"No ma'am. I'm just playing. When can I go home?"

"Home? Jason," she said as she fingered the wisps of hair peeking out from under the edge of the bandage that wrapped his head, "you've been a very sick little boy and you just woke up this morning. I think it's a little soon to talk about going home."

He grinned at her in a way that always made her go to mush inside. "But I feel fine. 'Cept my head still hurts a little. But only when I move it too much."

"Which is why you're going to have to stay in the hospital a few more days. But tell you what...?" She grinned at the crestfallen little boy. "Tonight, when we see Dr. Lowman, we'll ask her when she thinks you'll be well enough to go home. OK?" Then, waving her one good arm like an emcee, she said, "But if Jason can't go home, how about if I can bring home – or at least most of it – right here to Jason?"

"It still won't be as good as going home," he persisted. As if to emphasize his position, he ran his lower lip out in a pout similarly like the one he'd had on his face the first time Margaret got to look at him.

"Maybe not," she told him, emphasized with a no-nonsense look, "but it's the best deal you're gonna get here today. Take it or leave it."

"I guess I'll take it," he said in a quiet little voice that spoke legions about how disappointed he was. "But can I go home soon, Mommie?"

Because she understood how difficult it was for the child to accept all that had happened without some sort of idea when things would change, she smiled at him as she said, "Just as soon as Dr. Lowman says you can go home, I'll hire a limousine to drive you back to Carter's Crossroads."

"Really, Mommie?" the little boy asked with anxious eyes wide with anticipation. "Will you really?"

"I sure will," she promised and crossed her heart as if to seal the deal. "Now, how would you like to see Brian and Sally and Grammy and Grandee?"

"Are they here?"

"They sure are. That's where I've been. And they're very anxious to see you. Do you feel up to it?"

"Sure, Mommie. I feel up to anything if I can just see them."

On her way back to his hospital room, Margaret had stopped to confer with the Charge Nurse about allowing Jason to see his siblings and grandparents.

"It'll cause too much confusion if they all troop back here," the nurse told her. "After all, we still have some very sick children in these other rooms." Seeing Margaret's crestfallen face, she hastened to add, "But not to worry. Dr. Lowman anticipated this.

We'll get Jason into a wheelchair and you can take him out to the lobby where he can visit and talk as much as he wants." Then she caught herself, "Well, as much as he wants within reason, of course. After all, this is still a hospital, although if all our patients were as well off as Jason is right now, we'd be out of business."

"Is he really doing that well?" Margaret was almost afraid to ask. "Don't give me false hope, please."

The nurse placed her hands on her hips and said, "Jason isn't fully back to normal, but there's no doubt he's going to make it. The doctor has ordered that he be moved to the floor later to-day, if his vitals are still holding strong."

"This is GREAT news. I can't tell you what this means." *Thank You, Lord. Oh, thank You, Lord.*

"So," the nurse continued, "shall we go take one Jason Haywood for a ride he'll long remember?"

In a matter of minutes, the small boy was strapped into a pint-size wheel chair, covered with a blanket, and Margaret was pushing him up the hallway toward the double doors that would soon open to reveal his anxious family.

He's trembling. Is something wrong or is he just excited?

"You're shaking, Jason. Are you feeling bad?" *Maybe this is too much for him, all in the same day?*

"Unh-uh. I'm just excited. I hope I remember what they look like?"

Say what?

"Why wouldn't you remember?"

"'Cause I don't know how long it's been since I've seen them."

Margaret pushed a little faster, and when the double doors swung open, there were Brian and Sally, Grammy and Grandee, and Joe Busbee and P.C. who had arrived while she was getting

Jason ready for the family reunion. Joe and P.C. were holding one of the largest stuffed dogs Margaret had ever seen. *I sure am glad he doesn't have to be fed or cleaned up after!*

The next few minutes were a melee of excitement as the grandparents made over the little boy and his brother and sister brought him up to date on what was happening at school.

While all the visiting was going on, Margaret had withdrawn for a conference with Joe and P.C., who had found the hospital where Jim Deaton was a patient, and had stopped to see about him. "He was still pretty groggy, but not so much he couldn't ask about you," Joe explained. "Since he got shot early on, he didn't know anything about what happened afterward or whether you were safe or not."

The threesome walked to the window on the far wall, away from the children, and Margaret asked, "Who could ever have predicted it would come to this? I still can't believe it."

"Well you'd better believe it," P.C. quipped. "Because if you don't, the news media will jog your memory. Remember, it was just last night they had you on their six-o'clock news."

Just last night? Seems ancient ages ago, but P.C.'s right, it hasn't even been twelve hours. How quickly things can change completely.

"You're both right, of course. Today truly is the first day of the rest of my life. Nothing will ever be the same again.

CHAPTER SIXTEEN

True to her word, Dr. Lowman let Jason move out of ICU that same afternoon. When he questioned her about going home, she told him if he did OK until the next day and did everything she asked of him, she was going to let him go back to the hospital in Carter's Crossroads, where he'd need to stay for another three or four days before going home.

"But I'm already in the hospital in Carter's Crossroads?"

Dear Lord, he really doesn't realize where he is or how much time has passed.

"No, darling," she told him. "You're in Children's Hospital in Atlanta."

"Atlanta?" Neat. I've never been in the hospital in Atlanta before, have I, Mommie?"

"Only when you were born, son, and that was at a differ-ent hospital. This hospital only treats sick children; no grown-ups allowed," she said, mimicking the voice on the **Peanuts'** spe-cials that says "No dogs allowed."

Jason giggled. "You do that very well, Mommie."

"Good. Maybe I can get a job doing that."

The boy giggled again.

The Maxwells left with the two older Haywoods about mid-afternoon, after making Margaret promise to call if she needed anything.

"Thanks, Mama. You, too, Daddy. I know you don't like to drive in Atlanta, but I didn't want the children to find out about Don any other way."

"I agree," her father told her. "This was the best way. Now, do we let them go back to school tomorrow?"

Margaret thought for a minute, visualizing clearly the chaos that would probably be present after Don's sordid story had been talked all over town. At the same time, she knew that every-one in the family would have to endure a trial by fire before all that had happened was put to rest. "Send them on as if nothing happened. But be prepared if you have to go get them."

P.C. and Joe left shortly after the first group. "Everything is being handled at home, so don't you worry about anything," Joe assured her. "If you possibly can, you need to try to see the evening newscasts tonight. You need to know what's happening and what's being said.

In agreement that she did, Margaret left Jason's room later that afternoon while he was eating the evening meal. "I'll be back in a few minutes," she told him. "I've got an errand to handle. You be good... OK?"

Once in the waiting area, she tuned a TV that was playing

"Clifford the Big Red Dog" to a practically empty room, except for two men who appeared to be napping, to one of the network stations, just in time to catch the five o'clock newscast. The anchor was teasing the stories to come and she held her breath, until she heard him say, "We lead off the news tonight with an update on the man who shot an innocent bystander at Children's Hospital last night, then fortified himself in one wing of the building until S.W.A.T. team members brought him to his knees. We first reported on this at 6:00 o'clock this morning, and our reporter, Ashley Hornbeck, has spent the day working on the story, which is much more complex and bizarre than initial reports indicated. Ashley, what do you have for us tonight?"

Thank goodness they led with this. I can't be away from Jason's room very long. Margaret listened with horror as details she had yet to hear were revealed. The reporter gave the background on the story, including a clip from her news conference the previous afternoon and, much to her dismay, comments, complete with pictures, from several Carter's Crossroads residents.

It's obvious they're enjoying their fifteen minutes of fame.

The report closed with the information that Don was jailed in the local county jail. It listed the many charges against him and advised that the judge, especially upon learning that Don had escaped from the Carter's Crossroads jail before traveling to Atlanta, denied bond, despite protestations from his attorney regarding "Mr. Haywood's many contributions to his community."

"Mr. Haywood," the anchor continued when the camera was back on him, remains in the local jail, where jail officials say he is behaving like a mad man."

Exactly what I would expect.

She scurried back to Jason's room and later that evening, after they had played and watched some TV, Margaret insisted that it was time for him to get some rest. "Tomorrow is another day, and you remember what Dr. Lowman said. "You do what we tell you to do, and we can take you back to Carter's Crossroads tomorrow."

"Yeah, but it's back to the hospital there. I can't go home."

"Would you rather just stay here since you can't go home?"

"No...," he said softly. "It's just that I want to go home to sleep in my bed."

Does he mean his bed at the Red Bud Way house or at Grandee's? This poor child really does feel like he doesn't have a home.

"It won't be long," she promised, and said a silent thank you that he didn't pursue the subject further.

Later that night, when she went to bed down on the narrow bench bed provided for visiting parents, she realized how fortunate she had been to have the ICU parents' sleeping lounge. *Those recliners were a lot more comfortable than this hard thing I'm trying to sleep on tonight. But, I'm not complaining, Lord.*

Margaret wasn't sure if Jason awakened even more energetically than he'd been the day before, or if she was dragging more from having slept fitfully and not very restfully. Regardless of which was correct, she was as excited as Jason when Dr. Lowman told him they would transfer him back to Carter's Crossroads that afternoon.

"We have the ambulance scheduled for 1:30," she told Margaret. "And your hospital is expecting him. From the way they talked, I wouldn't be surprised to see yellow ribbons tied around every tree on the way in."

"But Mommie..." the boy wailed, "you said I could go home

in a limousine."

The doctor looked at her quizzically and Margaret could only look back with a helpless expression on her face.

"I'm sorry, Jason," the doctor told him gently. "But because you're still a patient you have to go in the ambulance." She turned to Margaret. "Insurance regulations require it. Our hands are tied."

"It's my fault," Margaret admitted. "I got exuberant last night and promised him a ride home in a limo." She grimaced. "Obviously I overstepped there."

The doctor looked helpless. "I wish I could change things, but I can't."

Margaret walked over to the little boy who was shedding silent tears, his body wracked with sobs. "Look, Jason. Stop crying and listen to Mommie." To her surprise, he did as she requested. As she looked into his red, swollen, tear-stained face, her heart gave a real lurch. "Listen. Sometimes we say or do things with the best of intent that can't happen. That's what we have here. I simply didn't think about you needing to ride back to the other hospital in an ambulance..."

Then inspiration hit. "Tell you what," she bargained. "You ride back in the ambulance this afternoon, and when you really get to come home, I'll still rent the limo. But you can ask some of your friends to ride with you. We'll have ice cream and cake and just have a really good time."

She could see the wheels turning in his head, processing her alternate proposal.

"OK, Mommie. That'll be fine. Let's see... I'll invite Richard and Carl and maybe Doug...

She left him planning his party and moved out into the hall with the doctor who asked, "How much does Jason know about the current trouble his dad is in?"

"Nothing as far as I know. He doesn't even know that Don was jailed at home because of what he did to him."

"It would be to his advantage not to learn any of this for a few more days."

"That'll be a good one in Carter's Crossroads."

"I figured as much. But try to keep as much information away from him as possible. You'll come back here to see me the day after he leaves your hospital. At that time I'll have found the counselor I want him to see, and we'll make you an appointment that day."

Brian and Sally never did say if they would participate.

"I'm going to want to see the counselor myself," she shared with the doctor. "And I've asked the other two if they'll consider talking to him. Or her. So far they haven't given me an answer."

"You've got a little time yet," the doctor assured her.

?

It was a hectic day, getting everything together and then getting the discharge. Margaret really began to question her judgment process when she learned she would not be allowed to ride in the ambulance back to Carter's Crossroads. Her father had volunteered to drive down and get her, but she had discouraged the idea, saying she'd just ride with Jason. In the end, she had to call him back and Jason had to leave ahead of her.

WHERE has my brain been? First I promise Jason a limo ride when I should have known better. Now, I've stranded myself here because I assumed that I and all our possessions could ride back in the ambulance. There's no way there was room in there for everyone and all this junk even if it were allowed.

Fearful of what Jason might hear when he got to the hospital ahead of her, Margaret was able to track down P.C., who promised to be at admitting when he arrived, and to stay by his side until Mr. Maxwell could drive into Atlanta and to get Margaret.

At least I resolved that problem. Or dare I be so bold as to think that, Lord?

By the time she finally spotted the city limits sign as they drove into Carter's Crossroads, Margaret felt like she had walked the distance from Atlanta. "I'm exhausted," she told her dad. "But I can't give up now."

However, as she was to learn when she reached the hospital and was directed to Jason's room, other plans had been made for her. It seemed that in her absence, her son and her friend had conspired against her. The plan was, they told her, that she would spend the evening with Jason. Then along about nine o'clock, P.C. would come in for the night and Margaret would go home to sleep in her bed.

As enticing as that sounds, I can't ask P.C. to make such a sacrifice. But when she protested to that effect, she was informed that it was out of her hands.

"Yeah, Mommie," her little boy crowed, "me and P.C...."

"P.C. and I..." she corrected him.

"Well, you know what I mean. We've got it all planned. Tonight, after everyone's asleep, we're going to raid the kitchen and fix us something good to eat." His pronouncement was delivered with all the seriousness he obviously felt their plans deserved.

"But you can't do that?" Margaret protested with the horror she felt obvious on her face. "P.C.! How could you? Now for sure I can't go back home to sleep tonight."

Her friend flashed her a look that clearly said "cool it." Then she turned to Jason. "Don't worry, friend. I'll explain everything to Mommie." She took Margaret by the hand. "Mommie! May I please speak to you out in the hall?"

Whether she wanted to go or not, she felt herself being pulled along. Once in the hall, P.C. was quick to explain that Joe would be coming by about the time Margaret left for home with banana splits for all of them. "That way his mind will be off you leaving."

"But P.C... raiding the hospital kitchen? I mean, really...,"

"Look, little mommie. When that kid got here, he was a basket of nerves, suddenly afraid to let them put him in a room unless you were here. I was desperate and the most outlandish thing I could think of was raiding the kitchen. So I went with it and in a matter of minutes, that little boy was giggling and talk-ing about it with so much anticipation he actually forgot to be frightened."

"Well... OK," Margaret said reluctantly.

"Sheesh," her friend protested. "The hospital staff handled it more calmly than you did!"

"You mean they know about it, too?"

"Thought it was a hoot!"

OK. I know when I'm beaten. "Just don't let me get here in the morning and find out you're both busted for the kitchen caper."

The attorney drew herself up with all the importance she could muster. "Puleeze... you seem to forget that I'm an officer of the court. I can't engage in that type behavior."

"Not in Georgia, you're not an officer of the court. So I guess I'd best go back to worrying." She shot P.C. a look that said "touché."

By the time Joe arrived just before nine o'clock with three super size banana splits, Margaret was too tired to argue about the wisdom of going home for the night. Her marathon days were catching up with her.

I've always been that way. I can move mountains in a crisis, for as long as it's necessary. But once things begin to level out and I put down the load, my whole body goes on strike and I'm not good for anything.

Her dad had followed Joe into the room, and he told Jason to sleep well, then led Margaret from the room. "P.C. will take good care of him. And I'm going to take good care of you. At home. In your room at our house."

"Thanks, Dad. I owe you."

"At the end of the day, we'll see who owes whom. For right now, don't sweat it. Just know how proud I am of the woman and mother you've become."

Tears sprang to her eyes unbidden. "Dad! Where did that come from? You're making me cry."

"Sorry about the tears," he replied, "but I realized yesterday that we don't tell those closest to us how we really feel sometimes until it's too late. I won't live forever, so I wanted to be sure you knew how very proud I am."

Margaret was too choked up with exhaustion, she told herself, to respond. Indeed, she said nothing until her dad was helping her get all her baggage unloaded and into the house. At one point she stood on tiptoe, which wasn't easy since her center of gravity was affected by the brace on her arm, and brushed his cheek with a kiss. "That's for being the man who gave me such an excellent pattern to follow."

Before she could even get her clothes off and into a gown, Margaret could feel sleep reaching for her and she was helpless to resist. "Thank you, P.C. You knew how badly I needed this," she whispered just before she closed her eyes.

And then she knew nothing.

෨

The room was very dark and she couldn't identify the source of the shaking she felt. A moment of terror passed over her... *Has Don somehow gotten out of jail and come here to kill me?* But she knew that couldn't be the case. Still, the shaking wouldn't stop. *Maybe it's an earthquake.*

"Margaret! Wake up. You've GOT to wake up!"

"Huh? Who wants...?" "Why?" *Every time I get to sleeping good, somebody wakes me up. I just wanna sleep!*

But the shaking continued and Margaret slowly forced her sleep-thickened eye lids open against their will. What she saw was her dad's face leaning over her again. Just as he had done only a few nights earlier.

"Wha... what is it, Dad? *Oh my gosh. Jason!* "Dad!" She struggled to get into a sitting position. "What's wrong with Jason? I knew I shouldn't have left him." She scrambled to get out of the bed and get to her clothes.

"No... not Jason. Jason's fine," her father said, not making much sense. *He doesn't look right. Oh, God, don't let him be having a heart attack. I need him too bad right now.* "Dad. What's wrong? You look horrible."

Her dad sat on the edge of her bed and offered her the cordless phone he held in his hand. "It's for you. It's the jail in Atlanta."

"The jail in Atlanta?" she asked, still in a sleep-drugged stupor. "I don't want to talk to them. Don's their problem."

"But they need to talk to you, and I think you'd better take it."

There was something about the way he said those words

that banished all the cobwebs in her brain. Without another word she accepted the phone.

"Hello?" she said hesitantly. *Don's probably pulled another one of his stunts. I don't know what they expect me to do about it. If they can't control him, I don't know how they expect me to.*

"Margaret Haywood?" a male voice inquired.

"Yes, I'm Margaret Haywood. Why are you calling me?"

"You're the wife of Don Haywood of Carter's Crossroads?"

"Yes, but why..?"

"Could you describe your husband, please?"

"Describe my husband? I'm afraid I don't understand. Won't you please tell me...?"

"Your husband, Mrs. Haywood? Can you describe him?" he asked again.

She realized the only way she was going to get answers was to play their game, so she began to rattle off Don's statistics.

When he was satisfied they were both speaking of the same person, he interrupted her. "I'm afraid there's been a problem here at the jail involving your husband."

"I'm not surprised," Margaret replied. "Only I don't know why you're calling me. We're separated and going to be divorced as soon as all the red tape can be cut."

"It's a little more complex than that, ma'am. Is the older gentleman who answered the phone still there with you?"

"Now you wait a minute...! That "older gentleman" you're referring to is my father and I'll not have you making insinuations!"

"Please calm down, Mrs. Haywood. I don't care who you're sleeping with – or in this case, not sleeping with. I was simply trying to determine that you weren't alone before I delivered the rest of my news."

"My dad is right here beside me, but I don't understand.

Why are you calling me because Don has thrown another of his tantrums?"

"It's not that, Mrs. Haywood. Your husband was involved in scuffle with another inmate about an hour ago."

"So?"

"It's rather awkward, Mrs. Haywood, but it seems that the other inmate, who was in the same cell pod as Mr. Haywood, made some rather... shall we say, deliberate sexual advances toward Mr. Haywood...,"

"I beg your pardon?" *Am I hearing what I think I am? This is ridiculous!*

"This isn't easy news to deliver," the jailer replied. "Bottom line: one prisoner was determined to have sex with Mr. Haywood and Mr. Haywood was equally determined that he wouldn't. They got into a pretty serious altercation, and I'm afraid Mr. Haywood lost."

"But I still don't understand why you're telling me this. I mean, do you have to have my consent to treat him to something? Don't you have an infirmary in the jail? Or is it serious enough that you need to take him to an ER?"

"That's not exactly our problem, Mrs. Haywood. We need you to come down here."

"In the middle of the night? Do you know what time it is?" *I don't even know what the time is, but it's too early to be driving back to Atlanta.*

"Yes ma'am, I do know what time it is. And I hate to inconvenience you, but we need you to come to Atlanta as quickly as possible. Even though you're getting a divorce, right now you are still closest next of kin."

"I still don't understand."

"I'm sorry, Mrs. Haywood, there's no easy way to do this.

Your husband has been rushed to the ER. He's in very critical condition."

That doesn't tell me a whole lot.

"Is...he... is my husband... is he alive?" *I never thought I'd be asking that question.*

"He was when he left here, Ma'am." The officer hesitated, a lapse of sound that echoed across the lines from Atlanta.

"But...?" Margaret inquired, suddenly aware of how icy she felt.

Without hesitation this time, the deputy offered, "If you or your children want to see him, I wouldn't waste any time getting here."

"It's... it's that critical?"

"With all due respects, Ma'am, he was more dead than alive."

Don dead? Impossible.

The officer's brusqueness returned. "If you or your children have any desire to say good-bye, I'd advise you not to wait."

Coming in 2009
Merry Heart

When Saralynn Reilly traveled to south Mississippi in the pages of *Broken Spirit*, readers from Oregon to Florida, from Maine to Minnesota and all across the south journeyed with her. Page by page, both women and men identified with this young woman and the crippling grief that threatened to consume her. They rejoiced with Saralynn as she found new family to replace those who had been so tragically lost, and shared with her in a personal way the new loss, the new anguish that she had to endure. Throughout the book, they were reminded once again that faith is nothing more than believing that God will do what He promises, and that when He answers prayer, He often uses ordinary human beings – you and me – who don't even realize they're part of a greater, much grander plan.

Saralynn's story continues in *Merry Heart*, as she begins her new life in Mississippi. Amidst the backdrop of newly found friends and family, and a growing acceptance of that which she alone cannot change, this courageous young woman discovers an gnawing emptiness that still exists within her. This next step on her spiritual journey also takes her to other parts of the deep south, where she finds still more of her genealogical heritage and the basis for her spiritual heritage.

You won't want to miss this next part of Saralynn's story, set amongst the magnolia blossoms, sweet tea, humid summer afternoons, and a family of God that allows Him to use them wherever they're needed.

Coming in 2009
Lift Up Mine Eyes

From the moment readers finished the final page of *Hear My Cry*, they clamored to know more. Specifically what happens to Margaret Haywood, the book's main character and also an unlikely domestic abuse victim. "What happens to Margaret?" they demanded. "I have to know!" Some of those answers were revealed in the second part of the story continued in *Paths of Judgment*. But with answers also came more questions about the fate of this courageous young mother who finally found the courage to confront the demon in her household and do something about it.

When readers reached the final page of *Paths of Judgment*, they found Margaret facing a set of circumstances unlike anything she had ever imagined. Readers, who found themselves uncomfortably in Margaret's shoes, were anxious for a solution to her problems. If she could prevail in the face of odds, so they could as well. More than one secretly-abused woman has written after reading about Margaret, "How did you know what goes on in MY house?" Through the knowledge that someone else understood, they found courage to face their own conflicts.

"I often forget it's a book," readers have said of Margaret's story. "You get inside the character so well." In the final chapter of this story of domestic violence, rescue and renewal, readers will again find themselves an integral part of Margaret's story. They'll suffer with her as she confronts, with the help of the God she's recently re-discovered, the new challenges and conflicts that would tear her down. They'll marvel at how she accepts that there are some things she cannot change, and want to emulate her as she emerges a survivor – bruised and hurting, but far from broken.

Coming in 2010

His Mercy Endureth

All journeys must come to an end, but with the conclusion comes a newness, an appreciation for what was, an awareness of what is. In *His Mercy Endureth*, the third and last part of Saralynn Reilly's story of love and loss, abandonment and grace begun in *Broken Spirit* and continued in *Merry Heart*, readers will be anxious to travel this last leg with the engaging young lady who has captured their hearts.

Every successful relationship, be it a marriage, a friendship, or a closer walk with Him who created everything, requires a divorce from self and an allegiance to another. This is a lesson that Saralynn must uncover for herself as the continues to walk in faith, secure in her newly-found belief, but uncertain of how to face the future.

Through the loving interaction of others, many of whom are answers to her prayers, she comes to appreciate and even embrace that walking with God doesn't ensure smooth passage, but that God Himself is the cushion between the walker and the rocky road.

"BearNekkid" Writing Workshops

Good writing – like good cooking or the works of a skilled craftsman – emerges from the depths of ones soul. Good writing, like good music, should have rhythm and flow, tempo changes and mood swings.

Writers are charged with creating so compelling a scene that readers find themselves ensnared in whatever is happening, without even realizing the transition. When it's ten degrees below zero, they will feel the biting cold on their exposed skin. The aroma of freshly-baked bread will assault their nostrils and their mouths will water for a hot, buttered slice.

To create such a believable work, writers must reach deep within themselves, while at the same time remaining invisible to their readers, who will forget that it's a book, and can smell the hot, fresh bread.

According to the late, great writer and humorist, Lewis Grizzard, "naked" means you don't have on any clothes; "nekkid" means you don't have on clothes AND you're up to something." That's about how it is when writing for the reader. To create a believable short story or fiction novel, the writer must bare his innermost feelings for all to see, and most definitely must be up to something!

Learn how to infuse your writing with a heaping portion of soul, and have fun doing it!

"BearNekkid" Writing Workshops and Retreats
Led by hands-on, publishing author John Shivers

www.johnshivers.com
jswriter@bellsouth.net

John Shivers

Word-Weaving Storyteller

John Shivers talks like he writes and writes in much the same manner as he speaks. Listeners to his tales of spending time with the cousins at his grandparents' home in the 1950's, yarns of the Cherokee Indians, or stories of the southern Appalachian Mountains well understand why he's been dubbed the "Word-Weaver."

And while he spins his yarns of yesterday, he's busy at his loom weaving yarns of many bright hues and textures. By the time he tells his last story, and his audience is making its way back from the far-away place where his stories have taken them, they can gaze upon a length of fabric as vivid and fraught with detail as the stories they've just heard.

John's word-weaving talents are available to civic and church groups and his selection of stories are suitable for children, youth and adults.

Contact John to schedule a storytelling session

www.johnshivers.com
jswriter@bellsouth.net

ABOUT THE AUTHOR

John Shivers
and His Ministry of Writing

When he was eleven years old, John Shivers decided his life's calling was to write. At age fourteen, he was earning a few dollars each week stringing for his hometown newspaper. At age nineteen, he felt a call to ministry but, unable to find total peace in the matter, continued to pursue his writing, going on to become the youngest newspaper editor/publisher in Georgia at age twenty-two.

However his dream and his goal was to become a publishing novelist, and in the thirty-some years that passed, while working for newspapers and magazines, he worked on first one book manuscript and then another. In 2005, his dream was realized, when his first book, **Hear My Cry**, was released. As the first volume in the Create My Soul Anew trilogy, this book introduced readers to an unlikely domestic violence victim named Margaret Haywood. What followed was an outpouring of response from readers across the country, many of whom were closeted abuse victims themselves, who confessed the truth to John, when their own, closest friends and family didn't know.

Through the response of these readers, John was able to see that the correlation between the award-winning writing skills God had given him and the ability to use those skills to minister to those who are hurting, whatever the reason.

"In my late teens," John told one reporter, "my concept of ministry would have been strictly defined by denominational walls and definitely confined by masonry walls. With my writing, however, I reach across denominational lines and work outside the church walls, to reach people where they are hurting."

John, his wife Elizabeth, and their cocker spaniel, Maddie, live on the family farm in Calhoun, Georgia, where John writes from a tree-top study with a view of the beautiful outdoors that God created to inspire him. John and Elizabeth are members of the Calhoun First United Methodist Church, and they have one daughter and son-in-law, two grandchildren and two granddogs.

John is a writer, using his talents for the God who so graciously gave him those skills, and ministering to those readers who need God's message that John's books contain.

www.johnshivers.com
jswriter@bellsouth.net